# DEEP AS THE DEAD

## THE MINDHUNTERS—BOOK 9

KYLIE BRANT

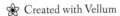 Created with Vellum

ALSO BY KYLIE BRANT

## ACKNOWLEDGMENTS

This book wouldn't have been written without the kind and generous help of a multitude of people. A big thanks goes out to vacation pals John and Sharon Barkhouse for being there to answer a barrage of questions about their province.

Canadian writing buddies Loreth Anne White and Pam Callow added necessary detail about their country and law enforcement procedure. I'll show my appreciation soon in the bar of your choice.

A huge debt is owed to my favorite retired coroner, Chris Herndon, who left her sick bed to answer questions about a severed tongue. That's dedication!

Keegan Davis is my go-to-guy for car information. Thanks so much for helping me catch a mistake in the story.

Much appreciation goes to D/CST Chris Gorman, Halifax Regional Police, for being a prompt source of answers to my never-ending questions regarding Canadian law enforcement process and procedures. Not sure what I would have done without you.

Christopher Grinter, Collection Manager of Entomology, California Academy of Sciences, was there at the beginning when the plot was just evolving, and our long conversation about weird insect behavior got the ball rolling. Many thanks for your input.

A big note of appreciation to Fred and Jane Hutchinson, owners, Irwin Lake Chalets, who never batted an eye when I contacted them about wanting to drop a body on their property <g>. Thank you for the descriptions and details about the area.

As always, the credit for details on cool gadgets and SWAT procedure goes to Kyle Hiller, Colonel/Training Manager, Hanford Patrol Training Academy. I want to shadow you for a month sometime!

Much gratitude to Jim Swauger, Binary Intelligence, Digital Forensics for your generosity of time and for solving a critical plot point for me.

Fiction comes with its own demands. My apologies in advance for those times when details, timelines and procedures get massaged or streamlined for plot purposes. And speaking of that...while Glooscap Caves on Cape Breton's Island is a real place, Devil's Fingers Caves is a product of my imagination.

The fault for any factual errors in the story rests with the author.

*For Sylvie Jeanne, who just has to flash that dimple to melt my heart.*

# CHAPTER ONE

*The way of the lord is a refuge for the blameless, but it is the ruin for those who do evil...* —Proverbs 10:29

FELIX SIMARD WATCHED his captor with an intensity fueled by hatred. The safety goggles gave the other man a cartoonish appearance, magnifying his protruding eyes and calling attention to his sloping brow and receding chin. His remaining strands of dark hair were carefully combed in a futile attempt to cover a blotchy bald spot. With his appearance and quick skittery movements, he resembled a cockroach. Felix regretted not killing him when he'd had the chance. Would have killed him, if they hadn't been interrupted. Then he wouldn't be here now, trussed up like a common street punk instead of the businessman he was.

Flames of humiliation seared him. Still, he hadn't built his empire on weakness. All he needed was one chance. And this time Felix would personally make sure Anis Tera didn't survive.

Felix knew that wasn't his captor's real name, because he'd had his people investigate him when he'd first come to Felix's attention over three years ago. Names hadn't been important. The fact that Tera had assumed he could get away with blackmail was. The man had gambled, and he'd lost badly.

Felix's chair was bolted to the floor, his hands and feet bound. Duct tape kept him from spitting the gag from his mouth. And yet he refused to allow himself to consider that now the tables might have been turned.

Tera turned off the machine he'd been bent over. Echoes of its shrill whine hung in the air for a few moments. He took off his heavy work gloves and ran a finger lightly across the edge of the utensil in his hand. Seemed satisfied. He didn't remove the goggles as he approached Felix.

"You remind me of my father, you know." Tera dragged over a portable spotlight and fussed over it a moment as he positioned it. When he flicked it on, Felix flinched and tried to turn his head away, but the blocks nailed to the chair on either side of his head made movement impossible. "Like you, he thought brute force was power. Bullies always do." A small smile played across his lips. "But you're both wrong. *Information* is power. That's how I first learned of you three and a half years ago. It's what brought you here this evening, as my guest." He brought up his right hand, the item clutched in it glinting in the light's beam.

Felix stared at the weapon, a sliver of relief working through him when he saw the rounded edge. Not a knife at all, he realized with contempt. How had he managed to be brought down by such a pathetic creature?

Tera leaned his face close to his. "You'll think this is about revenge for nearly killing me three years ago. It's not.

I'm just the sword God has wielded. You told me once that you like to watch. You'll watch no more."

Comprehension slammed into Felix as the object neared his face. The first jolts of terror twisted through him. He squeezed his eyes shut tightly. Felt one of them being pried open.

His screams were no less violent for being silent.

# CHAPTER TWO

ICY NEEDLES of rain pricked his face as Ethan Manning cautiously descended the embankment above Nova Scotia's Shubenacadie River. Nature had carved the slope steep. The downpour had slicked it to treacherous. Around midnight the heavens had opened up in a driving torrent that showed no signs of abating five hours later. That would also play hell with the evidence, a thought even more troubling.

"Is there an easier way down?" Fellow Mountie Nyle Samuels's voice sounded from above him.

"Well, I'm not going to carry you." His booted foot slipped then, and Ethan swore, almost landing on his ass. He managed to right himself, barely, retaining his grip on his Maglite. Its beam stabbed ineffectually at the heavy cloak of pre-dawn darkness. Pinpoints of light clustered in a tight knot two hundred feet below. He just needed to focus on joining the others without breaking his neck.

An avalanche of mud slid down behind him and Ethan nearly lost his balance again. "Dammit, move over a few feet. You're right on top of me."

Nyle's voice sounded again, this time nearer. "But if I go down at least you'll break my fall."

Ethan gave a grim smile, one that quickly flickered out as he drew closer to the riverbank. Angry rainclouds scudded across the dark sky like battling warheads. Snippets of conversation drifted from the cluster of law enforcement below. Canopies had been erected, surrounded by four LED spotlights, their combined glow forming a dim oasis of light in the curtain of rain. Reaching the bottom, he heard a muttered obscenity behind him and nimbly jumped aside to avoid being bowled over as Nyle slid and rolled the remaining distance down the slope.

He switched his beam to the other agent's face. "I see you found the elevator."

"Shit." Nyle unfolded himself and stood, twisting around to gauge the damage. "I'm covered with mud, aren't I?"

Ethan played his flashlight over the man's navy rain poncho and pants, which were fully coated with the reddish-brown clay soil of the area. "Nah. Clean as a whistle."

"Dammit."

A figure peeled away from the tight group to approach them, flashlight in hand. "I'm Robert Treelor, RCMP, Halifax H division. You Manning and Samuels?"

Ethan's credentials hung from a lanyard around his neck, and he lifted them for the man to inspect. "I'm Manning. What do you have?"

His earlier flicker of humor had vanished, replaced by a sense of foreboding that had knotted his gut the moment the call had come in a few hours ago. The details that had been provided were compelling enough to have Ethan leaving the other three members of his team in New Brunswick and catching a red-eye flight to examine the scene. He was hoping this visit would be a wasted trip. But Treelor's demeanor did little to lessen his trepidation.

"The body was found by a local fisherman. Constable Benton was first on the scene. He brought in provincial RCMP officer Shel Nolte." The man nodded toward the cluster of figures standing in a tight group outside the tarp. "When he saw the condition of the corpse, Nolte rang up divisional headquarters, and we reached out to you. Helluva thing. Don't mind saying I haven't seen anything quite like it." The slanting rain poured off the man's slicker, forming a pool around his shoes. "The forensic identification unit investigators haven't come up with much."

One of the investigators, outfitted in a white boller suit, nitrile gloves and booties, was crouched on the riverbank. In this weather, with the number of people already around the scene, Ethan figured it'd take a miracle to come up with a shred of evidence they could use. "The medical examiner is with the body." Treelor led the way, skirting a spotlight to make a wide arc around the sagging police tape that had been strung on three sides to form an inner perimeter.

The ground there was a muddy swamp that sucked at Ethan's boots with every step. It was training rather than hope that'd had him shoving disposable shoe covers in his pocket before leaving the car. In all likelihood, there was no scene to worry about preserving. Nature had made sure of that.

He followed the officer to the farthest of three canopies where a trio of people squatted on a soggy tarp spread next to a body. All were clad in matching navy windbreakers with Medical Examiner emblazoned on the backs. Another forensic ident tech was photographing the body. The woman in the center sent a look over her shoulder. Her gray hair was plastered to her head and her glasses had tiny rivulets of moisture tracing down them. "Mary McFarland, Hants County Medical Examiner. I understand you're from RCMP national headquarters. Does federal have an interest in this victim?"

"Remains to be seen," Ethan replied.

She made a nearly imperceptible gesture and the two assistants flanking her rose and parted to allow Ethan and Nyle to crouch beside the body. He noticed approvingly that the hands had already been bagged. Male, he ascertained at a glance. Dark hair. Forty to forty-five years old, just under six feet, one hundred eighty pounds. Two jagged bloody holes were all that remained of the eyes and the mouth had been sewn shut with what looked like black fishing line.

"Could still be copycat," Nyle said in a low tone.

"Guess we'll find out at the autopsy." Ethan slanted a look at the ME. "Any idea about what was used to remove the eyes?"

Some in her position were maddeningly reticent, unwilling to tender any opinions until the body was back at the lab. McFarland was more forthcoming. "Not a knife," she said with certainty. "Something rounded that had been sharpened."

"Christ," Nyle muttered. "Like a spoon?"

"Possibly. Or a melon scooper. Did the trick." The two Mounties exchanged a glance. "If I'm going to lose this case tell me now before I haul him back to my morgue. Your other victims missing eyes?"

"No." Ethan's gaze traveled lower, lingered on the neat vertical stitching of the lips. "But the same job was done on the mouth."

McFarland nodded and got to her feet. "Will you be using the ME in Burnside on the investigation?"

He nodded. It'd be most efficient to use the pathology building minutes away from the RCMP divisional headquarters in Halifax.

The woman reached inside her jacket for her cell. "I'll give them a call and see how they want to handle the transport."

"Appreciate it."

Water streamed off the edge of the canvas and Ethan rose, giving a shake to dislodge the steady cascade running down the back of his neck. The woman withdrew to huddle under the far corner of the canopy as she made the call.

"If this is our guy, it's only been eight days since the last victim in New Brunswick." Nyle had resurrected a tissue from somewhere and was wiping ineffectually at the mud on his slicker as he spoke. "He's never moved this fast before. When's Gagnon coming through with the extra assistance?"

"Hopefully soon." The new commissioner had made plenty of promises two weeks ago when it had become clear that the most notorious serial killer in the country was active again after a three-year hiatus. Ethan was hoping the commissioner moved swiftly. He could use a larger task force in the field and more resources. What form of aid he'd get, however, remained a mystery.

He continued studying the body. Almost imagined he saw movement behind the mouth, the slightest flutter. His gut clenched, and he found himself hoping that Nyle was right, and the perpetrator had merely borrowed a sensational detail from their case. Because otherwise it meant the offender they sought was escalating rapidly. Which made it impossible to predict how soon he'd strike again.

*The next day*

ETHAN STARED out the window of the terminal at the Halifax Stanfield International Airport, mentally willing the passengers to disembark from the plane more quickly. Puddles punctuated the pavement. The rain continued intermittently and the ground was saturated. Even when there was a pause in the precipitation the air was a sticky, sweaty fist of humidity.

The itinerary Dr. Hayden had sent them included a layover in Philly, turning the trip from DC into a four-and-a-half-hour flight. He glanced at his watch again. The autopsy had been scheduled for a half hour ago. He'd tried his best to get the ME to reschedule it, but hadn't been able to sway the man. The recent victim had been wedged into the autopsy schedule as it was. Hopefully they'd get there in time for a verbal summary of the ME's findings. If, that was, the passengers were ever allowed off the aircraft.

It took effort to tamp down the frustration that threatened to surge. Gagnon had made good on his promise, but his idea of assistance differed greatly from what Ethan had had in mind. Instead of more resources and manpower, he'd gotten an *outside consultant*. A forensic profiler with a highly specialized scientific expertise that was likely to have minimal impact on their case. He couldn't have imagined a worse scenario if he'd tried.

"Talked to that buddy of mine from British Columbia that I told you about last night. The one who worked the Dr. Death case last year." Nyle took a piece of gum out of his trouser pocket and thumbed the wrapper off before popping the gum into his mouth, and wadding the paper in his fingers. "Gagnon brought in an outside consultant from the States that time, too, and from the same agency as this one. Raiker Forensics. But they're better known as—"

"The Mindhunters," Ethan finished tersely. "I'm aware." The issue he had with Gagnon's decision had nothing to do with the reputation of the agency the consultant came from. The agency's owner, Adam Raiker, was an ex-FBI profiler in the States who'd garnered near legendary status before he'd been captured and then escaped from the child killer he'd been trailing. The man had spent the last several years amassing a formidable group of experts in forensic specialties, and his private labs were said to be the best equipped in North America. Services with his company likely didn't come cheap. Ethan wondered how much this consultant was costing the Force, and tried not to think about what sort of resources they could have added to the investigation for that price.

Seeming oblivious to his mood, Nyle continued. "My friend said the consultant was instrumental to them solving the thing. He was a doctor, used to be an ME before going to work for the Mindhunters." There was more, but Ethan had stopped listening. He and Nyle had worked together before, and normally he overlooked the genial man's penchant for chattiness because he was a damn fine investigator. Right now, though, Samuels's words drifted by him as he shifted his attention from the plane to the trickle of passengers filing through the gate. Maybe he should catch a cab and head to the morgue himself. Conrad, the medical examiner, wasn't the type to wait around. Samuels could grab a cab and follow later, with—

"Think that's her?"

Ethan's gaze arrowed to the woman who'd paused to

speak to an airline attendant at the counter before heading their way.

A second ticked by. Two. Recognition flickered, followed by disbelief. It couldn't be. There was no way.

Then a mule kick of certainty hit him squarely in the chest. He didn't know how the hell it was possible, but there was no mistaking that Nordic blond hair, pulled back now in a businesslike twist at the base of her neck. As she drew closer he could see the contrast of those turquoise eyes against a creamy complexion that was no longer dusted with the freckles he used to count with the tip of his finger.

Dr. Alexa Hayden, their outside consultant. Shock held him frozen in place. Nyle headed toward the woman Ethan had once known as Alexa Grace Sellers Manning. Although he sincerely doubted that she'd kept his name for long after she'd left. A deluge of suppressed memories surged, threatening to swamp him. He battled them back, aided in part by the realization that there was no surprise mirrored in her expression. She'd known exactly who she'd be working with.

He was the one who'd walked into an emotional ambush.

The knowledge had the paralysis in his limbs dissipating and he caught up with Nyle. "Dr. Hayden?" At her nod, Nyle extended a hand. "RCMP officers Samuels and Manning. Welcome to Nova Scotia."

"Welcome *back*." Because he wasn't sure it was a good idea at the moment to touch her, Ethan tucked his hands in his jacket pockets. "Dr. Hayden lived here for a while."

Nyle's head swiveled from Alexa to Ethan. "You two know each other?"

"I lived in a Truro for a time when I was growing up."

Her steady gaze revealed nothing as she surveyed him. "Ethan. You look well."

And she looked... His fingers curled. Polished. Professional. As far removed as possible from the scared vulnerable teenager who'd once owned his heart. Before leaving it —and him—empty and aching.

"Been a long time." The observation served as a warning to himself. He barely remembered the impulsive teenager he'd once been, ruled by hormones and quixotic ideals. And in this woman, he saw no trace of the skittish too-serious girl who'd once looked at him with forever in her eyes.

That was a lifetime ago. The two of them were ancient history. The bodies piling up in the case were the present. With an ease born of long practice, he shoved the memories aside. Deliberately, he turned. Skirting the roped areas directing lines, he headed toward the front of the Customs area. "We'll expedite Customs and then head for the car. I've already arranged to have your luggage sent to the motel. If we hurry, we'll make part of the autopsy for our most recent victim."

And that postmortem had to be a helluva lot more compelling than conducting yet another on he and Lexie's spectacularly failed marriage.

As they trooped into the autopsy suite, Dr. Isaac Conrad briefly looked up from his subject lying on the stainless-steel table before pointedly glancing from them to the clock on the wall. His fingers didn't falter in their task of closing the Y cut on the corpse's chest, using thread not unlike that still intact on its lips. "You're just in time." There was a female technician standing silently next to him, camera in hand.

Alexa left her laptop case by the door and trailed the two Mounties into the room. They'd all donned shoe covers, gowns and gloves, the garb accentuating the slightly alien feeling she'd had ever since the plane landed. Ethan had warned them that Conrad had a reputation for being a stickler about his domain, as well as being meticulous about his job.

Ethan. Her stomach clutched as he led them to ring the table and made introductions. The man she'd thought she'd never see again. She'd had since last night to deal with the shock of realizing that their paths were about to cross, despite all the odds against it. Different countries and professions should have insulated her from the possibility. Yet here she was. And from the forbidding expression on his face when he'd recognized her, he shared her dismay.

A familiar guilt had her palms dampening inside the gloves. "Dr. Hayden will be consulting on our investigation," Ethan said, jolting her from her thoughts. "She joins us from Raiker Forensics in the States."

Dr. Conrad's brows rose at the mention of the company. "Welcome, Dr. Hayden. I've heard of your employer, of course. I had the pleasure of attending a symposium where a medical examiner from your agency was a speaker. Carstens, I believe his name was. It was quite illuminating. Are you in the medical field, as well?"

She shook her head. "My areas of expertise are forensic entomology and forensic psychology. But you're correct, Finn Carstens is very gifted."

"With two specialties to your credit, something tells me you're just as talented." He indicated the tall brown-haired woman standing beside him. "Reese Wilcox is one of our technicians. She's taking care of the photo log for this autopsy." He turned back toward the gurney. "Let's get to the subject that brings you here, shall we? We have before us a male, likely early to mid-forties, in relatively good health. He ate approximately four hours before death, a cheeseburger, fries and beer. He's minus his appendix and he's suffered a few broken bones over the years, most notably three ribs, his nose and his left humerus."

"We got a hit from the Regional Automated Fingerprint Identification Access System a couple of hours ago," Ethan inserted. "Our victim is Felix Harold Simard, last known address in Montreal." They had no idea yet what had brought the man to Nova Scotia, but Ethan had a request in for all transportation manifests into the province for the last two weeks. "I spoke to the detective who arrested him fourteen years ago. Simard was suspected of making and distributing snuff movies, where the female leads ended up violently murdered in the film. They weren't able to get him on that, but his use of underage girls in his porn films netted him a seven-year stretch in Archambault." He glanced at Alexa. "Detective Brighton also shared his aliases and known acquaintances."

Dr. Conrad jotted the name on a form attached to a clipboard. "I assume family members have been notified?"

Ethan inclined his head.

Alexa's gaze dropped to study the hands of the corpse. Big. Raw-boned with scarred knuckles. Simard might have worked in some sort of manual labor. Or had seen his share of fights.

"No signs of sexual assault?"

Dr. Conrad shook his head. In an aside Ethan told Alexa, "That's been true of all the victims, male and female."

She recalled reading that in the case summary on the plane ride. As a rule, she found sexual deviants less complicated to profile. Offenders like the one in this case were more challenging because the underlying motivation could be more difficult to nail down.

"Lacerations are visible on his wrists and ankles." The ME pointed to the areas in turn.

"He was restrained," she murmured.

"Definitely. By handcuffs or zip ties would be my guess, fastened tightly enough to cut into the skin. There are no defensive wounds, but he did suffer a contusion to the back of his head, severe enough that he might have lost consciousness. Although tests will confirm it, it appears his hands and fingers were thoroughly doused with bleach." Conrad lifted one of the victim's hands. The nails were cut painfully short.

"Oxygen bleach was used on the rest of the victims. What about his tox screen?"

Conrad's brows drew together at Ethan's question. Clearly, he was tiring of his narration being interrupted. "It will be several days before those results are in. There was, however, an injection site found on the left side of his neck." The man lightly touched the area on the corpse. Alexa saw the two Mounties exchange a glance. The investigative summary had included the two most recent homicides in New Brunswick less than two weeks ago. The killer preyed primarily on men, but there had been some female victims, as well. All had suffered a blitzkrieg style of attack, had Scopolamine in their systems and cause of death—although undetermined—was thought to be asphyxiation. Her gaze fell to the stitching on the lips. The most chilling similarity in the cases.

"Traces of adhesive were found on his cheeks, and a few

fibers in his mouth," the ME went on. "Likely he was gagged and his mouth taped shut prior to death. His death would have been agonizing—his eyes were removed while he was still alive. From the progress of the clotting properties, it appears that happened hours after the contusion on his head."

"The ME on scene thought the instrument used for that might have been a sharpened melon baller."

Alexa's normally strong stomach did a quick flip at Ethan's comment. Conrad pursed his lips for a moment, then nodded. "It'd be brutal, but effective. The muscles holding the eyeball in place needed to be severed, and the thinnest bones of the skull are right behind the eye socket. That said, they're strong enough to withstand a scalpel or ice pick...but look for yourselves."

She leaned forward simultaneously with the two men flanking her, thankful she'd remembered to dab Vicks VapoRub beneath her nostrils before entering the room. "See the uniform-sized holes through the eye sockets?" Conrad asked. "There are no repeated or tentative wounds. Just one hole, uniform in width, straight through to the brain."

"A drill." Nyle sounded as queasy as Alexa felt. "But he was dead by then, right? The removal of the eyeballs killed him?"

"No, indeed." Conrad straightened from his position over the body. "There's actually very little blood loss associated with enucleation—removal of the eyes. Most of that comes from the irritation to the eyelids. I opened the skull first. You can review the pictures if you care to. The cause of death was likely the long bit drill. It was used—for lack of a better phrase—to scramble the victim's brain."

Nothing in the files she'd reviewed on the plane had

prepared her for such savagery. A glance at Nyle and Ethan's faces told her that this was a new detail. At least Nyle's shock was easily discerned. Ethan's expression was closed. Inscrutable. With a jolt, she was reminded that as well as she'd known him as a teen, the man was a stranger to her. The thought shook her more than it should have.

"So..." She struggled to reroute her wayward thoughts, "the offender hasn't used this technique before." Ethan shook his head at her words, his gaze still trained on the victim's empty eye sockets. It could mean the perpetrator was escalating, she mused. Or that the victim represented something personal to the suspect. This kind of brutality went hand in hand with rage, which could be fueled by revenge. Greed. Jealousy. But she was having a hard time reconciling what had been done to this victim with the suspect's past attacks.

The ME took a small pair of scissors from the tray at his side. "I left this part until your arrival." He bent over to delicately cut the stitches seaming the corpse's lips. As if enjoying their rapt attention, he prolonged the act by pulling delicately at each freed stitch, laying the threads on a sterile cloth lining the tray to be examined later. The tech shot pictures of his actions. "Be sure and leave your email address. I'll send you the tentative report and photo log as soon as the toxicology results are back." He reached for a pair of forceps and pried open the mouth.

She leaned forward in anticipation as Conrad used a small penlight to peer into the cavity, his nose nearly touching the corpse's chin as he peered inside the mouth. "Reese, I'll want some pictures of this."

Nyle stepped aside so the tech could move closer to snap photos as the medical examiner gently extracted something from the mouth of the victim and set it on a second sterilized cloth on the tray beside the gurney.

"*Anisoptera*." Alexa stared at the dragonfly the ME extracted from the mouth of the victim. It was lifeless, its wings a brilliant blue with delicate shadings of green and violet. "May I?"

At Conrad's nod, she rounded the gurney and, lifting the paper with the insect in her gloved hands, crossed to the magnifying glass sitting on the nearby counter. She peered closely at the item. "*Rhyothemis fuliginosa*," she murmured. The vivid colored markings and the transparent tips on the front wings matched the photos in the file she'd read today. The terminal appendages identified it as male. According to the case summary, an identical insect had been left with each of the previous victims.

"You specialize in dragonflies?"

It was one of the few times Ethan had addressed her since she'd landed. "I read up on the case on the flight."

"You were always a quick study." She glanced over her shoulder to look at him then, and the slight smile on his lips was so familiar that for a moment she was transported back to the first time they'd met in the musty reading room in Colchester East-Hants Public Library.

*He'd sprawled into a seat beside her, lifting the cover of the book in her hand to read the title. "You're reading Voltaire...because you want to? Girl, you don't look sick, but I'm thinking of calling a doctor." The crooked smile that accompanied his words had sent her stomach into a slow roll, a corresponding heat sparking in her veins.*

"There's more here." Conrad lifted something else from the mouth and set it on the tray. Ethan shifted his attention to the item the ME had discovered and just that easily the moment was broken.

Alexa hauled in a deep steadying gulp of air, one she immediately regretted. Quick shallow breaths were the rule at an autopsy. Even the Vicks didn't kill the unmistakable odor of antiseptic layered over decomposition.

"The victims in New Brunswick had paper bags like that at the back of the mouth, too," Nyle informed her helpfully.

She went to stand next to the ME to look at the object he'd removed. "A mini wax paper glassine bag," she corrected absently, picking up a pair of tweezers on the tray to open it. "One of its uses is for insect samples." She reached inside and withdrew one of the minute specks, and carried it back to the counter where a microscope sat beside the magnifying glass she'd just used. Putting the sample on a slide, she slid it beneath the instrument and adjusted the lens to examine it.

"I think I had a motel bed infested with those once," Nyle observed, coming up to peer over her shoulder.

"It's a bat bug. Although bed bugs and bat bugs are virtually identical, bat bugs have longer hairs on the upper covering of the thorax." She frowned and stepped aside so Nyle could peer at the slide. "Only these last three recent victims have had a second sample inserted into their mouths?"

"It's a new development." Ethan's mouth was a hard line in his face. "We haven't figured out what it means."

"It's not unusual for an offender to adapt his MO as he evolves," she mused, staring at the victim again. "But changing his signature is a bit more uncommon."

"The killer has been inactive for three years," Nyle put in. "The Force believed he was dead or in prison."

"Until the New Brunswick homicides." Her words weren't a question.

Ethan nodded. "Simard is the first who had an identifiable manner of death. There are three other deviations noted with the newest victims. They were all tortured before they were killed. The timeline is escalating. And instead of just the dragonfly, he leaves behind a second insect sample." His gaze was unwavering. "Guess you've already realized that you're here to help us figure out what the killer is trying to tell us."

She nodded, intrigued. Without a word, she crossed the room to retrieve the laptop she'd left near the door. Returning with it, she swiftly extracted her computer and set it on the counter and turned it on. Belatedly, she turned to Dr. Conrad. "I hope you don't mind me using this area. I need to access a database to identify this particular species."

The man inclined his head and reached for the oscillating saw. He began to cut precisely into the corpse's skull, just below the hairline. Nyle, who appeared as garrulous as Ethan was taciturn, said, "You mean there's more than one type of these buggers?" He had to raise his voice to be heard over the whine of the power tool Conrad wielded.

"Several species, if I recall correctly. I just need to determine..." The thought trailed off, as she typed quickly, accessing the vast pictorial entomology database she'd been working on for Raiker's labs. The murmur of voices behind her faded as she found the collection she was looking for and brought up the pictures of each to compare with the sample on the slide. After several minutes, the shrill sound of the saw fading away, she rejoined the officers, whose discussion had turned to details of the composition of the thread used on the victims.

"We'll need to bag the stitches you removed so we can send them to the lab," Ethan said as Conrad peeled back the skin of Simard's face. "They can compare the thread used with the other..." His voice tapered off as he noticed her. "Did you identify the type of bug?"

"I did." A faint frown marred her brow. "It's an *Afrocimex constrictus*, an African bat bug. A parasite that feeds on Egyptian fruit bats."

"What the heck is it doing in Nova Scotia?" Nyle asked.

"That's what I'm wondering," Alexa said slowly. "Your killer is using a dragonfly from Southeast Asia as his calling card and with this victim he's added an insect indigenous to Africa. Both are illegal to bring into this country. He's either smuggling them himself or buying them on the black market."

Her gaze traveled past them, settled on the now faceless corpse, as if it could provide answers for the myriad questions its death raised. "As you know, serial crimes are all about the offender. To generalize a gender for now—it's *his* wants, his needs. Victim selection, manner of death...and in this case the items he leaves behind." She looked from Ethan to Nyle and back again. "The dragon fly is also about the offender. It tells us something about him or how he perceives his crimes. It goes to figure then that the second sample is all about the victim."

# CHAPTER THREE

AFTER LEAVING behind the pungent scent of the autopsy suite, Alexa welcomed the muggy air outside, even with the light mist falling. She knew from prior experience that the smells would permeate her clothes, her hair. The motel the Mounties were using was in Enfield, relatively close to the dump site and less than an hour's drive from the Halifax morgue. Although she'd only recently witnessed the inside of the victim's brain, and the damage the drill had done there, she was grateful for the sandwiches they picked up on the way to the motel. She'd turned down the snacks offered on the plane ride here. Her stomach had been a tangle of nerves, a sensation that returned every time Ethan's ice-blue gaze settled on her.

As she'd watched the scenery pass by her window on the way to the motel, Alexa had been struck anew by the geographical similarities between Nova Scotia and her home in Virginia. They had vivid green countryside, rolling hills, mountains and beaches in common. But this trip didn't feel like a homecoming. She had few good memories about her life here.

They ate in the room the two men were using as a workspace. Both beds had been moved out of the room and two long tables had been moved in, atop which was a jumble of file folders and two laptops. A whiteboard sat behind it, to which photos and diagrams had been affixed with magnets.

"We disseminated Simard's ID this morning through CPIC, Canadian Police Information Center, to all law enforcement agencies in the province," Ethan told her as he dug in the bag for a sandwich. "Simard's only next of kin was an elderly aunt. Since she's been notified, I also released his ID to the media, asking people to call a tip line if they recognize the victim. We need to establish a timeline for when he arrived in Nova Scotia to pin down how and when he met up with the unknown subject."

Alexa raised her brows, waiting for him to find his order before appropriating her sandwich and taking the remaining one to Nyle. "Discovering where Simard was kidnapped might help us zero in on the UNSUB's location, as well."

"Yeah. Simard's financials haven't come in yet." Ethan took another bite of the sandwich, swallowing before adding, "Credit-card records might make the search simpler."

Nyle ate in front of his computer, while scrolling through the day's emails.

Ethan finished first, wolfing down his sandwich while sending text messages with impressive one-handed dexterity. By the time he'd put down his cell, three-pointed his wrapper in the trash can, and turned to Alexa, she was only halfway done with her meal.

"I don't know how far you got through that file on the plane," he started.

"Are you offering a recap?" She picked up her napkin to

dab at her lips. "Please, go ahead." Last night had been spent in a meeting with Raiker after he'd tapped her for this assignment, and then bustling home to pack a bag. The files she'd looked at on the plane had included an overview of the crimes and more in-depth information about the ones that had occurred more recently in New Brunswick, but they were by no means complete. And honesty forced her to admit that she'd been unusually distracted on the journey. She had few pleasant memories of her time in Nova Scotia, and Ethan figured in most of those she did have. It would have been difficult enough just returning to the province. Mentally preparing herself for facing him the next day, working side by side with him on this case had been like staring at the headlight of the oncoming locomotive of her past.

There was little Raiker didn't know about his employees, so the meeting with him, as he'd probed her readiness for this case had been almost as grueling as seeing Ethan again. She'd managed to convince her boss that the past had no hold on her. There'd been moments since her arrival when that conviction had been sorely tested. She suspected Raiker knew that, too. He was still the foremost profiler in the States. The man was a human lie detector. Little could be hidden from him.

"...span of thirteen years he's killed fourteen victims, three of them in the last couple weeks." With a jolt, she redirected her focus on Ethan. "There was a three-year hiatus, so that was eleven in ten years until recently."

"Just over one a year until now." She thought about that for a moment. "If he's making up for the time away, perhaps he's now finished for a while. I'm sure you've checked prison records on recent releases. Passports and visa information for visitors to the country in the last few..." Recognizing the glint in his eye, she swallowed the rest of her words. "I was just thinking out loud."

"Inquiries are in progress. If I may continue?" His exaggerated politeness was more telling than a growl. She decided it would be wiser to finish her meal as he spoke. She picked up the remainder of her sandwich. Bit delicately into it.

"We've determined the offender approaches them from behind and is left-handed, based on the angle of the blows that initially incapacitate the victim and the side he chooses to inject them." Ethan prowled the space with long lithe strides, his activity a marked contrast to Nyle's loose-limbed slouch in the folding chair. "Until Simard, there'd been no discernible manner of death. We'd settled on possible asphyxiation. Or an undetectable drug that would stop the heart, using the same injection site as that used for administering the Scopolamine."

"Potassium would do the trick." Nyle's voice sounded remarkably cheerful. His gaze never left his computer screen.

She chewed pensively. Swallowed. "Those options say remarkably different things about your killer." Stopped to shoot him a guilty look. But he didn't seem irritated this time.

"How so?"

Twenty years and two degrees had imbued her with the confidence and experience she'd lacked in her youth. But having Ethan's intense pale-blue gaze on her brought a flush to her system that she'd been certain only yesterday that she'd outgrown. "You mentioned the torture was a new addition to the three most recent victims. Before that, other than the blow to the head, the others didn't show signs of untoward violence."

"No. And I see where you're going with this." He leaned a shoulder against the wall, his laser regard still trained on her. "There's a contrast between the brutality of the initial assault and the relative ease of suffocating the victim. But asphyxiation can be plenty brutal. Placing a pillow over one's face might take minutes, but if, say, he secured a plastic bag to the victim's head and waiting for the oxygen to be depleted it would take far longer and be much more unpleasant."

Because he was watching so closely Alexa suppressed the shudder that skated through her at the thought. "Still a sadistic death, yes." But something else was niggling at her, skating at the edges of her consciousness before dancing away again. "How long have you been assigned to this case?"

"I joined the task force five years ago."

"Don't let him go all modest on you," Nyle shot her grin over his shoulder. "The team came up empty-handed under the last lead investigator's sojourn. When The Tailor became active again, the new commissioner went with a new lead, plucking Sergeant Manning here from IHIT in Ottawa."

Alexa's brows skimmed upward. IHIT was Canada's elite homicide team. Ethan must have risen through the ranks of the RCMP to command a certain level of respect, despite his age. He'd be thirty-eight now. A year older than her. She didn't recall him ever mentioning an interest in police work. Of course, her occupation was a far cry from her beginnings as a biology undergrad, too.

Belatedly, she seized on the rest of Nyle's words. "The Tailor?"

Ethan looked pained, whether at the other man's compliment or her question she couldn't be sure. "The media loves their hooks. The detail about sewing the mouths of the victims shut leaked after the second victim was found."

"But not the reason why?"

"No, the insertion of the dragonfly has been kept quiet. Some of the victims have been engaged in criminal activities. Prostitution rings, organized crime...but others were just the opposite. We've got a doctor, a housewife, the mayor of a small town and almost zero overlap between any of them. He's struck in nearly every province in the country and one territory."

A vastly ambitious hunting ground, Alexa thought, finishing her sandwich and folding the wrapper into a neat square. "Did the other victims live near the dumpsites where they were found, or were they transported?"

He looked as though she'd surprised him with the question. "So far, all identified victims lived within an hour of where their bodies were discovered. Simard is an outlier. A Montreal resident found in Nova Scotia. We're still waiting for an ID on one of the victims recently found in New Brunswick."

"Male?" At his nod, Alexa continued, "And another one not in RAFIAS?" The lack of a hit in the national fingerprint system meant he'd never been arrested like many of the other victims.

"Hard to tell. His hands were burned so badly there was no way to pull a print from them."

She recalled the photo from the file she'd looked at on the plane. "The UNSUB obviously wasn't trying to prevent identification since he's never bothered with the other victims." She mulled the information over. "The file said the injuries didn't cause his death. And the other man found in New Brunswick...Albert Norton. He had the

number twenty-eight carved into his back." She considered
—and dismissed—the idea of a copycat killer. Ethan seemed
certain the details about the dragonfly had never been made
public. And the dragonfly was too specific to believe a
second person would also use it.

She creased the wrapper in her hand with a thumbnail.
Victim selection and offender motivation went hand in
hand. Right now, both were puzzling. "Is he striking at
random, with the intent to cover the entire country?
Maybe to strike fear into each area. That might be about
wielding power. No one is safe." She was thinking
out loud.

Nyle finally tore his attention away from the computer
and straddled his chair to face them. "We've considered
that," he put in. "Because we can find almost no connec-
tions between the victims, the task force has long thought
the offender might be someone who travels regularly. A
salesman, a long-distance trucker, something like that. Years
ago, they even got lists from trucking companies of
employees who made long runs and tried to match them to
the locations of the murders. Nothing came of it. As for
salesmen," he shrugged, "no way to track that, so it's another
unknown. And this case is chock-full of them." There was
an unfamiliar grim expression on his wide, normally genial
face.

"All of the bodies are found near ponds, marshes, rivers
or lakes. No ocean shoreline."

"Of course." She nodded at Ethan's remark as she got
up to cross to the trash to drop her wrapper in it. "And he
takes some care with the dumpsites, doesn't he? From the
most recent crime scene photo, it appears he selected a
placid area of the river, avoiding nearby rapids or the Bay of
Fundy tides."

"It's more isolated," Ethan pointed out, finally putting the cell down to look at her.

"There's that. But he also wouldn't want the body disturbed by rising tides. He's gone to a great deal of trouble with it. He *wants* you to find the dragonfly. He likely sews the lips of the victims shut to make sure his calling card isn't disturbed until the body is discovered." Yes, that would be important to him, Alexa mused. To take credit for the kill, or to taunt police, perhaps. "He leaves victims in areas near bodies of water where dragonflies are normally found. Except," she corrected herself as she made her way back to her chair at the desk pushed into the corner of the room, "you wouldn't find this particular dragonfly there because they're not indigenous to this part of the world."

"So why is that?" Ethan demanded. "What's he telling us by leaving it with his victims?"

The question had nagged at her since first hearing about the case. "It could be any number of things," she admitted, tucking back a strand of hair that escaped from the knot she'd fixed it in that morning. She saw Ethan track the action with his gaze and her fingers faltered. This collaboration wasn't going to work if his every look threatened to yank her twenty years in the past. It took a moment to regain her focus. "Maybe he's telling us where he's from."

"That lead was exhaustively examined at the beginning of the case. It didn't go anywhere."

She nodded, not at all bothered by Ethan's curt tone. "The *Rhyothemis fuliginosa* is beautiful. Exotic. The offender could be saying he's exotic, too. Different from anyone you might have tracked before. Or he's beautifying his victims. Dragonflies are symbols of transformation and rebirth. He might be saying that he's giving his victims new life."

"By killing them?"

Alexa inclined her head at Nyle's question. "It's a mistake to try to consider a serial offender's motive through a rational lens. Often, it only makes sense to them. Canada has slightly more lenient policies about importing insect samples than does the States, but it's heavily regulated and importation leaves a paper trail. Which I'm sure you've already looked into." She didn't wait for Ethan's nod before going on. "That leaves smuggling, which would easy enough, given the size of the cargo and maybe that's how he began. But now, he's probably either breeding the dragonflies or getting them from someone who is. There didn't appear to be any preservative substance on the sample at the morgue, although it will take more testing to be certain. It's been dead only a few days." She glanced at Ethan's face and guessed, "You already knew that."

"They brought in a forensic entomologist from a university several years ago who ran tests and told us the same thing. It was his guess that the offender believed he was transforming the victims in some way, as you said." Ethan stopped pacing long enough to slip out of his suit coat. He folded it and draped it over a chair before he began prowling the room again. "We have no descriptions of the killer. No witnesses. We've guessed he might be slight, shorter than average. He makes up for that disadvantage by attacking the victims from behind. At one time, we even considered with that manner of attack, the presumed methods of killing might mean we're looking for a woman."

"Except she'd still have to get the drugged victim to a vehicle and haul a body to the water..." The bothersome detail that had escaped her earlier finally snapped into place and she said slowly, "Or maybe it isn't about transformation at all."

She saw the look the two men exchanged as she surged from her chair, the act of moving helping to shift her thoughts into place. "Do you know what the fiercest predator on the planet is?"

"Uh...a lion? Maybe a cheetah. They're faster, right?"

Unlike Nyle, Ethan didn't hazard a guess. Just watched her with that pale unfathomable gaze. She strode across the room and back again, certainty growing with each step. "It's a dragonfly."

Ethan snorted. "A bug."

"You'd be surprised at just how vicious insects can be. In enclosures dragonflies are known to capture ninety to ninety-five percent of all their prey. They have the best vision on Earth. They're doubly effective as a great white and four times more so than a lion," she said with a nod in Nyle's direction. "They can see every angle except for behind them." She stopped behind Ethan. "And theirs is an ambush predation. They come up behind their prey and—" She reached out to gently touch him on the back of the head. Then snatched her hand away, her fingertips tingling from their gentle brush against his hair. "It never sees them coming."

Ethan turned his head to stare at her. "Blitzkrieg attacks," he muttered.

"Like the killer," she agreed. She took a step away to increase the distance between them. Then another. "Maybe you're right about his physical description. Similar to the dragonfly, he's been dismissed. Underestimated. People don't look beyond the surface to suspect what he's capable of. Until it's too late."

"An interesting theory." There was no inflection in Ethan's voice, but she could tell he was considering her words.

"The dragonfly is about him. The second insect is about the victim."

"So what's a bat bug tell us about Simard?"

"Something important the offender wants us to know about the man. I need pictures of the insects you took from the last two victims' mouths. I assume the samples are at the crime lab."

Ethan nodded. "All evidence goes to Ottawa."

Driven to get to work, she gathered up the laptop and briefcase she'd brought with her. Stopped and looked at Ethan. "Have my bags been delivered?"

"They should be in your room."

Nyle scrambled to find the file folder with the photos. "Here are the images." He rose and walked over to hand her the file in question, which she took before heading to the door. Her mind was already on her next task. The insect samples could prove invaluable in fine-tuning the latest victim selection. She frowned as she reached the door, and juggled the items in her hands as she reached for the knob. A false conclusion, however, could send them in a completely wrong direction. It was here that the scientist in her often struggled with the criminologist. She preferred basing her conclusion on solid—

"You'll need this."

Ethan's voice interrupted her thoughts. Halfway out the door, she turned. He'd followed her, holding her room card. Sheepishly, she took it from him. "Of course." He let her get to the hallway before stopping her again. "Alexa?"

She glanced back at him.

A smile was lurking at the corners of his mouth. "Your room is directly across the hall."

"Oh." Thoughts scattered, all she could do was stare at him. He'd once worn smiles more easily, she recalled dimly.

He'd used them to tease her out of her seriousness. They'd been a beacon in her otherwise dark existence—until they'd extinguished completely when their shared grief threatened to swallow them whole.

The memory carved a hollow in her stomach. She turned and made her way toward her room, wishing she didn't feel as though she was running away from something.

Again.

"She left in a hurry."

Nyle's observation had Ethan turning away from the closed door he was still staring at. "Her mind gets two steps ahead when she has hold of an idea." He headed for the seat at the desk she'd vacated. He had phone calls to make to the team he'd left in New Brunswick so he could catch up on the results of the investigation they'd left behind. He still had to update his superior on the team, Captain Campbell at RCMP headquarters tonight and set priorities for the daily briefing that would take place with the task force members tomorrow morning. "It can make her seem absent-minded, but she's crazy smart."

"I'd say that's a masterful understatement. I researched her after I called home last night. Figured you'd have done the same after Campbell contacted you with the news she'd be joining us."

Ethan's shoulders tightened at Nyle's words. When he'd gotten word from the brass yesterday, researching the expert consultant had been the last thing on his mind. Dealing with the news that there'd be neither more resources nor more personnel for the case, he'd spent hours after he and Nyle had parted drawing up priorities for the investigation and juggling them between the task force team members and local police.

Would it have helped if he'd checked out Dr. Hayden last night? He dug in his pocket for his cell. Maybe he'd have been better prepared for the shock of seeing her today. His gut clenched. But maybe not. There was really no way to adequately prepare for coming face to face with the biggest regret of his life.

"She's got double PhDs and board certifications in entomology and forensic psychology, you know that? That's amazing at her age. She's got to be brilliant. But you knew her, you said. You'd know all about that." Ethan felt Nyle's gaze on him as he read through the responses to his earlier text messages. "Were you guys in school together?"

"She was homeschooled." He'd realized too late that his knowledge of Alexa's life before their brief marriage was sketchy. Their chemistry had been too sudden, too overwhelming to allow room for much else. But he'd come to understand that she'd glossed over the areas of her life where the shadows dwelled. He'd had a lot of years to wonder what sort of damage that darkness had inflicted.

Seeing Nyle's expectant expression, he realized it was time to end this conversation. "I've got to check in with McManus." He'd left the other man as point in New Brunswick. "Anything come through on the lab tests today?"

"Tox screen on both New Brunswick victims. Scopolamine, just like we figured."

Ethan nodded, unsurprised. Five years ago, they'd wasted a lot of man-hours chasing leads on where the killer was getting the drug. They'd come up with nothing. Scopolamine wasn't a controlled substance. There were too many illicit avenues available on the street and the dark web to track anyone bent on buying the drug.

They'd met with a similar failure following up on the source of the thread used for the mouths. It was mass-produced and widely available, although they had determined the same type was used in each crime. So far, the killer had been smart and lucky. But Ethan was going to do his damnedest to make sure the man's good fortune ran out sooner, rather than later. And he wasn't going to let anything divert him from that end. Not even the woman he'd once promised to honor and cherish for the rest of their lives.

*Especially* not her.

⌇

A HAMMERING on the door jolted Alexa from the report she was typing on her laptop. Frowning, she got up and crossed the room. As she was about to unsecure the safety chain, however, a sliver of caution chased away the remnants of the work fog engulfing her. She checked the peephole in the door first. A micro-sized Ethan Manning filled it.

She took a moment to haul in a breath. If she'd indulged in a fantasy that she could consult on this case without ever having a single conversation with Ethan, alone, that fantasy was about to be shattered. Alexa unlatched the chain and pulled open the door. She made a point of looking at Ethan's hands. "Where'd you hide the battering ram?"

"Funny." He brushed by her as he entered the room, leaving her to shut the door behind him. "I saw the light under your door. I've been knocking for five minutes. Was starting to think you were unconscious."

"As you can see, I'm..." she began. And then stopped when he turned. Stared at her. "What?"

After a long moment, he cleared his throat. Looked away. "Your glasses. You must have been working."

Her brows raised. He was acting as strangely as she'd ever seen him. "Yes. I like to put my thoughts down in writing, because I'm—"

"Hopelessly visual," he finished. One corner of his mouth kicked up. "Yeah. I remember."

Her heart kicked faster as his expression lightened briefly. The tilt of his lips barely qualified as a smile; there and gone so quickly she might have imagined it. So, there was no reason—none at all—for the unsteadiness of her pulse.

"I've identified the insects left with the last two victims." Work. She seized on the distraction with a sense of relief. She crossed to the desk where she'd been sitting when he'd interrupted her and scrolled to the beginning of her notes on the computer screen. "Your unidentified New Brunswick victim had a *Melanophila Acuminata* in the glassine bag. Common name is fire bug or black fire beetle."

"Is it exotic, too?" He remained where he was just inside the door, as if rooted in place.

"Not really. It's indigenous to North America, Cuba, Europe and Asia."

Frustration flickered in his expression. "It doesn't sound like we're going to get a lead from the insect samples. At least not one that we can trace."

"Well, perhaps not directly," she admitted, slipping her reading glasses from her nose and folding them neatly. "As you said earlier, you'd exhausted the dragonflies as a lead years ago. And if none of the secondary samples were live samples, he could have gotten them from any number of collectors, or, more likely on the Internet. It'd be the most anonymous way to attain them." She saw the agreement on his face. A face that was leaner than she recalled. Harder. His hair was cropped short, darker now without the sun-streaked strands it used to have. The color was more of a contrast to his icy blue eyes. Ethan had been lithe and rangy as a teen, with an athletic build that had served him well in his obsession with sports. He'd grown into his wide shoulders, filling out in a way that hinted at hard muscle below the muted dark gray suit he still wore.

"What else?"

She blinked once and attempted to lasso her wayward thoughts. "Ah...the second victim was left with *Acanthaspis petax*, a member of the Reduviidae family. It's a type of assassin bug, and found in Africa and Malaysia."

He stared at her. "I figured you'd go into science someday. But the bug thing...still having a hard time wrapping my head around it."

Questions about her profession were far safer than the emotional quicksand of their past. Alexa seized on the topic gratefully. "I was in biology as an undergrad at Georgetown. One summer I got an internship at the body farm in Knoxville. I worked with the entomology team." She gave a small shrug. "I was hooked." Before then she'd always imagined herself working in a lab setting when she finished school. Perhaps teaching eventually. But her first introduction to forensics dictated a natural career course that eventually paired science and criminology.

"I've been working on something else." She turned to her laptop and pressed the print command. A moment later, the portable printer next to the computer began to buzz then spit out paper. "I believe the samples left with the victims tell us something about why they were selected. Insect behavior can be as fascinating as that of humans." Alexa's lips curved at his expression of distaste. "And insects predate people, so that says something about their ability to adapt and evolve. Take the African bat bug that was left with Simard. It's one of the insect families that practices traumatic insemination."

He looked warily intrigued. "Sounds painful."

"And often deadly. The female has a sexual tract, but it's rarely used. The male stabs the female through the abdomen with his needle-like genitalia, causing a wound that can cause infection and death." She tried to temper the enthusiasm in her voice. Not everyone was as fascinated as she was about her work. "Males will also mate with other males in the same way. Females adapted by developing a set of external grooves that guides the males to their genitalia. Males evolved similarly, except the grooves lead to the least critical area of their body, where they are most likely to survive a wound."

He remained silent for a moment. Then, "You're a bit scary."

Alexa grinned, and gathered the pages of her report, dug in the computer case for a paper clip and fastened them together before crossing the room to hand them to him. "The thing that clicked for me was Simard's criminal sheet. You said he filmed pornographic movies. Was suspected of making snuff films. Maybe we want to tug on that string a bit more. Violent sex that ends in death...the offender may have targeted him because of his pastimes."

He propped a shoulder against the door, began flipping through the papers in his hand. "Now would be as good a time as any to tell you I don't deal well with maybes."

"In science, we call it a hypothesis. Our investigation will prove or disprove it." Seeing the objection on his face, she hurried on. "I can take over that end of things."

Ethan looked unconvinced. "What about the other samples we found?"

"The unidentified victim in New Brunswick was the one left with the black fire beetle. They mate inside smoldering trees, like in forest fires." She paused a beat. "His hands were badly burned. The link between the type of torture he underwent and the secondary insect is unmistakable." She saw by the arrested expression on Ethan's face that he'd grasped the significance.

"So according to your idea that the victims are selected according to their pasts, our John Doe is what...an arsonist?"

Alexa lifted a shoulder. "Something to do with fire, possibly. Fireman. Arson investigator. Or maybe he was in the insurance field. But our unknown subject believes that the unidentified man, like the other victims, is deserving of his death. I think that's what the second insect and the torture tells us. It's part of the victimology."

"What about the second New Brunswick victim?" Ethan asked, folding his arms across his chest. Despite his pose, he didn't seem to be rejecting her theory outright. "Albert Norton."

A wave of exhaustion hit her then and she backed up a few steps to sit on the side of the bed. She snuck a look at the clock on the bedside table. She'd only slept about four hours last night. Fatigue hadn't been a problem while she was working, but now she could feel a crash coming on.

She nodded toward the report he still held. "The insect sample taken from his mouth was an *Arilus cristatus,* or wheel bug, of the Reduviidae or assassin bug family."

His gaze snapped to hers. "Assassin bug?"

"They're carnivorous predators. Great for the gardens because they feed on common pests that harm plants.

Norton had the number twenty-eight carved into his back. Does he have a record?"

"Nothing that stuck, but he's been hauled in twice in the last decade for questioning in homicide investigations."

A thrill of adrenaline zipped up her spine. "That bears more looking into."

"No shit." He rubbed the back of his neck. Stopped mid-action to look at her. "Of the three insect samples left with the victims, only one isn't common to this area. The one left with Simard. I'm guessing you think that's important."

"I do. He could have chosen a bat bug—or a bedbug for that matter—that's found locally. Like the torture, the selection of a more exotic insect singles Simard out. Something about the man was especially noteworthy to the offender. Or the UNSUB feels Simard is particularly heinous in some way." Pressing a hand against her mouth for a moment to stifle a yawn, Alexa said sheepishly, "Sorry. The long day is catching up with me."

"Then you'd better call it a night. I just stopped in to tell you that we have a briefing with Captain Campbell and the other members of the task force at seven-thirty. I hope that's not too early for you." It was plain from his tone that the statement was a formality.

"Of course not."

Ethan looked unconvinced. "You realize I'm talking a.m."

Her lips curved and she got up to cross to the desk, laying her reading glasses on it. "Believe it or not, I've come to terms with my violent dislike of mornings. We've learned to co-exist."

"Be packed, because we'll check out tomorrow. After the briefing, we'll be heading to Halifax to the divisional

RCMP headquarters. Now that we're finishing up with the Simard crime scene, it will be simpler to set up there with their resources closer to hand. The transportation manifests have come in and are waiting for us. I don't have to tell you, that's going to be a tedious task."

She winced a little. Just the prospect of poring over reams of passenger lists from airlines, cruises, trains, buses, and the ferry looking for Simard's name was more than a little daunting. "All right. Can we swing by the body dump-site before we leave?" It wasn't often that she was called to a case in time to see a crime scene first hand. Usually she had to rely on photos to familiarize herself with the site.

Alexa half-expected him to refuse. She wouldn't have insisted. It wasn't crucial for her to visit the location in person. But since the secondary sites didn't appear to be totally random, each would tell them something about the killer. And the ability to walk the ground the offender had, see what he'd seen, would be a rare opportunity for her prior to writing a profile.

But he surprised her by saying, "Forensic ident unit is finished with it, not that the rain left much for them to find. They also searched across the river for a few miles in case a boat was used, with similar results. Wouldn't hurt to take another look at the embankment. In five or six of the scenes, we did find indentations in the ground that lead us to believe he uses some sort of two-wheeled dolly to cart the body to the dumpsite. Figure the rain took care of any tracks, but wouldn't hurt to check again before I release the site. So, request granted."

She smiled. "I'm ridiculously pleased by the prospect. Especially since it puts off the manifest chore a little longer."

He didn't return her smile. Just continued to gaze at her,

long enough to have her shifting uncomfortably, her palms dampening. Awareness sprang to life, thrumming with a familiar electric spark. It'd always been like this between them, even when she was too young, too naïve to put a name to it. That chemistry should have expired, buried by a mountain of regret, shared anguish and pain. It shouldn't be spitting and sparking to life anew.

"Why?" The word seemed wrenched from him, his tone so low she had to strain to hear. Nevertheless, it reverberated through her like a plucked harpsichord string. Why what? He wasn't referring to her request, of that Alexa was certain. Why did she come? Or—more terrifying—was he referring to why she'd left?

Cowardly, she seized on the former. "I didn't realize who I'd be working with on the case when I first agreed to the job." But Raiker had known. The man made it his business to know everything about his employees, and their potential vulnerabilities. When he'd revealed Ethan's involvement as senior investigator, it had been all she could do to avoid flinching beneath Raiker's laser blue stare. But the man had sensed her immediate reaction. There was no hiding that sort of thing from the man who'd once been FBI's most respected profiler. She'd had to convince him, as well as herself, that her past wouldn't trip her up on this case.

Her first glimpse of Ethan had shaken that conviction to its core.

He still hadn't moved. "It was a long time ago." The words were meant as much for her as for him. "I told Raiker that I had no doubt the two of us could have a productive working relationship." If anything, his gaze went chillier at her words.

"You're right." His expression had shuttered. He turned

to open the door and headed through it. "It was a long time ago."

~

ALEXA LAY STILL, staring up at the ceiling of the motel room. Despite her exhaustion, sleep was elusive, evaporating each time it ebbed just within reach. And she knew exactly who she had to thank for that.

She closed her eyes to keep her gaze from searching the alarm clock on the bedside table. It didn't help to watch as the minutes awake slid into hours, and Alexa tried not to waste energy on fruitless behavior.

Behavior like dwelling on the past. It was rearing its head again, grasping at her with gnarled fingers. Experience had taught her there was no good to be had reliving it. But her usual defenses were in shambles at the moment.

Memories drifted into her mind like smoke under a door. She couldn't completely blame them on the conversation with Ethan. It was this place. Coming back to the province where she'd spent the unhappiest years of her life affected her more than she'd thought it would, despite her assertions otherwise to Raiker. Her boss had known better than she that her return would be fraught with emotional entanglements. Understanding his employees better than they knew themselves was one of his least beloved traits.

There was a small click each time the alarm clock flipped from one minute to the next. The sound was hypnotic. For some reason, it reminded her of the two books that made up her childhood. Before her mother had met Thomas Reisman. Click. Then after.

Turning to her other side in the bed, Alexa let the past crash over her. With the insight of adulthood, she could appreciate how difficult it had been for a single mother to raise a child on her own. There had never been a father in the picture. Their homes had been a series of apartments, each indistinguishable from the other. Cracked linoleum and counter tops. Uncertain heating systems. Refrigerators that only sporadically chilled the food. But her mom had made them home. There'd been laughter in those days, songs and games that had kept Alexa entertained and close to her mother's side. The few pictures she had from then showed the weariness behind Rebecca Sellers's smiles, but they were genuine enough.

That had all changed with Thomas Reisman.

Alexa shifted to her back again, tension creeping into her limbs. He'd been a deacon at their church when he'd begun paying attention to her mother, and Alexa had experienced a child's level of resentment. The man had started coming to their apartment and soon there was less time for games and songs and more focus on their "spiritual growth." Slowly, the man infiltrated every moment of her time with her mother. And one night when Rebecca sat Alexa down to explain, with a light of excitement in her expression, that she and Thomas had gotten married, that they were all moving to Nova Scotia where he'd have a church of his own, a knife of dread had twisted through Alexa.

In a couple of weeks, her mother had quit her job, packed up their meager belongings and they'd moved to Yarmouth. Then New Glasgow. Digby. None of the churches had been a good fit. The other pastors were jealous of Thomas. The churches too liberal. Not focused enough on biblical teachings. The next would be better. When she was fourteen, they'd gone to Truro where Thomas had started his own church. With each successive move, life had gotten more restrictive for Alexa. Everything about her past had slowly been chipped away by the stranger her mother had married. Even her name.

Deep breathing calmed the worst of the tightness in her chest. It'd been Reisman's idea to start calling her by her middle name. Grace. A solid, biblical name to live by. Her mother had agreed. She almost always agreed with Thomas, which had infuriated Alexa at the time. But she realized now that he'd been molding his wife as surely as he was her daughter. Slowly, day by day, Thomas Reisman erased the best part of Alexa's childhood.

There would be no more public schools. Her mother would homeschool her with true Christian values. Punishments became more frequent. More severe for the tiniest infraction. They were most often directed at her mother, but Alexa had felt the brunt of Reisman's belt, too.

*Turn away from sin! Turn or burn!* She could still hear the snap of the belt, the slicing agony as it had whipped against her skin, his words keeping pace with the rain of blows. And the worst had been her mother's betrayal, sitting in the corner of the kitchen, head bowed during the beating, reading a jumble of passages aloud from the Bible.

The back of her eyes burned, but there were no tears. She'd forgiven her mother long ago. Rebecca had been a victim, too. She'd never made it past the tenth grade, and Alexa knew now that abusers preyed on those weaker than themselves. More malleable.

When Rebecca had proved no match for her daughter's insatiable appetite for learning, Reisman had grudgingly agreed to allow Alexa to use the public library in the afternoons. It had become her escape, a tiny crack in the window to the world. Soon she was staying there until closing time most days. And that's where she'd met Ethan.

A sliver of the tension slipped away. When he'd teased

her name from her the first day they'd met, she'd never know what had compelled her to blurt out Alexa instead of Grace. Just hearing her first name spoken aloud had brought twin spears of relief and defiance. The door to her life before Reisman had been opened and she'd taken her first tiny step out of the shroud of darkness that had dropped over her life. There was no way she could have known then the brilliant joy Ethan would bring to her life.

Or that together they'd hurtle headlong toward unimaginable heartbreak.

CHAPTER FOUR

*Whoever conceals their sins does not prosper, but the one who confesses and renounces them finds mercy.* —Proverbs 28:13

IGNORING the tearing agony in his back, Anis Tera sat in front of his laptop and tracked the movements of his next victim. She'd arrived in Halifax yesterday. Right now, she was ensconced in the hotel's VIP suite, no doubt lounging in the cushy surroundings preparing for her next interview. Despite her less savory and little known pastimes, Jeanette Lawler was the popular host on the seamy *Exposé* show on WBCT. Her guests were plucked from the headlines: a man accused of breaking his wife's neck and dropping her from a three-story window; a woman claiming post-partum depression who'd smothered her twin sons; a grandmotherly ex-nurse charged with an Angel of Death case. The more sensational the situation, the more doggedly she pursued her potential guests, who, while given a public forum for pleading their cases, could also expect to have her turn on them midway through the show with a titillating revelation she claimed to have uncovered about them.

Given the personal history Lawler kept hidden, her hypocrisy was astounding. Her ambition had made her remarkably easy to fool. She'd flown here from Vancouver because she thought she was getting an exclusive with Armand Vance, a Toronto-based financier who was battling multiple indictments for security law violations.

Anis made it his business to learn everything there was to discover about Simard, so he knew the man had lost a bundle because of Vance. Like a chess master, Anis had made sure the supposed meeting between Lawler and Vance had reached Simard's trusted advisors. He hadn't made the mistake of contacting Simard directly; he'd learned his lesson last time, and it had nearly cost him his life.

The financier was nowhere close to Nova Scotia. But the elaborate ruse had brought both of Anis Tera's prey to one place. Simard had been dispatched. Lawler would be, soon.

Not bothering to check the hour, Anis punched in a familiar number.

"H'lo." The word was slurred by sleep.

"Your chores better have been completed before you turned in for the night."

Fear creeping into his voice, the kid said, "They were. All of them. We had a bad storm this afternoon. Stuff was hitting the roof and the side of the shed. There might be damage outside."

Anis's reaction was sharp. "Did the electricity go off?" He had a backup generator for that eventuality, but it was a struggle for the boy to start it alone. Desperation would have fueled his eventual success, though. He knew the price of failure.

"It just flickered a couple of times. I checked all the enclosures. The temperature is fine. It didn't affect the carcass count of the dragonflies."

"And the prey enclosures?" Anis felt a burst of impatience at the long hesitation that followed his words. He'd had the boy over two years after saving him from a flash flood that had swelled the stream in the woods near his property. The kid would have drowned if he hadn't been pulled out. For that, he owed Anis his life.

He was extracting full payment.

"I...think they're fine."

Lips pressed tightly together, he silently counted to ten. Just when he thought the boy's training was complete, the kid proved otherwise. The midges and mosquito populations needed to be monitored, because they were the dragonflies' food source. A daily allotment was entrapped in mesh containers and released into the dragonflies' enclosure. The life cycle was intricately woven.

"Check on them now."

He waited as the boy went to do his bidding, visualizing the scene unfurling on the other end of the phone. The shed's interior would be dimmed during night, so he'd have to flip on the overhead light above the enclosure, or use the lone flashlight from the supplies Anis left when he was away. The boy's thin bedroll would be in the corner next to the small refrigerator containing the sandwiches and bottled water. The boy had learned to eat and drink sparingly, because Anis's return date was always uncertain. Just as the kid had learned to stop talking about his former home and family and stupid dog. His life had been given a higher purpose as surely as Anis's had

"Yes, it's all okay."

He blew out a breath. "Good. Make sure everything stays that way." He disconnected and set the phone aside, the boy already fading from his mind. Anis had seen to the shed's security himself. It was well-insulated. There were no windows from which to escape. The Firefly cell left there for the kid to communicate with him was programmed to only accept or dial out only one number. The kid would be there when he got back. And his prized possessions would be alive. Thriving.

The hour was late, but Anis spent another hour prowling the Internet, trolling for future clients. The information people put online always amazed him. Credit card statements and banks were a treasure trove, and he eased in and out of their servers at will. He dealt in secrets. Everyone had them, a shameful part of their life that they would pay dearly to avoid having exposed. His was a lucrative occupation, and while the cost of avoiding exposure was costly, the opportunity also afforded his victims the chance to mend their ways.

He stretched, then stopped, grimacing, when the bruised and broken skin on his back ached and bled. With care, he rose, took off the burlap garment he wore and folded it before treating his wounds as best he could with antiseptic. The self-inflicted flaying had been punishment for the glow of satisfaction he'd felt after Simard's death. Anis's purpose was to exact impartial justice from those who refused to repent for their sins, not to sit in judgment or revel in his work. To do so would lower his actions to that of a simple murderer. He was so much more than that.

People thought they could hide their most shameful secrets from prying eyes. It was his sacred duty to ferret out the worst of the wickedness and exact the Lord's vengeance. Sins could only be forgiven once a penance had been exacted. But the most evil sinners who turned down that chance...their sins would be buried with them.

As deep as the dead.

## CHAPTER FIVE

ETHAN WELCOMED the morning bleary-eyed and surly-tempered. Sleep had been difficult to summon. Enough so that he'd finally given up at one point and gone back to work for a few hours, poring over the earliest homicides attributed to The Tailor, looking for ways the offender had evolved until his eyes burned and his brain could no longer process information. And even then, when he'd tried sleep again, it'd been a long time coming. And he knew the blame for his fitful slumber was the woman across the hall.

It had been the glasses that did it. When she opened the door, tendrils of hair spilling from the knot she'd put it in, reading glasses perched on her perfect nose, he'd had a technicolor image of the first time he'd seen her in the Truro library. When he'd spoken to her then, she'd taken off the glasses self-consciously, fiddling with the bows during the whole conversation. She'd since lost that self-consciousness. The glasses were different. But she was still gut wrenchingly sexy in them, and his response pissed him off.

His second marriage had been as ill-fated as the first. In the four years since it'd ended, there'd been women.

Nothing serious, because his batting average in that area wasn't exactly stellar. But it wasn't lack of female companionship that made him hyperaware of Alexa Hayden.

Hayden. The unfamiliar name meant she'd remarried. Which was yet another reason there shouldn't be even a hint of the personal between them. They'd both moved on. A chance meeting decades after they'd parted wouldn't change that.

An icy shower did nothing to improve his mood. Neither did his first glimpse of Alexa, when she slipped into the room they used for their conference area. The slight shadows under her eyes were probably due to her late night the last two evenings. He didn't flatter himself that she'd spent the hours she could have been sleeping last night tossing in the bed, her mind returning again and again to memories that should have been long forgotten.

Nyle had obviously risen earlier and purchased Danishes and coffee. Ethan set his laptop on the table, booted it up and set the briefing agenda next to it before making a beeline for the caffeine to grab a cup. The first scalding taste was much-needed fortification. The unexpected addition of Alexa Hayden to the team was a distraction he could ill-afford. And he was damn well not going to waste any more time delving into memories that had been locked away long ago.

He took another long gulp and decided to cut himself a break. It'd been less than twenty-four hours since he'd come face to face with the biggest regret of his life. A response was normal. But they had a killer to catch, and like it or not, Alexa was a member of his personnel-strapped task force. From now on, that was all she was.

Ethan turned to the laptop and opened the group video conference software. One by one, the rest of the task force appeared on the screen. Captain Campbell, based in Ottawa, his expression stoic as he waited for the newest update. Ian McManus, Steve Friedrich and Jonah Bannon, the team members left behind in New Brunswick. Steve, the youngest of the three, was unshaven and chugged from a water bottle like a dying man in a desert. Ian and Jonah were RCMP veterans ten and fifteen years Ethan's senior. Jonah held a coffee cup in a death grip, his bald dome glistening in the overhead lighting. They were using the conference room in New Brunswick's J Division RCMP Headquarters in Fredericton. Ian sat next to him, one foot bouncing in a show of nervous energy.

Captain Campbell spoke first. "Commissioner Gagnon wants another national news conference, Ethan. The press won't be put off indefinitely with daily written updates on the investigation. We need regular face time with the investigators to convey a forward progression in the case."

A dull throb started in Ethan's left temple. "I'll assist in that with all the information at my disposal."

"No, Gagnon also wants *you* in front of the cameras this time." Campbell's wiry gray hair always looked like he'd just run a frustrated hand through it. This morning was no exception. "You're the face of the investigation. Not that he expects you to fly back to Ottawa, of course. But you'll do a remote segment during the interview, once we get it set up. We'll work on what to release beforehand, of course."

The pain in Ethan's head increased. This likely meant dropping everything on a moment's notice and wasting a couple of hours in a news station. But he couldn't fault the commissioner's decision. The media was a fanged beast that had to be fed regularly during a high-profile case. The Tailor's return had made national headlines. It was good PR for them to shape the narrative as much as they could, calm the fears of a jittery public and convince the press that they had the matter well in hand. Based on the UNSUB's long criminal career so far, that would be an uphill battle.

"And we'll want Dr. Hayden at your side, of course," Campbell added.

"Of course." Ethan managed to keep the irony from his voice. Forward progression meant a show of all the resources the Force was throwing at the investigation; in this case, a fancy consultant from the States. Far better to have the media talking about those extra efforts than having them speculate that not enough was being done.

"That's all I have. I'll contact you when we have a date and time set up."

"I'd like to take this opportunity to introduce our consultant, Dr. Alexa Hayden." Ethan motioned Alexa over to sit next to him so they could more easily share the screen. "She's already identified the insects left with the last three victims and has developed a theory about the UNSUB's use of them and how they tie into the torture. I'll let her lay it out for you." He nudged the computer screen toward her.

"Good morning. I've written up my initial notes and they'll be added to the updated case file Officer Samuels will be uploading shortly. I'll give you a brief summary, however." Alexa appeared poised, despite being thrust into the spotlight without warning. She launched into a succinct account of her findings, and her conjecture about the offender's reasoning for both the insect and victim selection.

Ethan found himself focusing more on her impact on the other men than on her words. Steve stopped fidgeting with the water bottle, sitting up straighter. Ian, who invariably chose the most butt-ugly tie he could find as in silent protest for having to wear suits, smoothed a big paw over his eye-popping neon green and red tie and buttoned his suit jacket. Even the normally stoic Bannon appeared enrapt. Given the fact that the team members had been as unimpressed with Gagnon's decision for a consultant as Ethan, it wasn't hard to understand where their newfound interest stemmed from.

Alexa was clad in a tailored blue blouse and black slacks, her hair pulled back into a knot at her nape. She didn't have to try to capture male attention. She never had. Her unawareness of the impression she made on the opposite sex was genuine. Which was probably what made it so irresistible.

But resist was exactly what he was going to do, he reminded himself, shifting uncomfortably in the chair beside her. Her value to the team was the only thing that mattered. They'd done perfectly well going their own separate ways for twenty years. After the case was over, as far as he was concerned they could go twenty more.

"Interesting theory," Jonah put in, after she finished. "Especially in light of the fact that we got an alert from CPIC this morning about a missing person in New Brunswick. Details match our John Doe." He consulted a sheet in front of him. "Henry Paulus from Edmonton. According to a co-worker, he took a two-week vacation to go backpacking and camping in Fundy National Park. He never returned to work and no one has reported seeing him since."

"His co-worker reported it? Where does he work?"

"That's the thing." Jonah Bannon looked up at Ethan's question. "He's a firefighter for the city. He was part of a group that traveled to British Columbia to help battle the forest fire in the Kamloops region recently. I just faxed a photo of John Doe to Edmonton's police headquarters. Waiting to hear on the tentative ID."

Ethan slid a look at Alexa. She looked completely

composed at the news but he was feeling more than a little stunned. Sure, her idea had sounded plausible when she'd run it by him yesterday, but if the unidentified New Brunswick victim turned out to be Paulus, her theory became much more than speculation. And might give them their first solid lead on the UNSUB's motivation.

"Let me know as soon as you hear about the ID. If it does turn out to be Paulus, I want you to do some digging into his background. Dr. Hayden is speculating that the victims are selected because of some wrongdoing they are involved in. In this case, the most obvious conclusion in his situation is something arson-related." It was a well-known fact that a small percentage of fire fighters were active arsonists. The problem was so persistent that fire departments received training in identifying and preventing the phenomenon.

"If the ID is positive for your victim," Alexa moved closer to Ethan to share the screen, "a search of his home might be fruitful, especially his computer history and any forums he regularly visited. Keep in mind he may not have been a serial arsonist. Arson is also committed for profit, revenge, vandalism and to cover up other crimes." Ian McManus was nodding as he scribbled some notes. "We don't know exactly what the UNSUB was telling us about the victim. We're making educated guesses at this point."

"Seems like the offender is saying these guys deserved to die," Steve Friedrich said bluntly. "So why start leaving these clues now? Why weren't the previous victims tortured? Why didn't they have the second bug in their mouth? Is he choosing different types of targets this time around? Because not all those killed in the past had a criminal record."

"I think something significant happened to the UNSUB

during the three years he was inactive," Alexa responded. "It triggered his need to tell us why the victims were selected. He's likely excusing his actions, as you mentioned. Or setting up a dichotomy whereby he's telling us that his is a moral evil."

"They're worse than he is?"

She nodded in response to Steve's question. "Something like that, yes. I believe this offender has never struck at random, at all. And the one thing his victims may have in common is something in their history that the UNSUB finds unforgiveable. Perhaps something the victim was never suspected of doing."

"If we get a positive ID," Ethan said, "I want the three of you to split up the duties of notifying next-of-kin, obtaining necessary warrants and going through the victim's home and car. Check with DMV for his vehicle plates and search campgrounds near Fundy National Park, see if we can find his car. Talk to friends, neighbors, colleagues...I want to know everything about this guy. Text me regular updates. If the ID isn't a match, I'm going to want a sketch of our John Doe to use at the next news conference." They'd held off doing that until now out of consideration for the deceased's family members. "Someone knows this guy."

He glanced down at the agenda he'd put together. "We've identified the victim found in Nova Scotia as Felix Simard." He summarized the man's criminal past and the rumors about his involvement in the snuff movie industry. "Alexa believes changing the manner of death for this victim signifies his personal importance to the UNSUB. Our next task is developing a timeline of the events leading up to his death. The travel manifests have arrived for Nova Scotia New Brunswick. We'll be trying to find Simard's date of entry here, and also comparing passenger names for anyone who traveled to both provinces within the relevant window of time."

"I'll take our tasks today over yours, anytime." The two older officers nodded at Steve's remark.

Captain Campbell put in, "Seems like that's a chore that could be parceled out to local law enforcement departments, Sergeant."

"Believe me, I plan to hand it off to them as soon as possible," Ethan replied. "Just as soon as we look check the lists for Simard." He glanced down at his agenda. They'd hit the bullet points. Looking up, he said, "That's all I have for today. Any questions?"

Steve Friedrich waggled his fingers. "Just trying to wrap my head around this. Everything I've ever heard says serial offenders don't change their ritual. Their MO, yeah, evolves when it suits their need. But not their signature. Dr. Hayden seems to be saying just the opposite."

Alexa moved back into the screen. "What you're saying is correct, as far as it goes. Simard is an outlier because he was killed in a different manner. Maybe he and the offender had a relationship. Perhaps Simard's suspected occupation is a hot-button issue for the UNSUB. We're not going to know the answer to that until we get closer to the killer. However, the torture of the last three victims serves the offender's purpose, just as the addition of the second insect does. He wants us to know why they were chosen."

When she sat back, Ethan added, "I don't have to tell you that the clock is ticking. Either the UNSUB is finished and already on his way out of the area, or he's lingering to strike again." Five years ago, such a thought wouldn't have occurred. But that was before the offender went after multiple victims in a short period of time. "Either way, he has to be stopped." The expressions on the screen went grim. Because unspoken was the knowledge that had the last task force captured the UNSUB, another three lives would have been saved.

The briefing concluded, Alexa and Nyle gathered up their things while Ethan closed out of the group video window and took a moment to check the emails that had come in during the meeting. "Simard's financials," he said over his shoulder, a zip of excitement shooting up his spine.

Nyle came over to peer at his screen. "This just might save everyone a bunch of trouble."

"He'd have needed a credit card to reserve his room," Ethan muttered as he clicked on the copy of the most recent statement. But a quick scan of the transactions showed no travel or hotel arrangements. A search of the previous two months' statements was similarly fruitless.

"No credit cards in the aliases we were given?" Disappointment tinged Nyle's words.

"Apparently not." Which might well mean that Simard no longer used those aliases. "Still ways a person can use cash for an airline ticket, though." He clicked out of the statement and opened up the bank statement. He scrolled down rapidly, seeing frequent use of a debit card, but no transactions for travel arrangements. The account seemed to be mainly used for routine household payments.

Ethan went back and read through the email the forensic accountant had sent. "He almost certainly has another account. They're looking for a bitcoin wallet or something overseas." He'd reach out to the RCMP Montreal detachment for officers to dig into Simard's occupation and property holdings. If he was still in the porn business, he'd need a place to film. "Unless we're to believe he's left his more unsavory pastimes behind him, he's got some place he's conducting his business. In another name, probably and maybe he pays cash for those expenses."

"Or has an alias we know nothing about," Nyle said gloomily.

"Simard's selection as a victim likely means he continued that activity, or something similar," Alexa put in. "That's what the second insect sample left with him tells us."

Ethan nodded slowly. He'd delve further into Simard's financials later, looking for a possible link to the man's killer, but right now they were useless when it came to tracing Simard's final steps.

Nyle pursed his lips and, eyeing the last two doughnuts, picked up the box to carry to the car with him. "Guess that would have been too easy. We'll continue doing it the hard way. Wading through the leads that come in on the tip line from area motels."

Ethan had a half-dozen police officers running down those leads, but nothing had panned out yet. Maybe their lack of success meant Simard had been staying with a friend, or had been killed before he'd even checked into a hotel.

They were on the road heading to the dumpsite before Alexa spoke. "Do you think his hotel room could be the crime scene?" He shifted to look at her in the back seat, noting Nyle's stealthy move toward a second doughnut as the man drove.

"I doubt it. Too many people around. We've never found the crime scene in any of the other cases, although we've discovered a couple of the abduction sites—both alleyways, where traces of the victims' blood turned up. Which means the UNSUB had a lair close by, or, more likely, a vehicle to transport them to one. Given the autopsy results, maybe Simard was taken close to wherever he ate his last meal. Or near a bar where he'd stopped."

"That would make the offender highly adaptable, wouldn't it?" He raised a brow and waited for her to go on. "It'd be much easier to plan the abduction from a place he could scout ahead of time. But he'd have to react quickly if he's snatching them whenever he gets the opportunity." She frowned slightly before going on. "He stalks them. Physically, of course, prior to abduction, but almost definitely online, at first. We can discard the notion that the victims were chosen at random. This UNSUB seems to know too much about them, and we give up much more privacy than we intend to online. People tend to reveal themselves when they believe they're anonymous."

That was especially true of the darkest corners of the web, Alexa thought, where there were forums and chatrooms for every type of paraphilia. "I think we're looking at a killer with better than average technology skills. The victims may well be selected based on what he learns about them online. Then he learns their habits, where they go, what they do. Arming himself with that information gives him an advantage. He chooses the time and place of the abduction."

"So his motivation is to punish them? People he doesn't even know?" Nyle took a bite of his pastry.

"There's more to his motivation than that, I expect." There was a note of weariness in Alexa's answer. "There always is. And it makes sense only to the killer."

Minutes later Nyle slowed to pull over at the side of the road. "I hate to get too far off the road. Ground's still pretty soggy."

Ethan hadn't yet seen the dumpsite in the daylight, and took a moment to take in the scene. A gauzy morning fog was lifting off the Shubenacadie River below. The weatherman had forecast an extended break from the rain, but as they got out of the vehicle, the air felt damp. Not for the first time, Ethan wondered why this spot had been chosen. A bird's eye map of the river showed mostly flat land adjacent to it for miles, punctuated with stands of thickly wooded areas. There were far fewer steep embankments in this area along the river. Why would the offender choose the most difficult terrain to get to the river? Maybe that meant he'd used a boat. A canoe or flat bottomed fishing skiff would work. And it could have launched from anywhere upriver.

He tried—and failed—to imagine the UNSUB wrestling a body into a boat. But then, there was very little about the offender's actions that made sense to him. One of the things that had made Ethan a success in IHIT was his ability to put himself in the killer's mindset. This one, though, was in a category of his own.

He led the way, scanning for an easier place to descend than the way he and Nyle had found a couple nights ago. A moment later, that thought was wiped from his mind when his gaze settled on the sight below.

A tent was pitched along the river. Smack in the center of the sagging crime-scene tape that flapped gently in the slight morning breeze. It was enough to undo the slight improvement coffee had made to his disposition. Alexa forgotten for the moment, Ethan looked over his shoulder, caught Nyle's eye and jabbed an index finger to the right, while he veered left. They'd come at the tent's occupant from opposite directions.

His mind was racing as he descended the steep river bank with as much stealth as possible. There was almost zero chance that the killer had returned to the scene. There was an excellent possibility, however, that whoever had pitched that tent had done so with the express knowledge that he or she was compromising an active crime scene. And he wasn't in a particularly forgiving mood.

He was three-quarters of the way down the slope when the tent's entrance opened. A head poked out, followed by a thin lanky figure, all legs and elbows. A kid. Or, given his height, a teen. He stretched, then looked out over the river for a moment before turning back toward the tent. He caught sight of Ethan approaching and froze. Then he bolted to the right, tearing off along the riverbank with surprising speed. Ethan and Nyle gave chase.

If the kid wasn't on his school's track and field team, he was depriving them of real talent. He sailed over a fallen log with the ease of a hurdler and then headed for a thicket of overgrown bushes surrounding a dense copse of trees.

Ethan ran for exercise, focusing more on stamina than speed. The knee injury that had ended his hockey career had healed, but he'd never regain complete strength in it. Neither he nor Nyle were going to be able to outrun the kid, although the distance between them wasn't widening. Glancing at the other man, he pointed toward the thicket. The other Mountie grimaced, but plunged in after the kid. Ethan stopped, bending over to pick up three fist-sized rocks before speeding after the other two.

He ducked a thorny branch that could have raked at his face, but felt something catch on his suit jacket. Heard the rip when he tore away. When he came through the bushes, he could see the other officer, still stalwartly running after the kid, but lagging.

"Nyle!" He waited for the other officer to look back at him. "Move away." With alacrity, the man veered right and Ethan stopped. Hefted one of the rocks in his hand. Then cocked back and threw it at the fleeing kid. It hit him squarely in the back of one knee, which crumpled beneath him, taking him to the ground. Nyle raced over as the teen struggled to his feet and continued running, but he was limping now and the other Mountie easily caught up with him. He grabbed the kid's shirt, yanking him to a stop and was restraining him when Ethan jogged up to them.

Nyle's teeth flashed. "Impressive. Thought you were just a hockey plug. Didn't know you played baseball, too."

"My fastball was clocked at eighty-one miles per hour senior year. But I just lobbed that one to slow him down."

"That's police brutality," the boy said sullenly. His face was red from exertion and he had a bad case of acne, his hair shaved close on one side, with a hank of long brown hair hanging from the other. He gave his head a toss to get the hair out of his eyes. "It was a punk move."

"You think?" Ethan asked conversationally as they made their way back toward the tent, walking around the thicket this time. "Me, I tend to think of a punk as someone who runs away. Guess it's all a matter of perspective. What do you think, Nyle?"

The agent had one hand on the kid's bound arms and another on his shoulder as he guided him around the log the boy had sailed over earlier. "You know what a real punk move is? Deliberately setting up camp in an active crime scene."

The kid lifted a shoulder. "How were we supposed to know it was still active?"

"The police tape should have been a tip-off," Nyle was saying, but Ethan had seized on one word. *We.* Dammit. The kid wasn't alone.

He started running back toward the tent, although he had little hope that the boy's companion was still in the vicinity. There hadn't been any vehicles around as they'd approached the slope, and he tried to recall whether there'd been a boat of some sort. Ethan couldn't remember. Like a dog sighting a rabbit, once he'd seen the kid take off, his focus had only been chasing him down.

He burst out of the trees, scanning the shoreline. Then felt his blood freeze.

"I'm telling you, bitch. Let go or I'll knock you out cold."

There was a canoe in the water, ten feet or so from the bank. Another boy was standing in it, an oar cocked at a threatening angle. And Alexa... Jesus. She was waist-deep in the water, both hands grasping the stern of the canoe, walking backward as she pulled it and its occupant toward shore.

"I don't think that would be wise."

"Oh, really?" the kid sneered. "I swear to God, you take another step and I'll..."

Ethan opened his mouth to disrupt the scene. But before he could say a word, Alexa stopped. Then, with a quick twist of her hands, she flipped the canoe over. The kid dropped the oar, his arms wheeling comically as he hit the water. When he came up for air, sputtering and swearing, Alexa was behind him, wrenching one arm behind his shoulder blade and propelling him toward shore.

Ethan grinned, delighted. As a girl, she'd been intriguing. Delightful. Full of surprises. Some things hadn't changed.

The teen started to struggle. "Consider that a lesson," he called, strolling toward the two as the canoe floated down the river. "Never threaten a woman." Her shoes were on the shore. She must have toed them off before wading into the water.

He waited, fists propped on his hips until Nyle and Alexa had both kids back at the tent. Alexa and the boy she'd dumped in the water were soaked, and the kid was complaining bitterly. "That's a nine-hundred-dollar canoe. You gotta let me get it. My step-dad's gonna kill me."

"I'm betting he'll be unhappier when we show up at your place and tell him where we found you two camped today." The boys exchanged a glance. Relying on memories of his own teenage years, Ethan said "He didn't know you were camping at all, did he? What'd you do, tell your parents you were staying at the other's house and then come here instead?"

Canoe-boy was a half head shorter than his friend, with a thick crop of wet dark hair and what looked like a perpetual sneer on his face. "We didn't even see the tape. It was dark when we got here and pitched the tent. You can't prove otherwise."

Nyle snorted. "Try again, kid. You had to pull down one side of the perimeter tape to even get inside the area."

Smugly, he shook his head. "No, it's hanging pretty low from the rain. Easy to overlook it."

"Nyle, why don't you get some pictures?" Ethan gestured toward the tent and tried not to notice the way Alexa's wet black slacks clung to her thighs. "I'm sure their proud parents would be interested to know what their kids were up to last night." The other man stepped away from the kid they'd chased and dug his cell out of his pocket.

"Uh..." The tall kid's head bobbed as he looked at his friend and then at Ethan. "Listen, I know it was a dumbass move. We just did it on a dare."

"Shut up, Sean."

Ignoring his friend, the boy plowed on. "But my dad will ground me for like the whole rest of the summer if he finds out. We didn't mess things up. Anything still here had to be washed away by the rains. It's not like we spoiled any evidence."

"But you could have." The forensic ident investigators had returned in daylight after the body had been removed, but according to the call Ethan had gotten yesterday, their efforts had been in vain. Like the kid said, the rain had been an accomplice in destroying any physical evidence the offender might have left behind. Ethan had intended to remove the tape when they stopped here this morning. That didn't mean, however, that he was willing to cut these punks any slack. At the very least, he'd put a scare into them that might serve as a warning the next time they decided to insert themselves in a crime scene.

"Naw, those forensic ident guys are pretty thorough. And it's been raining for like four

days. Even footprints would've been wiped out."

Ethan cocked his head and studied the boy more closely. "You police now?" With the explosion of crime shows on TV, everyone was an expert these days.

Sean ducked his head. "No. My dad's a constable, though. That's why he'd rip me a new one if he heard about this. I know we shouldn't have done it. I'm just saying... there was no harm done. We come here a lot to fish during the day and sometimes camp out. It's the most isolated part of the river around here, so we don't have to worry about anyone bothering us."

Isolated came in handy if they'd come to engage in illegal activities. On the heels of the thought came another. Isolation might also have been what drew the offender to this spot. "Ever see anyone in the area?"

Sean shook his head. "The easiest way to this place is by water."

True enough, Ethan conceded silently. But the forensic

ident unit had searched the shoreline for nearly a mile downriver to no avail. The weather had destroyed any trace of the UNSUB.

"There was a van parked up there a few days ago, though," Sean continued. "Saw it when we were coming across in the canoe. Figured it was a couple fu—...uh... screwing or something."

Interest flaring, Ethan asked, "A van. Anyone in it?"

Shrugging, the boy said, "I don't know. Didn't really pay attention. I guess there was, because it was gone by the time we pulled the canoe to shore."

"What day was that?"

"Uh..." He screwed up his forehead. "Saturday?"

"Friday," the shorter kid put in with an air of resignation. "It was a white Ford Econoline with lettering on the side. Or maybe one of those magnetic signs that companies use. 2014 or older."

Ethan narrowed his eyes. "You got a better look at it than Sean?"

The sneer was back, in the kid's voice and his expression. "No, I just know the vehicle. My stepdad's got a plumbing business and had a van like that, except it was navy. He waited until 2015 to replace it because that's when Ford changed to the Transit."

To Nyle he said, "Take off Sean's cuffs." He reached in his pocket for his cell and snapped a couple of pictures of both boys. "Tell me your names."

"Rick Anthony," the shorter kid said resignedly. Ethan observed Sean's gaze darting to his friend and knew the kid had given him a false name. Being a smartass was going to get the kid in trouble, probably sooner rather than later.

"Sean Blanchett."

"Detective Samuels will take your addresses and phone

numbers in case we need to contact you again. Should we discover you gave us false information, we'll show your pictures at the local police station." Rick's expression stilled. "We'll be a lot less patient in that case."

"Uh...it's Rick Anthony...Sibbits." The kid turned to shade his eyes as he tracked the canoe's progress downriver. Then groaned. "Man, I gotta go. It's half a mile away already. How am I supposed to get to it?"

"You know how to swim, don't you? Give your information to Detective Samuels and you can go." The kid didn't wait another second. He reeled off his address and phone number before beelining for the river bank and descended it, his gaze trained on the canoe.

Nyle finished writing down the information then flipped his notebook shut. "You can join your friend," he told Sean. "But you need to start making better choices if you want to enjoy your freedom this summer."

Relief flashed over the boy's face. "I do. I mean, I will." He nearly tripped over his feet as he headed down the slope.

"I don't have a teenager yet," Nyle muttered, "but if either of my kids turn out like those two you might have to get me out of lock-up."

Alexa smiled. "Especially Rick. That attitude would be tough to live with."

Nyle eyed her with interest. "Do you have any children?"

She shook her head. "I was widowed before we could start a family."

Her words hit Ethan like a well-placed punch. Whatever he'd felt toward her after she'd left him, he would never have wished her more suffering. Surely there was a limit to how much loss one person should have to live through.

Switching his regard to Ethan, Nyle asked, "Think this will lead to anything?"

Ethan opened his mouth to respond, then lost his train of thought as Alexa peeled away from them. She retrieved her shoes, taking her cell out of one them, and balanced on one leg to slip one on, then the other. "It's a long shot," he said, forcing his gaze away from her. "Any number of people might park in a scenic area for a bit, take in the view." Or, he added silently, to find privacy for other types of activities. "And the UNSUB was just as likely to access the site by water as land. But let's take another look at the embankment. See if there are any indentations the rain didn't wipe away."

"Forensic ident guys would have found them if they were there," Nyle muttered, but he and Alexa fanned out from Ethan to examine the rocky slope.

A half hour later Ethan admitted failure. They headed back toward the vehicle.

"If the offender did drive into the province," Nyle said, "the only passenger list he'd show up on would be the ferry. But without a name, we have no way of identifying him."

"Right. We have the airline, bus and train manifests for entry into New Brunswick shortly before the victims there were killed. We can compare them to the ones for Nova Scotia and see if the same name pops on any of them."

"It has to be done," Nyle said resignedly as he rounded the hood of the car. "But that doesn't mean I'm looking forward to it."

Neither was Ethan. It was a mind-numbingly tedious task. Which pretty much summed up the nature of police work. Sporadic bouts of action punctuating days of dead-end interviews, or poring over documents and grainy video. Nine times out of ten the trail to the killer surfaced from one of the deadly dull chores. Maybe they'd catch a break this time around. They were certainly due one.

THEY STOPPED at a gas station so Alexa could change, and an hour later Ethan nosed the vehicle into the parking lot of RCMP's H Division Headquarters in Halifax's Burnside Industrial Park. The building was multi-leveled red brick, fronted by an arc of mirrored windows. It was minutes away from the forensic suites where they'd attended the autopsy. He pulled into a parking space in the crowded lot. "Captain Sedgewick is our contact here. He has the manifests and he'll allot us some workspace." His cell vibrated as he got out of the car and he answered it as he waited for Nyle and Alexa.

"Manning."

"Sergeant Manning, this is Officer Baxter of the Halifax Police Department. I'm in charge of the tip line handling the recent homicide victim's ID."

Adrenaline did a fast sprint up Ethan's spine. "Hello, Officer Baxter." He thumbed on the speakerphone as Alexa and Nyle joined him.

"I know we've been running down lots of false reports," the officer said, "and maybe this is just another one. A woman working as a maid at the Claremont Towers on Broadway called it in. No match on Simard's name or aliases, but she recognized the picture. Said he'd propositioned her when she went in to clean room seven-fifteen."

Ethan reminded himself how faulty eyewitness accounts could be. The reminder didn't temper his response. "When was this?"

"The call came in about ten minutes ago."

"Thanks. I'll look into it."

After getting the address of the hotel, Ethan disconnected, and looked the address up on his phone. GPS claimed it was twenty minutes away. He mentally tacked on another ten, fifteen minutes based on the traffic they'd experienced on the drive to headquarters.

"Even a dead end would be more exciting than poring over manifests," Nyle said hopefully.

"We can do both. You and Alexa go in and meet with Captain Sedgewick. I'll check this out. Probably be back in an hour to help out."

"Okay," Nyle agreed, "but Alexa and I are going to save the pages with the smallest print for you." She nodded in agreement.

The corner of his mouth pulling up, Ethan turned back toward the vehicle. "I'd expect nothing less."

"OBVIOUSLY, I can't offer to open the room, Sergeant." The hotel manager, Lon Haskell, was politely apologetic. "We can't be certain Louise identified room seven-fifteen's occupant correctly, and an error like that could cost us a guest."

"I understand that. But perhaps I can verify the maid's ID. Do you have security cameras on that floor?"

"Yes, of course." The hotel manager smoothed the garish pink paisley tie he'd paired with a sober black suit. "They're mounted at each end of the floor with another outside the elevators."

"I want to see the footage from the cameras for that floor beginning with the date Simmons checked in."

Relief flashed across the man's expression. "That I can arrange. If you'll follow me to security?" As they strode toward the bank of elevators in the lobby, Haskell pulled a radio from his pocket and spoke quietly into it.

Security turned out to be two cramped adjoining rooms on the far end of the fifth floor. Stepping through the doorway after Haskell, Ethan took in the rows of cameras that lined one wall. "Do you have the playback for seventh floor ready, Phil?" The manager addressed the young balding man who'd bounced up nervously at their entrance from his chair facing the screens.

"I've got the film from all seventh-floor cameras starting at four-twenty last Saturday, when you said Simmons had checked in."

"Concentrate on the camera near the elevator," Ethan said. Room seven-fifteen was likely in the middle of the floor, too far away for clear images on the cameras mounted at either end of the hall.

The younger man bent over a screen, punching some buttons to fast forward the digital footage on one screen. After a couple of minutes, he pressed another key to halt it. Backed it up for a moment and then stopped it again. "Here's four-twenty."

The three of them stood staring at the screen for long minutes. Every time the elevator doors opened, Ethan leaned forward to scan the faces of the disembarking passengers. It was exactly thirty-two minutes after four according to the time-stamp on the screen when the elevator doors slid open and three people stepped out, one a dark-haired man.

Identification was difficult from the man's profile alone. Ethan stared at the film. Turn toward the camera, dammit. A young blond woman took the elbow of the elderly woman at her side and led her slowly down the hall. The man turned his head to watch their progress, his gaze focused on the blonde. "There. Right there." Ethan stabbed his finger at the screen. "Halt it. Can you freeze it where his face is turned directly toward the camera?"

"Sergeant, I can do about anything with these cameras," Phil said happily, his fingers dancing over the keys. "State-of-the-art system, you know?" A moment later he had an image frozen, and then, focusing on the face, enlarged it, distorting the image a bit with each magnification.

But that didn't matter. Because it was still easy to tell that the man on the camera was Felix Simard.

HASKELL STOOD BEHIND ETHAN, wringing his hands. "I'd feel so much better if you had a warrant."

They stood outside room seven-fifteen, the manager making no move to open the door.

Ethan reached for professionalism. "Sir, I'm an officer of the law and I've made a positive ID on an image taken on your hotel camera that matches a homicide victim discovered yesterday. I can assure you, Mr. Simmons isn't his name and he's not able to complain about our accessing his room. He's deceased. Please open the door."

After a moment, Haskell handed the card to Ethan. Clearly he wanted to shield himself as much as possible from any repercussions. So much so, that when Ethan waved the card over the magic eye near the door handle and opened the door, Haskell merely held it open to watch Ethan's progress, but didn't step inside.

Forgetting the man, Ethan glanced inside the bathroom, noting the toiletry bag on the counter. He moved toward the closet wardrobe next to the TV, opened the doors, and found a navy suit hanging next to a lightweight dark, hooded jacket. Pulling a pair of plastic gloves from his suit pocket, he checked the pockets. The jacket yielded nothing save for a folded metal object. Withdrawing it, Ethan flicked the button in its center. A wicked-looking blade unfolded. He pursed his lips in a silent whistle and refolded the knife. Replaced it. It'd be easy enough to lift prints from the weapon that would verify his ID of Simard's image on the security footage.

A moment later he realized that wouldn't be necessary. The wallet in the suit pocket bore a driver's license in the name of John Simmons. But the image on it was Felix Simard.

Muscles tightening in anticipation, he moved to the black suitcase sitting on one of the beds. He rifled through it, tossing clothes aside until he came to a black zippered laptop case.

Satisfaction speared through him. It was likely password protected, but they'd see what the IT analysts could do with it. There was nothing else of note in the bag or the secreted zippered pockets. Ethan straightened and scanned the room consideringly. There were no overt signs that the room had been the primary crime scene. Hotels were public places, filled with people and security. The killer would have taken a risk, killing Simard here.

To be thorough, he headed in the direction of the bathroom. "Are you about done, Sergeant?" The manager's voice barely registered. "I don't mind saying, I continue to be uncomfortable with this entire process. I'd hate to have guests aware that we..." The words continued. Ethan wasn't listening. He lifted an arm toward the opaque shower curtain. His brain registered the slight movement behind it even as the curtain and rod plunged toward him, a figure behind it leaping out of the tub to shove Ethan hard against the counter.

The quarters were tight, and he was off-balance. He reached for his attacker, grappling with the plastic to find the opening of the curtain. A fist shot out, clipping Ethan on the jaw, before he grabbed for the curtain rod and drove it forward, hoping to knock his assailant off his feet as the back of his knees hit the tub.

He got a glimpse of the man as the curtain slid away in their struggle. Shaven head. Bearded. Heavily muscled. Swarthy. The stranger grabbed the rod to keep Ethan from pressing it against his windpipe. With a mighty shove, he wrenched it to the side and aimed a kick at Ethan's groin. When Ethan dodged to avoid it, the man used that moment to break free and charge for the door, Ethan a step behind him.

"What in the world...are you Mr. Simmons? My apologies for this..." The stranger grabbed Haskell and pushed him violently into Ethan, taking advantage of the few moments it took the men to disentangle to sprint toward the exit at the end of the hall.

"Sergeant, what in heaven's name..."

"Your radio!" Ethan snapped, already reaching for the instrument clipped to Haskell's belt. "What channel for Phil in security?"

The hotel manager was white-faced and shaking. "This is highly unusual. Highly..."

"The channel!" Radio in hand Ethan was already in pursuit.

"Three-one-nine. But you can't just take that..."

Ethan reached the door the attacker had gone through and began descending the stairs three at a time. He pressed the code that Haskell had given him. "Phil. I need Phil on the cameras. Now!"

There was a scuffling noise, and the man he'd talked to earlier came on, his voice surprised. "Mr. Haskell?"

"RCMP Sergeant Manning. We've got a person of interest who just went through the east stairs on floor seven. Caucasian. Five-nine. Two hundred pounds. Dark complected. Shaven head. Black beard. Jeans and dark windbreaker." Ethan passed floor five. Started toward four. "I assume he descended, but he may have gone up first instead. I need camera angles that would catch the exits on each floor. Any door to the outside from the lobby. Find him."

"Yes, sir." Ethan ran by a woman in pink spandex who was power-walking the stairs, and she jumped to the side to avoid being bowled over, then shot him a filthy look.

"No cameras in the stairwells, I assume?" He rounded the third-floor steps and headed toward the second.

"No, sir, but once he leaves it we'll...wait, I think I've spotted him! Navy jacket. Looks like he could bench-press a Volkswagen?"

Remembering the punch he'd taken from a ham-sized fist, Ethan said, "Sounds about right." He took the stairs to the main floor at a rapid pace.

"He's speed-walking across the lobby, as we speak. Heading toward the west exit, which leads to Salem Boulevard."

Shit. "Cameras on the outside of the building?" Ethan jumped down the remaining steps, the force of his landing singing up his spine. Yanking open the door, he burst into the lobby and ran toward the exit Phil had mentioned.

"Yes, sir. Adjust that angle," Phil muttered in an aside. "He's heading north on the sidewalk adjacent to the hotel.

Stepping into the street...might be hailing a cab, sir. There's a line of them across the street."

Dodging the clusters of people, Ethan ran for the doors and hit the street, looking for the man in vain.

"He's halfway down the block. Ducked down behind cab number three seventy-three as he's getting in the backseat. I'm going to lose sight of him as soon as they move."

"You've done enough. Thanks." The traffic had thinned a bit since Ethan had arrived at the hotel. He ran into the street, his action rewarded by a litany of horns. One vehicle braked to a violent stop inches from him. Banging a hand on its hood, he darted by, his focus trained on the cab holding the stranger as it pulled away from the curb. He had one last glimpse of his assailant as the man turned and shot his middle finger into the air before the taxi rounded the corner.

# CHAPTER SIX

"COULD they make this print any smaller? I swear my eyes are bleeding."

Alexa gave Nyle a commiserating smile. They'd started with all the airline passenger lists for three days preceding Simard's death, dividing them up between them. Each page had to be checked for the name of the victim, all of his documented aliases and the names of his known acquaintances. It was laborious work. When they found nothing, Nyle began cross-checking the pages against the airline manifests for visitors into New Brunswick for a few days prior to the first victim being found there.

Alexa began to put the more recent pages she'd scanned back in order when a name seemed to jump off the front sheet at her. She'd missed it before, but this time its familiarity sparked a memory. She turned to her laptop to bring up the briefing notes Ethan distributed each day.

"Mikiel Fornier," she said slowly.

Nyle lifted his gaze from his work. "Fornier?" He thought for a moment. "That's the name of one of Simard's buddies, right? At least it was back when he was arrested fourteen years ago."

"Look at this." She nudged the manifest page toward him, her finger stabbing at the name. "He appears on the passenger manifest for JetCanada. He arrived at the Halifax airport a few hours ago." Logic suppressed her initial surge of excitement. "Of course, there may be several people with the same name."

"True enough," he muttered. "But what's his city of origin?" They peered at the page, then simultaneously, "Montreal." Alexa's gaze met Nyle's. "Same city as Simard."

"Maybe something, maybe nothing." But he pushed away from the table and headed for the door, the urgency in his movements belying his nonchalant tone. "The airline's PNR is a personal name record for all passengers. It has information that isn't on the manifests. I'm going to Sedgewick's office to see if we can access those details. Good catch, Alexa."

She looked at the remaining pile in front of Nyle's empty seat without enthusiasm. To give her eyes a break, she took a moment to pick up her phone and text Ethan. *A Mikiel Fornier from Montreal flew in this a.m. Confirming ID as Simard's acquaintance.* As she pressed send, she noted the time. It had been nearly two hours since Ethan had left them, which should surely be more than enough time for him to check out the tip at the hotel and be back.

Unless the maid's lead was valid. She frowned. But if that were true, he'd have surely alerted them. She pushed away the niggling sense of concern and returned to the airline lists. When Nyle burst through the door thirty minutes later waving a sheet of paper, she was more than ready for the interruption.

"PNR yielded a date and place of birth, which matches the Mikiel Fornier who's a known acquaintance of Simard. Even got a photo, courtesy of his most recent arrest two years ago." He slapped the paper down in front of Alexa.

The image was a mugshot, showing a beefy man with a bullet-shaped shaven head and bushy black beard. A prison tat adorned the side of his neck. She took out her phone and took a picture of the image, sending it to Ethan with the message *Confirmed. Mikiel Fornier.* "Do you think Simard sent for him? Or that they had plans to meet here?"

Nyle sank back into the seat he'd vacated earlier. "Maybe he came looking for him. We just ID'd Simard's identity yesterday morning."

"Have you heard from Ethan?"

Nyle shook his head and reached for a pile of manifests. "No. He hasn't even responded to my messages about Fornier. If I didn't know better, I'd say he's deliberately avoiding us until we get this chore finished without him."

ETHAN NOW WISHED for the traffic he'd cursed only a short time ago. The taxi containing his assailant was moving freely. It'd be held up only by traffic lights. As he gave chase on foot, he drew his cell out and pressed the number for his contact in the Halifax Police Department. Muttered an epithet as the cab turned right on a red light.

"Lieutenant Martin."

"It's RCMP Sergeant Manning. I'm heading east on foot after a person of interest on Cortail Street and Sixty-Seventh. Yellow cab number three seventy-three. I need patrol cars in the area to give pursuit." Martin wasted no time asking questions. Ethan could hear him radioing the message to the patrol cars. "I'm uncertain whether he's armed." He gave a brief description of his attacker. "The cab just turned north on the next block." With a burst of energy, he sped down the sidewalk, dodging pedestrians and strollers as he raced toward the corner to keep the vehicle in eyesight.

"Vehicle heading north on Montrose Street between Sixty-Seventh and Sixty-Eighth," Martin repeated.

"Unit two-four-six responding. I have a visual." Ethan heard the faint response of a patrolman on Martin's radio.

"RCMP officer in the vicinity in foot pursuit." Then Martin spoke into the phone again. "We've got units converging on the area."

"Thanks." He rounded the corner and headed north. "I see a department vehicle." With an eye on the traffic, he darted into the street. On the opposite sidewalk, he ran as fast as he was able, charging through a queue of thirsty patrons waiting for their coffee outside a Timmie's and nearly barreled into a couple of workmen in tan uniforms unloading a truck outside a restaurant. A siren split the air, the sound welcome to his ears. He could see the cab a block ahead now, and it was stopped, a uniformed officer approaching the driver's door. Then the passenger door on the opposite side burst open, and Ethan's attacker lunged out. He raced away from the car, heading directly for Ethan.

When the man saw Ethan coming, he veered to the right and ran through a shop doorway. The officer immediately gave pursuit, so Ethan, energy flagging, rounded the corner to cover the alley, drawing his weapon as he did so. The stranger burst through the back door of one of the buildings and headed his way, only to stumble to a halt when he saw Ethan,

"Hands in the air! RCMP!"

He could almost see the man weighing his options before he turned and fled the other direction. As he did, the officer who pursued him stepped through the rear door of the building the man had used. "Stop! Police!"

The bearded man stumbled to a halt, turning slowly, his arms half-raised, chest heaving.

"Sergeant Manning, RCMP." With his free hand, Ethan reached for his credentials and held them high for the uniformed officer to see. "Go ahead and cuff him. We'll take him in for questioning."

"Yes, Sergeant." The younger officer fastened cuffs on the larger man who was staring balefully at Ethan.

"What's your name?" The stranger didn't answer. Ethan put his weapon away and searched the man quickly. Found no ID or phone, but there was a large knife strapped to his ankle. Ethan disarmed him. "You're being arrested for assaulting a law enforcement officer and breaking and entering." Once he'd recited the man's rights, the patrol officer told Ethan, "Be glad to give you a ride."

His breathing still a bit labored, he nodded. "That's an offer I won't turn down."

ALEXA AND NYLE followed Ethan as he strolled into the interview room holding a slim file folder. The man Ethan had found in Simard's room was no longer in handcuffs. He was sitting in a chair where he'd spent the last hour and a half after his booking. It wasn't until they'd been en route to the police department that Ethan had seen the messages from Alexa and Nyle and summoned them to join him downtown.

Ethan checked to make sure the camera video-taping the interview was turned on. Then he dragged a chair away from the table opposite the man and sank into it, flipping open the file folder he held. Alexa positioned herself behind him against the wall. "Mikiel Fornier." There was a flicker in the other man's eyes that might have been recognition, but he said nothing. Taking the mugshot photo out of the folder, Ethan slid it across to the man. "Not a great likeness, but undeniably you."

Fornier's gaze flicked to the image and then back to Ethan, still silent.

"We know you're an associate of Felix Simard. We know Simard traveled to the province recently under the name John Simmons." Ethan's tone was grim. "You found a way to enter his hotel room illegally, which, as you'll recall, is where we first became acquainted." He fingered the bruise forming on his jaw. The man saw the gesture and gave a satisfied smile. "What were you doing there?"

Fornier flexed his hands. Each knuckle had a tattoo on it. Prison tats, like the one on his neck. The man was built like a short squat wall. Alexa hated to think about the physical altercation that had transpired between him and Ethan.

"I want a lawyer." They were the first words he'd spoken since they'd walked into the room.

"We'll be happy to facilitate that. Do you have someone in mind, or shall we contact Legal Aid?" Without waiting for an answer, Ethan reached into the folder again. He withdrew an array of crime-scene photos of Simard and splayed them before the other man. "As you can see from the pictures, you arrived too late to speak to your friend."

This time, there was no mistaking the man's reaction His dark eyes widened with shock as he studied each photo in turn. His big hands fisted on the table. "Who...who did this?"

"Assuming it wasn't you."

Eyes flashing, the man said, "I can show you my airline ticket stub. I arrived here only this morning."

"As a matter of fact, we know that. What we don't know, what you still haven't told us is why you flew in today."

The man's gaze fell to the photos again. He picked up one that showed a close-up of Simard's missing eyes. "He didn't answer his phone," he murmured, dropping the picture suddenly as if it burned him. "Felix is never out of communication. How long has he been dead?"

"His body was discovered early Monday morning. What was he doing in Nova Scotia?"

The man lifted a shoulder. "He had business here. I don't know what it was."

He was lying, Alexa thought. And he didn't make much of an effort to conceal it.

Ethan leaned back in his chair and surveyed the man. "I've got you for assaulting a law enforcement officer. With your record, that will likely put you back in prison. Maybe you've been missing it. You've been out for...what?" He opened the file and consulted some notes. "Five years now? Some cooperation here could work in your favor."

The man seemed to consider the offer. "What kind of cooperation?"

Nodding toward the pictures on the table, Ethan said, "Did Simard have enemies? Anyone you might know who would do this?"

Fornier's lip curled beneath the bushy beard. "All successful men have enemies. But one who would dare do this to Felix? No. It was a random killing. It must have been. You will find the killer. Or I will."

Ethan shot a look over his shoulder. "Dr. Hayden? Care to weigh in here?"

"It wasn't random." Alexa spoke for the first time, drawing the man's gaze to her. "He was targeted. And what was done to him was very personal. You can see from the pictures that his eyes were removed. But what you can't see is that a power drill was used to bore through the sockets into his brain." Shock flickered across the man's face, to be replaced by menace. "Someone hated him. Enough to torture him before his death. That sort of brutality speaks of violent emotion. Revenge. Rage. Both are highly personal, indeed. So, if you know of anyone capable of this, you need to tell us."

"First you guarantee a deal that my cooperation will mean there will be no charges." Fornier settled his heft more comfortably in his chair. "Then...maybe I have some information to share."

"Nyle." Ethan didn't turn his head as the other officer left the room. Alexa was a little stunned at how effortlessly Ethan had led Fornier to exactly this place. They'd already spoken with Risa Wilson, a Crown prosecutor who was watching the interview on a monitor nearby. Given the status of this case, and Fornier's close alliance with Simard, Wilson had agreed to streamline the process. She and Ethan had collaborated on the interview questions.

Ten minutes ticked by. The room was getting uncomfortably warm. Temperature settings were sometimes used to discomfit a recalcitrant arrestee in interview rooms in the States. She wondered if that was the case here. A few minutes later, the door opened again, and Nyle returned with Wilson. The woman approached the table and laid a bundle of paper-clipped sheets on it.

"Mr. Fornier." Her voice was crisp and as no-nonsense as her dark dress and sensible shoes. "This agreement is contingent upon you sharing information that helps advance the investigation into the death of Felix Simard. In return for your cooperation, no charges will be brought in relation to your altercation with Sergeant Manning. That includes assault on a police officer and flight from a peace officer. If you provide false details, or if you're deemed uncooperative, this agreement is void. Do you understand?"

"Yeah." The man took the pen she held out and scrawled his name on the last page as if he'd done this before.

Wilson nodded at Ethan as she took the signed papers and left the room again.

"So." Ethan withdrew a yellow legal pad and pen from the file folder. He pushed them across the table toward the other man. "Simard had enemies, you said. Just like all businessmen. Write down their names."

Slowly, Fournier reached for the pen. "There's a difference between enemies and people who could have done this." He indicated the pictures still displayed before him. "A bullet is easier. Or a knife." But he bent over the paper and wrote down some names. After he'd finished, he shoved the pad back across the table.

"When was the last time you spoke with Simard?"

Fornier scratched his chin through the beard and thought for a moment. "He arrived on Saturday afternoon. He was hoping to meet with an acquaintance here this week. I last talked to him Sunday, about noon. I called him back Monday and got no answer. I needed to tell him there was a problem. This man...the hotel where we thought he was staying had no record of his reservation."

"The man's name?"

Hesitating for a moment, Fornier finally said, "Armand Vance."

Nyle and Ethan exchanged a glance. "The embattled financier, Armand Vance? Simard knew him?"

With a twist of his lips, the other man shrugged. "He hoped to set up a meeting. We learned Vance would be in Nova Scotia this week. Felix lost money investing with him."

"But Armand isn't here?"

"No. That's what I was calling Felix about. I went to Toronto and checked for myself. Armand Vance never left the city. We had good intelligence that he was going to do so. Perhaps he changed his mind."

Alexa wondered if she was the only one who ascribed a sinister motive to Simard's attempted "meeting" with Vance.

"But you were never able to give him that information."

Fornier slowly swung his head back and forth. "Felix was no longer answering his phone by Monday. Today I got on a plane to come look for him. And met you." He nodded toward Ethan.

"Did he say anything else when you spoke with him?" There was a note of impatience in Ethan's voice. Alexa wasn't surprised. So far, the man had revealed little of value.

"We spoke of business. Some...matters I was taking care of in his absence. He mentioned that he thought he'd seen someone we both knew. I convinced him that was impossible." His tone was tinged with derision.

"Is that person on this list?" Ethan asked.

Fornier snorted. "No. He's a nobody. A pest who tried

to make trouble for Felix years ago. We caught up with him then and convinced him that blackmail didn't pay. He wouldn't show his face around either of us again if he's even still alive." He grinned widely, his teeth very white against the black beard. "He didn't seem a healthy sort."

"When did you last have dealings with the man?"

"Two...no, three years ago, maybe."

"And his name?"

An expression of contempt crossed Fornier's face. "I never learned his real name. He said it was Anis Tera, which of course was fake."

A shock zipped down Alexa's spine. "Anis Tera? You're sure?"

"Of course." The man flexed his hands again, his gaze wandering insultingly down her figure. "As certain as I am that he lied about that, as well as many other things."

She pushed away from the wall to approach the table, aware that Ethan was sending her a questioning glance. "And he tried to blackmail Simard three years ago. How did that occur?"

"He is what we call a piss-ant. He thought he was being very clever by contacting Felix through an anonymous email server, with messages that disappeared minutes after opening." Fornier curled his lip. "We convinced him that Felix couldn't wire the blackmail money because police were monitoring his accounts. A cash transaction was arranged. We set the bait, and he took it."

She stared at him for a moment, her mind racing. "And Simard thought the man was here. When was that?"

"Saturday evening. Felix said he saw him driving by in a white van. But as I told him, that is impossible."

"And why is that?"

"Because this person who calls himself Anis Tera is not

a man. He had to hide behind a computer to make his threats. He would never have the courage to approach Felix again."

She nodded as if she understood. "Because he's a piss-ant."

Fornier folded his arms across his chest. "Exactly that. A cockroach. Anis Tera doesn't have the nerve or the strength to do something like that." He nodded at the photos in front of him.

"Mr. Fornier, we're going to have you work with a sketch artist to come up with a likeness of the man you knew as Anis Tera." Nyle left the room silently. Ethan continued, "In the meantime, I want you to tell us everything you recall about him."

The other man looked at both of them askance. "You're wasting your time, I'm telling you. He wouldn't have the balls to come near Felix again." A sly smile crossed his face. "And I know that for a fact."

THEY HUDDLED with Lieutenant Martin in the room next door, where the man had been watching the interview on CCTV with the Crown prosecutor. "Edouard Cote is an accomplished forensic artist," he was telling them. "He can often tease out physical descriptions from the most recalcitrant witnesses."

Ethan wished he could share the lieutenant's optimism. They'd spent several minutes trying to get details about Tera's appearance before leaving Fornier. He'd come up with little more than short, weak, and brown hair. Cote was going to need to be gifted indeed to develop a sketch they could use.

In the meantime, the requested warrant had arrived for Simard's effects at the hotel. At Ethan's request, Martin had sent a couple of men to pick them up. The laptop would be overnighted to the Ottawa crime lab. Even if it had been replaced since the blackmail messages three years ago, there might be information regarding the man's business that he was sure the Montreal police would find interesting.

He slanted a look at Alexa. "You zeroed in on Fornier as soon as he mentioned the alias Anis Tera." And it *was* an alias; they could be fairly sure of that. A quick search of the Internet revealed no Canadian by that name.

"Anis. That's Swedish, isn't it?" put in Martin.

"Anis Tera. *Anisoptera*. It's the scientific infraorder name for dragonflies."

"Holy shit," Ethan muttered. "I perked up when Fornier mentioned the white van Simard thought was following him. But that name...you're right. It's too damn similar not to be him." They'd never released the information about the insect samples in the victim's mouths, although the media pressed them for more details nearly every interview. The cautious side of him tempered his flare of excitement, but he couldn't prevent a lick of adrenaline from spreading through his veins. They'd had suspects before on the earlier task force. But this fit too neatly for it to fizzle the way the others had.

"Just this morning some kids reported spotting a 2014 or older white Ford Econoline above the embankment of the crime scene," Ethan told Lieutenant Martin. The other man's eyes widened in understanding. "And now Fornier reveals that Simard mentioned seeing this Tera in a white van. That can't be a coincidence."

"If the UNSUB drove the vehicle from New Brunswick, there are limited ways into Nova Scotia," Nyle said, as

Ethan opened his laptop and brought up a map of the province. "His second victim was in Fredericton, and he needed to come to Halifax for Simard."

"Fastest driving route would be from Fredericton to Moncton, where he'd catch the Trans-Canada Highway," muttered Ethan as he scanned the map he'd brought up. "That has tolls, though." Which meant cameras. "It would be nearly two and half hours longer to circumvent the toll roads and drive to the St. John's ferry. Nyle." The other man was peering at the computer over his shoulder. "Check where the highway cameras are for the roads on all these routes."

"Highway traffic cameras won't show driver images," Nyle warned. As Ethan straightened from the computer, the other man took his place. "But the cameras at the toll roads...yeah, maybe..." He began typing.

"I have some men I can put at your disposal," Lieutenant Martin put in.

"Thanks. I'm sure we can use them." But he needed to talk to Captain Campbell, immediately. Ethan looked at Alexa. "The kids spotted the van on Friday. Simard saw it Saturday evening."

"And he was dead early Monday morning."

Ethan nodded. He needed to issue a BOLO alert on the van, which wasn't going to be easy without a license plate. If the UNSUB was still in the province, they wanted to prevent him from leaving.

His mind was racing. They had the Anis Tera alias to give to all transportation centers to stop the UNSUB from buying a ticket to leave Nova Scotia. But he was under no allusions that the man had only one alias. "No reason for him to still be in the vicinity." There was a burn of frustration at the possibility that the man might have already escaped them. "Unless…"

She picked up his thought. "Unless he's planning on a second victim here."

He took his phone out and pressed the numbers to call Campbell.

"Ethan?" He looked at Alexa questioningly, his cell already up to his ear. "We need more information from Fornier about the intel that brought Simard here. There should be a safety check done on Vance, and anyone else included in that intelligence."

"You're right."

Campbell came on the phone then. "I was just about to call you, Manning. That press conference has been set for today, in less than three hours."

Somehow Ethan had managed to put the prospect of a news conference out of his head. Wincing, he said, "Maybe we should hold off. We've got a person of interest in the case, and I need all the resources you can bring to bear to shut off his possible routes out of the province. If he is still here, I want to keep it that way."

CHAPTER SEVEN

*For all have sinned and fall short of the glory of God.* —
Romans 3:23

THE TV in the room was on. Noiseless chatter that Anis
tuned out but for the occasional glance. His focus was on
his quarry, and she was proving more troublesome than he'd
expected.

He read again the email Jeanette Lawler had responded
with when, posing as Armand Vance, Anis has asked to
reschedule the interview until tomorrow morning. Such
rudeness! So very sure of herself and her place in the world.
Which, she appeared to believe, was a lofty perch above
other mortals.

"'Pride goeth before destruction, and a haughty spirit
before a fall,'" he murmured as he composed a reply. She'd
eventually agree, of course. A one-on-one with Armand
Vance was too good a scoop to pass up. No doubt she was
envisioning an even more brutal takedown for Vance in the
interview that would never transpire. Anis smiled as he
pushed his chair away from the computer. If people weren't

so predictable, so imperfect, he'd be able to lay down the sword he carried for the Lord.

He'd give her an hour and then head toward her hotel again to watch for her exit. Lawler craved the night scene. The clubs and godless music. She'd remained in her room most of the time she'd been here, preparing for the phony interview with Vance. Anis was betting she was chafing at the solitude. Sometime tonight, she'd go on the prowl. And that's when he'd take her.

Anis plucked the room service menu from beneath the phone on the desk and flipped it open. He'd panicked when Simard had seemed to recognize him when he'd been tailing him. Enough so that he had immediately driven the van back to the storage garage he'd arranged for and rented a car instead. Perhaps he'd use the car tonight for Lawler. He considered the possibility as he scanned the limited menu items. The rental was a mid-sized roomy sedan with a large trunk. It would be less noticeable than the van.

First, he'd eat. And then he'd begin his cleansing ritual that would ready him to do God's work tonight.

But something on the TV screen caught his attention. He reached for the remote to turn up the sound. "...and now here's RCMP Commissioner Reginald Gagnon with an update on the on-going manhunt for Canada's most notorious serial killer."

A sober-looking man with an angular face and deep-set eyes stepped before a microphone. There was an imposing-looking building in the background. The news conference took place on its steps. "Today, our task force positively ID'd the John Doe found in the Fundy National Park as Henry Paulus of Edmonton. According to co-workers Paulus was on a two-week vacation for hiking and backpacking."

A photo of the man appeared on the screen. "If anyone

came into contact with him in the park and has information to share, they should call the number at the bottom of the screen. I want to assure the public that we've made the manhunt for this killer a top priority. To that end, we've brought an outside forensic consultant on board who has expertise in areas of value to our investigation. Dr. Alexa Hayden is working closely with our task force."

It was amazing, Anis thought, his attention drifting, how much the man could say about how little they had to go on. Anis had begun his godly crusade thirteen years ago. In that time, he'd seen more than his share of these updates, all spinning inconsequential details and leads that would go nowhere. His was a battle blessed by God. The right- eousness of his work shielded him from capture.

He returned to the menu. Anis never made the mistake of eating too much before a night of judgment. Fresh fruit and a lean cut of meat with a salad, he decided. He placed the order and hung up the phone, glancing back at the TV disinterestedly.

The Commissioner was saying, "...I'll let task force leader Sergeant Ethan Manning handle the update in the case." A square appeared at the top right corner of the screen indicating that the man would be joining them from a remote location. A vapid-looking anchor asked avidly, "Sergeant Manning, what can you tell us about the ongoing search for The Tailor?"

Anis grimaced at the stupid ill-fitting nickname. The sergeant was a sober-faced man, who looked surprisingly young to be at the helm of an investigation this important. Anis had researched him when he'd read the news of the task force reforming. Nothing in what he'd discovered about the officer had been noteworthy. Investigators came and went. None had gotten close to him. They never would.

"We have a person of interest in the case that we're pursuing for questioning," Manning was saying. "This sketch was developed by an eyewitness who has had dealings with the man." A drawing showed on the screen. Anis peered closely at it before he burst into laughter. Was that supposed to be *him*? Oh, that was too rich. The sketch portrayed a male who could have been in his late thirties or forties. The face was unremarkable. It was much wider than Anis's, with a full mouth, abnormally small ears and wide forehead. He chuckled again in genuine amusement.

His gaze went to the woman standing behind Manning's left shoulder and all humor abruptly vanished. Her hair was very blonde, pulled away from an exquisite face, exposing fine features which were arranged in a serious expression. Who was she? His pulse sped up as he stared at her. Not a cop, he could tell that much. He remembered the commissioner mentioning a private consultant earlier. He turned to his laptop and typed in a search, bringing up several news stories about the investigation. Impatiently, he skimmed one after another until he found the information he was looking for.

Dr. Alexa Hayden...consultant from a forensics agency in the state...He scanned the article rapidly, and, finding little more of interest, he closed out of that window and opened another. He typed in her name. Was shocked when the page filled with hits. His meal forgotten, Anis read through several articles before he sat back, aware that his heart was hammering in his chest.

The woman wore several hats, it seemed, but the one that interested him most was her background in entomology. An unfamiliar heat suffused him. He looked at the TV again, but the news had moved on to yet another sensational story. No matter. His focus shifted back to his laptop. The letters after her name represented advanced degrees in more than one field. She wasn't self-taught like he was. But surely she'd specialized in entomology because she had the same fascination for insects as he did. She would understand the message he left with each of the the bodies.

Delight unfurled within him. He wondered if, like him, her interest in insects had developed in childhood. But hopefully, not a childhood like his, locked in a root cellar too much of the time with no companionship but the bugs that found their way into the space. He'd like to think that her affinity for the insect world came about more naturally.

Anis continued his online search, reading about her background and schooling on various bios for different organizations she belonged to. There were scholarly articles she'd authored, none of which were of interest to him. He also disregarded the information about the agency she worked for. It was personal information he was after, and that was in short supply. She appeared to live near Washington, DC. But then he found yet another short bio that stated she was originally from Canada.

A feeling of rightness settled over him. It was similar to the sensation he'd had when he'd rescued the boy from the flooded stream on his property. He'd known he was going to take him home with him, instead of returning him to his parents as soon as he'd seen him in the raging water. Alexa Hayden filled him with a similar sense of purpose. There was more research to be done.

But Anis Tera already knew their fates were linked.

# CHAPTER EIGHT

"CAUGHT THE PRESS CONFERENCE." Nyle looked up from the computer in the conference room at RCMP headquarters in Halifax, which was fast becoming their point of operations. The building was nearly empty, save for this area. "Sort of surprised the brass didn't pressure you to release your profile while they had you on TV."

Alexa grimaced as she strolled into the room. "They tried. We had a phone conference with Captain Campbell prior, and he shared that request from the Commissioner. It took some doing, but I convinced them it would be of little value to the public." She hadn't been surprised by the request. It was a common one from law-enforcement departments seeking to calm a jittery public. "Profiles are tools so investigators better understand the offender they're tracking. Using them in media communications is just a glitzy bone to throw a public that spends too much time watching Hollywood's idea of investigative work."

Nyle let loose a surprised laugh. "Agreed. But I'm surprised you managed to change their minds."

"I had help from Ethan," she admitted as she drew a

chair out from the conference table and sank into it. She couldn't be completely sure whether it was because Ethan held profiles in low esteem, or if he agreed that making the information public was useless.

"Where is he now?"

"Holed up with Captain Sedgewick." And he'd been on the phone the entire drive over, giving directives to the other task force members and the police personnel on loan from Halifax PD.

"I heard he was in contact with Toronto police," Nyle said. "They've located Armand

Vance and have spoken to him?"

Her stomach rumbled. With a jolt, she realized they hadn't eaten since this morning. "Yes. Vance denies that he ever had any plans to travel to Nova Scotia, which, apparently would be a violation of his interim judicial release before trial. When I spoke with Fornier again, he claimed his intel said Vance was coming here secretly for a taping of Jeanette Lawler's *Exposé* show."

"So the information was bait to get Simard to Halifax."

She nodded. "It seems so." Not for the first time she thought about how familiar the UNSUB was with his victim. He'd known exactly what it would take to draw Simard to Nova Scotia. "I still don't understand why the offender didn't attack Simard in Ontario. That makes him the first victim who was killed outside his home province."

Nyle pushed away from his laptop, where it appeared he was accessing the DMV website and jotting down information for owners of older Econoline white cargo vans. The list was depressingly long, and probably a waste of time. But they couldn't rule out the possibility that the UNSUB resided in the province. He could have decided to entice Simard here because it was the offender's home turf.

"Lots of details about Simard's killings were different than the other victims," he reminded her. "I got the idea from Fornier that they hurt this Anis Tera quite badly once they caught up with him after his blackmail attempt. If Tera is the UNSUB, he might have sought to avoid Montreal, where he could be recognized."

"And where Simard had muscle at his disposal." Alexa glanced at the door, wondering what was keeping Ethan. "You're right, it could have been an attempt to isolate him. To level the playing field." She tapped a finger against the table as she thought. "Before the New Brunswick victims, the UNSUB had been inactive for three years. Fornier claims they had dealings with Anis Tera about that long ago."

Nyle nodded slowly, rubbing his chin. "Actually, I'm surprised he didn't kill him. Nothing we know about Simard paints him as the forgiving type."

And if Alexa had read Fornier correctly, the man enjoyed brutality for its own sake. "If Anis Tera is the offender we're after, maybe his injuries were severe enough to keep him inactive for three years."

"You think this escalation is just him making up for lost time?"

"Whatever triggered him—maybe near-fatal injuries if indeed it's Anis Tera—might have created this urgency in him. Perhaps even a near rage. He feels justified in his killings, remember. And how inherently unfair it must have seemed to him to suffer so."

Nyle snorted. "Unfair. That's a good one. So, is he done here or not?"

The door opened, and Ethan walked in on Nyle's question. "I don't know," Alexa admitted. "But I'd feel a lot better if we knew that Jeanette Lawler was safely at home."

The woman might have been part of the elaborate ruse used to bring Simard to Nova Scotia, as Vance was. At least Alexa hoped so. She'd researched the reporter on the way back here, while Ethan had driven and spoken on the phone the entire way. Lawler resided in Vancouver, but she often flew to where her guests lived and filmed on location.

"We need food. And a truckload of Timmies," Ethan announced as he pulled out a chair and dropped into it.

Alexa smiled. It'd been a long time since she'd heard the uniquely Canadian word for the coffee from the popular Tim Hortons chain. "I could get on board with that. Especially the food."

Ethan loosened his tie, which looked as though it had been mangled since the press conference. "To catch you up, I now have the commissioner's assurances that all evidence from this case will go to the front of the queue in the labs."

Nyle looked as impressed as Alexa felt. If the crime lab in Ottawa was anything like the ones in the States, evidence could languish for weeks or longer waiting to be processed. It wasn't unheard of for a case to go to trial before the forensic tests were completed. "He's also assigned two forensic analysts to work specifically with the task force. One is IT, which should come in handy with these new victims' computers and other technology devices."

"But not cell phones," she recalled.

"We have none in evidence because the UNSUB has always made damn sure to get rid of them. He probably deactivated them immediately to avoid being tracked." Ethan stifled a yawn with the back of his hand. "However, we've gotten the previous victims' phone records. There's never been a number on them that could be traced back to the offender." He took his cell out again. This time, Alexa noted, he was looking up pizza places. "We have a stop-and-search authorization for any white van fitting our description at each exit route from the country. Commissioner Gagnon wouldn't permit it province-wide at this time."

Nyle muttered a curse and Ethan nodded in agreement. "He said we needed irrefutable evidence linking the van to the offender before he'd inconvenience the public to that extent."

"At least now we can hope to contain the offender," Alexa murmured, transfixed for a moment by the sight of Ethan's undoing the top button of his shirt. She attempted to slam the door shut on the mental images that threatened. Was unsuccessful.

*His fingers moving down the back of her flowered sundress in the front seat of his used Impala, undoing zippers and snaps with a finesse belied by his years. Of his hands moving...everywhere. His touch leaving a path of fire on her skin.*

Mortified by her wayward thoughts, she tore her gaze away. She hadn't recalled those moments in too many years to count. What would elicit them now?

But she knew the answer to that. It was this place. Ethan's proximity. Both of which made a lie out of her assurances to Raiker that there were no memories here to trip her up. At least, she hadn't thought so.

"*If* we're right and the UNSUB is this Anis Tera that Fornier mentioned. And *if* he hasn't dumped the van and is still in the province—" Ethan broke off to order a pizza at the takeout place that answered. Through charm and intimidation, he managed to convince them to have the driver pick up the coffee, as well. Alexa's lips quirked. His powers of persuasion had always been legendary. How else had he talked her into a relationship that moved outside the library walls and into his world? One that had been utterly foreign to her, but with Ethan as her guide, so completely irresistible.

When he hung up, he picked up the conversation where he'd left off. "Fornier said Simard arrived here on Sunday. We know the offender's time frame—the last New Brunswick victim was two weeks ago. The chance of the highway and toll-road cameras still having images from that long ago is minimal, but we do have a request in for those images." He scrubbed both hands over his face for a moment before dropping them to regard them again. "Next moves?"

"I've been pulling names of owners of vans like the kids described this morning." Nyle shoved the list he'd been making toward Ethan. "I assume you have someone from the team in New Brunswick doing the same?"

He nodded, picked up the sheaf of papers and studied them. "McManus. But until we get a clearer connection that it is the UNSUB in that vehicle, chasing down all these owners isn't the best use of our time."

"My priority is a safety check on Jeanette Lawler," Alexa said. She couldn't put aside the nagging concern that had been growing inside her since they'd talked to Fornier earlier. "How long ago did you speak to the Vancouver RCMP?"

Ethan glanced at the clock on the wall. "You heard me calling them in the car. That was...what? A half hour ago?"

His words did nothing to allay her anxiety. Vance was an unwitting player in the ruse to draw Simard here. It was possible that Lawler was, too. But she wanted to be certain. "Do we still have the manifests we were looking at earlier today?"

Nyle jerked his head to a box near the door. "I packaged them up to be sent downtown. Ethan said Lieutenant

Martin would assign a couple of his men to them. Should go a lot faster now that they no longer have to look for names associated with Simard. They just need to cross-check the incoming New Brunswick and Nova Scotia passenger lists for names of people who entered both provinces in the window we've defined."

"So it shouldn't take long at all for us to look only at the airline manifests for the last week or so and examine them for Jeanette Lawler's name."

The glint in Ethan's eyes told her he wasn't keen on the idea. But after a moment, he sighed. "Fine. We'll check them over pizza. And hope that we get a call before we're through, informing us that Jeanette Lawler is safe and sound in her own province."

It was Nyle who made the discovery. Still on his first coffee, but midway through his third slice of meat-lover's pizza, he paused, the slice halfway to his mouth. "Jeanette Lawler. Dammit."

The food she'd consumed turned to a cold brick in Alexa's stomach. "She flew in?"

Ethan's chair scraped as he pushed it back and bounded out of it to round the table to peer at the manifest in front of Nyle. "Monday afternoon." His mouth flattening, he whirled on his heel, grabbing for the phone in his pocket. "Keep looking," he snapped over his shoulder. "Make sure she hasn't left the province again."

Alexa flipped to the beginning of the pile in front of her and skimmed the pages for today. Yesterday. A frigid finger of ice traced down her spine as she quickly scanned the pages. Nothing in the offender profile she'd shared with the task force this morning had offered specifics on the reason for his escalation. After meeting Fornier, she could guess what had triggered the UNSUB. But she still had no idea if he'd selected more victims.

Or whether he had Jeanette Lawler in his sights.

"How DID you even discover the hotel where we're staying?" Parker Bixby, the tall emaciated looking cameraman of *Exposé* looked more annoyed than concerned when he made his eventual descent to the Piedmont Hotel lobby a couple of hours later. "No one is supposed to give that information out. There'll be a big kerfuffle over this, I promise you."

"Jeanette Lawler," Ethan interrupted. "Where is she?"

"Who did you say you worked for again?"

Ethan studied the man. Whatever he'd been imbibing in his room was likely illegal in this country. His pupils were dilated and his speech overly enunciated. "Royal Mounted Canadian Police," he repeated slowly. "We have reason to believe Lawler may be targeted by someone wishing to do her harm."

"Oh, dear." A vacant smile tilted the man's lips. "Those numbers are myriad, I'm afraid."

Ethan took a step closer and tamped down an urge to grab the man by his shiny purple shirt. "Call her."

The woman hadn't responded to their messages or those from the administrative assistant who'd finally been tracked down by Vancouver RCMP officers and persuaded to give up her boss's number. The reluctant assistant had eventually shared the name of the hotel where the crew was staying, but Lawler wasn't answering the phone in her room, either. Nor had she responded to repeated knocks on her door

"Me?" The man trilled a laugh, throwing his head back to show a protruding Adam's apple. "She isn't likely to answer a call from me, either." Still chuckling, he lowered his voice conspiratorially. "She's got her party panties on by this time, and her colleagues are the last ones she wants to talk to."

When Ethan only looked at him, the man gave a theatrical sigh. "Fine." He made a show of drawing his cell out of the back pocket of his tight black jeans and languidly punching in a number. Ethan could feel the impatience rolling off Alexa and Nyle at his side. It mirrored his. It was like a giant clock had lodged in his head, and he was watching the minutes tick off while waiting on the self-important idiot before him.

"See?" Bixby held up the phone so Ethan could hear the voice mail message. Then he disconnected and wedged the phone back into his pocket. "She's been working like a madwoman for the last few days finalizing the interview we came to this godforsaken province for. Then it got postponed today. Jeanette was pissed. Beyond pissed, actually. Thinks the guest is disrespecting her, which is a dangerous game to play with the host of *Exposé*. She's going to be out for blood when we shoot tomorrow."

"The guest is Armand Vance?"

He abruptly sobered. "How'd you know that? Did Cindy give out that information, too? Oh, that girl is so fired...."

"How did Vance contact her today?"

Bixby lifted a bony shoulder. "Email, I assume. I mean, Jeanette mentioned a couple of times that the man couldn't be bothered to have a phone conversation. Which is pretty arrogant, considering the guy is probably going to spend the next decade in prison."

"Listen carefully." Ethan's voice was hard, slicing through the man's ramblings. "Armand Vance is not in Nova Scotia. He doesn't know anything about this interview. Lawler was scammed by someone who lured her here."

Finally, the seriousness of the situation seemed to dawn on him. "Lured? But who? How?" He shook his head. "We're very careful to double-check these things."

"When did you last see her?"

"Five or so? There are just four of us here. Joey, the producer, Stella, who does makeup and hair, Jeanette and me."

"Is Stella here?"

"Probably. Girl gets room service every night." He rolled his eyes. "You ask me, she could stand a little socializing."

"Call her. Get her down here." They needed to question both the woman and Bixby, zeroing in on a list of Lawler's potential enemies. After the man had obeyed, Ethan reached into his suit jacket and brought out a copy of the sketch the forensic artist had done. Unfolded it and showed it the other man. "Have you seen this individual before?"

Bixby squinted at it. "Hard to say. Sort of looks like half the people you pass on the street, doesn't he? Doesn't look familiar, though."

Ethan tamped down his rising frustration. "Was the original contact set up by email, too?"

Spreading his hands, the man said, "I assume so. With the type of guests we schedule, the set-up is often hush-hush, but usually there are phone calls. Not this time, though."

He caught Alexa's glance. Recognized what she was

thinking. Fornier had mentioned Anis Tera using emails that disappeared. But the man wouldn't have utilized that technique when masquerading as a potential guest for the show. Lawler's computer might give them valuable information.

"Any idea who Jeanette Lawler might be with right now?"

This time the man's shrug seemed sincere. "We don't really hang outside of work hours. I know Jeanette stayed in the last few nights we've been here, and that's not usual for her. I'm assuming she caught some dinner and then went out for a night on the town. Joey probably did the same, although they wouldn't be together because they both hunt the same prey."

The word was unfortunate, given the circumstances. "What do you mean?"

"Pretty young boys." Parker smirked. "Jeanette likes her music loud, her drinks strong, and her men barely legal. Find the clubs in town that offer all three, and you'll likely find Jeanette."

Ethan stepped away and used his phone to look up Lawler's cell phone provider. Then he placed a call to them. The exigent circumstances were urgent enough to waive a warrant. He requested a phone ping to get Lawler's location, then looked up when Nyle made a subtle gesture toward Bixby. Ethan nodded. The man had given them all he could. He could be dismissed.

A moment later Ethan disconnected, cursing his luck. "Lawler's phone is dead or shut off."

"So now what?" Alexa asked.

He placed a call to Lieutenant Martin as he answered her. "We get a group of officers together and spread out."

It was a far cry from the clubs in Vancouver. Jeanette brushed her hair back over her shoulder and leaned against the bar as she scanned the occupants. In this dress, sitting down wasn't an option. The place was only three-quarters full. But it was early yet. Barely ten. And the dim lighting, the music pumping through the speakers and the better-than-average-looking bartender who'd yet to charge her for a drink tempted her to give this place a chance.

Jeanette picked up her phone, intent on looking up other clubs in case she wanted to ditch this one later. Discovering the cell dead, she set it back on the bar, disgruntled. She'd already forgotten the club names from her earlier research.

She turned to catch the bartender's eye. He hurried over. Definitely attentive. A possibility if she struck out with the younger patrons. "What time do things get going in here?"

"Wednesday nights aren't usually our busiest." He crossed his arms and leaned over them across the bar, raising his voice to be heard over the music. "But we've been having Hump Days specials to draw in the crowds. Give it another hour, it'll be shoulder to shoulder in here. You gonna stick around?"

"I don't know." She twirled the straw of her drink between two fingers. The guy didn't seem to recognize her, which was a plus. The place was dimly lit enough that maybe no one else would either. Not the way she was dressed.

"I think you should." Someone called to the bartender, and he shot them a quick look before turning to smile at her again. "Take my word for it. You won't be sorry."

~

ETHAN USED his credentials to avoid the line and cover charge at Zoomey's nightclub. When he and Alexa walked inside, the lights and sounds that met them was an assault on the senses.

She reared back a little at the visual onslaught. The place was a gyrating wall of people, the strobes making them look like a solid mass of human JELL-O, jiggling and moving to the heart-pumping bass beat.

They were constantly jostled as they attempted to move forward. To ensure they weren't separated, Ethan slipped his arm around Alexa's waist. Tried to ignore the zing of electricity that touching her elicited. She turned her head at that moment, her hair brushing his jaw. "And people come here for *fun*?"

A hard smile of agreement settled on his lips. It wouldn't be his idea of entertainment either, although there'd been a time years earlier when he'd tried the club scene. Paying for overpriced liquor and leaving stained with others' drinks and vomit had lost its allure in a hurry.

A loose-hipped young man who'd obviously been over-served danced up to them, his hand on Alexa's arm. "Dance with me, gorgeous." He exerted enough force to pull her forward a few steps.

Ethan's brows lowered. "Back. Off." He doubted the man could hear him, but something in his stance had the other guy glancing in his direction. What he saw in Ethan's expression made him release Alexa and retreating quickly into the mob behind him.

As Ethan forced their way forward, it soon became apparent that the crowd parted naturally for the woman at his side. Not so much for the two of them. He turned a shoulder into the mass of people and wedged a hole for them to pass through. In the ten minutes it took them to make their way to the vicinity of the bar, no fewer than three guys tried to halt Alexa's progress.

Which was exactly the reason he'd insisted the two of them pair up for the search for Lawler. Alexa had made no secret of her annoyance. They could cover twice as much area if they split up, she'd insisted. An assurance that now proved false. Alone, she would have been accosted continually.

The people were lined up three and four deep waiting for service. Ethan was about to flash his credentials again when Alexa slipped away from him and headed to a group of raucous young men draped over the bar a few feet away. He watched as they turned as one at her presence and parted like the Red Sea for Moses.

Ethan shook his head, unwillingly amused. Maybe he'd underestimated her after all. He took a moment to scan the room behind him. More crowded than the other establishments they'd been to, but the places seemed to get more jammed with the passing hours. It was going to be impossible to pick a lone woman out of the masses at tables, booths and the dance floor. It was going to take forever to search the whole area.

He faced the bar again and saw a bartender leaning attentively toward Alexa as she showed him what was likely a copy of Jeanette Lawler's professional photo. The man with the bar rag leaned forward to take a long look before nodding. He later shrugged at something Alexa said and waved an arm at the mob that had to be a violation of the fire code. As she fought her way back to him, Ethan stepped in front of a harried-looking waitress balancing a tray of drinks.

"Have you seen this woman tonight?"

She barely gave the picture a glance. "Not that I recall, but look around. She could be anywhere."

Alexa reached Ethan's side then. "According to the bartender, she was here earlier. But he hasn't seen her recently."

Which meant she may have left, or she was among the sea of occupants. With a mental sigh, he nodded. "We'll look here first."

"We split up."

He opened his mouth to argue, then shut it again and nodded. She could go where he couldn't. And she'd already proven that she was more than adept than he at garnering the attention needed to show people the picture. Men would be far more likely to notice the woman in the image than another female would. And Alexa had already proven that she had no trouble eliciting male cooperation.

For some reason, that thought wasn't comforting.

THE BARTENDER WAS RIGHT. The place drew a decent crowd and there were more than enough young men here to take advantage of the Hump Day specials. Jeanette was glad she hadn't left earlier. Now it was time to narrow her focus because she had to be up early for the interview tomorrow, which meant a short night in bed with her favored selection.

She was squeezed into a booth with five prospects, and she needed to choose while she could still focus. One of the enterprising souls had hooked his finger in the narrow strap of her dress and lowered it to write his number on the back of her shoulder with a Sharpie. She didn't bother telling him that whoever she took home tonight wasn't going to get a callback.

As if they recognized that she was on the prowl, all of the young men were plying her with drinks and what they probably thought passed for witty conversation. The conversation was part sophomoric laughter and part one-upmanship, with lines thrown in from the latest juvenile movie that guys always thought was hilarious.

It was one of the downfalls of selecting outside her age group, but as long as she made her choice early enough in the night, she could overlook a few faults. She studied each of them in turn and decided that when it came time to make her exit, she'd just grab the one that seemed soberest. Because she definitely wasn't.

He was going to have to do all the work. Laughter spilled from her lips, and she clapped a hand over her mouth, shocked. The guys seemed to take her amusement as encouragement. Their voices rose and their gestures grew wild. A drink was knocked over, which of course landed straight in her lap to pool in her bare thighs. She'd forgotten her vow earlier not to sit in the dress. Right now, it resembled a short glittering shirt.

"Shit, I'm sorry, I'm sorry." One of the young men reached over to sop up the liquid with a damp napkin. His hand lingered where it met bare skin, then skated upward. She batted it away. He was out of the running, she decided, disgruntled. Not only a slob but one who'd take every advantage as well.

"I'm going to the restroom." She grabbed the small purse she'd brought.

"We'll save your place," one proclaimed.

"On my lap," another said.

"On my face," one of the others put in and then of course they all laughed like the young fools they were.

Morons. Jeanette weaved through the wall of bodies, barely managing to avoid a flailing arm from one of the dancers. "Here, don't forget your drink," someone said. She didn't even turn around. If she ever did get to the ladies' room, she wouldn't be returning to that table of dickheads.

But suddenly the drink was in her hand, and she looked down at it, before scanning the moving crowd behind her. Her benefactor was lost in the ocean of people, but he was right about one thing. There was no reason to leave a half-full Crown and coke behind. Especially when it'd been free.

She managed to make her way to the back corner of the structure, groaning when she saw the line to the ladies' room. Now that she'd stood up, she needed to pee as well as mop herself off. Propping herself against the wall behind a girl who really shouldn't have been wearing the middriff top and Daisy Dukes she was sporting, Jeanette sipped at the drink and looked around. She remembered the bartender from earlier and craned her neck trying to get a look at him. But he wouldn't be off for hours, and there was no way she was going to last much longer.

There was a guy leaning on the bar. A little older than she liked them, but she appreciated the day's scruff of beard, as dark as his hair. In the next moment, a woman next to him craned her neck to see what he was looking at, and, noting Jeanette's interest, flipped her the bird.

She was tempted to take the guy home, just to prove that she could. She was Jeanette Fucking Lawler! Sure, she might have come from nothing, but she'd clawed her way to a good place now. Bitch at the bar would never rise as far as she had.

The queue moved infinitesimally. As soon as she got close enough, she was going to invade the men's room and the fuck with everyone else. A new couple entered the bar. Their faces appeared and disappeared in the swell of people, but the man pushed his way through the crowd with determined intent.

She felt a spark of interest, and tipped her glass to her mouth again, studying him over the rim. He wouldn't be able to see her in the crowded hallway so she could spy on him to her heart's content. Wide shoulders. Trim hips. A face that looked hard. Experienced. A trickle of regret traced down her spine. Not her type, unfortunately. She liked to be in control, and he looked like he had a hard time giving it up.

Her gaze flicked to the woman at his side. Buttoned up. Smoothly professional. An odd type of look to wear to a place like this. Her focus returned to the man. There was an air of familiarity about him...something recent... Then the two were lost to sight as patrons crowded past them to the front entrance.

"Ouch! Dammit!" She slapped a hand to her neck where the sting had occurred and whirled on the woman behind her. "What the hell did you do to me?"

The woman gave her a push, which, given the way they were packed inside the hallway, reverberated all the way up the line. "I didn't do anything, bitch."

Guys were starting to line up near them, which meant the men's room would be as impossible to get into as the women's.

"You poked me with something." Her vision blurred and she swayed, slapping a hand on the wall again for balance. Jeanette didn't feel good. Not at all. There was something wrong with her equilibrium, and her eyes wouldn't focus.

"You're drunk, bitch." Another shove, and this time she stumbled, dropping her drink on the floor. The glass shattered. One of the flying shards jabbed at her ankle. It felt just like what had stabbed her neck. She reached up to finger the site that still stung. "Go home before you barf on your skyscraper heels."

"Don't mind her. She's not feeling well, are you love? Here, now." Her arm was lifted, draped over narrow shoulders. She was propelled forward, through the mob in the hallway that had swelled dramatically since she'd first walked back here.

One of the guys from the table. Her thoughts were scattered. Probably thought they'd get... She searched for the word as she teetered on her high heels. Plucky. Fucky. Lucky. She wanted to smile in triumph at finding the word, but the man at her side was making her move too fast. Slow down she wanted to tell him, and managed to turn her gaze toward him.

Oh, shit. Not one of the boy toy prospects at all. Not even close. This guy was a stranger. And he was old, with gray bushy hair and a matching mustache that looked like something from a Halloween costume. With her heels, he barely came up to her shoulder. Nausea rose, and she thought she was going to be sick. Hell, no, she wasn't going anywhere with this guy.

"Get...away. Get...off...me." The floor tilted beneath her and she nearly face-planted. And then there was a door with a big red warning sign on it. You couldn't get out this way. She stopped and ducked her head, managing to dislodge his arm, but it was back a moment later, and the door was opening in front of them.

"Not much longer," the cheery voice sounded. "A little tap on the head and we'll get you all curled in, nice and cozy."

No alarm sounded when they stumbled through the door. She wished for an alarm. She wished everyone would look. Because something was very wrong and she couldn't even manage to scream.

# CHAPTER NINE

*For God will bring every deed into judgment, with every*
*secret thing, whether good or evil.*
—Ecclesiastes 12:14

"WELL, you were a bit of extra trouble." Anis Tera kept his voice cheerful. A soldier of the Lord didn't complain about doing God's work. "But the rental car came in handy. This van would have been much more visible in that dark alley."

He'd secured his guest to the chair in the van, her mouth taped shut for the moment. He'd had plenty of time to hide the car away in some nearby brush once he'd gotten her safely inside the larger vehicle. The storage garages were in as remote an area as he could find, worth the extra time traveling because he'd never seen anyone around at night. Although he'd had Jeanette Lawler's demise planned for nearly a year, the car wasn't the only deviation he was contemplating.

His pulse raced as he considered the enormity of the change. Was it worth the risk? Was he allowing his newest obsession to counter his usual reason?

It was a real possibility. Anis's crusade required focus and strict adherence to the plan. Already he'd used more time than he could afford to discover everything he could learn about Dr. Alexa Hayden because he knew the Lord had put her in his path for a reason. Just as he'd realized the meaning of the boy's appearance in the river, and immediately recognized what God meant him to do, there had been a similar zap of rightness when he'd seen Hayden on TV today. It had only grown stronger the more he learned about her.

God had sent him a helpmate. Lawler started struggling, trying to call for help, but he paid her no mind as he drew his favorite scalpel from its sheath. What else could Hayden's sudden arrival in his life mean? A woman trained in the insect field he loved. One who knew how to look into a man's deepest heart and see the pain that had set him on his path.

One who would stand beside him once she came to understand the holiness of his mission.

"There's still much to be done," he murmured, as he approached the woman in the chair. Not so much more for Jeanette Lawler, of course, but he needed to learn everything he could about Alexa Hayden. Each new detail that emerged from his research just seemed more preordained. So, he was going to allow himself a small variance from his previous plan tonight. Alexa Hayden had once lived in Truro, so that'd be Jeanette Lawler's final resting place. Hayden wouldn't recognize the significance. Not yet. But he'd soon change that.

"Maybe I slipped too much into your drink." Lawler's struggles were weak, futile. When he occasionally used the liquid Scopolamine before the injection, the kidnapping went more smoothly. But it was hard to judge the proper dosage for someone who had drunk as much as Lawler had this evening.

He pulled up a metal stool and sat down in front of her. Watched her eyes try to focus on the instruments in his hand. "We've had dealings before, Jeanette. I tried to keep my word, but you...you did not. Once you paid the fifty thousand four years ago, I never bothered you again, did I? But I watched you, just as I said I would. After your penance, you were to turn away from your sins forever. But you're still finding young vulnerable girls, aren't you? So easy in your profession. Because you're a seedy celebrity of sorts, they contact you, filling your ears with hero worship. And you. So altruistic. You get close to the girls, act as a mentor. And then provide their names and addresses to a man who'll scoop them up for use in the sex market."

She was crying now, fat tears that traced down her cheeks. Anis watched her, unmoved. The satisfaction he usually felt while carrying out his mission was strangely absent. Instead, the thrum of excitement in his veins was reserved for the woman who would gaze upon Lawler's body. And try to make sense of it.

Did Alexa realize the holiness of his cause? Did she guess at his noble calling? He ripped the duct tape off Lawler's mouth. Immediately she opened her mouth to scream, and he leaned forward to jam the stainless steel dental gag inside it. She reared back, tried to spit it out, but her head was held in place by the binding around her neck and the large blocks on either side of her face. It was a struggle, but he managed to work the instrument into place. Then he picked up the next two tools. He reached into her mouth with the forceps to clamp on her tongue. Drew it out.

The guttural sounds she was making were lost on Anis.

As he sliced at her tongue with the scalpel, he could only think of Alexa Hayden.

# CHAPTER TEN

"THAT'S IT." Ethan disconnected the call and shoved his cell back into his pocket with barely concealed frustration. "Officer Mallard was the last to check in. We covered the busiest clubs in the city. No one saw Jeanette Lawler."

The trepidation in the pit of Alexa's stomach knotted. They were standing in the lobby of the Piedmont Hotel, where Lawler's crew was staying. She, Ethan and Nyle had returned here after they'd covered the clubs on their lists. The woman could have left an establishment before the team had started the search. She could have gone home with someone. She hadn't returned here. Lawler wasn't responding to phone calls to her room or repeated hammering at her door.

"Nothing says she would have brought her date back to her room." Nyle's face flushed a bit at the euphemism for a one-night stand.

"Right." Ethan's voice was flat. "No way to be sure for a few more hours." A few of the clubs stayed open until four a.m.

"We may as well get rooms here. We'll just need to

come back in a few hours." Alexa stifled a yawn. It seemed cavalier to allow exhaustion to override her concern for Lawler. But there was nothing to be done now but wait. And hope.

Ethan's expression lightened. "I look forward to explaining my expense report for a night in the most expensive hotel in Halifax."

"At this point, I'd spring for a room on my own dime. Not that I expect to sleep much."

Ethan nodded at Nyle's words. "I'll get us checked in. We all need to rest. It's going to be a short night."

BUT IN CONTRAST to Ethan's earlier words, sleep proved elusive for Alexa. There were too many questions flashing into her mind. Too much second-guessing.

It was the what-ifs that proved to be the most disturbing.

After a couple of hours, she surrendered and took her laptop out of its case. Booted it up. There were a dozen constructive things she could be doing, not the least of which was catching up on correspondence and updating the offender profile victimology pattern.

She tackled the emails first. Communications from Raiker's agency and members of this task force were formatted so they would come directly to her phone, but others that she used for social and professional networks had to be accessed online. She quickly scrolled through the emails for the different accounts. Found nothing that was pressing.

She opened the final one, which was used only for emails from her professional organizations and for media inquiries. There were four new messages in the inbox. A yawn overtook her as she clicked on the top one. Perhaps she'd given up on sleep too soon. Maybe there was time to salvage an hour or two....

Her stomach did a slow roll as she read the message.

*Hello, Alexa. I hope you don't mind the familiarity. I don't know you well yet, but now that my mission here is accomplished, I'll be remedying that soon. I knew as soon as I saw you on television yesterday that your being here was preordained. What a delight that we have so much in common. You cannot yet understand that I've been appointed a prophet to the nations. But soon.... You will know me.*

She wasted precious seconds staring at the message in shock before she finally leaped up, grabbed the laptop and her key card before rushing out the door.

Ethan was two rooms away. She pounded on his door, her eyes glued to the screen as if the message would disappear before her eyes. And perhaps it would. Fornier had mentioned something about Anis Tera sending emails that later vanished.

"What?" Ethan stood framed in the open door, clad in nothing but a pair of gym shorts. His tone was grim, but his expression was alert. Perhaps, like her, he'd been unable to sleep.

"He emailed me." Alexa brushed by him to enter the room and sat on the edge of the rumpled bed, indicating the laptop she held.

"Who?"

"The offender." She felt an unfamiliar rush of impatience. "He used my professional account that's public, although rarely used..."

Ethan was at her side, sinking down next her before she

finished the sentence. "How can you be sure it's him?" She waited for him to read the message. Watched his expression go from grim to dangerous. He bounced from the bed, crossed the bedside table for his phone and returned to take a picture of the screen. Then he reached out to press the reply command. The screen went blank.

"It's gone." Alexa closed out of the window and returned to the inbox, but the message had disappeared. "Just like Fornier said. Vanishing emails. Forensic IT analysts can do something with this, right? Maybe track down the sender?"

He stared at her. "I think you're missing the most critical point. He reached out to you. That means he has you in his sights."

"Yes. Well..." She couldn't say that the idea didn't discomfit her on several levels, but the psychologist in her was oddly thrilled. "Do you realize how much we can learn about him if he continues to communicate with me?"

Ethan's face went thunderous. He picked up the phone and pressed a speed-dial number. "Yes, we're about to learn that you're his newest obsession. Excuse me if I don't share your enthusiasm at the prospect." He spoke a few terse words into the phone and then disconnected.

"He said his mission here was accomplished." Her stomach did a slow roll. "Do you think he's saying that Jeanette Lawler is dead?"

"We're soon going to find out."

She glanced at the time in the upper corner of her laptop. Nearly six-thirty. They could check again whether the woman had returned in the last couple of hours. But a bitter sense of foreboding told her what they would discover.

The tap at the door was light. Ethan immediately got up

and pulled it open. Nyle walked in. "He messaged you? That's not good, Alexa. It means he's focused on you now."

"Communications from him offer a rare opportunity to figure out what he's thinking. How he thinks. That can only help us catch him."

Her words only made Nyle's expression turn mutinous, but she knew she was right. Something was niggling at her about the email, tugging at a long-forgotten memory.

Ethan held out his phone to show Nyle the picture he'd taken of the message and Alexa swiftly reread it. The wording was slightly formal, but that wasn't what had captured her attention. "A prophet to the nations. That's from the Bible, I think."

"Just another way of excusing his behavior," Nyle noted.

"Possibly." She chased after the dim memory in her mind. Thomas Reisman had drilled Bible verses into her from the moment he'd entered her life. As if the ability to regurgitate obscure quotes made up for the fact that he didn't live the words. Not any of them.

"Before...something...the womb," she murmured, staring into space, trying to recall the verse. "Before I formed you...in the womb I knew you...and before you were born, I consecrated you; I appointed you a prophet to the nations," she finished in a rush. "Jeremiah, chapter one, verse five."

"Someone's got delusions of grandeur," mumbled Nyle.

Ethan looked at her long enough to have her glancing away. When it came to the time she'd spent under Thomas Reisman's roof, he knew some of what happened. He'd never known all. "This is a critical breakthrough for his profile," she insisted. "We've known he's an organized offender, but haven't understood his motivation. Perhaps the homicides are enacted because of his own twisted sense of justice."

"So...God told him to do it?"

She ignored the hint of derision in Ethan's tone. "He wouldn't be the first to claim God told him to kill," she reminded him. "More than that, he thinks he's been chosen for this task."

"You'll need a new laptop, which will have to be backed up with all your important files." Ethan was texting again. "I'm going to want to FedEx your computer to the Ottawa lab."

The thought of losing her computer didn't come without a pang, but it was no more than she'd expected. "I have flash drives in my computer bag. I can always—" Her voice broke off then as another email landed in the inbox on the screen before her. A dart of trepidation arrowed through her.

"Guys..." But both men were already at her side. As Alexa reached out to open the message, she noticed rather distantly that her fingers were trembling. This message was only one line. But it was enough to turn her bones to ice.

*Jeanette rests in a place familiar to you.*

Ethan's curse was long, imaginative and brutal. "Nyle, wake up Lawler's crew. Check her room." But they all knew what he'd find. While they'd been out searching for the woman last night, she'd likely already been in the clutches of a madman. The officer all but raced out the door.

"He's engaging you. Making you part of this." Ethan's tone was even, but urgency layered beneath his words. He sank down next to her again, and when his hand reached for hers, squeezed, she welcomed its strength.

"Yes. Not ideal, of course."

"God." He gave a half laugh and released her hand to

jam his fingers through his hair. "That's got to be the under-statement of the year."

"Think of it as another tool in the investigation. The message said familiar to me. I haven't been in Canada for twenty years. Nothing is *familiar*."

"He's researched you. Probably started when he saw you at the press conference. He's talking about Truro, isn't he? That's the last place you lived." He paused a beat. "At least while in Nova Scotia."

But most of the landmarks were unfamiliar to her. Reisman had kept her sheltered. Imprisoned, was how it'd felt at the time. The library had been her refuge, where unbeknownst to her mother or Thomas, Alexa had not only studied but tutored several local students. She'd passed online Advanced Placement classes in every subject, and by the time she was seventeen she'd acquired two years of college credits. The elderly lady next door had given her an old ten-speed bike, which had offered Alexa her first taste of freedom. And still she'd rarely been outside the city limits until she'd met Ethan.

Ethan had changed everything.

"Victoria Park," she said doubtfully, tugging her focus back to the present. She'd ridden through it once or twice on her bike but had never dared to take the time to explore it. "The falls would be too public and difficult to access, but there are streams in the area."

"There are. It's also four hundred or so acres." Without asking, he turned her computer toward him and keyed in a search. Looked stunned at the results. "Look at the number of waterways in Colchester County."

She peered over. Felt her heart drop. "Well, I suppose that's to be expected. In Nova Scotia, one is never more than fifteen minutes away from a body of water. There has to be a way to narrow down the search."

His mouth was flat. "We can choose a couple of places and expand from there. It'll still take hours." Unspoken was the fact that it could take longer than that. Even days. "I have to speak to the Colchester County detachment of RCMP. And the local Police Service. We need manpower. Possibly even an organized search party."

Alexa was silent. The urgency in her veins had nothing to do with the possibility of finding Jeanette Lawler alive. The UNSUB's last message had removed the final vestige of hope.

TWO TEAMS WERE FORMED, the larger one focused on Victoria Park, with the other searching nearby Irwin Lake. Each had a Search-and-Rescue canine, which had been given a possession of Lawler's to establish her scent. Ethan had started the dog and handler on one end of the shoreline, he and Alexa on the other. The lake was only a kilometer long and a third of a kilometer wide. With the SAR unit, the two of them could handle this and the other small lakes in the vicinity.

Alexa was at his side. She was silent, but her silence spoke volumes.

"The two of us could cover twice as much ground if we split up."

It was a recycled argument. She'd used logic, and then irritation when Ethan had first apprised her of the plan. Neither worked. "It's too dangerous. The UNSUB contacted you directly. He could have remained near the body, waiting for you to come. It's stupid not to take precautions."

"Only if they make sense."

They'd left the stretch of the lake with cottages and houses built close to shore for the end of the search. The offender had always left the bodies in remote areas up until now. But everything was upended as of this morning. The killer had never reached out before. He'd never tried to engage a member of the task force.

"Contacting you was an aberration." Ethan stepped over a tree limb and turned to give her a hand. Ignoring it, she hopped over on her own. "When offenders suddenly change their behavior, we damn well better be cautious." And he wasn't going to take chances with her safety. He might not want to crack open the vault of their past together, but he wasn't going to put her at risk, either.

That was all there was to the protective instincts that had surged to the surface. Ethan told himself that and tried to believe it.

"That defies logic. He could hardly be lying in wait at every one of the rivers, streams and lakes in the area."

Her reasoning might be sound, but his reaction came from a visceral place, not a logical one. Contrary to his vow just days ago to keep his distance, it appeared as though he'd have to keep Alexa near him at all times. His unwillingness to dredge up the past paled compared to the need to keep her safe, even if her job did sometimes place her in similar situations.

"What did your husband think of you going to work for the Mindhunters?" He regretted the question as soon as it left his mouth. More so when she shot him a quick, startled look.

"I've worked for Raiker for five years. Danny died the

year before I took the job." The smile on her lips was wistful. "His cancer was in remission when we got married. It came back with a vengeance six months later. He was gone six weeks' shy of our third anniversary. I thought then about what your dad told us. That none of us get through life unscathed. It was difficult to hear at the time, but he was right. We all have to find a way to live with pain without letting it define us."

A bird shrieked overhead as Ethan bent to pick up a branch in their path and threw it toward the woods. He didn't want to remember the conversation she referred to. Out of self-preservation those memories were buried deep. They seeped out despite his best defenses at times, usually picking the midnight hours to haunt. When mistakes were magnified and regret sliced deep.

"What about you?" When he cocked a brow, she elucidated. "Are you married?"

"Divorced." He wondered how long it would be before he could say the word without an accompanying flood of relief. "Charlene was fond of saying that she'd married a hockey player, not a Mountie. After a knee injury cut short my time on the team, she never really adjusted to our new lifestyle." Mostly because of the vast difference in paychecks for the two professions. He gave a mental shrug. She deserved credit for knowing what she wanted. And it had been readily apparent that what she didn't want was a washed-up hockey player, no matter what job he chose afterward.

"And you were surprised at the career choices I made." There was a teasing note in her tone. Apparently, she was over her pique of minutes ago. Alexa had never been one to hold onto a grudge.

"I had a lot of time to think when I was in rehab for my

knee. I wanted to do something that would make a difference. I haven't regretted it."

The sand rimming the lake gave way to a grassy shoreline, hemmed by thick trees. The grass was tall enough that
something lying in it wouldn't be visible from a distance.
Across the lake, the shore was punctuated with dwellings,
but this part was undeveloped. Next to them was a marshy
area where reeds rose from the water like fingers pointing
accusingly at the sky.

A couple of flat-bottomed fishing boats dotted the
placid water. The stillness of the scene would have been
peaceful if it not for the reason they were here.

He even recognized the area ahead of them. "Were you
ever out here when you lived in Truro? We'd have keggers
sometimes, deeper in the woods there." He indicated the
crowded cluster of trees that stood like silent sentinels just
feet away from the water. "A pulp company leased a lot of
the land on this side of the lake back then. There weren't
near as many houses here either. No one to care what we
were up to."

"No, I was never here. And I can honestly say I never
attended a kegger in my life."

He wasn't surprised. "Another shameful void in your
childhood."

Her expression was sober as she nodded. "The voids
were myriad."

Ethan had thought her pampered when they first met.
Part of an overprotective family that sought to keep the
world at a distance lest it proves too unpleasant for their
precious daughter. His first impression couldn't have been
further from the truth, but he hadn't known that until later.
She'd been unlike any girl he'd met before, and he'd been
captivated. It had taken persuasion, the likes of which he'd

never had to use before even to get her to meet him outside of the library. Then he'd lured her to football games. Hockey matches. Baseball games. Once or twice he'd even managed to get her to agree to accompany him to a party, although she'd never seemed comfortable in crowds. She'd been stingy with the details she'd revealed about her home life, but he'd sensed a darkness there that was the polar opposite of his own family—his father an outspoken single dad raising three rambunctious boys on his own.

He could see the handler and the dog at the far side of the lake. They were covering a quarter of the perimeter themselves. The search-and-rescue animal didn't have to rely on visual cues. With three hundred million olfactory receptors in its nose, the hound was more valuable than having an additional half dozen people on the site.

Alexa veered farther away from him to avoid a soggy area of ground. "When I recognized the words from the Bible verse in the offender's message this morning, I couldn't help thinking of Reisman."

"Your st—your mother's husband?" Not her stepfather, he recalled. She'd always been adamant about that. Nothing about the man's treatment of her had been the least bit parental.

She nodded. "Some people will use religion to rationalize anything. Abuse, murder, discrimination, war. Reisman used it as a weapon to force my mother and me into the roles he decreed proper. If my suspicion about the UNSUB is correct, he may see himself as an emissary with a holy justification for his deeds."

"And how does knowing that help us catch him?"

Her voice was unperturbed. "By allowing us to think like the offender. Calculate his responses. Predict his actions based on what we know about his motivation."

Ethan knew her words made sense. He stepped over a painted turtle making its way to the water's edge at a torturously slow pace. What he didn't know was how they explained the offender's sudden focus on Alexa. And what that fixation might mean for her safety.

"We're attracting attention."

He looked across the lake. Several people had come out onto docks to watch them. The two boats he'd seen earlier were now making their way closer to where the SAR handler was positioned. "Inevitable, I guess." They came to a place where a copse of trees grew right at the water's edge. Ethan went instantly alert. There were several areas like this around the lake. This one was the sort of spot he'd expect the offender to have chosen. Although it was directly across from a row of cottages, the tree line offered privacy.

They slowed, scanning the ground carefully. Ethan was so intent on the task that he started when three quick blasts of a whistle split the air.

The search was over. Jeanette Lawler's body had been discovered.

"Thanks for your help."

Ivan Swant, the dog's handler, nodded at Ethan's words. "A successful mission isn't always a happy one." He looked over his shoulder at the body for a moment. "I'm going to take Hudson back to his kennel. I don't want to contaminate the scene. I wish you good luck finding the guy who's doing this, Sergeant, I truly do. Hate to think about a monster like that on the loose." The man turned and made his way back up to through the woods to the road beyond. And Ethan turned to look at the what the "monster" had wrought.

The body was lying on its back, limbs perfectly straight, staring sightlessly at the cloudless blue sky. The red sequined dress was a garish splash of color against the tall grass. Eyes were intact, Ethan noted absently, and he approached from an angle, preserving what would become the inner perimeter of the crime scene. The ground was still moist after the rains of the last few days. They had a chance of getting a decent footprint. As he drew closer to the body, he thought he could see grooves in the soft ground beyond, spaced about two feet apart. He pointed them out to Alexa.

She shaded her eyes to peer at them. "The case file said the UNSUB was thought to have used a dolly to transport bodies to the scene before."

"We haven't ruled out boats in some of the scenes, but yeah, that's what we've figured. Haven't always found the evidence, though." He crouched down near the body. "No outward sign of torture. But we can't be sure until the ME gets a look at her."

"I wish I didn't feel certain we'll find something," Alexa said quietly. There was pity in her voice, in her expression, as she gazed down at what was left of Lawler. "He changed his ritual with the last three victims to better justify his cause. I don't see him changing it again, so soon."

Her throat worked, and instinctively he knew what she was thinking. "On IHIT, I'm used to being called to crime scenes. But with an offender like this, there's occasionally an opportunity to prevent another victim. Sometimes we're too late," he said softly. "Those times are the worst part of my job." Their gazes met a second in mutual understanding. And then a movement in the corner of his eye had him whirling toward the lake.

"Sir, back that boat up! Now! Have a little respect."

The rubbernecker in the fishing skiff was drifting as

close as he dared, a camera phone aimed at the victim. Mentally cursing, Ethan moved into the water and positioned himself so that he was blocking the body. He'd already called a halt to the search at Victoria Park and summoned a forensic ident unit. Nyle was on his way, and he'd bring crime-scene tape and tarps. They'd have to get creative and rig up a barrier to keep the public from getting too close to the scene.

They may have been unable to get to Lawler in time to save her from the killer. But they could at least lend her some privacy in death.

"ETHAN HAS SET today's briefing for..." Cell pressed to his ear, Nyle raised his brows at Alexa.

"...seven p.m.," she supplied.

"...seven p.m. He'll be at the crime scene until the forensic ident guys are done. If you have updates that are time-sensitive before then, contact him as needed. Yeah." Nyle's mouth flattened as he listened. "It was a tough one." He disconnected a moment later and slipped the phone into his suit pocket. "Ian McManus. They're still working the highway cameras in New Brunswick, as well as interviews with the two victims' acquaintances."

Nyle leaned over her and opened the glove box, taking out a small notebook and pen to hand to her. "You're going to need these." They got out of the car. They'd driven to the side of the lake sprinkled with cottages and cabins. "Start at opposite ends?"

Alexa nodded. It was doubtful that anyone had seen anything. The UNSUB had likely been here sometime hours past midnight when most would have been asleep in their beds. But there were fewer than a dozen dwellings. It wouldn't take long to talk to all the inhabitants.

She knocked at the first door and received no response. Recalling the attention the crime scene had received, she rounded the house to look out back. A couple stood at the end of the dock. When she stepped onto it, they turned to look at her.

"You're...I saw you across the lake." A tall, slender woman with black hair clubbed back in a short ponytail approached her. "Is that a body over there?"

Alexa gave a mental sigh. She was going to be facing as many questions as she asked. "I'm sorry to say there's been a homicide."

The woman's mouth made an "O" but the interest in her eyes was avid. "Do you know who it is? Who did it?"

"The victim's name won't be released until next of kin have been notified." Alexa didn't attempt to answer the second question. There was no way she wanted to get into that conversation. "We're talking to everyone who lives in the vicinity. Did you see or hear anything unusual last night?"

"We don't live here. Just renting for a week." A man with thinning blond hair lowered the binoculars he had in his hands and turned to face Alexa. "Came for the peace and quiet. This is the most exciting thing that's happened since we arrived." Their names were Doug and Cindy Heathcliff, they told her. And after redirecting their focus time and again from details of the murder to her questions, Alexa was finally convinced they knew nothing.

The next house was more of the same. And the one after it. Although a few people were out on the lake, most were apparently going to spend the better part of their day watching the forensic ident team work.

The exception was the cabin midway down the row of houses. Nyle was already next door. After a desultory knock at the door, Alexa headed to the back. But there she found a mother in the water with her three young children, splashing and playing on inner tubes. It took some discretion for Alexa to state her reason for being there while being aware of the children in proximity.

"Well, thanks for not shouting your questions in front of the children," the woman, who introduced herself as Sam Quinton, said after Alexa stated her purpose. Quinton wore a no-nonsense black one-piece and toweled her short dark hair vigorously as she kept a watchful eye on the kids. "I have a pretty good indication what's going on across the lake, and I don't want the children to get wind of it. God, a murder! Here!" She shook her head, a few stray droplets spraying out from the gesture. "You can't get away from it anywhere, can you? This dissolution of the social fabric. It's endemic."

"Were you out at all late yesterday evening?"

The woman rolled her eyes. "Like on the town, you mean? Fat chance, with these three. Biggest social event in our lives is taking them to the dentist."

Alexa smiled politely. "Maybe you saw a light or some activity from your window or patio door...?"

Quinton should her shook her head. "I sleep like the dead. And so, unfortunately, does my husband. Because he never knows just how late Grayson stays out at night." She broke off for a moment to shout, "Bradley, absolutely not! You do not hold your sister's head under water!" She turned back to Alexa. "Twenty-three years old, sleeps all day and doesn't lift a finger. Forget about paying rent. My step-son, not my husband."

A flicker of hope ignited in Alexa. "So your stepson was out late last night?"

"If he weren't, it'd be the first night all summer. He's inside. Still sleeping, as I said."

"I knocked earlier." Alexa looked back toward the rental. "There was no answer."

A grim smile tilted her lips. "Oh, I can fix that." She walked a few steps toward the dock and leaned to pick up her cell phone, keyed in a number. After several moments, she said, "Oh, Grayson, it's Sam. I'm so very sorry to wake you." Her expression was positively gleeful. "But there's someone out here with RCMP who would like to speak to you. What? Oh, I'm sorry, I'm not certain exactly what she wants. But we're out back when you care to join us." She cut off the call and gave a satisfied smile. "I don't think he'll be long."

Not quite sure what to say in the face of those family dynamics, Alexa waited silently. As the woman had indicated, it was only a few minutes before a tall, thin young man, clad only in athletic shorts, stumbled out the back door of the house, pulling a T-shirt over his head. Alexa went to meet him. "Grayson Quinton?"

"Uh, yeah." He looked like he could still be in high school, with a scraggly goatee and patchy facial hair. "I don't know what Shorty Roder told you, but I already promised to pay for the damages."

Surveying him, Alexa was half glad she didn't have to get to the bottom of that story. "I understand you were out last night. What time did you get home?"

With a sidelong glance at his stepmother, he said, "Uh, right around midnight, I think."

"It's important to be accurate with any information you share with the RCMP, Grayson," Sam said virtuously.

"Uh, yeah, you know it might've been later than that. I sort of lost track of time."

Reaching for her rapidly fraying patience, Alexa said, "How much later?"

Shifting from one bare foot to the other, he said, "Maybe...it could have been three or three-thirty."

"Did you see anyone as you got closer to the lake? Cars or people that stood out?"

"Not really, I guess. I was pretty..." With a quick look at his stepmother, he seemed to amend his words. "...tired. Didn't notice much of anything. Oh. Except I stopped on the way to take a piss."

"Grayson, honestly! Your language!" Quinton scolded.

He lifted a narrow shoulder. "Couldn't wait 'til I got home, so I pulled off onto one of the logging roads on the west side of the lake. Got out for a couple of minutes and then headed here."

Alexa was fast coming to share Sam Quinton's opinion of the stepson. "Did you see anyone?"

He swung his head slowly from one side to the other. "There was hardly any other traffic most of the way home. But when I stopped to pee, there was a vehicle of some sort parked on that road, deeper into the trees. I figured it belonged to Andersen's logging company. I didn't notice anyone around it, though."

Nyle must have finished next door and was now rounding the house to join Alexa. "What sort of vehicle?" she asked.

"Um...I didn't get a great look at it." Grayson folded his arms across his bony chest.

"I mean, was it equipment the company might use? A car? What?"

"Oh. No, it wasn't logging machinery. But it wasn't a car

either. Too big. Like a van or something, I guess. Not a minivan like Sam drives, though." There was disdain in his tone. "A bigger one like businesses use."

Alexa could tell by the falter in Nyle's step that he was close enough to hear what the young man had said. "Did you notice a color?" she persisted.

"White maybe or some other light shade. Oh, hey!" He finally seemed aware of his surroundings and gazed at the scene across the water. "What's going on over there?"

# CHAPTER ELEVEN

THE PATH the killer had taken was easy to follow.

After updating Ethan about Grayson Quinton's observations from the night before, they had the young man show them to the spot where he'd stopped last night on the way home. Leaving him in the back seat of the vehicle, Alexa and Nyle followed the twisted, rutted logging road through the woods. It was little more than a wide, leaf-lined path through the trees, following a meandering trail toward the lake.

"Look." Alexa stopped and pointed to another area where the grooves from dual tire tracks were clear for several yards.

Nyle took out his phone and crouched down to take pictures of them. They'd found several other areas where the twin depressions were visible, as well as a clear set of tire treads from the vehicle parked there last night. "The forensic ident unit will have to head over here once they finish up at the dumpsite," he said, rising. "They can make casts of these tracks."

"Which won't lead us to him."

"Well, no." They continued on their way again. "But once we catch him with the van and a dolly in his possession with tires that match these prints, it's one more irrefutable piece of evidence against him." He looked at her then, a glint of concern in his gaze. "How are you doing, Alexa? Being contacted by a killer is enough to shake anyone up a bit."

"It's also a remarkable opportunity to learn more about the UNSUB. To glean details about him that he doesn't even realize he's giving." She stepped over an area still muddy from the rains a couple of days ago. "It's a profiler's dream. The more I understand him, the better I can help you catch him."

Slanted sunlight pierced the canopy of trees overhead. The quiet buzz of insects and occasional bird calls added to the tranquility of the spot, a marked contrast to the scene ahead. As they walked, Alexa tried to imagine the area only hours earlier, when it would have been shrouded in darkness. Bats swooping low in the shadows. The occasional gleam from the eyes of night animals. The screech of predators meeting prey.

And the ultimate predator wheeling Lawler's body down this same path.

The body would have to be well secured to the dolly, Alexa mused. And he'd have needed light of some sort. Not a flashlight; his hands wouldn't be free. So perhaps a miner's hat with the spotlight affixed to it, affording him a narrow beam to split the darkness.

*Jeanette rests in a place familiar to you.*

The recollection of his words was like an icy finger against her nape. Yesterday's press conference had been late in the afternoon, just hours before he tracked and killed Jeanette Lawler. But in the intervening time, he'd managed to do at least some cursory research on Alexa. Enough, at least, to track down the last place she'd lived in Nova Scotia.

But he hadn't learned much about her. At least, not yet. She'd never been here before. She had rarely been outside the town when they'd lived here. There'd been no family vacations or outings. No picnics by nearby lakes.

But now that his mission in the province was accomplished, he'd have time to do a more thorough job looking into her past. They'd speculated that the UNSUB stalked his victims online. That he used the Internet and possibly the dark web to learn their vices and extort them. Despite her response to Nyle earlier, Alexa wasn't certain she was ready for what the offender was sure to dredge up.

The trail tapered to an end. They continued walking straight. After another fifty feet, they stepped out of the tree line into a grassy area. To their right, they could see Ethan and the white-suited evidence team two hundred feet ahead at the water's edge. More people had arrived and circled the body. The ME and assistants.

They skirted the police tape that had been strung as a perimeter as they made their way to Ethan. He had his cell pressed to his ear as they approached. Alexa wondered if it felt like a permanent attachment these days. He disconnected the call moments later and stepped away from his position near the body to approach them.

"We've got the kid in the car," Nyle began without preamble. "Took him a couple of tries, but he led us to the logging road where he saw the van parked last night. It's the right place, too. The forensic ident unit will be able to get casts from the tire treads we found. Plus, there are visible dolly tire marks for several feet in spots leading through the woods toward the lake where."

A glint of excitement in his eyes, Ethan said, "Good job.

I'll dispatch some officers to cordon off the road until the team finishes and can get up there." He led them farther away. Lowering his voice, he said, "With this latest verification of the vehicle link to the case, I've been in contact with Captain Campbell and lobbied for a province-wide stop-and-search of every Econoline van older than 2014. He agreed and received the go-ahead from Gagnon. The order's gone out on the province-wide law enforcement system."

A thrum of adrenaline began in Alexa's veins. That was an extensive security net to stop vehicles similar to the offender's. If he were seen by a patrol cop anywhere, they'd have him.

"He's struck twice in Halifax. Maybe his base of operations is there."

Ethan nodded grimly. "Unsurprisingly, the two local officers working on the manifests found no one named Anis Tera entering the province. The name doesn't appear on the ferry passenger list either."

"And the ferries don't have much usable information anyway," Nyle said, "since they don't keep copies of the photo ID passengers have to show or include models of vehicles."

Ethan nodded. "Which is why it's his most likely method of entry into the province. We suspected that Anis Tera is an alias. The UNSUB is probably using a different name now. We still need to comb through the toll-road camera images that have come in, just in case. We released the image the sketch artist did with Fornier to the media. The tip line hasn't elicited anything of value yet."

Alexa wasn't surprised. The drawing had shown a person with no discernible features. He'd been an everyman...outstanding only in his ordinariness. Often releasing the work of forensic artists brought forth a flood of worthless calls about exes' boyfriends, annoying neighbors, and dead-beat relatives. But each of the tips had to be checked out, which required a lot of man-hours. "A matching vehicle photo from a toll road camera might get us the plate and driver image."

"A plate number would lead to a driver license photo, which will be a helluva better likeness than the forensic sketch appears to be," Ethan agreed. "We'll need an updated profile for the briefing this evening." Alexa nodded. "The two of you can work out of the RCMP Colchester County detachment. I'll catch a ride back when we wrap things up here. Alexa knows where the car is parked."

Ethan stopped, sent a glance back to where the body laid. "As soon as next of kin have been notified, we'll release her photo to the media with a note that anyone who saw her last night or early this morning needs to call the tip line."

"You think we have a chance of discovering where he snatched her from." Alexa's words weren't a question.

"We know the general vicinity she was in. Just need a witness or two to pinpoint it for us." And if a witness came forward who'd seen something of value, that could turn out to be the break they were seeking.

"Sergeant."

He turned away then as someone from the medical examiner's office called to him, and Alexa and Nyle headed back toward the woods. "Think Quinton got tired of waiting for us and walked home?"

She smiled and shook her head. "Something tells me he's not that ambitious."

~

AFTER THEY DROPPED Grayson Quinton off, they headed toward Truro. "You know," Nyle said, "I can't remember the last time we ate. Sleep I can go without, but food? Not so much."

"I'd trade sleep for food any day, but in this case, I'd be willing to..." The vehicle rolled by a cemetery dotted with drooping willows and massive oaks, and her heart twinged.

"...be willing to...?"

Alexa's attention returned to Nyle. "I could eat," she admitted. "But first, would you drop me off somewhere? I can walk to the headquarters and meet you."

"Don't be ridiculous. Where do you want to go?"

"Heavenly Angels cemetery. It's just outside of town on the east side. I can direct you." She didn't meet his searching look. But he was surprisingly circumspect when he said, "You get me there, and I'll give you a few minutes while I pick up sandwiches or something. Then I swing back and pick you up. Will that be enough time?"

She shot him a grateful look. "Yes. Plenty of time."

ALEXA WALKED through the cast-iron gates of the cemetery. She'd been unable to recall when or what she'd eaten yesterday, but had had no problem helping Nyle get here. The dusty details had survived in long-term memory, unused until now, but easy to pluck at the exact moment they were needed.

As a teen, she'd been here several times when a member of their church had died. Alexa didn't know the exact area where she'd find the marker she was looking for, but she headed for the newest section of the cemetery, where the burials she'd been to had taken place. Then she walked up and down the rows quickly, peering at the names on the markers as she went by. It took only ten minutes to find the object of her search. A simple flat marker that read:


Rebecca Ann Reisman
Dutiful wife to Thomas Reisman
1956-2001


ALEXA STARED AT THE STONE, her eyes burning. Of course, there was no mention of Rebecca's daughter. Her husband had seen to that. The flare of resentment in her chest ignited anew. Even in death, Rebecca's existence was framed only by her service to him.

She wouldn't even have known about her mother's death if not for Willa Satler, the elderly neighbor that had lived next door. The woman had eventually found the number Alexa had left with her and contacted her, a month after the fact, once Willa had returned from an extended stay with her daughter in Amherst. Rebecca had died of breast cancer, the woman had confided, with a pitying tone. No one had even known she had it until she died. There hadn't taken treatments.

Which certainly had been Reisman's doing. Alexa couldn't recall a single time she'd received medical care after he'd entered their lives. A weak body was a sign of a weak spirit. No need for science when they could pray the sickness away.

Alexa crouched down, fingers reaching out to trace her mother's name. When she'd needed her mother most, Rebecca hadn't been there for her. But Alexa had long since forgiven the woman for that. She understood now how abusers worked. Isolating their victims. Cutting them off from support systems. Denying them a life outside their control. Alexa's biggest sorrow was that she hadn't been able to convince her mom to take even a tiny step away from Reisman's watchful eye. His power over the woman had been absolute.

She wondered now if that's what had frightened her the most about the passion that had flared to life between her and Ethan. It had started instantly. Burned fiercely. It had blinded them both to consequences and caution. The pull had been so strong, so powerful, that leaving him had taken more strength than she'd known she possessed. And the regrets of that action would linger, despite knowing she'd made the right choice.

In the space of fifteen months, Alexa had lost everything. Everyone.

*I'm sorry, Mom.* A drop of moisture fell on the marker. It took a moment for her to realize it was a tear. *I'm so, so sorry.*

ALEXA LOOKED up from her laptop. Stretched. She was feeling good about the changes she'd made to the profile. Even so, she'd sent a message to Raiker asking for a consult. He was on a case somewhere in Kentucky, so his response time would be uncertain. She'd been a little surprised to hear that he was in the field. Since his wife had suffered near-fatal injuries a couple of years ago, he'd stayed close to home.

When she'd finished with the changes, she copied all her files to flash drives so Ethan could have the laptop overnighted to the crime lab in Ottawa. Then she made some calls and arranged for a new laptop and a tablet to be delivered to the hotel they hadn't checked out of in Halifax.

"How are you doing over there?" she asked Nyle.

"I've got four white cargo vans fitting our description so far from the toll cameras in the date window we established. Still not done."

They'd long since finished the sandwiches Nyle had bought before returning to the cemetery gates. He hadn't asked about her trip there, and she appreciated his discretion. Given his sweet tooth, it hadn't been a total surprise to find the bakery sack alongside the one with the sandwiches, but she was grateful for the cookies, too.

Even as she had the thought, he reached to draw another double-chocolate-chip cookie out of the bag. "That better not be the last one," she warned with a smile.

"Would I do that? There's another. But I wouldn't advise you leaving it unattended much longer."

Taking him at his word, she snagged the bag and rescued the treat. Bit into it. A moment later, her enjoyment was ruined by a sudden thought. "Do you think Ethan has eaten?" Maybe they should run a meal out to him and the crew.

"I've never known him to go without food for too long. Don't worry. He's probably sent someone to town for—"

The door to the postage-stamp room they'd given opened. RCMP Lieutenant John Brookings stepped inside holding a takeout container.

"Is that for us?" Nyle joked. "Because it has been a couple of hours since we ate, if you don't count the baked goods."

"One of the officers reporting for shift a few minutes ago saw a youngster on a bike set it on the hood of your car and pedal away." It wasn't until he stepped farther into the room that Alexa noted that he wore a grim expression on his face and nitrile gloves on his hands. He nodded in her direction. "This has your name on it."

Her stomach clenched in trepidation. The man put it on the table in front of them. "You don't have to look inside if you'd prefer not to."

ALEXA. Her name was written across the top in block letters with a black marker. "I'll chance it."

He reached out and opened the tab on the container. Raised the lid. Alexa stared in shock, a wave of revulsion nearly choking her.

It was impossible to tell the origin of the bloody organ inside. But Alexa didn't need tests to guess that it was human. And it didn't take much imagination to predict from whom it had come. Nyle uttered a vile oath, which sounded foreign coming from him. "Maybe they'll be able to lift a print from the container," she said in as steady a tone as she could manage.

"That's a question for the lab guys. If he ate a meal earlier from this container or left DNA anywhere in it, that would help nail him." Brookings said.

*If the offender's DNA were in the country's CODIS system it would*, Alexa thought. But if not, it would be yet another piece of evidence that would cement the case against the UNSUB only once he was arrested.

"We'll know for sure what that is after the autopsy." Nyle's jaw was tight. "But it looks an awful lot like a tongue."

Brookings nodded. "That's my guess, too."

Alexa risked another look. It would make an awful sort of sense. Jeanette Lawler had made her career exposing people to the public eye. If Fornier was to be believed, it would have been a secret of Lawler's that had brought her to the attention of the UNSUB.

"I had one of my men download the feed from the security camera in the area where you were parked. I'll have a picture of the kid in minutes."

"It's not that big a town." Nyle stood. "Someone is going to know him."

"I can lend you a couple of officers if you want to show the pictures door-to-door. I'll take that." Brookings picked up the Styrofoam box again. "Probably should keep this refrigerated until Sergeant Manning decides what he wants to be done with it."

THE GRAINY IMAGE from the film showed a young boy of nine or ten. Alexa thought of a quicker way to search for him than going door to door. Instead, she and Nyle would try the elementary schools in town. It was the third week in June, so chances were the principals would still be there.

They struck out at the first school. Hit gold with the second. "It looks like one of the Udall boys," Michael Whisp, the short, stout principal told them, peering at the photo through his reading glasses. "Ernest, Douglas, Patrick...can never keep them straight. But I can give you his address."

"That would be extremely helpful."

The man disappeared into the outer office and came back a few minutes later with a card, which he handed to them. "There you go. I appreciate the gravity of the situation surrounding this inquiry, but go easy on the boy, please. All three of them are good kids. High-spirited, but they tend to run free at home."

"He's not in trouble," Alexa hastened to assure the man. "We just want to ask him some questions."

"He might be in trouble," Nyle muttered, as they walked back to the car and got in.

"The child was just a tool." Alexa fastened her seatbelt. "The UNSUB used him to get to us. Now we might be able to use the child to get to *him*."

Finding the lad was easier said than done. They went to the address listed on the card the principal had given them. There was no answer when they rang the bell. The next-door neighbor was walking toward her car in the drive. Seeing them, she gave a friendly wave. "Mark and Janet are both at work," she called.

Alexa descended the steps again. "We're looking for one of their sons." She held out the picture for the woman to view while Nyle flashed his credentials.

"Patrick? What'd he do?"

One had to wonder the about the boys' pastimes when that was the first thing that came from the woman's mouth. "Nothing, really. He just might have seen something that could help us."

"Oh." The woman smiled. "Whew. Well, those three don't spend much time at home in the summer. I do know they are all ungrounded at the moment, which makes me suspect that they're at the public pool. Do you know where that is?"

"I'm sure we can find it. Thank you."

The woman got into her car and backed out of the drive as Nyle and Alexa walked to their vehicle. Before they got in it, however, a boy on a green bike wearing a blue cap zipped by. He jumped off his bike, letting it fall to the ground in the yard and sped up the steps to the house, slipping something off his neck. A key, Alexa noted as she and

Nyle walked toward the house again. The boy disappeared inside. As they approached the porch, he was already running down the steps, something in his hand.

He came to a stop when he saw them. "Hi." He surveyed them warily from beneath the brim of his Toronto Blue Jays cap, a mop of tousled blond hair showing around the edges. "I'm not allowed to buy anything."

Nyle pulled out his credentials again and held them up for him. The boy's expression went wary.

"We'd like to ask you about the delivery you made at the RCMP building on Pictou Road not long ago."

"I just left a sandwich there."

Alexa and Nyle exchanged a glance. "You're not in trouble," she said, giving him a friendly smile. "Did you look inside the container?"

He shook his head. She saw now he held a pass in his hand. He must have needed it for the swimming pool. "He said not to open it, or it would get stale."

"I just want to know who to thank for the delicious meal." The snort Nyle made was barely audible.

"I don't know the guy. He gave me this." Digging in the pocket of his shorts, the boy pulled out a wadded-up ten-dollar bill. "He told me what car to put it on. Made me recite the license number four times like I'm some sort of idiot or something." He rolled his eyes.

A chill prickled Alexa's skin as she and Nyle exchanged a look. The offender knew the license number of the vehicle they drove. Had he left town at all after dumping Lawler's body? The prospect was disturbing.

"Can you tell me what he looked like?"

Patrick shrugged. "Like a regular guy. Not that tall. Not as tall as him." He pointed at Nyle. "Not as big, either.

Skinny, but he had long sleeves on so I couldn't see if he had muscles."

Nyle peeled away from them, pulling his cell from his pocket and walking off a few paces to make a call. Alexa said, "What color hair did he have?"

"Gray," he surprised her by saying. "And a gray mustache. But I think it was a wig. The hair, I mean. Because when he was walking away, he was fixing it, like great-grandma does when she wakes up from a nap. Sort of like this." He reached his hands up like he was tugging at his hair.

"You're very observant." Her pulse quickened with excitement. At this rate, the boy would provide a better source than Fornier had. "Was he as tall as me?"

He eyed her critically. "Probably an inch or two taller."

"What color were his eyes?"

His shrug was a quick bounce of his shoulders. "He had sunglasses on. Long pants and a long-sleeve Toronto Blue Jays T-shirt. In the *summer*."

"Where did you see happen to see him?"

"At Fredo's Sandwich shop. I mean, he was in the parking lot, and I was next door at the bakery getting some cookies." He looked guilty for a moment. Rushed on. "I ate them there because if my brothers saw them, there'd be nothing but crumbs left. And when I picked up my bike, he came over and asked if I wanted to make ten bucks. I said sure."

"Did he get into a vehicle?"

He shook his head, dashing her hopes. "No, he was walking. After he gave me the sandwich, he went back between the two buildings. I figured that's why he didn't take the food to the car himself. Because he didn't want to walk all the way out there. Maybe because of his sore leg."

An inner alert sounded. "He had a sore leg?"

"I guess because he limped. Sort of like this." The boy gave an energetic imitation down the sidewalk and back. "Not a bad limp like I had after I broke my leg and first got the cast off. More like the way I moved a few weeks later after it'd healed."

The kid was impressively alert. "Which leg was it?"

He slapped his right thigh. "Just like the one I broke."

"You've done a good job," Alexa said sincerely. "We won't take any more of your time at the moment. You're free to go."

But he didn't sprint for his bike like she thought he would. "Are you Alexa?"

"I am."

"Don't you know who this guy is? I mean, why would he buy you a sandwich if he doesn't know you?"

"If it's who I think it is, we haven't met." Nyle rejoined them. "But I know about him."

He smiled impishly. "My brother Doug bought Tara Marvin a slice of pizza because he thought she was hot. Maybe this guy likes you."

The thought had her mouth drying out. It was all she could do to force the words out. "That's a thought. Thanks again for your help."

This time he lost no time gathering up his bike, jumping on it and pedaling off.

"It would be worthwhile for that young man to sit down with a forensic sketch artist," Alexa informed Nyle. "He's eagle-eyed, and he saw the offender minutes ago rather than three years like Fornier. I'd like to get a second sketch and compare the two."

Nyle nodded. "I just called Ethan. He's contacting the Halifax RCMP and requesting Cote's services again. He's also sending extra officers from the scene over to help do a patrol for the van in the vicinity."

"Let me guess." She turned toward the car. "We're on camera duty again."

He nodded. "We'll check the businesses the kid mentioned and other ones in the vicinity for security cameras. Then it's back to our tasks from earlier this afternoon."

A sense of urgency filled her. If Anis Tera had been caught on camera in town in the last couple of hours, they wouldn't need a forensic artist. They'd have the first picture of The Tailor in the history of the case.

THREE HOURS LATER, they were back at the RCMP head-quarters in Halifax, preparing for the day's briefing that would begin in twenty minutes. Alexa had a feeling that she looked worse for wear. The long hours without sleep were beginning to take a toll. But working practically around the clock hadn't prevented Jeanette Lawler's death.

That failure weighed heavily.

Ethan strode into the conference area they were using for the meeting, his cell clutched in his hand and his expression forbidding. "Commissioner Gagnon," he said, by way of explanation, and pressed a button before setting the phone on the table between them. "You're on speaker-phone, Commissioner. Dr. Hayden is with me."

"Doctor. Thank you for your efforts on the task force." Gagnon's voice was brisk but sincere. I wanted to hear your thoughts about the UNSUB's communication with you. Is this an encouraging development? Or is he playing a cat-and-mouse game with us?"

She flicked a glance at Ethan's expression, which hadn't lightened. She could only guess at the phone conversation before it had included her. "Nothing in the profile I've developed leads me to believe that the offender had planned to change his behavior. Now that he has, however, he will attempt to manipulate us, yes."

"And what do you think precipitated the change?"

A bit discomfited, she said, "I believe it was my appearance at the press conference that did so, sir. We know the UNSUB researches his victims exhaustively. He might have been intrigued by my specialty in entomology, given his interest in that area."

"Sergeant Manning believes he has an unhealthy fixation on you."

Ah. The reason for the temper radiating off Ethan was now becoming clear. "I wouldn't disagree. That doesn't mean we can't use it to our advantage."

A note of satisfaction entered the commissioner's voice. "That's what I wanted to hear you say. Of course, we don't expect you to take any unnecessary risks. But as long as you're comfortable, I'd like you to use his new focus on you as a way to expand the investigation. Tomorrow I'll call another press conference, for which the two of you will again be miked in remotely. I want you to speak directly to the offender. You know best what to say to say to him. But use his newfound fixation to draw him out."

"Exactly what I would suggest myself, sir."

"Excellent." There was no mistaking the note of finality in the man's tone. "Ethan? Did you have anything else to add?"

"No, sir."

"Then Captain Campbell will contact you before the

conference to discuss what information you're ready to make public. I won't keep you."

They said their goodbyes and disconnected.

Ethan slipped the phone in his pocket, careful not to make eye contact with Alexa. But she could sense his disapproval. He didn't have to state it. She already knew that she was in for some heated discussion over on this subject.

For now, though, Ethan and an RCMP officer busied themselves hooking up the video conference software. The equipment was a far cry from what they had available in the hotel room yesterday morning. There was a large screen hanging in the center of the wall and three mikes set up before each of Ethan's, Alexa's and Nyle's places at the table. Within minutes, familiar faces filled the screen. The remainder of the task force team.

Ethan walked back and took his place at the table between Alexa and Nyle. "Welcome, everyone."

There were subdued murmurs from the rest of the officers. "Tough break on Lawler," Ian McManus said, and the other two agents nodded.

"It was. We had the people out on the street, in the clubs, but..." Ethan shook his head. "Hard to know whether we missed her in the crowds or if she'd left by the time we hit the places."

"To be that close," muttered Steve Friedrich, who was clean-shaven today, but somehow still looked slightly disheveled.

"Pretty damn frustrating," Ethan agreed. "Some of you have updated me throughout the day, but to keep everyone on the same page, why don't you summarize your findings?"

Ian McManus started. "Jonah and I caught up with an ex-girlfriend of Norton's." The second New Brunswick victim, Alexa recalled. With the assassin bug in his mouth.

"And there's a reason for she's an ex because she hates the guy's guts. She clapped when we told her he was dead. Claims that she didn't know anything about how he made a living. Said when they were living together, he'd sometimes disappear for days and then reappear, saying he'd been 'working.' She did know that whatever he was doing during that time, he got paid in bitcoin for it."

He looked down to consult some papers in front of him before continuing. "Five years ago she says he claimed someone was trying to blackmail him. He wouldn't tell her for what, but he was stomping around and threatening to kill whoever it was."

"That sounds like what Fornier told us about Anis Tera and Simard," Nyle said.

"That's what I thought. We found two computers at Norton's apartment when we searched it, so hopefully, the forensic IT guys will find something on the older model."

Jonah Bannon spoke next. "I spent the day interviewing Henry Paulus's colleagues and the chief at the fire department where he worked. The chief was real defensive about any hints that Paulus might have been a firebug. Guess he figures that reflects on him since he hired the guy. We didn't get too much from the other firefighters, except two who admitted that they'd heard Paulus make some remarks that had them wondering. Edmonton had a half-dozen suspicious fires the previous year, all businesses. For every one of them, the owner was alibied tight. Out somewhere in public surrounded by people the night their places burned down."

"You think he was an arsonist for hire?"

Jonah nodded his shaved head at Ethan's question. "Both of his colleagues brought up the possibility without any prompting from me."

It was Steve Friedrich's turn. "I chased down the latest

leads from the tip line we set up for anyone who might have seen our white cargo van in the vicinity of Fundy National Park while Paulus was there. It was a bust, as expected."

"As always, I appreciate your efforts. We got the go-ahead for a province-wide stop-and-search of every older white Econoline van. You can track the ones in New Brunswick. We're looking for alibis for all four recent homicides." The three Mounties nodded in unison. "Nyle has finished with the toll-road cameras which catch vehicles entering Nova Scotia from New Brunswick on both driving routes. He'll pass those on. Same protocol. Any of the owners farther than a couple of hours away from can be left to local RCMP departments."

"Did you find anything of value at the crime scene?" McManus asked.

"The forensic ident unit got clear casts of tire marks left by the van," Ethan told them. He told them about the witness who'd led Nyle and Alexa there. "We also got some tire prints from what might have been a dolly and some footprints behind it. He would have wheeled the body through the woods and down to the water's edge. It's all more evidence to build the case against the offender, once he's in custody."

He looked at Nyle, who took the opportunity to fill in the other men about the delivery to Alexa that day.

"This isn't good, Doc." The two older men flanking Steve nodded at his statement. "I mean, I'm not the profiler here, but once this guy starts engaging with a member of the task force, stuff gets freaky."

Smiling slightly, Alexa said, "That's a pretty good description of today's events." Not for the life of her would she show just how much the delivery had shaken her. "But I look at it a bit differently. An offender changing his behavior after sticking with it so rigidly for years is indeed alarming. It can precede an escalation, or make him harder to predict. But it also offers opportunities to get inside his head a bit more. One thing I gleaned from his written communication today is that we might have an offender who believes he's doing God's work."

The expressions on the officers' faces showed just how unimpressed they were by that. "They all have some cop-out motivation," Jonah remarked.

"Yes, one that absolves them of responsibility. But I want to tug on that thread a bit more. I might be able to use it when I communicate with the UNSUB directly. This deviation is useful to us because he's now taking risks that he never has before. To have that...object delivered today, he had to linger in the vicinity of the dump site. Or he returned to the area," Alexa corrected herself. "We have no way of knowing if he went back to his lair first. He spoke to someone who can offer a description. We may yet find a local business that picked him up on a security camera." She and Nyle had gone to all the local businesses and asked them to check their feeds for the van or a man fitting Patrick's description. "When he strays outside his usual comfort zone, he's more apt to make mistakes. And one of them might help us catch him."

"He's using a disguise, as I've noted in the update I sent you," Ethan put in. "And according to our young witness, he has a limp. Right leg. That's a detail we didn't have before."

Alexa wondered for the first time if the injury to the UNSUB's leg came at Fornier's hand.

"Are you having a forensic artist work with the wit?" This from Jonah.

Ethan nodded. "The boy's parents agreed to bring him

to  Halifax  RCMP  tomorrow  morning  for  that appointment."

"Maybe you'll get it in time to include it in tomorrow's press conference."

"If it's available we'll use it. Even with the wig and mustache the offender sported, it gives us another drawing of the guy. The more accurate the sketches are, the more he's going to feel like the walls are closing in on him." Ethan's voice held a note of certainty. "We've got descriptions of him and the vehicle he drives. The net is getting tighter, gentlemen. When he realizes that, he's going to panic. And when that happens, we'll be there."

# CHAPTER TWELVE

IT WAS DISTURBING to be back at the hotel where they'd spent a sleepless night after searching for Lawler. They'd returned much too late to consider switching to a less-expensive place. That would have to wait until morning. But Alexa wouldn't be sorry to leave this reminder of their failure to save the UNSUB's latest victim.

Jeanette Lawler's next of kin had been notified. The ripples that radiated from death were far-reaching, touching family, friends, colleagues, employers. And in Lawler's case, an entire viewing audience. That wouldn't occur to the UNSUB. Lack of empathy was ingrained in his psyche. For the offender, Lawler's life began and ended with him.

After agreeing on their meet time the next morning, Ethan, Alexa and Nyle went their separate ways. She figured the men had to be as exhausted as she was. She collected the new laptop and tablet that she'd had delivered there, then returned to her room to shower. After ordering room service, she set up the devices and plugged in the flash drive to transfer her files to the computer before starting on her press conference remarks for tomorrow. She worked for a couple of hours, revising and fine-tuning her statement until she set the task aside. No doubt there would be further changes before she and Ethan went on air. And if he had his way, her portion would be scrapped altogether.

Ethan. His feelings about Gagnon's orders had been all too easy to read. As a consultant, Alexa had butted heads with members of an investigation before. It wasn't unusual for the brass and the agents on the ground to have far different ideas about her role in the case. She almost always sided with the investigators; they were the ones closest to the case. In those instances, she went to bat for them with the administration, as she had when Ethan had warned against releasing the profile. But in this case, she agreed with Gagnon. If the UNSUB continued to communicate with her, it would be for his own reasons. And she'd engage, to further the investigation.

Which meant she'd better get used to Ethan's disapproval.

A ringing sound emanated from the new laptop. It took a moment for Alexa to realize it was the alert for an incoming FaceTime call. Recognizing Adam Raiker's number, she answered promptly.

"Thank you for getting back to me. I was surprised to hear that you were in the field."

Raiker surveyed her with his familiar laser-blue gaze. "Jaid and I agreed that it was time for us to start resuming our normal routines. Or, what used to be normal. We've got a child predator case in Lexington. Another victim recently snatched. Clock is ticking."

Alexa winced slightly. She wondered if the case brought back memories of her employer's last case for the Bureau when he'd been captured by the child killer he'd been tracking, and tortured before he'd overpowered his captor and killed him.

And then she realized she already knew that answer. Adam Raiker saw the reminders of that case every time he looked in the mirror. The black eyepatch over the eye he'd lost, the scar that traced across his neck, the one running down one cheek, the others on the backs of his hands. He'd never shown a hint of self-consciousness about them. Survival was the ultimate trade-off.

"What's going on with your case?"

Succinctly, Alexa updated him. Raiker had been intrigued from the first when contacted by the RCMP Commissioner. An UNSUB that had been on the loose for over a decade was a unique challenge.

His brows drew together. "So he's communicated with you three times."

"If you count his 'gift' today."

"Of course that counts. Under other circumstances, I'd say he's thumbing his nose at the investigators. But that would be out of character for him. And I don't get that impression from his first communication with you."

"Nor do I."

"He's going to reach out again. Sooner, rather than later. This isn't about an offender taunting the police—he wants to *connect* with you, Alexa, on a personal level. Your shared interest might have been enough to whet his fixation. Your looks likely didn't hurt." Typical Raiker, his words held no flattery, but were stated as blunt fact. "This is a unique chance to discover more about him. But don't underestimate the danger this puts you in. You've learned that he first reaches out to his victims by blackmailing them for some perceived sin. He won't stray far from his long practice."

"He's going to dig into my background. Look for something he can use." She'd known it already. But having her certainty put into words had a greasy layer of nausea pooling in her stomach.

Raiker nodded. "You may represent a deviation in his signature, but he's going to abide by that ritual as much as possible. He'll be compelled to."

"He's not going to find any blackmail material in my past." Heartrending loss, perhaps. But not major crimes.

Her employer was shaking his head. "You're applying logic to a person who isn't rational. Whatever he discovers, his perception won't be grounded in reality. You're a square peg, yes. But he's going to try to work you into the familiar round hole he has for his victims. Continue developing that possible religious link. If it proves tenable, it's a tool you can use to engage or manipulate him."

They chatted a few more minutes about her piece for the press conference tomorrow, with Raiker suggesting some tweaks before they disconnected.

It was barely nine, but none of them had slept much the night before. She got up, readied for bed and then switched off the light. Slipped between the covers.

Exhaustion had unconsciousness approaching quickly. When the alert sounded on her phone, Alexa was already dozing. It was a struggle at first to break free of the sticky fingers of sleep. So tempting to ignore the intrusion. In the next moment, her brain clicked on and she sat straight up, grabbing the cell from the bedside table.

After Anis Tera had contacted her yesterday, she'd set that email addy to send an alert for each new email. This could be a professional contact. She already knew it wouldn't be. When she pressed the inbox button, the same set of letters and numbers appeared from the message sender. The subject header read, TRURO.

She called Ethan's cell. He answered on the first ring. "There's another message." She said nothing more. She knew she didn't have to. Alexa quickly pulled on yoga pants and a cami and then opened the door. Ethan walked in, his expression grim. He was still fully dressed, minus the suit jacket and tie.

"What's it say?"

"I haven't opened it yet." She went to the desk and used the tablet to bring up the email addy the offender was using. "When I ordered a new laptop, I got a tablet, too. I don't want any chance for him to access my files." She didn't think that was possible by just opening the email yesterday. But that didn't mean future communications would be as secure.

"Good idea." He came over to watch over her shoulder. "I think you'd have to click on a link for that to happen, but no use taking risks."

She clicked on the email. It took long seconds for the message to open. This time there was no text. Only a photo. Alexa hissed in a breath, the muscles in her belly twisting.

"Son of a bitch." Ethan's low tone was lethal.

The photo was of her, taken this afternoon. She was standing, half-turned. The image was a little blurry, as if it had caught her in mid-motion. Alexa knew the exact moment it'd been taken. After she'd risen from her mother's grave and readied to leave.

"Where was this snapped?"

"This afternoon at Heavenly Angels Cemetery. My mother's buried there."

"He *followed* you?"

The sense of violation was overwhelming. The one moment she'd had with her mother in twenty years had been tainted by the presence of a madman. "We know he's familiar with our vehicle, since he had the boy repeat the license number of the car he was to make the delivery to." She tried to recall any vehicle in the vicinity of the cemetery. Failed. "Maybe we're wrong about the van." Because there was no way they would have missed *that*.

"The forensic ident guys casted the tread prints and measured them. The vehicle that left them has a longer wheelbase than a car or a pickup."

She looked over her shoulder at him. "Well, he didn't follow us to the east side of town on foot. He has a second vehicle."

Ethan gave a slow nod. "That would explain a lot. Why chance having the van in the same vicinity as the body he carried it in when there are police swarming the area?"

"He feels invisible," she murmured, her mind racing. "Because he's been overlooked all his life. And he's been operating with impunity for years. Maybe long enough to convince himself that he *can't* be caught." Perhaps there was a religious aspect to that, too, if the UNSUB thought his was holy work, he may believe it'd been blessed by the God he claimed to be serving.

"I won't take that as a dig," Ethan said wryly and her gaze flew to his again. Was aware for the first time of how close their faces were.

"I'm trying to think like he does."

"Then think about what this is." He tapped the screen, before reaching for his phone to take close-up pictures of the image. Alexa stared at the spot he'd indicated. She'd barely noticed it before, so caught up with the fact that the offender had been close enough to witness her vulnerability in the cemetery.

An image had been photoshopped onto her right shoulder. Insects, of course. She slipped out of her chair and went to her briefcase. Hurried back with a magnifying glass. Examining the enlarged image, she said wonderingly, "Termites."

Ethan looked up from his phone. "What would the significance of that be? Do you think he's identifying the second insect sample in Lawler's mouth?"

Alexa shook her head, trying to shove aside her burgeoning trepidation. "This will be more personal." She opened her laptop and brought up the database to double check for accuracy. She wasn't mistaken. But the symbolism still escaped her.

"The email has vanished." Ethan straightened. "I'm going to go print this." Alexa barely noticed him leave. She was already immersed in looking up facts about the insects, rapidly reading article after article. When he returned, she looked up.

"The image is of a male and female sample of *Kalotermes flavicollis*. They're a species of Dampwood termites."

Ethan crossed to drop one of the images he'd printed off onto the desk. "So what's he telling you? That you and he can destroy buildings and construct your own world together?"

"I'm not exactly certain," she admitted. "The fact that he included both male and female is probably significant. They may represent him and me." And she'd never admit how squeamish that made her feel. "Termites are social creatures with a definite caste system. There's the king and queen, the workers, alates and soldiers. The king and queen mate for life and are responsible for reproduction. They populate the entire colony." She frowned. "They're also the only ones in the colony that develop eyes, although they don't have a strong visual sense." She wasn't sure if that fact was important. It was critical not to read too much into the possible symbolism.

"Christ, Alexa." Ethan stared at her with something between horror and distaste in his expression. "You've got to see how frightening his focus on you is. And, from a non-bug enthusiast, damn creepy."

That drew a smile from her. "Well, it's certainly unique."

"Unique, hell." The concern in his voice was impossible to miss. "I think it's further proof that encouraging this fixation on you is a mistake. To use it the way Gagnon urged you to do, to draw the guy out."

They'd come full circle. "I'm familiar with your feelings on the topic."

The fact that she said nothing else had him clenching his jaw. But he visibly reined in his temper. Tucked it away. A quality he'd perfected in adulthood. "It's a moot point," he managed to say evenly. "The brass has spoken." He looked down at the images he held. "How long were you at the cemetery?"

"Not long. Twenty minutes maybe."

"Were you alone there?"

She sat down on the edge of the bed and tried to recall. "I really don't remember," she said finally. "I didn't notice any people or cars around when I was trying to find the grave, or when I was walking out again. And I would have, I'm sure of it." She thought for another minute. "But it's an old cemetery. Lots of vaults and oversized monuments." And the possibility that the offender had lurked behind one of them, spying on her, had a new chill breaking out of her skin. "Roads flank the cemetery, with gates on either end. My guess is he followed us, passing by when Nyle let me off and then he returned on the other road. If he parked the vehicle and took the picture from over there, I wouldn't have noticed."

But she resented the intrusion. Fiercely.

Ethan looked away. The images were still clutched in one hand. He shoved his free hand in his pocket. "I'm sorry about your mom."

Surprisingly, her eyes filled. It'd been a long time since she'd shed tears over her mother. She'd lost her a little at a time from the moment Thomas Reisman entered their lives. But it'd been a long day, one steeped in emotion. "Thank you."

"How'd she die?"

"Breast cancer, from what I heard. Untreated, of course." She heard the bitterness in her tone. Was helpless to control it. "I'm sure her husband convinced her the power of prayer was greater than any medical treatment could be."

"When did it happen?" He sat gingerly down on the bed next to her.

"Fifteen months after we left Truro." The last time Alexa had seen her mother there had been censure in her eyes. Judgment on her lips. Alexa didn't think she'd realized until that moment just how thoroughly Reisman had transformed the woman.

"Did you ever...reconnect?"

He'd once known how badly her mother's rejection had hurt her. Because although she'd never shared all, she'd opened up more to Ethan than anyone else. He may not have understood but he'd sympathized. And he'd hurt, once upon a time, when she hurt.

The memories were a slippery slope. One misstep and a deluge of unwanted recollections would flood forth. The emotions roiling and careening inside her were unwelcome.

Alexa had thought they were dealt with. Properly identified, processed and tucked neatly away to be examined occasionally with a clinical detachment. She pressed a fist to her mouth. Tried to formulate an answer.

"I tried once. I had the neighbor's number. Willa Satler. A bit of a busybody, but she was kind to me. I called her and she agreed to speak to my mother sometime when Reisman was out. She told my mom she had my number and that she could use her phone to call me." After all these years, the memory still had fangs. "She declined." *She turned her face from God, now our faces are turned from her.*

"She was completely under her husband's thumb."

"I thought so at the time," Alexa said wearily. "But it was more than that. Like an abuse victim, which of course she was. Or someone brainwashed by a cult. He just...erased her, a tiny bit every day. Until there was really nothing of her there anymore. Just what he'd remade her into."

"You and she both got robbed. You of a childhood. Her of a life."

His words were no more than the truth. But Alexa had gotten out, and her escape was wrapped up in Ethan all those years ago. Rebecca Reisman had never gotten the chance.

It was easy to be reminded, sitting next to him, of the attraction he'd held for her all those years ago. Alexa could have resisted the teenage Adonis looks, the confidence and slight swagger of a boy used to female attention. But beneath it all, she'd discovered a generous heart and a capacity for caring that had been its own seduction. His sense of adventure had awakened her own. It was little wonder that, although she'd stepped cautiously, she'd fallen hard and fast.

"My dad moved from here when he retired. Went to Kingston, Ontario."

She froze, sensing a trap. "I hope he's well," she said carefully.

"I figured you knew, since the two of you have been corresponding since you left."

Her gaze snapped to meet his. "How did…"

Ethan's expression was neutral. "I found a letter in his desk when he had heart surgery about ten years ago and we were taking care of things for him. It was clear you'd kept in touch."

She could understand if Ethan regarded that as a betrayal. But he didn't seem angry. More… resigned.

"I asked him about it later when he was feeling better, and he told me the whole thing. How he'd given you the money to leave when you went to him. He said 'Son, the girl had her mind made up. I wasn't going to let her go without making sure she'd be safe.'"

Her heart shredded all over again. "He's a good man."

"He is. I was pretty pissed at him for a while but I finally figured he was right." His expression had gone bleak. "You were set on leaving."

"You know why." The whisper felt like it was torn from her.

"I know what you said. Hell, maybe in another twenty years, I'll even agree with your logic." He bounced up from the bed, as if compelled to move. "All I knew then was first there was a baby, and then there wasn't. First I had a wife, and then I didn't."

Had she really ever believed they could work together on the case and not have this conversation? It was all too easy to be transported back twenty years. To feel anew the heartbreak of losing their baby girl only weeks before they should have been holding her in their arms. The months afterward, sleepwalking through the pain and loss. Before Alexa had come to the one decision that would be best for Ethan. "You were exhausted from your studies, hockey, and the part-time job. We both knew you were good enough to go pro. Your coach told you that. The only thing holding you back was me."

"You were my wife." His face, his tone, was just as implacable as it'd been back then.

"But I wouldn't have been if not for the baby. We both know that," she added gently. "Some things are absolutes. The grass is green. The sky is blue. And Ethan Manning will always, always do the right thing." In that way, his career choice made perfect sense. "You couldn't see beyond your sense of duty. But once I removed that obligation, I knew your future would get a lot brighter." That's what she'd told him at the time, and she'd been right. With her gone, he could quit the part-time job. Concentrate on the sport and his classes. And three years after she was gone he'd been a second-round draft pick. He'd had the life he'd always said he wanted.

"Replaying the same argument from back then is just as useless now." There was a heat in his pale blue eyes. A dangerous burn. "It shouldn't matter. Do you know how many times since you've come that I've reminded myself of that? We were kids. It wasn't real, it wouldn't have lasted. I told myself the same things whenever I allowed myself to think of you. And then you showed up here, and everything I'd been telling myself explodes in my face. Because there's still something there, and you're lying to yourself if you won't admit it."

Her heart beat a rapid tattoo in her chest. Ethan's words had alarms shrilling in the recesses of her mind. They were a demand for honesty that would be much more comfortable to dodge.

"I've been trying like hell to deny it." A hard smile crossed Ethan's lips. "Damn you, Alexa Grace." He dropped down on the bed beside her again, his face dizzyingly close. "Twenty years wasn't long enough to get you out of my head."

When his lips touched hers, her hand lifted of its own accord to cup his jaw. It was leaner now. Harder than it'd been the last time they'd touched. And she knew this was a mistake. It had to be. But Alexa wasn't going to waste a second regretting it.

Her lips parted beneath his and his fingers speared into her hair as he angled his face closer to take advantage. There'd been so few indulgences in her life. She wasn't going to deny herself this one.

She'd known the kiss of the boy but not the man. It was the hint of familiarity that drew her, the foreign demand that left her craving more. His tongue entered her mouth in a slow seductive glide. Alexa could feel his arm around her as she floated backward. It wasn't until the mattress was at her back that she realized, much too dimly, that he'd lowered her to the bed. Her hand slid to his nape as she urged him closer, her tongue doing battle with his.

This didn't feel like catching a nostalgic piece of her past and pulling it close. No, it was different between them. *They* were different. Ethan's mouth ate at hers with a hunger that torched her own. With him, she held nothing back. Instead, she gave herself over and poured herself into the kiss.

There was heat there, heady and familiar, but the faint hint of desperation was new. As if each of them realized they were hurtling toward disaster, and as one they hit the accelerator. The weight of him, half settled over her, had flame licking up her spine. There was no slow buildup. Just a brutal punch of desire that shook her with its urgency.

She raked his bottom lip with her teeth, and the tiny bit of savagery unleased his own. Their breaths mingled, tongues tangled and teeth clashed as the world fell away to allow only for the kick of passion.

Alexa would never know which of them stilled first. Not because reason had returned. It took several seconds for that. When it did, comprehension followed.

Her phone had sounded again.

They both rose, but Ethan's longer reach snagged her cell first to bring to her. And still it took a moment for her eyes to clear. For the fog of desire to dissipate. "There's another message," she said.

Alexa surged from the bed and crossed to the desk where she'd left the tablet. It was still open to her inbox. She recognized the sender. But this time, there was no subject. Just a jpeg icon to click on.

The picture that opened was old. Faded. A young woman with big hair and a bright smile holding a toddler. Alexa had never seen the photo before, but she recognized her mom as the subject. Which meant the child was her.

She had no idea who would have taken the photo. There had never been any dad or grandparents in her life. But that wasn't the most disturbing thing about the image. Alexa had few snapshots from her childhood. This wasn't among them.

But she knew exactly where the picture had come from. And the realization had a cold trickle of dread snaking down her spine.

"You don't have to do this." Ethan sent a troubled glance across the front seat of the vehicle. Alexa had said very little on the way to Truro from Halifax. She saw now that her silence had worried him.

She summoned a wan smile. "Actually, I do."

Her sleep last night had been fitful. The second picture the UNSUB had sent had rocked her more than she'd like to admit. Ethan had realized it, and hadn't pressed her about it. He'd been, in fact, so solicitous that it had taken an hour to convince him she'd be fine if he went back to his own room. The evening might have turned out much differently if not for the offender's timing. And Alexa still wasn't sure how she felt about that.

Ethan turned the car off. Waited quietly while she stared at the house where she'd spent the last years of her childhood. She supposed everything in a person's past shrank when confronted through the lens of time. The house seemed smaller, but it had never appeared this unkempt. The sidewalk leading up to the two cement steps had cracked and heaved in places. What remained of the lawn needed mowing. The siding on the home was chipped and faded, the trim stripped nearly bare of color. The entire structure seemed to tilt a bit, like a tired old man.

Ethan had never been inside; she'd made sure of that. It had taken weeks for him to convince her to see him outside of the library. Even longer to persuade her to accept a ride from him. If it was nice weather, they'd put her bike in the trunk and she'd insist that he let her out a few blocks away so she could ride it home. In the winter, she'd walk that distance. Always, he'd drive around the block a few times until he saw her safely inside the door. He'd had a strong Galahad streak, even as a teen.

"I tried to imagine back then. What life was like for you

in there." He gestured at the house. "I know I never came close to the reality."

"It was...sad." A pervasive hopelessness had seemed to reside inside, almost like another living breathing member of the family. As if Reisman's disenchantment with the downward spiral of his career had taken form and sprang to life. The more disappointed he was, the harder life became for Alexa's mother.

She shook off the memories and drew a fortifying breath. "He won't talk to you. He has no respect for the authorities. They were called often enough when I was still at home. I notified them a few times myself." No charges were ever filed for the domestic disturbances. He knew they never would be. Her mother had been much too indoctrinated by then for that. "But you start the conversation. Show your credentials. And we'll see where it goes from there." The conversation would deteriorate as soon as he recognized her, Alexa knew. But she was long past the age when his words could move her.

She opened her car door and got out, waiting for Ethan to do the same. When he rounded the hood of the vehicle, they walked toward the house she'd once sworn she'd never return to.

The screen door was minus a window, and it rattled when Ethan knocked on it. A long minute stretched before he repeated the gesture, harder this time. His fist was raised to try again before the inside door swung open wide enough to show a man in the wedge of space.

Alexa's first thought was that the last two decades hadn't been kind to Thomas Reisman. Like the house, he was showing signs of age. His once tall, spare frame had become slightly stooped, his thinness bordering on skeletal. Wisps of hair clung stubbornly to his head in random gray tufts. He glared at them suspiciously through glasses he'd never worn before. A bottle of orange juice was clutched in one hand. "What do you want?"

"RCMP Sergeant Manning and my associate, Dr. Alexa Hayden." Ethan held up his credentials and let the man study them before he raised his gaze to the two of them.

Alexa braced herself for the outburst she knew would be forthcoming. But the man only repeated, "What do you want?"

"Did you have a visitor yesterday, Mr. Reisman? A stranger, perhaps?"

Reisman pursed his lips. "'You shall also love the stranger, for you were strangers in the land of Egypt.'"

They waited, but when he said nothing further, Ethan pressed, "So someone did come here yesterday?"

"That's my business, isn't it?"

"Actually, it's ours." Ethan's voice hardened. "We're conducting a homicide investigation and we have reason to believe the perpetrator is the person who appeared at your door. We want to talk to you about that."

"I have nothing to say." Reisman took a step back, as if making to close the door, and the realization hit Alexa like a fist to the solar plexus.

He didn't recognize her.

Somehow, the possibility had never occurred. But it should have. She'd never been more than a mouth to feed when she'd been living there. Another mind to bend and mold into his idea of a pious young woman. He'd kept her in line with beatings when she was younger, but he'd grown wilier by the time she was a teen. Any hint of less than total obedience from Alexa would be taken out on her mother. Once Alexa had realized that, Reisman had the control over her that he'd always sought.

She knew if she didn't stop him, he'd shut the door on them and nothing would compel him to reopen it. She couldn't allow that to happen.

"He was asking questions about me, wasn't he? And you welcomed him into your home. Shared our history as if you'd known him for years."

The man visibly started and then stared hard at her, his lips moving silently. "Alexa *Hayden*? It's you, isn't it, Grace?" His mouth twisted into an ugly sneer. And that, too, was familiar. "You found yet another man to marry you? Your type always finds a soft place to land."

"My *type* earned doctorates in forensic entomology and forensic psychology." She kept her voice hard. It was always a mistake to show any sign of weakness to the man. He'd used it as a weapon to bludgeon her with.

"'Pride goeth before a fall.'"

"Your empty platitudes are just that. You were asked about the conversation with a stranger who came to your house yesterday." The only way the UNSUB could have seen that photo was if he'd come here. And once Reisman started spouting Bible verses, the offender would have known just how to play the man. If Alexa was correct about the killer's motivation, the two men might be kindred spirits. Both used religion to condone their actions.

"I've never had much use for the police." The man glowered at Ethan. "Always butting their noses into people's private business."

"You can answer our questions here, or come with us to the RCMP detachment to explain why you're covering for a man who has killed fifteen people," she said crisply. And watched the comprehension belatedly filter into his expression, before he shook his head in disbelief.

"A murderer? I don't believe you. You were always a

wicked girl, refusing to embrace the light I brought into your life. And you ended up exactly as I always expected. A penniless, pregnant tramp who slept with anyone who crooked a finger. Drove your mother to an early death, not that you'd care about that."

It was no more than she expected from him. But Ethan opened the screen and took a step toward the man, who must have sensed the threat in the movement. He shrank away. "Be very careful," Ethan warned in a deceptively quiet voice. "She's not a child anymore, to be bullied by the likes of you. She's offered you a choice, and it's one you need to make now."

Reisman angled his jaw. "Who said anyone stopped here?" he asked Alexa truculently.

"I say. Because you gave him a photo of my mother and me. Or showed it to him and he took a picture of it. And then he shared it with me, and I knew immediately where he'd gotten it."

"I didn't give him any of the pictures. They were Rebecca's and now they belong to me." Alexa couldn't believe he'd even kept any old photos. Certainly, he couldn't claim sentimental attachment. To Thomas Reisman, Rebecca's life had begun the moment he'd walked into it. Nothing that had happened before was of consequence. Including Alexa.

"But you showed them to him," she prompted. Her hand curled around the wrought-iron railing on the side of the steps. "Did he ask you to?"

"He came in the afternoon. Two or so. I was taking a nap. He said that he knew you, that the two of you had met and were becoming friends. He knew you'd grown up in Truro and wanted to pay his respects. You wouldn't understand anything about respect," he said to Alexa bitterly. "I don't believe all these lies you're telling about him. It was obvious that he was a godly man. A good man."

"Because he could match you in Bible verses?"

"'The soothing tongue is a tree of life, but a perverse tongue crushes the spirit.' I brought him a glass of water and we spoke of biblical things." Reisman's voice went sly. "I told him what a disappointment you'd been to us. How wickedly you'd turned away from the Lord. He understood, he said. He had family of his own. And yes, he wanted to see pictures of you. Asked a lot of questions about your life before I lifted Rebecca and you out of poverty and showed you the path toward God."

"Did he introduce himself?"

The man cocked his head. "Anas. Anos. Anis. I think he said Anis. Anis Tera."

A hard clutch of nerves tangled in Alexa's belly. The UNSUB had used the same name when he'd contacted Simard. The offender had to know they'd come to talk to Reisman. He must be confident there was no way to tie the alias to his true identity. Certainly, the team's attempts to do so had been unsuccessful. But the alias was important to him; it closely entwined the insect predator he emulated with his own acts.

"You say he was here around two?"

Reisman answered Ethan sullenly. "I said about then. I don't know precisely. We spoke a while out here before I invited him inside."

A serial killer had elicited an invitation to step inside Reisman's home. His wife's daughter had been met with vitriol. The irony was jarring.

"What did he look like?" she asked. She hadn't looked forward to this meeting, and she desperately wanted it over now.

Reisman shrugged. "Not that tall. Maybe this high." He touched his shoulder. Alexa made a mental measurement. That would make the offender no more than five feet six inches, which contradicted the five feet eight inches two other witnesses had pegged him at.

"What color was his hair?"

"Blond, I think."

She and Ethan exchanged a glance. "Thomas." Alexis deliberately gentled her voice. "I don't remember you wearing glasses."

"Macular degeneration," he admitted. "But that doesn't mean I couldn't see a man sitting not three feet away from me."

Depending on the progression of the disease, it could mean exactly that. "Did you see him get into a car?"

He shook his head definitely. "I walked him to the door and he thanked me for my time, and shared a Bible verse with me. And then I watched him walk away. He didn't get into a vehicle."

"Which way did he go?"

In answer to Ethan's question Reisman pointed east, but his gaze settled on Alexa. "He wanted to know all about you and I told him. Every bit. All your sins. Your willful lack of repentance." His smile was sly. "I don't believe he left here with a very good impression of you."

# CHAPTER THIRTEEN

*There is none righteous; no, not one.* —Romans 3:10

ANIS TERA LINGERED over his breakfast of coffee and a sweet pastry. This was one of those times that it was a blessing to have the sort of face that blended into a crowd. Today, he wore a baseball cap pulled low over his eyes, on top of a scraggly brown wig that hung below his earlobes. The patchy mustache and goatee were itchy, but in service to the Lord, sacrifices must be made.

Today's treat was a rare indulgence for him. Over the top of his newspaper he watched people in the coffee shop bustle about with their orders, finding places to sit with friends or family. A few of them, like him, were alone. He approved of that. Only those who weren't at peace with themselves feared solitude.

There was a big splashy news article about Jeanette Lawler's body being discovered, followed by a few smaller ones filled with juicy tidbits from her sordid show. Anis read the first article carefully. There was mention of a canine unit, and a professional photo of Lawler, along with a plea for anyone who'd seen her last night to call a police line.

He pursed his lips as he considered the development. It had happened before, over the years, and the tactic had yielded nothing. Given the crowd in the club and the pains he'd taken with his appearance, Anis wasn't worried.

He picked up the pastry and bit into with relish. At first he'd lived in fear of being found out, but his paranoia had long since dissipated. He'd had some close calls with his subjects a time or two, but never with the police. He'd thought he was lucky until the truth had been revealed to him: The Lord was paving the way for Anis's holy work.

Still, care had to be taken. Anis worried about whether he'd overstepped caution yesterday. He'd never tarried after a mission like he was now. There had never been a reason. Alexa Hayden had changed everything.

So, he'd had to change, as well.

Sipping from his to-go cup, he contemplated the actions he'd taken yesterday. Dangerous, but he'd mitigated the risk. The van had been safely stowed away while it was still dark, and he'd switched vehicles before returning to Truro. He'd stayed away from cameras and had only been seen by a kid and an old man, neither of whom would be good witnesses. And what could they tell the police, anyway? That they'd spoken to a man decades older than Anis. Wearing clothes he'd already thrown away.

No. The police would yip excitedly about the sightings, but in the end, they'd have nothing new. The risk was balanced by what he'd gained—information on Alexa Hayden.

A small smile tilted his lips. Had she gasped when she'd seen his gift to her? Had she realized his power? The police would test the container, of course. And they'd find prints.

Possibly DNA. But both would belong to the person who'd thrown the to-go box in the Dumpster for him to fish out. His smile grew at the thought of them wasting labor and time testing the container. Possibly chasing down the poor sap who'd discarded it and hauling him in.

Licking the last of the pastry frosting from his fingers, he reached for a napkin, looking idly out the window while he wiped his fingers. He froze. The street beyond the sidewalk outside was busy. But there was a van very much like his pulled to a stop beside the opposite curb. A patrol car, lights still flashing, was parked behind it, and a uniformed officer was approaching the driver's window.

His heart beat faster. Coincidence? He might have thought so had he not passed a similar scene on his way back to Halifax yesterday. He couldn't afford to ignore the possibility that the police might have a description of his van.

How? There was no way to know. But he hadn't remained free this long by ignoring warning signs such as these. He'd been spooked when Simard had looked right at him when he'd been surveilling the man. He'd seemed to recognize Anis despite the simple disguise he'd been wearing. After that, he'd rented a car and started adopting a different appearance.

Now those precautions appeared serendipitous. A signal of the Lord's hand directing his actions.

He'd have to leave the van behind when he left Nova Scotia. The thought was accompanied by a pang, one he immediately shoved aside. He'd salvage the contents he could carry in the car, but he'd burn the Econoline and the magnetic signs he'd used on it, destroying any chance the police could get evidence from the vehicle even if they happened to look.

How long had they had the description of the van? Perhaps remaining in the province longer than he normally would had saved him from detection. If so, he had Alexa Hayden to thank for that.

Alexa. He picked up his cup, drank slowly. It was her job to try to understand him, and yes, that gave him a thrill. Now he understood her, as well. While it was disappointing that she'd rejected a solid godly upbringing, he was used to discovering that the most innocent facades masked hideous sinners. He was prepared to offer her a chance at redemption. Plans to that end were already taking shape. She'd be wise to take the opportunity he'd offer. For penance. For peace.

Because if she didn't... He drained his cup. Set it down and got up from the table. If she refused the light, he'd have no choice but to condemn her to darkness.

# CHAPTER FOURTEEN

"THE INTERVIEW with Reisman was sort of a bust." Ethan slanted a glance at Alexa, who seemed too still, too damn pale to his eye. The man was a snake, and it'd been all Ethan could do to allow him to spit his venom at Alexa. In the end, little new information had been revealed, so the scene had been unnecessary. She'd suffered too many hits, coming too fast together. He didn't doubt her strength; he knew better than most what she'd been through. But even the strongest person had a breaking point.

She shook her head. "Nothing that gives us a new perspective on the offender is wasted. Reisman revealed far more to the UNSUB than he gleaned in their meeting, that's true enough. But I'm stuck on the comment Anis Tera made about having a family."

Ethan glanced at the clock on the dash. They wouldn't make Lawler's autopsy. He'd known that. But Nyle had gone and hopefully they'd hit the tail end of it. "Isn't that just something he'd say to get Reisman comfortable? Like the way he spouted Bible verses."

She turned a bit in her seat to face him, her expression

becoming more animated. "Yes, very possibly. But most people couldn't have gone to see the man on a pretense and done the same. Few are familiar enough with random Bible quotes to use them as freely as he did when he spoke to Reisman. So today wasn't a waste. It verified my belief that the UNSUB uses religion to condone his behavior. That he steeps himself him a faith-based system. I think he may have been raised in a family that adhered to a strict religious upbringing. He got the foundation from somewhere, before he perverted it into a rationalization he uses now."

"So, was he blowing smoke about having a family?"

"I can't be sure," she admitted, pushing her hair back over her shoulder. She'd worn it down today. With her hair loosened, she seemed younger. More vulnerable. He had a feeling that she'd been running late this morning. Maybe she hadn't slept well last night. God knew, he hadn't.

A slow heat bloomed low in his gut and he shifted uncomfortably. Ethan had gotten used to living his life by the book the last few years. Life had thrown him enough curves that he'd come to welcome some predictability. But there'd been nothing predictable about his response to her last night. Nothing expected about him throwing caution to the winds and diving headlong into the fire.

Maybe he could have forgiven himself the lapse had he discovered that the chemistry had been inflated by memory. That the intervening years had burned it out.

Maybe—his hands clenched on the wheel—she could have pulled away. But she hadn't. Instead, she'd kissed him back. And that had sealed his complete loss of reason.

"A-and...you didn't hear a thing I said."

He looked at her blankly. "What?"

Her lips curved. "Do you still zone out thinking about hockey statistics, or is your mind on the case?"

He seized on the excuse she'd offered. "Just thinking it was wise for us to talk to Reisman's neighbors after we left his house. The lady two doors down gave a description of the UNSUB as he walked away that was a lot closer to the one we got from the kid yesterday. What were you saying?"

"You asked if I thought the offender really had a family. I wouldn't give the remark a lot of credence, given the context in which it was made. But it does raise an interesting question."

"Not all serial offenders are lonesome losers without a support system in place."

Her brows shot up. "Someone's been paying attention. Yes, you're right. This offender is perfectly capable of juggling two lives and keeping them separate. I don't have an opinion on whether or not he has a family. There's just not enough information."

And that, Ethan thought, as he pulled into the parking lot for the Burnside morgue in Halifax, could be the summary of the case so far against this offender. Maybe Dr. Conrad could give them a few more details.

The skull on Jeanette Lawler's body was being sewn up by one of Conrad's techs when Ethan and Alexa entered the autopsy suite. Nyle and the ME were hunched over something at the back counter. The officer sent a look over his shoulder. "Didn't think you were going to make it." He searched their faces. "Learn anything important?"

"Nothing we didn't already know." Like the UNSUB's obsession with Alexa was causing him to take the sort of risks he'd avoided throughout his criminal career. Which told Ethan that the offender had much more in mind for her than a few communications. It was exactly that fear that had him wanting to keep her in the background of the investigation, despite Gagnon's wishes.

She brushed by Ethan with the laptop and briefcase she'd grabbed from the front seat to join the men in back. "What'd you find in the victim's mouth?"

"She was minus her tongue, which Officer Samuels informed me you already knew about." Conrad looked at her over the top of the glasses perched on his nose. "That's a very personal message the killer sent to you. What do you think he was trying to tell you?"

"I assume he wants to go steady."

"You need to take his focus on you seriously," Ethan said, more sharply than he intended. The two other men nodded soberly.

Alexa blew out a breath and set her laptop on the counter. Booted it up. "He wanted to get my attention. Sending the tongue to me was him showing off. 'Look at what I can do. See my power?' So, when I go on TV today, I'll acknowledge that power. Play to his ego. And do everything I can to continue to draw him out. Because the more risks he takes, the more likely it is that he'll screw up."

Conrad stared at Ethan. "I trust your men will see to her safety."

"That's the plan." One meeting with Alexa and even the recalcitrant ME's protective instincts had risen to the surface. Giving a mental head shake, Ethan came to a stop behind her. There was something about her that drew men in, had them rising to her defense. And she was as oblivious to that trait now as she'd been as a girl.

"You received the organ? I sent it over yesterday from Truro."

Conrad nodded. "DNA tests will be run, of course, but the cutting marks match. It'd been removed by a small sharp blade. A scalpel perhaps. Or possibly a skinning and caping knife. It's not especially easy to cut the tongue out. Hence the slicing, chopping and sawing marks I found. I found a contusion on her scalp beneath her hair, on the left rear portion of the skull. Not nearly as much force used for the head wound compared to the first victim you brought me."

"Because she was already impaired by alcohol, maybe," Nyle put in. He moved aside to allow Alexa more room.

"Or she was weaker and less difficult to overpower." Ethan positioned himself to Alexa's left. The familiar dragonfly was lying on a sterile cloth in front of her. But it was the contents of the glassine bag she held that he was interested in. She used a pair of forceps to withdraw one insect from it and laid it beside the dragonfly. Conrad handed her a magnifying glass.

"Jesus," Ethan muttered. He couldn't get used to the nonchalant way she handled the bugs. And this was a big one even without the magnification. Not that he was squeamish about that sort of thing. "Is that some sort of cockroach?"

"Looks like a relative of the grasshopper," Nyle observed, peering closely.

"Your guess is closer than Ethan's. It's a good-sized specimen," Alexa set the glass down and sent Ethan a sly smile, half-lifting the paper towel the bug rested on toward him. "Did you want a closer look?"

He remained rooted in place, but it took effort not to move away. "Brat. What is that thing?"

"*Anabrus simplex*. The common name is Mormon cricket, but it's actually a katydid, not a cricket at all. They're flightless, except when they're craving protein and salt, during which time they swarm and are quite destructive to crops." She reached into her briefcase and took out her reading glasses, putting them on before leaning forward and bringing up several articles about the insects, clicking out of each before he was even half way done skimming it. "Found in the range areas of North America. Ah."

She went silent then, long enough for Nyle to say, "Well?"

"They're known to cannibalize members of their own species, usually, again, when craving protein and salt. The slowest and weakest, of course, are the likeliest candidates." She tapped an index finger thoughtfully against the counter.

"Well, that sort of makes sense, given the removal of the tongue." When everyone looked at Nyle, he flushed. "I mean...given Lawler's profession. She was known for inviting high-profile controversial guests and then pulling the rug out from under them during the show. That's predatory behavior, if you ask me."

"You have to consider how the UNSUB would view it." Ethan looked at Alexa. "He wouldn't have sympathy for the type of guests Lawler had on. Few people would. So, I don't see this as retribution for her treating people unkindly on her show."

"The Mormon crickets prey on the slowest and weakest among their species," she repeated. Then went silent for a moment as if thinking. Finally, she said, "I don't know if the UNSUB is saying Lawler secretly preyed on other people in some way, or on females in particular. But whatever her perceived sin, he saw it as worthy of death."

Ethan looked at the ME. "Sorry for hijacking the procedure here."

The man waved a hand. "I'll admit to being a bit fascinated. I had an insect collection when I was a kid." That was actually a thing? Ethan wisely swallowed the question as the man went on. "As I was telling Officer Samuels earlier, tox screens will take a couple of days, but Lawler's blood alcohol level was two point oh three, which is well beyond the legal definition of impairment. She ate approximately six hours prior to her death, which may be when she consumed the wine she drank."

"Most of the clubs closed at three-thirty. A few at four," Ethan said. And they'd missed her at every one of them.

"Like Simard, her hands had been treated with bleach and the nails clipped." Dr. Conrad strode back to the stainless-steel table on which Lawler's corpse laid. "No defensive wounds are present. Manner of death is unclear."

"So she didn't die from having her tongue cut out."

"It's possible a person could die from having the lingual artery severed, if that person had no assistance and was unable to stem the bleeding. However, the removal of the tongue occurred only minutes before death." Conrad leaned down to inspect the sutures around the skull, before straightening again. "As your colleague will tell you, I found three sets of numbers written on her shoulder in what appears to be ink from a pen. Two of the numerals were worn off."

"A phone number?" Ethan's gaze shot to Nyle's. "And you didn't lead with that?"

The other officer smiled smugly, holding up a sheet upon which he'd jotted the digits. Two spaces were empty.

"Can I see?" Ethan asked the ME.

Seeming more amenable than he'd been the last time they'd been here, Conrad waved him over. He levered the body upward so Ethan could peer at the writing. "Definitely seems like a phone number," he murmured. The two last digits were indecipherable, although there was still ink visible. He stepped back, looked at Alexa. "What are the chances the offender wrote those digits?"

She cocked her head as if considering for a moment. "I

don't recall anything in the file similar to this. I think it's unlikely to be from him. With whom would he be communicating? He already has access to me. If he wanted to send a number, he'd do so."

Ethan nodded. It would have represented another deviation for the offender. Not that he hadn't engaged in his share of them in recent days, but those had all involved Alexa in some way. Which was the source of the simmering worry that had lodged in the back of his mind.

No, these numbers were likely related to Lawler's night out before her death. And given the activities Bixby had indicated she engaged in on such nights, someone who was interested in her might written them.

And he very much wanted to talk to that person.

He thanked the ME. After Alexa collected her things, they left the suite and headed for the parking lot. As soon as he reached an area with cell-phone reception, Ethan texted the rest of his team in New Brunswick. He needed them here. If there were still interviews to conduct, one of the men could stay in the other province and finish them, but he could the additional assistance for the most recent victims. The tip line they'd established might just be about to pay off. They needed more bodies to conduct the most promising interviews.

"How are you planning to use the partial phone number written on the body?" Nyle asked as they walked outside into the bright sunlight. "No way we get a warrant on all the possible variations."

"One hundred."

Both men's heads swiveled toward Alexa. "That's how many combinations there would be after filling in the missing digits."

"She used to tutor me in math," Ethan told Nyle.

Alexa smiled. "I did not."

"You could have. You just refused."

They'd reached the car. "You didn't need help with any subject. You just used that as a reason to keep talking to me."

"Mad skills with the ladies even back then, eh?" Nyle laughed.

"She did help me with English a couple of times." Ethan unlocked the car, and they got in. "She used to read Voltaire. For *fun*."

Nyle feigned a shudder. Looked at Alexa over the seat as he fastened his seat belt. "What's wrong with you?"

"The numbers?" she reminded them patiently.

Ethan returned his attention to the case as he drove out of the parking lot. "We can computer-generate all the possible combinations of the phone numbers." He ignored the muttered remark from the back about doing the exercise in his head. "Then we can leave automated messages for the recipients to call our tip line if they saw her last night."

"We'd still have to double-check on all the numbers that don't call in, but that would be a faster way to hear from potential witnesses," Nyle noted.

"I called one of the officers manning the tip line on the way back from Truro. He's forwarding a list of the updated messages every few hours. I say we prioritize those and take some of the interviews ourselves." Lawler's photo and the message to the public had appeared in local papers this morning. Sifting through the deluge of calls to find the ones worth checking out would be a chore of its own.

"I guess you haven't heard the news about the memorial service," Nyle said.

A hard knot of trepidation formed in the pit of Ethan's belly. He wasn't a big fan of surprises. "Enlighten me."

"It was Conrad's tech that mentioned it to me," Nyle informed him. "Apparently, there's a movement afoot to have a candlelight vigil this evening in Victoria Park in memory of The Tailor's two most recent victims."

Ethan looked at Alexa in the rearview mirror. Caught her gaze on him. "Will he be there?"

"Ordinarily, I'd say no," she answered slowly. "I think it's unusual for this UNSUB to stay in the area after a kill. He calls the homicides a 'mission.' And that doesn't sound like someone who would get a rush from standing around and reveling in the emotional aftermath the way some killers do. I think the bigger question is...do we want to try and lure him there?"

"I'M STILL NOT sure about this," Ethan muttered later that afternoon. They were sitting in an interview room at the Halifax RCMP divisional headquarters, waiting to be summoned for their remote appearance on a national newscast. As before, the setup had been left to Gagnon's office. This time, the filming would take place on scene, rather than at the television station.

"Captain Campbell seemed to think that trying to lure the UNSUB to the memorial vigil was low-risk," Alexa reminded him. She'd put her hair up again before their arrival here and donned a black jacket that matched her slacks. The makeup artist that he'd sent away had found a more willing subject in her. Once again, her smooth, polished demeanor was intact. He found himself preferring her appearance this morning. "You'll have ample time to get preparations in place. And I'll be surrounded by a police presence."

He was aware of the advantages and disadvantages of the operation. He and Nyle and Alexa had debated them thoroughly before the conversation with Campbell. It had reached the point where Ethan had to ask himself whether he'd have the same reservations if Alexa weren't involved. The answer was uncomfortable. She changed everything, and he couldn't allow that. He'd sworn from the beginning that she wouldn't be a distraction in this case. It was time he started remembering that vow.

When he'd spoken to Gagnon yesterday, Ethan had been adamant that Alexa not use the news conference to try to connect with the UNSUB. He hadn't wanted to cement the UNSUB's obsession with her. But like it or not, the connection was already happening, on the offender's terms. As much as it pained him to admit it, it was time to shift the balance of control. He had to reluctantly accept that fact that Alexa could help toward that end.

"We're ready for you." A harried-looking woman led them quickly down the hallway, and out the front doors. Then she spent more time than he thought necessary positioning them for optimal impact outside the building while avoiding a glare from the banks of windows.

He ignored the cameras and tried not to fiddle with his ear mic, which he found damn annoying.

A moment later, the mic was activated. "...here with us now in Halifax, RCMP Sergeant Ethan Manning, lead investigator and Dr. Alexa Hayden, the profiler consulting on the case. Sergeant Manning, can you speak to your attempts to rescue Jeanette Lawler yesterday evening?"

He kept his remarks brief, factual and undramatic, ending with, "We want to extend our condolences to the victim's family, and assure them that we are actively pursuing a number of leads to bring the killer to justice."

"And what can you tell us about those leads, Sergeant?"

"We now have a second sketch of the person of interest in this case." He knew that the drawing Patrick had worked on with the forensic artist this morning and the one Fornier did were now showing on the screen. "This man changes his appearance as he moves about in public. If you see this individual, do not approach him. Instead, quickly call the number on the screen."

"Thank you, Sergeant. And now here's a picture of the latest victim, Jeanette Lawler."

"We know Jeanette Lawler was in downtown Halifax last night at a nightclub. People saw her. Spoke to her." His voice was grim. "They might have seen her killer, as well. We ask that you please call the tip line if you have anything to report from yesterday evening. Your statement might be all we need to close in on this killer." He hoped the UNSUB was watching. He hoped like hell the man wondered and worried about being seen the night before.

"And Dr. Hayden, you've had time to study this madman who has struck all across Canada." Ethan struggled to keep his face impassive. There was no way to keep sensationalism from creeping into the newscast. "What have you learned about him that will aid in the investigation?"

Ethan tensed, but beside him, Alexa appeared calm. Composed. "I understand this offender like no one else can. I know what drives him. He realizes that every deed will be brought into judgment. Every secret thing. His mission is over. Like a weary soldier returning from battle, he can put down his sword. Only then will he find true peace."

The viewing audience wouldn't comprehend. But Alexa's message would make perfect sense to the offender they sought.

"Thank you, Doctor. Sergeant, I understand that there is a vigil in Victoria Park at nine o'clock this evening for the most recent victims. Will your team be there to pay your respects?"

"We will be, yes."

"Thank you, Sergeant. I return now to Commissioner Gagnon, who..."

Ethan's ear mic cut out. He knew from last time that the people from the news station freaked if he tried to remove the equipment himself. So, he waited impatiently for a technician to take care of that before he and Alexa made their way inside the building again. They went to find Nyle, who was sitting in the interview room they'd just vacated, with sacks of food surrounding him.

Ethan regarded him soberly. "Are you some kind of sandwich wizard? Do you know a conjuring spell that summons them out of thin air?"

"Don't be ridiculous." The man shoved a sandwich into his mouth. Chewed. "My magical powers are reserved for baked goods. I had this stuff delivered. Met them at the back entrance."

Alexa took a ham on rye with a decided lack of enthusiasm. "Don't you guys ever eat anything green?"

Nyle gave her a puzzled look. "You mean...like green M&Ms?"

She rolled her eyes and sat down, unwrapping her food. Ethan, decidedly less fussy, grabbed one of the meals and took a seat, pulling out his phone. Moments later, he turned his laptop on and scrolled through the latest list the tip-line officer had sent, starring the ones he deemed most promising. He took pictures of them on his cell and texted them to Nyle. "Here. You and Alexa start on the interviews for people responding to the newspaper article this morning that had Lawler's picture. The newscast we just filmed won't show for—" he checked the clock on the wall, "—another two and a half hours. If better tips come in from that, I'll let you know."

"What's your next step?" Nyle wanted to know.

Ethan's temples began to throb just thinking about the next few hours. "I'm going to take those phone numbers we computer-generated and arrange for a voice message to be sent to each. Then I'll organize the police presence for the vigil tonight. If Alexa's little spiel about the offender worked, he's not going to be able to pass up being there. And if he does come, we need to be prepared for it."

THE FIRST THREE calls they followed up on required more time to drive to than the interviews themselves. But slowly, Alexa and Nyle were constructing a timeline for Lawler's last few hours. They spoke to the waitress who served her at an upscale restaurant; a person working the door at a club she'd attended around nine, which she'd exited shortly later; and an Uber driver who'd delivered her to the restaurant, and chatted with her about the Halifax nightlife.

The fourth interview was with someone Alexa had already met. Dennis Jeffries, the bartender at Zoomey's.

"I almost didn't call. I mean, I remember you coming in and showing me that picture." Jeffries nodded at Alexa. After Nyle had contacted the man about his message to the tip line, they'd arranged to meet at a Timmie's in the man's neighborhood. Alexa hadn't turned down the opportunity to caffeinate. "I told you then she'd been there. But then I thought, hey, maybe you'd have more questions, so..." He shrugged, wrapping both hands around his coffee to-go cup.

"It's not every day that you talk to someone who comes in and find out they're dead a few hours later. Makes you think, you know?"

"What can you tell us about her?" Alexa asked.

"She arrived a bit before ten." He reached up a hand to push back the hair that kept flopping onto his forehead. "We talked a little bit. She'd already stopped at some of the clubs. Wanted to know when things would get going. I had the feeling she was looking for action."

"What kind of action?"

He shrugged at Nyle's question. "Same kind most people want. Crowds, dancing, music, lights. And maybe to hook up. She had that vibe about her. Not that I'm judging," he hastened to say.

"And did it look like she was successful? At finding a partner?"

He shrugged again. "So maybe for a little while, before things got wild, I thought I'd be the lucky guy. But it got super busy, and I lost sight of her. Which means she either ended up leaving, or she was at a table or booth that was being waited on."

"Can you give us the names and numbers of the other bartenders and waitresses on that night?" Alexa asked.

He looked stricken. "Oh, man, no, I can't drag them into this. I mean, naw, I can't."

"We can get them from your employer."

Alexa knew Nyle would only do so if they had evidence that Zoomey's was indeed the place where Lawler had met with the offender.

"Hold on a minute." He pulled out his phone and started texting furiously, a long enough message that Alexa was left wondering why he didn't just place a call. When he finished, he set the cell down and looked up. "Zaila works at the club, too. She'd have been working the floor. I asked if she'd agree to talk to you. That's all I can do, okay? I mean, I have to work with these people." His words were interrupted by an alert. He picked up the cell again and gave a smile of relief. "She says okay. I don't know if she has any information, but she'll meet up if you can do it in the next hour."

Nyle nodded. "That works. Before we go, though, we want you to look at a couple sketches." He took out the two drawings of the offender and laid them out in front of Jeffries.

To his credit, the man looked them over carefully. Then he finally lifted a shoulder. "Not going to lie, I remember the females. Unless it's some asshole who causes trouble for us. This guy—" he tapped the sketch Patrick had helped supply, "—is not our usual clientele. At least, not when things get going. We draw a younger crowd."

"The hair and mustache were probably fake. Think of this face," Nyle tapped the second sketch, "with this hair." He touched the first drawing.

But Jeffries shrugged. "Like I said...I remember the pretty girls. And the bonus of my job is there are lots of pretty girls."

ZAILA HAD a round face with heavily made-up eyes and black hair tipped with pink. They'd had to drive across the city to the place she'd set to meet with them. The only parking they could find was blocks away. Nyle and Alexa were out of breath by the time they walked into the seedy diner and slid into the booth opposite her.

"Dennis showed us your picture," Alexa said when the woman looked up in surprise.

"Yeah, Dennis. What'd he get me into?" She picked up a sugar packet from a bowl placed in the center of the table. Fiddled with it.

"Nothing too worrisome." Nyle put a picture of Lawler on the table in front of the woman. "Do you recall seeing her in Zoomey's Thursday night?"

The woman made a box with her fingers, centered it around Lawler's face, blocking out the hair. "Yeah," she said finally. "She was there. I know faces. I'm an art student at NSCAD." She surveyed the picture critically. "Makeup was different. Less polished, more glam, if you know what I mean. Don't recall what she was wearing or anything. Me, I see faces."

On cue, Nyle produced the sketches of the offender. "How about him? Remember seeing him?"

She shook her head. "He might have stood out, too, because we cater to a younger crowd." Which was similar to what the bartender had told them. "Once in a while, you get an older guy in there with a lot younger girlfriend, but that's not the norm."

"Did you see this woman with anyone throughout the night?"

Zaila rolled her eyes. "Saw her with lots of people. All guys. A good twenty years younger than her, you ask me. She was dancing earlier, but last time I noticed she was sitting in a booth with a bunch of guys, pretty smashed. It looked like they were buying all the drinks." She grimaced. "They'd had plenty, too."

"Do you know what time that was?" Alexa asked.

"There is only two times that matter in that place." The woman smirked. "The time I have to be at work and closing time. Seriously, the place is busiest on the weekends, but Wednesdays and Thursdays can be crazy, too. There's never enough staff, and we work our asses off. I don't notice the time. Oh." She seemed to remember something. "Except I know I waited on that booth right before the band's first break, which would have been about eleven-thirty. I try to time my rounds because otherwise the floor gets too congested, with people going to the restrooms and trying to get to the bar. It was the last time I remember seeing her."

Alexa exchanged a look with Nyle. Here was another point for the timeline of Lawler's last night. She and Ethan had been there about one. But they still didn't know if the woman had left before then.

"How about the guys in the booth with her? Did you recognize any of them?" she asked.

"I've seen a couple of them before. One had some trouble at the club a few months back. Got kicked out for a while." She thought for a moment. Shook her head. "Maybe Duncan knows. He was the bouncer we had back then. I'll ask him."

"Please call my number if you discover his name." Nyle slid one of his cards across the cracked vinyl table toward her. "We appreciate your time."

"Yeah." Zaila stood up, hefted a large hobo bag onto her shoulder. "Figured with something like this, you gotta get involved, right? Plus, Dennis is pretty hot and I don't mind him owing me a favor." Giving them a surprisingly impish smile, she walked away.

The bartender they'd just interviewed? Hot? Alexis suddenly felt very old. There was, she supposed, no accounting for taste. "Who's next?"

Nyle checked his cell. "Ethan wants us back at head-quarters by seven. Which is another hour. It'll take us almost that long to get there. We'd better head out. Unless you want to catch a quick bite first."

Alexa looked around the diner. She wasn't especially fastidious, but she was willing to guess the sanitation here was sketchy, at best. "I think I'll pass." She slid out of the booth and headed toward the door. She was anxious to get an update about the plans for the memorial this evening. Alexa couldn't be sure the offender would attend. But if her remarks at the press conference resonated with him on any level, she thought he might be unable to resist appearing tonight.

# CHAPTER FIFTEEN

"WHAT DO YOU MEAN, I'm not going?"

Alexa's words were delivered in a decidedly dangerous tone, one Ethan had never heard from her. He decided the best way to meet her temper—which, admittedly, he'd expected—was with logic. "We have a stand-in for you. Dara Lavoie, an officer from the Halifax PD vice unit. It's one of the steps I've taken to mitigate the risk."

"Oh, they didn't have an officer to stand in for you?" Alexa looked around the table in the conference room. "Or Nyle?" A few of the other RCMP officers in the room shuffled their feet. A couple looked amused. "I didn't realize I'd been removed from the task force."

"I'm going with police presence only," he said evenly. "We know if the UNSUB does show up, it will be because of you. He's never shown interest in these types of events before. Our efforts have to be focused on sighting him, and then chasing him down if he is spotted. We're better equipped to do that if we don't have to worry about guarding you, as well."

She gave a nod as if in agreement. Ethan knew better

than to buy it. "And you think this offender, who is showing signs of obsession, who even visited my childhood home to get information about me, will be fooled by your stand-in and hang around long enough for you to swoop him up."

This wasn't a conversation he wanted to be having in public. His tone clipped, Ethan replied, "All he has to do is appear. I've worked with the city to employ barricades and parking areas in such a way as to cut him off as much as possible from his vehicle. The officers will be equipped with body cameras. As soon as he gets close enough to realize Lavoie isn't you, hopefully, one of us will have spotted him."

She subsided, but he didn't fool himself into believing that she was in agreement. The temper was all but radiating off her. Ethan couldn't allow himself to be moved by it. His decision was a no-brainer. Lavoie bore a passing resemblance to Alexa, more in coloring and height than appearance. But he'd have officers crowding her, as if in protection, so her face would be difficult to see. The offender would have to draw close to realize it wasn't Alexa.

"There will be uniforms there whose only duties are crowd control for the event. They have been advised of our presence and purpose. I'll also have officers armed with sketches assigned to the Park Lane parking garage." He turned to a whiteboard mounted on the wall to which he'd affixed a map of Victoria Park, where the vigil would take place. It was a long and narrow area directly across the street from the Public Gardens. A red marker had been used to mark the memorial fountain at the south end. Blue indicated where he'd have officers stationed. "Officer Lavoie and two uniforms will be stationed here." He pointed to an X he'd made to the side of the fountain. "The park is bordered on all four sides by public streets, which works to our advantage. The UNSUB will have to be somewhere in this arc—" he pointed to yet another line he'd drawn, "—to see Alexa's stand-in. Questions?"

He answered the few raised by the RCMP officers in the room. Was well aware that Alexa remained silent. "Now for the equipment. We've set up a bridge call number which all officers can dial into from their phones. The number is on the bottom of the whiteboard." The advantage would be the discretion it offered. No one would think twice of seeing someone with a cell to his ear. The downside was often the amount of background noise that resulted. "Everyone will use a body camera. I want images of anyone that looks suspicious." He gave each of the assembled officers their positions. "Equipment is on the table by the door. Sign it out and bring it back in the same condition. The brass knows where you live."

There were a few chuckles. The red tape necessary to request equipment was a well-known nightmare. The ramifications for bringing it back in less-than-pristine working order was even more so.

"We'll meet near the fountain and take up our positions. I'll see you there." It took another few minutes for the RCMP officers to clear the room. It didn't escape Ethan that Nyle hurried to join them, leaving Ethan and Alexa alone. *Coward.*

"I had food brought in before you and Nyle returned." His words were met with a frosty stare. "I ordered you a salad. It's in the refrigerator in the staff room."

"What," she enunciated perfectly, "do you think the offender's reaction is going to be when he realizes he was duped? How is that going to impact the relationship I've tried to forge with him?"

He folded his arms across his chest. It'd been a long day. He had hours left ahead of him. Engaging in a battle of wills with Alexa was not going to be part of it. "I thought of that. Weighed it against the possibility of catching him tonight and decided to take the chance."

She shook her head. "Catching him could occur with or without me there. You're allowing personal feelings to get in the way of your decision-making."

She'd finally goaded him into a response. "You know what?" He took two quick steps toward the table and slapped his palms on it, leaning over them toward her. "I don't give a damn. This guy is unpredictable. He's obsessed with you, and there's no history of him engaging in this type of behavior. Who knows what the hell he's capable of? He could stage a distraction in the park, something to panic the crowd then use the resulting chaos to make a move on you. So, sue me, I don't want to put you at risk. And, fortunately for *my personal feelings*, this is a situation where I don't have to."

He immediately regretted his outburst, even before he noticed the flare of reaction in her eyes. Having Alexa join the task force had been like taking a fastball to the gut. But he was dealing with it. If she only knew just how damn much energy he put into trying not to allow personal feelings to override professional ones, maybe she'd be a bit more cooperative. He'd be concerned about the safety of any civilian consultant on his team, but the fact that it was Alexa in the crosshairs was a major factor in his decision to use a stand-in.

But he wasn't anywhere close to admitting that out loud.

"What am I supposed to be doing in the meantime?" The ire in her words was an improvement over her earlier show of temper. Whatever other changes Alexa had undergone in the last twenty years, she still couldn't hang on to a mad, which was a trait he'd always appreciated.

"I'll leave my computer booted up so you can check the hourly updates I'm getting on the tip line." He straightened and fetched the laptop, turning it on and opening his email for her. "You can follow up with phone calls to the callers you prioritize. Tomorrow we can interview any you think have usable information."

Alexa didn't look excited about the task, but at least she was no longer arguing.

"If you hear from the offender again, I want to know immediately." When she nodded, he glanced at the clock. "I have to go." He grabbed up the equipment he'd set aside for himself and headed for the door, restraining an urge to look back at her. Knowing she was safe at RCMP headquarters was going to make it a whole lot easier to concentrate on the job ahead. And he wasn't going to apologize for that.

IF THE SALAD was meant as a peace offering, it was a miserable failure. Alexa finally gave up after a few bites and went to Ethan's computer, scrolling through the most promising leads that had come in since Lawler's picture had been released that morning. The chore was preferable to watching the clock, trying to figure out what was happening downtown while she was stuck here.

Dutifully, she returned several phone calls from the tip line and took notes of the conversations. None resulted in any new details. Feeling like she was spinning her wheels, Alexa glanced at the clock. It wasn't even eight-thirty yet. She set her pen down in disgust. The solitary task gave her too much time to think. About the UNSUB. The vigil.

About Ethan.

She tried to push thoughts of him away, but they returned despite her efforts, drawn like metal filings to a magnet. Alexa wished she could summon a fraction of her earlier irritation with him. Annoyance was far easier to deal with than the welter of feeling she experienced every time she recalled their kiss.

It'd been an aberration on both their parts. A mistake not to be repeated. But knowing that didn't calm the jitter in her pulse every time she recalled the instant heat that had sparked to life. The inexplicable chemistry between them was still there. Immediate. Combustible. And it would have been far safer for her equilibrium if she'd never learned that.

Her cell pinged. She looked at it and saw a forwarded text message from Nyle. Zaila had contacted him with the name of one of the Zoomey's customers seen with Lawler last night. The one who'd been banned from the premises for a while. Bobby Kantor.

Immediately deciding Kantor was more interesting than the task she'd been engaged in, she looked him up on social media sites. There were three people with that name, only one in this province. Although his posts weren't publicly available on Facebook, his friends list and his city of residence were. He lived in Dartmouth, across the harbor from Halifax.

Another idea occurred. Alexa closed out of that search window and looked Kantor up on the four-one-one site. Not only did it list his name and address, it also published his cell-phone number. It was a little appalling, she thought, just how little privacy people had these days. But in this case, it might be useful.

Alexa tapped his number into her cell. No answer. Realizing that people often didn't pick up when they didn't recognize the incoming caller, she hesitated, running through options. Grimaced when she realized which would likely have the quickest results.

Swiftly, she undid her hair and arranged it around her shoulders. Pursed her lips and took a selfie, which she texted to Kantor with the message: *Were you in Zoomey's last night? So was I! Call me.* She added her number and prepared to wait. If this had no result, she'd be forced to leave a message and leave it until tomorrow to follow up.

She returned to the list on Ethan's computer. Responded to a couple of people who'd left messages there before she had an alert for an incoming text. Elation filled her when she realized it was from Kantor.

*Did we talk? I was pretty wasted. Had to be or I'd remember you!*

*I'm Alexa. Call me*, she responded. Moments later, the cell rang in her hand. She answered it immediately.

"Alexa. A pretty name for a pretty lady."

"Bobby Kantor. My name is Dr. Alexa Hayden, and I'm working with the RCMP." There was an audible gulp on the other end. "By now you've heard about The Tailor's most recent homicide victim found in Truro yesterday. We know she was at Zoomey's before her death, and so were you. We'd like to have a conversation about what you may have seen."

"Man, I don't know anything about that. I mean, yeah, I was there last night." It was easy to figure out the young man was dissembling. "I don't remember much...like I said. I don't think I could be any help."

"We've spoken to wait staff at the club who identified you as someone in a booth with the victim," Alexa said crisply. "You're not in any trouble here, Bobby. But we do need to speak to you to establish a timeline of the victim's last hours."

"Ah...I just don't know when I could manage that. I'm leaving tomorrow for a week's vacation."

Her stomach plummeted. "Then how about right now? I'm sure you can understand that this is a matter of urgency."

"I guess."

"I'll come to you," she promised rashly. If the offender showed up this evening, it would be at Victoria Park, not in Dartmouth. Ethan could hardly complain about the risk. Although she had no doubt he'd have plenty to say about it.

"I'm packing, so I can't spare much time."

"Just name a public place close to you."

"Um...there's a Timmie's on the corner across from my apartment."

Of course there was. Alexa smiled. "Give me the address and thirty minutes. I have to get an Uber."

ETHAN SCANNED THE PARK AGAIN. Full, and getting more so. Although they'd gotten there at seven-thirty, there'd already been people congregating. The uniformed officers had arrived first. The event was supposed to begin in fifteen more minutes.

He continued moving about the perimeter, careful not to make eye contact with the plainclothes officers. He held his cell to his ear. "Number six, man at your three o'clock. Jeans, cap, gray T-shirt, dark backpack." He continued walking, watching from the corner of his eye as his officer moved in the direction he'd indicated. Ethan walked by the female officer acting as a decoy for Alexa. The two uniforms beside her were doing a good job angling their bodies in such a way that her face was mostly hidden.

"Number six clear." The officer's voice sounded in his ear. Ethan continued, rounding the fountain and looking toward the street. A few people were entering the park from this end, as well. He was grateful the park was small. It would have been impossible to monitor otherwise.

An older man was tottering toward the fountain with the help of a cane. Ethan veered closer to him to get a better look. Even bent over the way the man was, the height would be about right for the offender.

But once Ethan got nearer, he mentally dismissed the man. The UNSUB might have a penchant for disguises, but he couldn't replicate the age stamped on the elderly man's face.

"Position one." A voice sounded in Ethan's ear. "Red shirt, black pants, sunglasses. Heading in your direction."

Sunglasses? At this time of night? Ethan quickened his step, searching the crowd until he spied the person in question and made his way toward him. And it was a male, he ascertained as he drew closer. The height was right. The figure was wider than the description they had of the UNSUB, but it would be simple enough to make that change to an appearance. Ethan just needed to jockey around enough so he could see the face.

Once he had, however, he could see the man was much younger than he'd expected. "Number One clear."

The organizers of the event were behind him now, standing directly in front of the fountain. One of the women wielded a microphone, which let out an ear-splitting shriek when she attempted to speak into it.

Ethan winced. Kept walking. It occurred to him that if the UNSUB was as cautious as normal, he'd wait until full dark to join the vigil. Making it that much more challenging to pick him out of a crowd.

"Yeah, that's her." Kantor studied the photo of Lawler that Alexa set in front of him. "She looked even hotter last night. Wow, is she really dead? Me and my friends were all hitting on her, buying her drinks and stuff. I'd have bet money she was going home with one of us."

"What happened?"

He shrugged. "I don't remember. We were all getting wasted. She went to the bathroom, I think. We'd just bought drinks." He stopped. Frowned. "Maybe she took hers with her. Anyway, she never came back to the table. Hunter went looking for her after a while, but that place was packed."

"What time was this?"

"Twelve-thirty or so? I'm not really sure."

She took copies of the sketches of the offender from her computer bag and laid them out in front of him. "Did you see this man there last night?"

He lifted a shoulder. "Wouldn't have noticed him if I had. I go there for the women."

Alexa gave a mental sigh and put the drawings away. "Who else was with you?" When he gave her four other names, she asked, "Do you have their phone numbers?"

"Oh, man, they're going to hate me for this."

Alexa narrowed her eyes. "Yes, I can see what an imposition this is. How terribly inconvenient for you that the woman you were hoping to sleep with last night died. Horribly inconsiderate of her."

"Oh, hey, I didn't mean that." Dejectedly, Kantor began

scrolling through his contacts. "You got a pen or something?"

She reached into the computer bag she'd brought with her and drew out a pen. Snagged a napkin from the dispenser in the middle of the table and slid both toward him. "Add their first and last names too." Laboriously, he copied the numbers onto the napkin. "How long after she went to the bathroom did Hunter go looking for her?"

"I don't know." He shoved the napkin across the table to her. "Half an hour or so? I think he had to pi—take a leak, too, because he was gone for a while. When he got back the rest of us had decided to leave. We went to another club a few blocks away. The Sphere."

She glanced at the phone numbers. Froze when she noticed the third one.

The first eight numbers on it matched the ones on Jeanette Lawler's shoulder. Alexa read the name next to it. Hunter Owens.

"Where were you all sitting in the booth in relation to Jeanette Lawler?"

Bobby shoved his hand through his hair as he thought. "She was on the outside. Then Hunter. He was getting a little handsy with her. Spilled a drink in her lap and pissed her off when he tried to wipe it up. But that's Hunter. Then me. Sam. Ben. Parker."

"Did anyone else go to find Lawler when she left the booth?"

He swung his head back and forth. "It was louder than hell in there. Hunter was the one who was plastered up against her. Thought he had the best chance with her because of it, but then he spilled that drink, she went to the restroom, and the rest of us started talking about getting out of there." He craned his head so he could see the clock on the wall. "Can I go now?"

"Not yet. I need you to call this number. Hunter Owens." She tapped his name on the list. "He'll pick up for you."

Resignedly, he looked at the name she was indicating. "He was heading downtown tonight. Called me earlier and wanted me to come. I'll text him." Alexa watched him type a message in all caps. *URGENT. CALL ME.* Alexa appreciated the sentiment.

According to Kantor, Lawler had left the booth around twelve-thirty. She and Ethan had been to that club shortly after one. With the time of death pegged between two and three a.m., it was looking more and more like Zoomey's was the place Lawler had met up with the offender.

"We could go inside. I'd buy you a drink."

Alexa surveyed Hunter Owens impassively. It was rare for her to take an immediate dislike to someone, but she'd learned to rely on her first impressions. And Owens struck her as a too-too type. Too handsome, too smooth and much too sure of himself. The sort of entitled jerk she'd met on more occasions than she could count. It didn't surprise her in the least that Kantor had mentioned Owens thought he'd had the best shot with Lawler. His sort never lacked confidence.

"Did Bobby Kantor tell you about what happened to the woman sitting with you guys last night?" They were on the sidewalk in front of yet another club. Owens had agreed to meet her outside it.

"Yeah. That blew my mind." As he bent his head to talk

to her, he subtly angled his body closer. "Someone we just spoke to yesterday...dead." He shook his head sorrowfully. Alexa wished she didn't believe it was feigned.

"Just to be clear..." She bent down and brought out the woman's photo. "This is the woman you spoke to?" She used the opportunity to shift a few inches away. The guy had a smarmy vibe.

Owens nodded solemnly. "That's her. She seemed really sweet. Friendly. All of us hit it off."

"Is that why you wrote your name on her shoulder? Because you were 'hitting it off?'" It was a bluff. All Alexa knew was that his number was one of a hundred possible phone numbers. But she saw by his expression that she'd been correct.

He shrugged, laughed a little. "Yeah. It was a joke. See, I wanted to give Jeanette my number, but her phone was dead. So..." He shrugged. "She was sitting right next to me. I wrote her on her back instead. She didn't mind," he hastened to add. "She was laughing, too."

"So the two of you were getting along." Alexa was in no mood to prolong this conversation. "You must have been surprised when she didn't come back to the table."

Something shifted slightly in his expression before he blanked it. Alexa had the feeling that surprise hadn't been the emotion he'd experienced.

"I was worried about her when she didn't return," he said piously, reaching out a

hand to lean against the red-brick front. "It was pretty crazy in there. The lines to the restrooms were ridiculous, and I didn't see her in them when I checked. But then I ducked out the back—"

"You went out the back door?"

"Yeah. It says it's alarmed, but it isn't." He gave her a

smile that was meant to be charming. "Most of them aren't. Guys sometimes skip the queues and use the alley around back to ah...relieve themselves."

"So that's what you did when you didn't see Lawler."

"I said I didn't see her in line," he corrected her, reaching up with his free hand to smooth his gelled hair. "I was in a sort of in a doorway, behind the Dumpster, taking leak. And when I looked up, I saw her in the alley, hanging all over some other guy."

Everything inside Alexa stilled. "Another man?"

"Yeah." And this time, he didn't attempt to keep the disgust from his expression. "I mean, I'm not saying she owed me anything just because I bought her a few drinks, but it was still pretty shitty for her to leave with someone else and not even tell me."

"Did they see you?"

"I don't know. Didn't seem to."

"Did you tell your friends about what you'd seen?"

"I don't remember. When I got back, they were ready to leave, so I went with them."

Alexa bent and got the sketches of the UNSUB from her bag and showed them to Owens. "Is this the man she was with?"

"I didn't see him from the front. And hey, this guy is *old*." He shook one of the sketches.

"We think he was wearing a wig in that one. What did you mean when you said Jeanette was hanging on him?"

It was the wrong question to ask. Owens took the opportunity to demonstrate, leaning heavily on her, one arm thrown around her shoulders. "Sort of like this." Alexa gave him an elbow jab that had him dropping his arm and stepping away, but not without a self-satisfied grin on his face,

"She was pretty drunk. I suppose he could have been helping her to the car."

The blood began to pound in her veins. "A car. Not a van?"

"What? No, it was a car. Toyota Camry, I think. Black or navy...hard to tell in the dark."

"But you could see well enough to know the make?"

"I drive a red Camry so I recognized it. I can tell you it had a light interior, though. Saw it when the dome light went on."

"Which door did he open?"

Owens thought a moment. "Back driver side. Which is weird now that I think about it. Unless she was so drunk, he was just going to have her lay..." His eyes widened. "Hey, you don't think...that couldn't have been the killer, could it?"

Handsome, Alexa thought again. But maybe not too bright. "Yes. I think that's likely."

THE LAST PASTOR HAD SPOKEN. The people in the park were holding candles high, singing a hymn and swaying to the music. Ethan supposed it would be a moving sight, had he not been on the watch for a killer.

A fruitless effort so far.

The candles that had been given out by the sponsors of the event did provide one service: they lit up the face of the person holding them. Ethan and his men were crisscrossing through the crowd in a grid pattern now. Looking at faces. Watching those who held no candles at all.

He thought again about the odds of the UNSUB coming. Although it was out of character, an obsession could compel a person to take risks they ordinarily wouldn't. Risks that just might get the man nearer to Alexa.

He looked in the direction of her stand-in. The offender would have to get fairly close to Dara now to identify her. Maybe he'd never shown up. Perhaps he'd wait to make his move when she was leaving. Frustration mounted. And maybe this whole thing had been a complete waste of time.

Moments after he had the thought, three loud reports sounded behind him. "Gun!" a male voice shouted. He whirled, pulling his weapon in one smooth move. People began screaming, pushing at each other in their rush to get away. Candles were dropped in the frenzy. A few sparked and flamed in the grass. He ran toward the fountain where he'd last seen Dara and the uniforms. They were spreading out in an arc across the southeast corner, weapons drawn.

Ethan mentally cursed. "Position two," he said into the phone, "reassume your original stance." Without waiting for them to do so, he continued, "It's a distraction. Look for someone approaching Lavoie." Pandemonium reigned for a few minutes. One uniformed officer was shouting into a megaphone, trying to bring order to the exodus. Others were rushing to put out the small fires that had sprung up where the candles had been abandoned or aiding people who had fallen.

There were no wounded as far as he could tell. Because there hadn't been a gun at all. To Ethan's trained ear, the noise had likely been firecrackers. A planned distraction.

Because, Ethan thought as he ran through the jostling crowd, this was the effect the offender had wanted. Exactly this.

There. The uniforms had resumed position around Lavoie, probably too late. A figure was peeling sharply away from the trio and heading diagonally for the nearby street.

"Positions eight and nine. Southeast corner behind the fountain. Dark pants and cap. Oversized gray shirt." He holstered his weapon, running now, but he was slowed by people fleeing the area. With relief, he saw two of officers racing in his direction. "Spread out. Cut him off."

But once out of the park the figure sprinted across traffic, dodging cars. Tires shrieked as the vehicles jerked to a stop. Horns blared. Ethan and his men followed suit. The stranger ran down a block and then veered into an alley.

"Position eight take the street on the south side of the buildings. Nine opposite." Ethan's cell was still at his ear. He winced as he banged his hip against the car that had barely avoided mowing him down, and headed down the shadowy passageway in search of the stranger.

He pulled his weapon again. He had no way to be certain the man he was chasing was the UNSUB. But the stranger had run, and that was suspicious in and of itself. He flattened himself against the wall of a building and moved swiftly down the alley, swinging around at every doorway, weapon ready.

He kicked through piles of rubbish piled high enough to conceal someone. The Dumpster was pressed up against the wall of a building. He moved around the three free sides before flipping open the lid. Checked inside. A foul odor emanated. Ethan pulled out his cell and turned on the flashlight app. The receptacle was full. He watched for several moments. Was there the barest movement inside? Could be a rat.

Or it could be a two-legged rodent. Ethan lowered the lid, keeping an eye on the Dumpster as he quickly finished searching the rest of the alley, before backtracking, checking the entrances into the buildings that lined it. The doors were all locked.

Meechum and Kelly were waiting at the end of the alley. Ethan tucked his phone in his pocket and silently waved them toward the Dumpster. It was large, made of hard plastic instead of steel, with a split top. He positioned himself at the back end, while the other two men took the front

Ethan held up fingers for a silent countdown. Three. Two. One. In unison, the three of them heaved and pulled at the container, finally managing to tip it forward, its contents spilling onto the ground.

Ethan pulled his weapon and crouched down in front of it, while the other two officer flipped the lids up. "You'll need to crawl out. Slowly," he said conversationally to the figure cowering inside. "Because I'm sure as hell not coming inside to get you."

THE STENCH EMANATING from the man on the other side of the table in the Halifax PD room was enough to turn Ethan's stomach. He had a feeling that just his brush with the Dumpster had left a similar smell clinging to his clothes. *The glamour of the job*, he thought sourly, *just never quit*. Not to mention the frustration. Because whoever it was that they'd hauled back to the police head-quarters, it was easy enough to see that it wasn't the UNSUB they sought.

"I didn't do nothing wrong," the man insisted stubbornly. He had a few days' growth of beard on his jaw and was missing his front teeth. He'd refused to give a name and carried no ID. He did, however, eagerly drink the can of Pepsi Meechum had fetched for him, objecting angrily when the officer took it away before he finished it. The officer would lift a print. If the stranger were in the system, they'd find out soon enough.

"Then why did you run?" asked Ethan logically.

"'Cuz you was chasing me!"

"You had firecrackers in your pocket when we searched you. You deliberately caused a commotion that could have caused serious injury to a panicked crowd. There is any number of charges we could bring." He paused, letting that sink in for a moment before continuing. "Maybe it wasn't your idea, though. If that's the case, you need to let us know."

"She said it was just a prank. No one would get hurt."

Ethan stilled. "She?"

"The old lady who stopped me on her way to the park. She said there was a service going on over there. Gave me ten bucks to light the firecrackers when it got dark."

"An old lady did that."

Stubbornly, the man nodded. He looked like he was in his mid-sixties, Ethan figured, although a hard life had a way of carving years onto a face prematurely. "She had long brown curly hair and a big hat on. One of those long flowered dresses with a sweater over it." He lowered his voice. "She wasn't much to look at. A woman her age shouldn't wear her hair that long, you ask me."

Son of a bitch. It didn't take much imagination to know the man had talked to the UNSUB. Ethan thought quickly. If they were lucky, maybe one of the video cameras around the park had picked up the offender. But he needed more.

He took copies of the two sketches out of his pocket and showed them to the man, who studied each intently before slowly shaking his head. "These are men. I talked to a lady."

"Look at the faces," Ethan instructed slowly. "Are any

of them the same shape as the woman you saw? Are the noses or mouths similar?"

The man's jaw dropped. He stabbed a finger at the sketch Patrick, the boy in Truro, had helped develop. "You know what? If this didn't have a mustache, and maybe longer hair, it could almost look like the lady's brother!"

"There. That's her. Him." Ethan, Nyle and the officers who'd manned the video cameras were in a conference room at the police department. A TV and video equipment had been carried in and hooked up so they could watch the feed from each of the cameras. They were fast-forwarding through most of it, slowing it only when something of interest came up.

Like a woman in a flowered dress and large hat.

"Matches the description Rogers gave us." Joe Rogers, the man they'd flushed out of the Dumpster. Meechum had gotten a hit on his prints. A vagrant, with a few bumps for public intox. Exactly the type of person who would jump at the chance to make a few bucks with no questions asked.

"She didn't come to the park alone," pointed out the officer who'd operated that camera. "She was with another couple, which is why I didn't think anything of it. They walked in together, and she stuck with them, at least in this frame."

Ethan stole a look at the clock on the wall. He was glad he'd had Nyle run the debriefing after the vigil before joining them. They were going to be here half the night as it was. The last time Ethan had checked his phone, he'd found a text from Alexa. She'd headed back to the hotel hours ago. Had been gone when Nyle had checked in the equipment back at the RCMP headquarters. It was just as well. Maybe one of them would get a few hours' sleep tonight.

"Okay, let's look at the next one." It was a laborious process. They were going through all the films, watching enough on each to piece together the UNSUB's progress from the moment he entered the park. Ethan noted how he inched closer and closer to the front, as if in search of a better view. Each time he changed position he was careful to attach himself to someone nearby. He'd known that a single attendee would draw more attention than one in a group, although once the park had gotten congested, it was hard to tell the difference.

An hour later, Ethan jabbed a finger at the screen. "And there he is after the firecrackers went off." The crowd was scattering, but the UNSUB was moving with a single-minded focus toward Alexa's stand-in.

"You can see the limp now," Nyle murmured.

"Not enough to slow him down much, but it's there," Ethan agreed. Patrick had proven to be their most observant witness so far. "What's that? In his hand?" Without breaking stride, the UNSUB had reached into the purse he carried and taken something out.

"Let me see if I can enlarge it." The officer running the film paused it, backed up to the spot Ethan had indicated and zoomed in. The larger image was fuzzy. But there was no mistaking something long and narrow extending from the offender's closed hand.

"A needle." Ethan sat back in his chair, half-stunned. Had the UNSUB thought he'd have a chance at Alexa in a park full of cops? "Resume the film." He watched the offender approach Lavoie and the uniforms. Saw the trio break apart, drawing their weapons and facing the crowd. Ethan bit back a curse when the figure in the long flowered dress stopped. The UNSUB abruptly changed course and attached himself to a passel of vigil-goers and was lost in the mob.

He scrubbed both hands over his face. The offender had gotten close enough to see that they'd used a female decoy. It was all too easy to imagine a far different scene if Alexa had been at the park. If the two uniforms on either side of her had broken rank, as they had in the film. Leaving her exposed for a few instants. He still didn't understand, even in that scenario, how the UNSUB had hoped to get her away from the area without being observed. But it hammered home to him just how far adrift the man was from his usual behavior.

And his unpredictability just heightened the danger.

"Let's pick him up from his exit." The videos were changed and they tracked the man being jostled in the throng as he made his way back toward the other end of the park. They weren't able to get a full-figure shot until he veered toward the opposite end, head tipped down as if in a purposeful effort to avoid the camera the nearby plain-clothes officer held. He reached into his purse with a now-empty hand. Withdrew... Ethan squinted. Car keys? He watched until the offender cut away from the park and walked quickly down the street.

"Back up to where we saw him take the keys out of the purse," Ethan ordered. Once the officer had obeyed, he said, "Zoom in there."

A key was held pointed outward. Ready for use. Had the man been parked nearby? That was the area where Rogers had said he'd been approached.

"Looks like an insignia on the keychain," Nyle observed. He was closer to the screen than Ethan was. "Can you enhance just that area?"

"Getting beyond my technical skills," the officer replied, but he attempted to do so. He got down and pressed his face almost against the screen to peer at it. "Can't quite make it out, but the shape of it...does it remind anyone else of the CarsNow rental logo?"

# CHAPTER SIXTEEN

*...Behold, you have sinned against the Lord, and be sure your sin will find you out.*
—Numbers 32:23

FRUSTRATION ATE at Anis Tera like a fanged beast, feeding in the night. He paced his motel room in a fit of temper, fists clenched. Praying hadn't lessened his sense of failure. Or his anger.

Alexa had betrayed him. And that made him feel like a fool.

Yes, it'd been a mistake to stray from the plan he'd been carefully developing. But he'd been transfixed by her message at the latest press conference. No mere mortal could comprehend his holy crusade, but she understood that it *was* holy. That he was Christ's soldier. She'd said as much.

*Like a weary soldier returning from battle, he can put down his sword.* And if that wasn't enough of a code, she'd included parts from one of his favorite Bible quotes: *For*

*God will bring every deed into judgment, with every secret thing, whether good or evil.*

She'd signaled her awareness of the divine purpose that drove him. His fist clenched at his side as he crossed the room. Back again. Yes, he'd been exultant when he'd heard the words, shared specifically with him. It was like listening to music only the two of them could hear. Had anyone ever understood him before in his life? Certainly not the man who called himself his father. And not even later, when he'd been removed from that home and lived with the pastor and his wife for a time. While the minister had done his best to show Anis the way of the Lord, he'd never once tried to comprehend what was in Anis's heart.

He'd been certain she'd be at the vigil. The RCMP sergeant had said as much. She was part of the task force, was she not? What possible reason would there be to keep her away?

Anis knew the answer to that question. He'd been outwitted, and the thought was infuriating. Lured like an ant to a picnic, he'd responded as the police had figured he would.

But they hadn't trapped him, had they? His fingers uncurled, and a hint of the tension that had been riding him dissipated. Of course not. Because God's cloak of protection shielded him from the machinations of the police. He allowed himself a tiny smile. Was the sergeant as frustrated as Anis right now? Oh, more so. He'd have to be very angry that Anis had evaded him once again.

Calmer, Anis sat on the edge of the bed. Had Alexa known of the attempt to catch him? Had she perhaps suggested it? It wasn't undue pride that had him doubting it. She wanted to meet as much as he did. She thought it would be on her terms.

But she was very wrong about that. The Lord would choose the time and date and filter His wishes through Anis.

And he, Christ's soldier, would either redeem Alexa...or destroy her.

His cell rang. He only received calls from one person. And never when there was good news. Anis snatched up the phone. "Is everything all right with the dragonflies?"

The boy's voice on the other end was timid. Weak. "Yes, everything's fine. But I'm out of sandwiches and fruit. I ran out yesterday. When are you coming back?"

A measure of tension escaped him. His beauties were safe. That was all that mattered. His voice cold, he said, "I told you to ration the food carefully. You disobeyed, and going hungry is the price for that."

"I'm out of water, too." The boy's voice was piteous. "I've been drinking out of the hose we keep the pond filled with, but I need to eat. Will you be back soon?"

His mind racing, Anis said, "No." He'd left the boy extra food, but he'd never been gone this long before. Hadn't planned on it this time, but the assigned had changed. Alexa Hayden had revised everything.

There was an ample supply of water with the hose, but how long could the boy go without food? No more than a few days, probably. And if he were no longer able to take care of the insects, Anis's collection would be destroyed by the time he returned. He couldn't risk that.

There was only one option. "The door that I use to enter the shed leads to a garage where I keep a freezer."

"But it's locked."

"Of course the door's locked, fool," Anis said impatiently. "Turn on the light in the enclosure and go to the door. The code to the keypad is eight-six-four-zero. Can you remember that?"

"Eight-six-four-zero." There was newfound life in the kid's voice. He probably thought he'd find a way out from the garage. He'd soon learn that it was every bit as secure as the shed was.

He had the kid repeat the code a few more times. "Don't touch anything else in the garage. I'll know if you do. You'll be severely punished if you disobey again."

"I won't."

Anis hung up, his earlier frustration returning. This was the plight of fathers everywhere, he supposed. To be saddled with ungrateful children who couldn't think for themselves. He'd warned the boy to ration the food. Now he'd have to eat whatever he could unthaw from the freezer, and eat it raw. Nearly starving would provide a well-learned lesson.

LOGAN CREPT to the door that he hadn't dared touch in over a year. The man had once entered through it when he was lurking on the other side, trying to figure out how to get out. The door had slammed into his head, knocking him to the ground. That had earned him a goose egg on his forehead and a vicious beating. After that, he'd remained on the other side of the shed as ordered, tending to the enclosure.

But he'd never stopped looking for a way out.

There were no windows. No light except the one that lit the enclosure where the dragonflies were kept. It was on during the day and dimmed at night. He'd explored his prison many times. There was only the single door that had always been locked.

His hands shook so badly it took him two times to punch in the key code correctly. The garage was between the shed and the small house. He'd been in the home once when Anis Tera had rescued him from the flooding. He'd fetched a blanket and gave Logan an ice-cream bar. The man had pretended to call his parents and then asked Logan if he wanted to see something beautiful.

That's when he'd taken him to the shed, where Logan had been kept ever since.

When the green light flashed on the keypad, his hand closed around the knob. Fear trickled down his spine, despite the man's words on the phone. When his parents were training Sadie, Logan's dog, she'd worn a collar that had shocked her whenever she got too close to the edge of their yard. Later, she hadn't needed a collar. She still couldn't be lured out off of the property, not even with her favorite treat.

Logan didn't have a collar, but he felt like Sadie now. Too scared to go outside his territory.

Finally, his stiff fingers turned the knob. He was panting as if he'd run a race as he slowly pushed the door open. More darkness met him. He squinted into the shadows. There would be a light switch somewhere. He tried to remember from the one time he'd been here. Like a dumb kid, he'd just been happy with his ice cream, thinking that his parents would be coming to pick him up soon. He hadn't known then that the ordinary-looking man who'd been kind enough to save him from drowning was really a monster.

Logan made his way across the interior of the garage, hands out in front of him like a blind person until he reached the opposite side. He felt along the wall for the door to the house. And then searched beside it. There. With a feeling of triumph, he flipped the switch, and dim light split the darkness.

The sight of the small freezer sitting on the other side of the door had him salivating. He rushed over to it and opened the lid. His stomach growled in hunger at the sight of the packaged food inside. No ice cream, but there were sandwiches sitting on the top in a Ziploc bag. He took it out and rummaged around inside for more. Most of the contents were packaged meat. Hamburger and pork chops and chicken. Logan felt a little queasy thinking about having to unthaw some of it and eat it raw, but he would if he had to.

For now, he took the sandwiches and closed the lid. Then he scanned the rest of the interior. His dad's garage was messy, with tools and overflowing shelves everywhere. If Logan had a tool, he could find a way out of the garage. Or into the house, and out a window or door there.

But the garage was tidy. There wasn't a workbench with a pegboard hanging above it. There were no shelves, stuffed to overflowing. A small TV hung on the wall with a DVR player beneath it on a small table. Logan's uncle had a big-screen TV in his garage, with chairs and a sofa just like a room in the house. He called it his man cave.

If this was the stranger's man cave, it was pretty pathetic.

He went to check out the row of tall metal cupboards with double doors along one wall. Logan crossed to them and yanked on the doors, but they were locked.

Then he turned his attention to the door that led to the house. That, too, was secured. A little desperate, he went to examine the double garage doors. Not automatic like the ones that went up at the touch of a button at his house. They were wooden doors that swung outward with a big wooden bar on the outside to keep them locked. He remembered seeing it when the man had first brought him here.

Logan set down the sandwiches and pushed against the doors. They didn't move. He backed up a few feet, then ran up and rammed them with his shoulder. Pain sang through him.

It dawned on him then. He'd been allowed out of his prison, into a jail of another sort.

Tears welled in his eyes, and he bent to pick up the bag of sandwiches before trudging over to turn off the light. The man taught him prayers and made him repeat them regularly. He would never know that Logan prayed every night that somehow he'd get out of this place.

His hand on the light switch, he hesitated and looked at the TV again. Maybe the man watched movies out here. But there were no chairs or a couch like there would be in the house. He didn't know why anyone would watch a movie when they couldn't sit down.

He crept closer to the TV. Logan hadn't seen a movie in...however long he'd been here. He wouldn't even care if the man only had old ones. And maybe the TV worked alone. Maybe Logan could actually see some cartoons or shows on it before the man came home.

The thought of getting caught doing so made his stomach hurt. But the temptation was too great to ignore. He went closer and picked up the remote. Turned the TV on. It showed nothing but static, no matter the channel. He should have known.

But when he checked the DVD player, there was a DVD inside. Without much hope, he spent a few minutes figuring out how to make the thing work. He clicked through the TV channels until he found the one that showed the movie.

He grimaced. It looked like a horror movie. Logan's big brother, Kevin always called him a baby, but he didn't like to watch scary films. They gave him nightmares.

And this...he backed away. Something was wrong with this movie. A man had a plastic bag over his head, taped around his throat. He was sitting in some kind of chair and couldn't move. The guy was sucking in air in the bag until the plastic was plastered against his mouth. Logan watched in horrified fascination until the man stopped breathing.

After a few minutes, there was a pause in the film. Then moments later, the movie flickered to life again. Only this time there was a different man sitting in the same chair. The clear bag was over his head, and his eyes bugged out as he tried to get air.

Logan finally realized the truth. These weren't movies. And the men weren't actors. The guys on the disc were really dead. Someone had put the bags over their heads. Someone had watched them die.

And Logan already knew who had filmed their deaths. Anis Tera. The same man who had rescued him from the flooded stream and then locked him up in the shed. The one who'd almost let him starve to death.

He was backing away from the TV now. So fast that he tripped over his feet and landed on his butt. When the man on the screen slumped forward, his eyes wide and staring inside the clear bag, Logan opened his mouth and began to scream.

# CHAPTER SEVENTEEN

WHEN SERGEANTS IAN MCMANUS AND JONAH BANNON walked into the briefing at the RCMP headquarters the next morning, Alexa was the only one in the room who seemed surprised. There'd been no conversation on the way here from the hotel. Ethan had been on the phone the whole time while Nyle drove. There had, however, been coffee, and Alexa was grateful for that.

She smiled when the two newcomers seated themselves on either side of her. "Good to meet you in person, Doc," Ian said gruffly. His tie today was eye-popping fuschia with a pink and purple flamingo on it.

"I thought you'd be taller," deadpanned Jonah.

Alexa laughed. "I used to be. Ethan chewed a couple of inches off me yesterday."

Ethan looked up, the phone still pressed to his ear and frowned in their direction.

"He's got to realize he can't treat civilian consultants the way he does the rest of us," Jonah remarked. "Especially when you don't have inches to spare."

Nyle fiddled with the video conferencing equipment. It

seemed odd, once it was turned on, to see only two partici-pants instead of four. Steve Friedrich and Captain Campbell.

"Feels sort of lonely on this side," remarked the wise-cracking Friedrich.

"Believe me, it was nothing you said," replied Jonah. "Or wait, maybe it was."

"Gentlemen." The Captain looked sober. "I'm anxious to hear about what went down in Victoria Park last night."

Alexa leaned forward. She'd heard only the barest details from Nyle on the way here this morning. But as Ethan recounted the events from last night, a cold pool of dread pooled in her stomach.

They'd been right. The offender had taken the opportu-nity the vigil offered and shown up.

"We believe he came armed with Scopolamine," Ethan said grimly. "When he first started to approach the stand-in, he was holding what looked like a needle."

Alexa's trepidation intensified. Not for what might have happened. She didn't waste time on could-haves. No, her foreboding was reserved for the evidence of the UNSUB's recklessness. She'd seen the map Ethan had put up yester-day. It was a green space smack dab in an urban area, with streets bordering all four sides of it. Yes, there were plenty of trees, but she didn't think there was enough cover that he could have possibly expected to escape detection.

Either he'd quickly hit upon a foolproof plan, or he'd taken an incredible risk. The type that had, until the last few days, been foreign to him.

"...IT to get us a clearer picture of the keys he was hold-ing. One of the officers spotted an insignia on it that might be the CarsNow logo, but we need to be certain before we get a production order for the rental records."

"Oh." She snapped to attention. "When we do get that order, we'll be looking for a Toyota Camry. Black or navy, with a light-colored interior." She smiled in satisfaction when all the men stared at her. "After Ethan gets done filling you in on the events of last night, I'll tell you about *my* evening."

"AND THIS IS why I don't like to let you out of my sight," Ethan muttered, as he and Alexa walked to the IT area in the Halifax RCMP facility.

"You have to realize how illogical that is," she remarked airily, "when you're the one who refused to let me go with you last night."

"I specifically told you to stay here and answer messages left on the tip line." He wasn't angry, not exactly, but she'd describe his mood as smoldering.

"You didn't tell me to stay here." They descended the stairway. "You *assumed* I'd stay since I had no way of getting home with everyone gone. So as long as I was going to have to summon an Uber anyway, you can hardly quibble that I took one to conduct some interviews in person."

"I think you'd be surprised by what I can find to quibble about in that plan." He was silent for a few moments as they walked down the hallway to the IT offices. "How sure did Owens seem about the vehicle?"

"He was useless when it came to describing the person with Lawler, but was unshakeable when it came to the car. I'm sure that's a guy thing. Said he drove a red one like it."

"I may need to talk to him."

"I hope you do." She rather liked the idea of Owens

coming up against Ethan's implacable persona instead of a woman he thought he could charm.

Ethan stopped suddenly enough that Alexa bumped into him. "Looking for Officer Peters."

The area was a rabbit warren of desks, with electronic equipment taking up the rest of the available space. "You've found him." A stocky balding man stood up and gave them a wave. "I've got some photos for you. Blew up that insignia on the keychain from the video you sent over." Alexa and Ethan headed for the man's desk and looked at the sheets he'd spread out on it. "Here's the clearest I could get." It was a close-up of a logo, taken, Alexa knew, from this morning's briefing, of the UNSUB's keychain. It was still fuzzy enough to make positive ID uncertain.

"I looked on a site we keep of product logos and insignias. I downloaded the ones I think looked close, blew them up to the right size for comparison." He sat down at the desk and tapped a few keys on his laptop. The insignias appeared. He picked up the image taken from last night's film and held it up to each on the screen by turn.

"The interlocking 'C' and 'N,'" Ethan said certainly.

"It's the closest," Peters agreed. "The item on the film was too small and too far away to enhance without losing detail in the picture. But here," he reached an index finger to trace the photo he'd made, "you've got a half-arc, straight lines on either side of the bottom letter with a diagonal. That looks like the insignia you have. Here's another with a 'C' and 'H' for some fashion designer and her products." He brought the appropriate image up on the screen. "But going with the law of probability, a rental car agency is far more likely to put their logo on a keychain tag than some fancy designer who sells purses for what I spend on groceries every month." He handed the image to Ethan. "Does that help at all?

"Helps a lot. Thank you." Ethan and Alexa turned to make their way back upstairs. "With this and what you came up with last night, we've got enough to get a production order," Ethan told her. "That will require the agencies to produce data and records about their clients for the last few days."

Her eyes lit up. "This could be the lead we've been waiting for."

Ethan didn't answer. He'd seen too many similar leads fizzle at the end to allow himself to hope. But if they were going to catch a break in this case, this would be the time for it.

There were six CarsNow rental agencies in Nova Scotia, mostly congregated around Halifax and its suburbs. The one outlier was in New Glasgow, over an hour and a half away. The team would spread out, armed with copies of the production warrant and pictures of the offender. For once Alexa didn't protest sticking with Ethan. He wasn't sure if that was progress or if she was as wiped out by last night as he was. They would visit the agency in Dartmouth, go back to the RCMP headquarters to check the license numbers against the photo IDs in the DMV database, and if they were unsuccessful, they'd drive to New Glasgow.

While Ethan drove, Alexa brought up the company's site on her phone. A map appeared, with the colored markers where their rental agencies were. "We know Fornier said Simard thought he'd seen Anis Tera in a white van the day before he died. Maybe that spooked the

UNSUB. It might have been the moment he decided to get a rental."

"Which then gave him *two* vehicles he had to deal with." Ethan braked suddenly to avoid a running into a driver turning against a red light. "Our patrols have discovered nothing with the stop-and-checks they've been running. So he's keeping the van out of sight somewhere."

"Except when he uses it for the homicides."

"Except then," Ethan agreed grimly.

"Which brings up a point." She half-turned in the seat to look at him. "According to Owens, the offender used a car to pick up Lawler. But his van was spotted by Grayson Quinton at the lake that night. Which means he transported her to wherever he was keeping the van, then drove that to the dumpsite."

Ethan slowed to pay at the toll station before crossing the McKay bridge that would take them to Dartmouth. "If the offender thought Simard would recognize the Econoline, he probably used the rental to snatch him, too. I can't see him just leaving the van out in the open in a motel parking lot. He seems too cautious for that."

"These days, he could get a residential rental through Airbnb or a similar site. He might have a local home with a garage he's staying in."

It was feasible, Ethan supposed, keeping a close eye on the bridge traffic. There were too damn many possibilities, which was the problem. It seemed reasonable to assume that the UNSUB would stay in the vicinity since both victims were snatched from there. But it was impossible to know how far outside the metro area he might have strayed.

One would think that the offender would want to avoid people as much as possible. Which would make a remote two- or three-star motel attractive to him. One where there weren't a lot of questions asked, and no one cared much about the occupants' comings and goings. Which, Ethan supposed, could also be said for an isolated rental property.

"Are you thinking what I'm thinking?"

"What?"

"Why..." she pounded lightly on her knee with a closed fist for emphasis. "...does he need the van at all? Yes, he likely drove it into Nova Scotia from New Brunswick. But once he had the rental, it seems like a car would be less noticeable."

"Spaciousness," he suggested, but now that she had him thinking about it, he was wondering the same thing. "We know he often uses a dolly to get the bodies from the vehicle to the dumpsite."

"Okay, so he puts the body in the trunk and the dolly in the back seat," she said logically. She bent over her phone. A quick glance told him she was looking up the measurements of dollies. His mouth quirked. Scientific to the end.

"Privacy. No windows for anyone to look inside."

"Or maybe," Alexa said slowly, "it is space he needs."

Ethan slowed to a stop for a red light. "I think I said that. There are supplies he'd carry with him. The insects. Tape. Plastic bags. We know he had a power drill and scalpels or knives for the last two victims."

She was still staring at her phone. This time she was searching the dimensions of the Econoline cargo vans. After a few minutes, Alexa murmured, "He could haul a lot in that big a vehicle."

"Again, that's what I—"

She raised her head to look at him. "But maybe he's using it for more than that. Maybe it's his kill site."

A knot of tension formed at the top of his spine. "No way to prove that." At least, he thought grimly, accelerating when the light turned green, not until they found the vehicle and had the forensic ident guys go through it.

"Obviously. But it would explain why you've never found the kill site for any of the homicides." She was getting excited about her idea now. It sounded in her voice. "He's killed in all seasons. In most of the provinces and territories. Many times, it had to have been in places with which he's unfamiliar. No primary crime scene lessens the chances of leaving evidence behind. And it'd be one less thing to have to scout ahead of time."

"He'd still have to keep the van somewhere isolated when he killed them." But her idea wasn't totally without merit. The problem was, it was all speculation, which this case had plenty of. It was facts and evidence that were in short supply.

Ethan remembered something he'd meant to discuss with Alexa. "I expected the UNSUB to reach out to you after the vigil." Accelerating after he left the bridge, he glanced over at her. "I figured he'd be agitated by the way things went down. We could see in the film the exact moment he must have realized that Lavoie wasn't you."

The expression on Alexa's face was more telling than a shout. He thought it wise to ignore it. The video clip showing the moment the UNSUB had approached the stand-in was chilling. Because Ethan couldn't be certain the officers wouldn't have behaved the same way if it had been Alexa there. Leaving her exposed and vulnerable. How close would the offender have gotten to her before their attention had returned to the woman they were supposed to be guarding? "I thought he'd contact you again if only to castigate you for not being at the park."

She nodded slowly. "I feared how he might react if he discovered the decoy. But I expected him to respond in some way. I don't think he would have felt threatened by the way the evening transpired. He would have seen it as going according to plan, up until the point when he realized I wasn't there."

"What do you think the UNSUB's silence means?"

"It's worrisome," she admitted. "Not contacting me shows a self-discipline I didn't expect. Because I think I reached him with the press conference message. He's regrouping somewhere, considering his options. He may decide that these risks aren't worth it and try to get out of the province."

Somehow Ethan doubted it. "You don't believe that."

She hesitated. "I'm not sure. If four homicides in a short amount of time are him catching up for time lost, that says one thing about him. But I think it's more than that. I'm guessing that the injuries he sustained at Fornier's hand acted as a trigger that caused his escalation. If I had to make a prediction...right now he's planning his next move."

"I DON'T KNOW." Molly, the young woman who'd greeted them with a cheery smile as they entered the Dartmouth CarsNow agency now sported a worried frown as she perused the production order Ethan handed her. "I mean... I've never seen one of these things." She waved at the sheet of paper. "And my supervisor isn't in yet, and I'd be in a lot of trouble if I didn't follow procedure."

"You'll be in more trouble if you ignore the order, which has been duly signed by a justice of the peace." Ethan tapped the signature at the bottom. "What this says is you supply all client records for a window of four days." Simard had seen the offender on Saturday. Owens had spotted

Lawler being helped into a car outside Zoomey's after midnight Thursday morning. "It narrows it down to Toyota Camrys, dark-color exterior with a light interior."

"I don't know," Molly said again, doubtfully. "My supervisor is a real...I mean he can be difficult. And if I screw up one more time, I think he's going to get rid of me."

"Chances are he'll know what a production order means." Alexa gave her a friendly smile. "And if he doesn't, I'm sure he has a boss to report to, and that person will. You won't get in any trouble for following the law."

"I wish I was as sure as you are." But she sat down at her desk and began bringing up records. "Do you want drivers of both genders?"

"Yes," Ethan and Alexa responded simultaneously. After last night, Ethan wasn't certain what to expect. If the offender had obtained the license at a DMV station and given a false name and a phony address, the picture would be that of a man. It was far harder to pull that sort of charade in clear view of a DMV attendant.

But if he'd obtained false ID...people who forged documents for a living would have no compunction about someone attempting to disguise his gender.

"You got it." The printer on her desk began to whir. "We've been pretty busy," Molly said chattily. "What with the nice weather and it being tourist season. More and more people are asking for the small SUVs, but I always tell them, the mid-sized sedans are often roomier for luggage."

"Were you working those days?" Alexa asked.

Molly nodded. "All of them. My day off is Wednesday."

Alexa had brought in copies of the offender sketches, and she unfolded them now, holding them up for the young woman to see. "Do you happen to remember seeing someone who looked like either of these drawings?"

The young woman looked up briefly from her task and smiled delightedly. "Hey, yeah, I recognize him." She tapped the sketch Patrick had helped develop. "Can't remember his name, but he complimented me on my tattoo." She stopped to slip her lightweight cardigan down her arm a bit to bare a shoulder emblazoned with an intricately detailed butterfly. "I just got this because it was pretty, but he told me all about it, like the real scientific name, but I can't remember that. He said it was... Let me think." She tapped a finger against her chin. "He called it a Luzon Peacock Swallowtail." She pronounced the name carefully. "Said it was from the Philippines. We had a nice long talk about it. It's endangered, you know."

Ethan stilled. "What day would that have been?"

"Um...Saturday? Or Sunday, maybe. I told him he sure seemed to know a lot about butterflies and sort of teased him that maybe he should get a tattoo, too. But he said he liked dragonflies better."

"Robert Merkel."

Ethan sat back in his chair, stunned elation filling him. They'd gone back to the RCMP building in Halifax and inputted the drivers' license numbers from the rental agency into the DMV site, which in turn emailed copies of the corresponding licenses. The copy of the photo ID he'd printed out was eerily close to the second sketch of the offender, with gray hair and a mustache.

"License is phony," Ian said as he and Jonah crowded around to look at the sheet. "Seventy years old? No way a septuagenarian is hauling dead bodies through forests and down embankments."

"Septuagenarian?" Jonah Bannon chuckled. "You've been doing those Word-a-Day challenges again?"

"I know words." Ian sounded offended. "And a Bridgewater, Nova Scotia address? He's struck as far away as British Columbia. Until his most recent spree, he's never been this far east before."

"Even a phony name might leave a trail," Alexa said. She was trying to mask her excitement at the development, but she was all but bouncing in her chair next to Ethan. "And we have his matching credit card information."

"We do indeed." Ethan turned to Ian. "See if you can match the name to the ferry passenger manifest. We have lists from the days following the New Brunswick homicides."

"Where are they?"

Ethan jerked a thumb at the corner of the room where the boxes of manifests had been stacked when they were returned by the Halifax PD. The other man looked at them resignedly before getting up to obey.

To Jonah, he said, "Send out a BOLO alert for the description we have of the offender's rental car and plate number." A BOLO would result in a much more targeted search than the stop-and-check for the white van.

The door to the room pushed open, and Nyle walked in. "All I have to say is, the CarsNow branch at the airport is the most disorganized…" He looked from face to the next. "You got him already?"

Ethan caught him up on the morning's events and then added, "We need a warrant on Merkel's financials. I'm especially interested in that credit card. He used it for the rental. He may have put the motel where he's staying on it, as well."

"If he went to dives and showed enough cash, he probably could have avoided using a card," Nyle pointed out.

"We'll soon find out."

"What do you want me to do?" Alexa asked.

"Research," Ethan told her. "We need to learn everything we can about Robert Merkel of Bridgewater."

"Okay, the warrant on the Merkel credit card has been processed with the highest priority stamp, whatever that means." The near-silence the group had been working in for the last hour and a half was splintered by Nyle's return. Ethan noticed with amusement the man held a bakery box in his hand. The officer had a serious sweet tooth. Once they had this case solved, they might have to stage an intervention.

"It means the brass in Ottawa is getting personally involved in the process." Which Ethan hoped was going to get them a rapid response.

"What'd you learn?" Nyle set the box on the table in the corner and as if on cue, Ian and Jonah got up and beelined for it.

"There's no Robert Merkel listed on the ferry passenger manifests," Ian McManus responded. He peered into the box and grabbed a napkin with which to make his selection. "Since the UNSUB also didn't show up on the toll-road cameras, he probably used a different ID for the ferry."

"The BOLO alert for the offender's rental went province-wide." Jonah Bannon nudged McManus aside and studied the contents of the bakery box intently. "It's might just be a matter of time at this point. He could be spotted driving anywhere."

*Could* be, Ethan thought grimly. But the alerts depended on manpower and location. If the offender stuck to back roads, his chances of being seen by a cop plummeted drastically. But the noose around the province was tightening. "The address of the Robert Merkel in Bridgewater matches that given on the rental agreement and the driver's license." Ethan rolled his shoulders, working the knots out of them before getting out of his chair to see if Nyle had brought any brownies.

"If you study that license photo closely, it appears that the offender used something on his face to make him look older. But he still doesn't look seventy." As if unwilling to join the fray at the table holding the baked goods, Alexa remained seated. "If, as we believe, he drove into the province, it would make sense to have a driver's license name that's in the system. If he got pulled over for any reason, the first thing the patrolman would do is run the license."

With a tinge of satisfaction Ethan discovered there were, indeed brownies. He selected two and set one down in front of Alexa as he made his way back to his chair.

Her lips curved slightly. "Double fudge? You've got a good memory."

His hand paused with the treat halfway to his mouth. The mental image swamped him, summoned by her words. It'd been his birthday, just a few weeks after they'd met, and when he'd joined her at the library after school, she'd surprised him with brownies from the local bakery. One had a candle on top.

*If it's not double fudge, it's not worth eating. Make a wish, Ethan.*

His wish, of course, had included her. She'd already taken up residence in his mind. His heart. With the strength of a seventeen-year-old's single-minded passion, she'd been the focus of all his desires. As a teenager, he hadn't had the experience to realize that sometimes getting exactly what he wanted could still end in heartbreak.

Shaken by the subconscious reminder, he continued to his seat. Redirected his attention. "The Bridgewater Merkel is a former minister of a church in town. Retired two years ago, a time that corresponds with his wife's death. According to the local RCMP officers I spoke with there, he spends November through March in Naples, Florida where his brother lives."

"Leaving his residence unoccupied."

"Any kids?" Nyle asked.

"One son." Alexa picked up the thread of conversation. "Carl Merkel. He's hopped around the country a bit. Vancouver. Toronto. Quebec City. Most recently Calgary." She paused to take a bite of the brownie in front of her. Chewed. "Interestingly enough, he works for West Transport."

There was a moment of silence in the room. "The largest trucking company in the nation." Nyle's words weren't a question.

Ethan could guess what the man was thinking. There'd been a time when the team had seriously considered that the UNSUB's occupation took him to different parts of the country. A trucker. A salesman. With Alexa's input, they'd laid to rest the theory that the victims had been chosen at random. But Carl Merkel's job still gave him pause.

"Robert Merkel is currently in a local nursing home with a broken hip," Ethan said. "He's been recuperating there for over a month, according to the Bridgewater RCMP officer I spoke to. He had no social media accounts that we could find, but the brother in Florida often posts pictures of them together down there. And Merkel's daughter-in-law has tweeted regular updates of her father-in-law's progress in rehab. It's possible the UNSUB could keep tabs him through those avenues to learn when the place would be empty."

"According to one of the local RCMP officers, Merkel and his wife were foster parents for about fifteen years," Alexa put in. "Who knows? Maybe the offender gets a fake ID to match whichever area he's going to strike in. And if so, it's not implausible he might choose someone he's familiar with."

"I've alerted police in Calgary, and they've paid a visit to the Carl Merkel's home using a pretext excuse. According to his wife, he's on his way to Winnipeg for a convention. With what we've discovered, I think Robert Merkel's residence requires a closer look." Bridgewater was just over an hour from Halifax. It was unlikely, but not out of the question that the UNSUB had used the Merkel address as his base of operations here. "The closest Emergency Response Team would come out of Halifax, so I've spoken to Captain Sedgewick about arranging that for us." Ethan looked at his team soberly. "We'll roll out with the tactical team in a couple of hours. Whether or not we find the offender in residence, if he's been occupying the place, there will be evidence of that."

"Friedrich is going to be so pissed he missed out on an ERT raid." An unfamiliar smile flashed across Jonah's normally sober expression. "Are Gagnon and Campbell updated?"

Ethan nodded. He'd spent most of the last hour on the phone updating the brass as their research progressed. "They're on board with our plan." But they'd have plenty of questions if the team came up empty-handed after the raid. The offender's communications with Alexa had given them much-needed insight into the UNSUB. The longer he went without contacting her again, the more Ethan's foreboding grew. It'd be damn difficult for the man to get out of the province right now. So, either he was plotting his next homicide, or he was planning another attempt to get close to Alexa.

Either way, Ethan had a feeling their time was running out.

FIVE HOURS LATER, Alexa was seated inside the ERT command vehicle. One of the team members sat in front of a screen, which showed a one-story older home, white with green trim. There was an attached single garage and what looked like a small shed in the backyard. The house was located a mile or so outside of town. The vehicle was parked well down the road.

"How are we able to see this?" she asked. They couldn't see the house from the command post.

"Cameras with wireless playback capabilities are affixed to the tactical team members' helmets," the officer explained. "The video is fed to this computer. The screen will split for the different feeds coming in We can even loop in other law enforcement from remote locations if we need to."

Alexa fell into silence once more. Ethan and his officers had huddled with the ERT commander for what had seemed like an eternity. Sitting here waiting allowed her too much time to think about what could go wrong. If the offender were inside, he could be armed. Not that he'd be any match for a tactical team, but he could get shots off before being eliminated as a threat. Someone could still get hurt.

That someone could be Ethan.

A sick tangle of nausea tightened in her stomach. He'd be at the tail end of the unit. Logic dictated that his risk would be minimal. It was a mistake to underestimate an UNSUB, but equally important not to endow him with superhuman qualities. He'd be outgunned by the tactical unit's firepower.

But illogical or not, worry chased across her mind like frantic little ants. It'd be easy to dismiss it as the same concern she'd have for any of the men assembled outside.

Easy, but not honest.

Alexa had taken the optimistic stance that proximity to Ethan would lay to rest the ghosts from their pasts. She'd convinced herself she'd made the right decision to leave all those years ago. To allow him the life he'd always planned before duty and obligation had dictated another path. But working closely with him was chipping away at her long-held conviction and wreaking havoc on the emotional peace she'd finally achieved. And after their kiss, she'd started to fear that she wasn't going to escape their second parting unscathed either.

In the next moment, the scene on screen exploded into action. The ERT unit members, swarmed across the street, into the yard, surrounding the house. The first member on the steps used a breaching device to knock the door off its hinges. Then the entry team members raced inside.

Alexa held her breath. It was eerie to see the interior of the strange home. The front room was empty. As was the kitchen. Shouts of "Clear!" were heard as other members covered the house. But to Alexa, it had a feeling of vacancy. As if waiting for its owner to return.

"The house and basement are empty," the officer at the screen said several minutes later. "There's a shed out back that still requires checking."

The unit members inside the home were searching the rooms. She knew they'd be looking for anything that suggested recent occupancy. Evidence that the offender had been inside.

As she watched the screen intently, she was able to pick out Ethan even before he lifted the shield on his helmet. Something in his stance gave him away. It was his aura of command, she supposed. The slight swagger of youth had solidified into a projection of authority, which had been honed by experience.

"Shed outside is clear."

The camera was back in the front room of the house. She saw now that there was a walker parked next to a recliner.

Alexa settled more comfortable on her stool while the team members conducted their examination of the premises. Their movements were methodical, but no longer urgent. Ethan turned when another team member called to him. Followed the other man. Alexa's mind drifted to the offender. What did his sudden silence signify? Had he selected Robert Merkel at random, or was there a connection there?

The UNSUB had the technical skills to wander in and out of people's online lives, she mused as she watched team members tipping over furniture and going through drawers, cupboards and shelves. That could have been how the offender settled on Merkel in Bridgewater for his false ID.

But there could also be a more personal link. And it was that possibility that had Alexa hoping to speak to the real Robert Merkel in person.

~

ALEXA STOOD in a cluster with Nyle, Jonah and Ian outside the vehicle as the ERT team members filed out of the residence. The front door hung out of kilter, useless. It would have to be boarded up, along with any other entry points that had been used.

Ethan stood a distance away, consulting with the ERT commander and an RCMP officer from the local detachment. If he was disappointed by the results of the raid, it didn't show on his impassive expression.

"Too much to ask for that the UNSUB would be sitting in there on his computer, screwing up someone else's life while the team burst in on him," Ian said glumly, smoothing a hand down his garish tie. "Didn't expect it, but it'd sure be nice to catch a break in this case."

"We still have all the exits from the country blocked." Alexa rubbed the small of her back. The stool she'd been perched on for the last couple of hours hadn't been the epitome of comfort. "The ferry and Coast Guard have been alerted and have his pictures. As have the airlines, trains, cruise ships..."

"...but if he gets as far as the toll road to New Brunswick, picking up his image on the camera after the fact won't do us much good," Ian countered. "We have to count on the vehicle being recognized and pulled over before he gets that far."

"What if this is his home province?" Jonah Bannon's question hung in the air between them. "He could go back to his house. Abandon the rental, hide the van and no one would know the difference."

"Except for the release of the sketches." The UNSUB knew they had the drawings because they'd been made public. But he wouldn't know the team had one of his fake identities, and the makes of the vehicles he was driving. That, Alexa mused, could lead him to believe he could safely leave the province while leading him right into a trap.

"What's to say he doesn't just abandon the car and the Econoline, don a disguise to match yet another ID and take a bus? A train or airplane?" Nyle was slowly scrolling through his emails on his cell. "Let's face it. Witnesses haven't been great at IDing this guy. No reason to think ticket agents would be any better."

"I don't think he'll leave the van behind if he can avoid it." Alexa didn't go into the reasoning that she'd shared with Ethan earlier that day. She almost wished she could believe that the UNSUB would leave the province soon. But there was some instinct much more primitive than logic that told her he wasn't done here.

"Well, all is not lost." Nyle sounded a bit more cheerful as he looked up from his cell. "Someone at the top must have pulled some strings, because I've already got the records for the credit card statement in Merkel's name." He was silent for a moment as he looked it over. "The user signed up for online-only statements. It looks like payments were made that way, too." He shook his head in bemusement. "That's one way to keep the person at that address unaware that another card has been taken out in his name."

Alexa frowned. "I don't understand. The cards would still be delivered to Merkel's address."

Nyle wagged a finger at her. "You're not thinking deviously enough. Merkel's name and address were listed on the phony license. But while the name matched on the credit card, the address given to the credit card company doesn't. It's still in Nova Scotia..." He paused while he tapped in a search. After a few moments, he said, "The address given on the credit card information doesn't show up in a search. So, he likely used a mail forwarding service."

"Which would send his mail to the address of his choice, while shielding his location," she said slowly.

"And," Ian added, "tracking down mail forwarding services is almost impossible."

"But you still have the transactions, right?" Jonah went to Nyle's side and peered down at his screen. "Where'd he use the credit card most recently, aside from the car rental agency?"

Nyle scanned the statement. "Only two transactions. Gas stations." His mouth flattened. "Both in New Brunswick. One in Edmonton and the other in Fredericton." The three men looked at each other. "Where the two victims there were from." Jonah peered over Nyle's shoulder. "What are the dates for those... Shit."

"Edmonton date is two days before Henry Paulus left for his backpacking trip. The Fredericton date is the day before Albert Norton disappeared." McManus picked up his cell and started texting. "Steve can check the gas station security cameras. Lots of times those places reuse the tapes after a week or so, but you never know."

Ethan strode over. "The ERT team found a few clothes in one of the bedrooms that appear to belong to a male. Different size than those in the master bedroom. One of the T-shirts is from Fundy National Park." He smiled grimly when Jonah's brows shot up. "A couple of local RCMP officers will accompany us to Merkel's nursing home. I'm anxious to talk to this guy myself."

# CHAPTER EIGHTEEN

ROBERT MERKEL still cut an imposing figure, even seated in a wheelchair. Over six foot, barrel-chested with a full shock of white hair and matching bushy eyebrows, he glowered at the team as they filed in to take chairs lined up before him.

"If there's damage to my house, I want to know who's going to take care of it," he thundered. "Someone's going to pay for the damages, and it's not going to be me."

"We'll cover the expenses," Ethan told him. He'd run that by Campbell and follow-up to make sure it happened. "In the meantime, the entrances to your home are being repaired as we speak." The doorways were being replaced with plywood sheets until new doors were purchased. He doubted that news would calm the man down much.

"I still don't have an explanation for what happened." The man thumped his cane on the floor for emphasis. "Whose genius idea was this? What'd you think, that a seventy-year-old man was running a meth lab in his basement?"

Ethan leaned forward in his chair. "Mr. Merkel, your

name and address showed up on an ID bearing your name used by a dangerous criminal we're tracking. When we checked out your identity and discovered you hadn't been inhabiting the house for weeks, we had to entertain the possibility that someone else could be there in your absence. I understand that you spend your winters in Florida and are gone months at a time."

"Yes, but even though my home is outside of town, I have my share of nosy neighbors," the older man scoffed. Clearly, he hadn't forgiven the intrusion into his house. "Can't throw a stone without hitting one of them. Wouldn't take long for someone to notice if a stranger was coming and going from my home."

"Can you explain the clothes in a much smaller size in the blue bedroom? One of the T-shirts bore a New Brunswick logo."

He looked puzzled for a moment. "That room used to belong to my son, Carl. He lived in New Brunswick for his first job. He was here a few weeks ago when I landed myself in the hospital with this bum hip. He must have left some things at the house. Haven't been back there, so I can't say."

It was a shot in the dark, but Ethan asked, "Do you have a photo of your son?"

It took several moments for the man to shift position in the chair enough to dig into his back pocket for his wallet. He extracted a picture and held it out. Ethan got up to look at it. The image showed a couple posed with two children. The man looked nothing like the offender's sketches or the photo on the fake license.

Ethan handed the picture back and then drew out a copy of the fake driver's license photo from his pocket. Unfolding it, he showed it to the man. "Have you seen this man before?"

The older man stared at it intently before slowly shaking his head. "Don't recognize him, but I don't know everyone in town. Is he local?"

"Probably not." Ethan decided to begin wrapping things up. "Have you been notified by any companies that your personal information has been breached? Perhaps at a merchant or hacked online?"

Merkel let out a hearty laugh. "Son, unless they break into the Old Age Security or Canada Pension Plan systems, I'm safe. I've never had a credit card in my life. If I can't pay cash for something, I don't buy it. That's the problem with the country today. Too many people are buying things on credit, putting all their business out there for anyone to grab. I had something similar happen...oh, must have been twenty years ago or so. Someone used my ID to try to buy a car. Caught him red-handed, of course. Turned out to be one of the foster kids we had thirty years ago or so." He shook his head sorrowfully. "You try to do God's work, and that's how you get repaid."

"Mr. Merkel," Alexa spoke for the first time, giving the older man a friendly smile. I'm Dr. Alexa Hayden, a consultant on this case. Can you tell us more about your foster children?"

"Which ones? We probably fostered forty, forty-five over the years. Mostly males, because I know how to talk to boys, having had a son. I'm a pastor, and I thought if I could bring God's word to children desperately in need of it, I'd be doing the Lord's work." He shook his head sorrowfully, "I did what I could but these kids...just a stream of sad stories from miserable backgrounds. A few went back home, but most bounced around in foster homes until they aged out of the system."

"I imagine you have quite a few stories from those days,"

Alexa said encouragingly. Her manner would calm the most volatile of subjects. Ethan watched the fiery-tempered older man from a few minutes ago visibly relax under her questioning.

"More stories than I can remember. Claire, my wife, used tell me to write them down, but truthfully, they were more heartbreaking than joyful. We had such a revolving door of kids for so many years, I just couldn't keep the names straight. I'd given them a name from the Bible that began with their first initial. Sort of as a memory device. But it was always the Biblical one I'd recall when I needed to. Claire was better at that kind of thing."

"Did you ever have a foster child who was fascinated by insects?"

Merkel raised a hand. "Boys and bugs. They go together, don't they? Why, I remember one time, we had a kid who asked for a jar to catch a Banded Garden Spider to bring inside for a pet. Then there was another boy who could spout the Latin name for any insect you could imagine. I put that knack of his to good use by having him memorizing his prayers in Latin." He thumped his cane again. "A talent like that is a gift from the Lord and should be used to serve Him. He begged and pleaded one year for an ant farm for his birthday to keep in his room. I said absolutely not. He was already bringing all sorts of creatures into the house when we weren't looking. But Claire...she had a soft heart. Found one at a garage sale and wrapped it up for him. Which turned out to be a mistake, just like I told her it would be. The dog got into the room and jumped up on the table, knocking the glass case off. Ants all over the house. Finally had to call an exterminator."

A buzz of interest started in Ethan's veins. "Do you recall that boy's name?"

The question brought the man up short. His eyelids drooped, and his lips moved silently as if running through an ancient list decades old. Which he likely was. Finally, he said, "I sure don't. Not even the Biblical name I gave him. It's been too long ago."

And they'd have almost zero luck getting those records opened by Nova Scotia's Child Protection Services to jog his memory, Ethan knew. He sent a surreptitious glance at the clock on the wall beyond the older man. "Well, thank you for your cooperation..."

But Alexa wasn't done. "What about your son?" she asked the man. "Would he remember the boy?"

"Carl would have been out of the house by then. I could call him if you like, but he wouldn't have known any of these kids."

"Would you, please?"

Ethan slid a glance at Alexa. She was spinning her wheels on what was very likely a dead end, but another few minutes here wouldn't hurt. A nursing home assistant brought Merkel's cell to him, and he placed the call. On his other side, Jonah Bannon pulled out his phone and started researching mail forwarding addresses. Which was likely another long shot. Ethan felt a bolt of frustration twist through him. They were inching closer to the offender, but he remained tantalizingly out of reach. Even with the safeguards they had in place, Ethan was well aware of the dangers the UNSUB still presented. His gaze went involuntarily to the woman beside him. Danger to Alexa included.

"That's it!" Ethan's attention jerked to Merkel. He wore a broad grin as he listened some more before saying, "I can't believe you recall all that." There was another moment of silence. Then the man chuckled. "You've got your mother's memory, son. Thank the Lord for that." Ethan's impatience reared while the man chatted for another minute before disconnecting and smiling triumphantly at Alexa.

"Carl remembers the whole ant story. He'd graduated from the university before the kid was there, but it happened in his old bedroom, so he took an interest." He laughed again, pleased that he'd finally placed the memory with his son's help. "Adam Ant, Carl called him. Guess he has his own memory devices. Neither of us recalls his real name, but that should be easy enough to discover. Carl reminded me that there was a big write-up in the papers when the kid went back home to live with his birth father. The man used to lock the boy in the cellar. Then he went and had himself a heart attack, and no one found him or the boy for days." He shook his head sorrowfully. "Like I said earlier, not many happy stories to remember from those times."

"WHILE HIS FATHER lay dead in the room above him, Amos Tillman, age eleven, survived for over a week, drinking only the water that dripped from overhead leaky pipes in the cellar." Alexa scrolled down on her cell to read the next paragraph of the article. "The boy was canny enough to throw a scrap of wood through the lone window high in the wall, breaking it out so he could call for help. Unfortunately..." she scrolled again. "...no one heard his pitiful cries. But a small rabbit fell through the broken glass on day three, and a bird flew in later in the week. The animals would become meals for the starving boy."

Ethan slanted a look at her. "So now you're going to tell me that the trauma he underwent in childhood would explain him growing up to kill fifteen people?"

Alexa clicked on the next article her search had brought up. "I'm perfectly aware that we haven't definitively linked Amos Tillman to this offender. But it's a name that bears checking out, and yes, his childhood is significant. Profiles are most valuable when they focus on the individual offender's behavior and motivation, rather than relying on generalizations. But it's also true that the FBI has found a correlation of childhood abuse among serial killers."

She checked the side mirror. They'd taken two cars to Bridgewater, and the other three officers followed in the vehicle behind them. "Of course, far more people who underwent similar traumas didn't grow up to become murderers. It's all about the individual's perception of what happened to him."

Her tone grew teasing. "And by the way, don't think I missed your reaction when Mr. Merkel spoke about the spider one of the foster children wanted to bring into the house."

"What? I did not react. Spiders don't bother me." He slowed as a red sports car zipped into their lane.

"Really?" Skepticism dripped from her words. "Have you developed a new-found affinity for them? Because I remember once you wouldn't get in your car until I caught the daddy long legs that was..."

"Okay, okay." He reached over to put his hand over her face and gave a gentle push. "We agreed a long time ago you'd take care of spiders and I was the designated bat killer. Bats are bigger than spiders. Much more heroic."

"So you promised," she breathed under her breath, "but it's not like we ever put it to the test."

When Ethan shot her a grin, she saw twin reflections of herself in his mirrored sunglasses. "You'll just have to take my word for it."

Her heart squeezed in her chest. His smile lightened a face that was far more somber than she remembered. Gave it a carefree look that was so reminiscent of the seventeen-year-old boy she'd fallen in love with that it took her breath. It'd be easy to believe that, as an isolated, emotionally damaged teen, she'd been susceptible to the first boy who showed interest. But there had been plenty of males who'd approached her. Ethan was the only one, however, who'd sneaked past her wary guard.

He was the only one who'd stolen her heart.

She stared blindly at the article open on her cell. It'd been easy to convince herself for the last couple of decades that their story was a combination of teenage chemistry and lack of experience. But it was far harder to reconcile that explanation with the feelings he could still awake in her now. And those feelings had alarms shrilling in her mind.

"If...and it's a major if," Ethan said, "Tillman does turn out to be The Tailor, what significance does his past play in the homicides?"

Grateful for the interruption to her thoughts, Alexa looked up. "An interesting question. His stay with Merkel could have established his foundation in religion. One that evolved and mutated over the years to fit his growing need to strike out at others."

"You've suspected the offender was using God to justify his actions since his first communication."

Alexa nodded. "Of course, there have been plenty of killers who claim God or Satan told them to kill. They're referred to as visionary killers. Most of them have suffered a psychotic break. I wouldn't place the UNSUB in that category, however."

"But you just said..."

"He uses God as a justification. But in reality, this is a

control-driven killer. And yes, if the offender turns out to be Tillman, his past does explain where his need for control originated. He had none throughout his childhood. A father who abused him and nearly killed him. A revolving door of foster homes and group homes, if these articles are to be believed. Then add Fornier's observations about the man he knew as Anis Tera. Weak. Insignificant." She turned in her seat to more fully face Ethan. "By acquiring technological expertise with computers and the Internet, the offender learned to control others. Think of the secrets that are buried online. All the evidence that exists of alleged misdeeds. First he made his victims pay for his silence. He can rationalize that by looking at his actions as an offer of penance or redemption. But it no more than extortion."

"And killing them for continuing their misdeeds was murder," Ethan said grimly.

"Which he'll again justify. But despite shrouding his acts in faith, make no mistake, his actions are about *him*. His wants. His needs." She stopped, struck by a sudden thought.

"What?"

"You said you had been following the premise that the killer was someone who traveled widely. A sensible theory given the seeming randomness of the attacks, and the vast territory covered." She stopped a moment to collect her thoughts before going on. "Most serial killers don't kill out of state. Or, in Canada's case, outside their home province or territory. Most stay within their comfort zones. They like the familiar."

"So this UNSUB is atypical."

"In this particular instance, yes. They may gain confidence later on and venture farther away from home—" She broke off that thought as another occurred. "The first victim was from Ashville, Manitoba, right? The body was found near the Assiniboine River."

"You could give Merkel memory lessons," Ethan noted.

"When you get back to the Halifax RCMP headquarters you'll be running Tillman's name through the national crime database."

His mouth quirked up. "Will I?"

She waved a hand. "Just the quick check I did online shows fewer than ten people in the country with that name. The Tillman that stayed with Merkel shouldn't be that hard to trace. And I'd look for one who lived in Manitoba within easy driving distance of that river at the date of the first homicide or some time earlier."

"Because when he was first learning, he'd go to a place he knew?"

She nodded. "Someplace close to him. Subconsciously, he may have chosen his first victim based on his comfort zone. That's why it makes so much sense to me that he used the van as his—for lack of a better phrase—kill space. By using it, he's bringing a measure of that comfort zone with him, even when he's far from home." He'd still have to arrange the scene where he snatched his victims. Select the area for the dump sites. But he cut his risk by not leaving a primary crime scene. Alexa wondered if that was solely designed for his own ease or to avoid detection.

"So if he started near his own residence, what was his purpose for returning to one of his childhood homes? Why take a risk by choosing Merkel's name for an ID?"

She shook her head impatiently. "Don't you see? He's returning to another anchor point. He spent his formative years in Nova Scotia. The UNSUB knew he couldn't chance taking Simard in the man's home city. He had to lure him far away from Fornier, or other hired muscle. By including Lawler in the ruse, he got two of his victims to the same location using the same pretense. It was the likely the biggest challenge he's undertaken. It makes sense that he'd stack the deck in his favor by getting both of them out of their familiar surroundings while returning to a place known to him. He'd have weighed the safety of making a return. He probably knew Claire Merkel was dead. Maybe he's kept tabs on the couple. He had to have known there was little chance Pastor Merkel would remember him."

The man couldn't even be bothered to learn the names of the foster children under his care. It hadn't escaped Alexa that the pastor's habit of bestowing Biblical names on the boys was not unlike Reisman insisting on calling her by her middle name. She wondered if it had ever occurred to Merkel that he was robbing the kids of a piece of their identity.

"But he didn't count on Merkel's son. It sounds like you've already decided Tillman is our guy." Ethan reached up a finger to settle his sunglasses more securely.

"We'll know more in the next few hours." Because Alexa didn't doubt that once back at the RCMP in Halifax, they'd be learning everything there was to know about the Adam Tillman who'd lived with Pastor Merkel.

The pieces fit. They didn't know yet if the facts did. But one way or another, they were soon going to learn if they finally had the identity of the killer called The Tailor.

"Meat lovers and taco pizzas. The dinner of champions."

Alexa raised a weary gaze to view Ian coming through

the door to the conference room bearing two pizza boxes and a sack. "What is it with you guys and carbs?"

"We've also got protein covered," the officer said virtuously. "You could use more protein. And carbs. They both build muscle."

"Carbs also build fat."

"You know what lettuce builds? Nothing." He reached into the sack and brought out a clear plastic container and waved it at her. "But I got you a salad anyway."

Touched, she said, "Thank you." She half rose from her seat to snag it and the plastic silverware he handed her.

Ian gave her a concerned look as she opened the container. "Seriously. How are you planning to keep your strength up?"

"I am planning," Alexa said, as she stabbed her first bite of salad, "to eat all of this. And then grab a slice of pizza."

"That a girl," he said approvingly, before turning around and waving an arm to fight off Nyle and Jonah. "Let me set it down first. Geez, you're like a pack of dogs."

"I don't think two counts as a pack, but the description is still oddly fitting." Ethan walked into the room, looked amused.

"Just looking to help," Nyle said as he stole one of the boxes away from the other officer and strode quickly to the table at the front of the room. "His age slows him down."

"I can still run a six-minute mile, so unless you can beat that, no cracks about my age."

"Only if there's a beer waiting at the end of the run," Jonah joked.

As the men bickered good-naturedly, Ethan ambled over to where Alexa sat. He'd shed his suit jacket at some point, along with his tie. His jaw was stubbled, giving him a slightly rakish look.

Firmly corralling her observations, Alexa asked, "You spoke to Captain Campbell?"

He nodded. "Once we have the list of Tillmans narrowed down, we'll reach out to local law enforcement for a closer look. I also checked in with Steve Friedrich. He visited the gas stations where the UNSUB used the credit card. The camera images were a bust. Both places record over old images every week or two, just as we figured."

Alexa spoke in between bites. "We've found eight Amos Tillmans in the country. One, a man in his eighties, recently died. Two others are late sixties to early seventies. I think we can eliminate them, as well. Another is a teenager. So, we have four prospects."

"I've got a DMV request for each of those Tillmans." Jonah turned from the table, three huge slices of pizza piled on a paper plate that was crumpling under the weight. "Just waiting to get copies of the licenses back."

"This time of night, we might be waiting a while," Ian said around the pizza he was chewing.

"Better get up here and eat before these guys inhale both pies," Nyle advised Ethan.

Apparently viewing it as a real threat, Ethan moved toward the food.

Alexa continued to eat her salad methodically. It was nearly eight p.m. She wasn't sure how much longer the officers planned to work, but she was hoping they'd call it a day soon. She thought she had a fair amount of stamina, but the late hours they'd spent in recent days were starting to take a toll.

It was a sign of her exhaustion that she didn't immediately react when the tablet next to her pinged. A moment later, the significance hit her, and she froze, her fork halfway to her mouth.

Dropping the silverware, Alexa hurriedly logged into her professional email account. Her stomach twisted when she saw the familiar combination of numbers and symbols where the sender's name should be.

She opened the message and clicked on the image gif in the body. Then gasped quietly as the picture took shape. A single black and white photo of a flat headstone already showing the wear of years. An angel was etched around the date, with the text below it:

Olivia Rose Manning
Infant daughter of Ethan and Alexa Manning

ALEXA WAS aware of the sidelong glances Ethan was sending her way as he drove, but with Nyle in the back seat, he retained his silence. She channeled all her concentration toward locking down the emotion that was churning inside her until she was alone. Compartmentalizing her feelings. Her grief. Sealing them off so they couldn't rise up to swallow her whole.

She'd become an expert on all of that twenty years ago.

Nyle kept up a running commentary all the way back to the hotel. It helped to focus on his words. Consider them with a fierce intensity that didn't allow other thoughts to intrude. Certainly not dead babies. Not daughters who were fiercely loved even in the womb. Ones who never got to draw a breath outside it.

She drew in a strangled breath. Released it shakily.

"You okay?" Ethan murmured.

She nodded, beyond words. Like an injured animal, she

needed solitude to tend to her wounds, to gather her defenses and mend them layer by layer.

When Ethan pulled into the hotel parking lot, she gathered her briefcase which held her notes, laptop and tablet. "See you in the morning." She had her door opened and was exiting before Ethan had the vehicle in park.

"Well, she's sure in..." She didn't hear the rest of Nyle's statement. With single-minded focus, she headed for her room. For privacy.

And once inside it, once she'd locked the door with a shaky hand and set her briefcase on the floor, she leaned heavily against the door. Then slid down it when her knees would no longer hold her upright.

That *bastard*.

The tears that she'd been willing back sprang forth in a helpless, involuntary flood. She was usually stronger, but the image had blindsided her. The UNSUB was looking for a reaction. She knew that. He was expecting to catch her off-guard, vulnerable. God help her, at the moment, she was both.

Minutes ticked by before she was able to stem the tears through sheer force of will. The grief couldn't be controlled as easily. Her inner fortitude had been constructed brick by brick over the last two decades. It shielded her from reliving the paralyzing hurt. The brutal sense of loss that could still throb anew in moments when she least expected it.

It was the callousness of the message that had her steeling her spine. *I know you.* That's what the offender was telling her. *You have no secrets from me.* She wiped her eyes with the back of her hand and struggled to her feet. He was wrong, of course. He could learn a bit about her past, but she knew far more about him than he did her.

And she was going to use what she knew to bring him down.

She jerked when there was a quiet knock on her door. Knew who it would be.

"Alexa." Ethan's voice was quiet. "Are you okay?"

"I'm fine." And she would be. She just needed another minute or two alone. When she channeled the regrets from a lifetime ago into anger, she'd be stronger. Invulnerable.

"Open the door."

"Ethan." She breathed his name out in frustration. In defeat. She couldn't keep this latest communication from him even if she wanted to. It was part of the case. An intricately sticky piece of their past that now was entwined in the investigation. One that laid bare their shared regret that had lasted a lifetime.

She undid the latch and opened the door. Ethan's gaze swept her once, then returned to her face. His expression softened. "What's wrong?"

Alexa turned away from his concern. It would weaken her, return her to the quaking mass she'd been moments ago. She needed to maintain control, and that was tougher do facing the one man who'd know if she was dissembling.

"There's been another communication." She crouched to retrieve her briefcase and carried it to the desk, using the precious moments to summon the resilience she'd briefly surrendered.

"What? When? At the headquarters," he answered his own question. "Before we called it a night. I knew you were too quiet in the car."

"Yes. Well." She bent over the tablet and brought up the email again. Discovered she didn't yet have the fortitude to look at the image again. "He wanted a reaction. He's becoming more personal. Trying to show me that he's in control. That I have no secrets from him." And because she didn't want Ethan to be caught unaware as she'd been, she turned and laid her hand on his arm. "He knows about Olivia."

The muscles beneath her fingers bunched as he stared at the photo on the screen for long moments. Then he swore, a long ugly string of obscenities. "Fuck this guy."

He shrugged off her hand and shoved away from the table, turning to stride to the window. The curtains were still open. Lights glowed in the distance below, the city adorned in gaudy sparkles. "He doesn't know shit. How could he?"

She hadn't gotten that far yet but considered the question now. There was no way the offender could have accessed her long-ago medical records. He wouldn't know about her hospital stay or the condition that had caused the stillbirth. And since she hadn't spoken to her family since she'd left Truro, Reisman couldn't have revealed any details either.

A chill skated through her veins. Reisman may not have known facts, but that wouldn't have stopped him from gleefully filling in the gaps of his knowledge with the ugliest speculation imaginable.

"You're right. He had no way to learn the specifics." She remembered what Raiker had told her on their phone call. *You're a square peg, yes. But he's going to try to work you into the familiar round hole he has for his victims.* If the UNSUB believed he'd discovered a significant transgression in her past, the next step would be blackmail.

But she suspected it'd be emotional rather monetary extortion.

"What's he trying to do with this? Where would he even have gotten that image? There's no way he traveled to

Ottawa." Ethan hadn't turned away from the window. His tone was lethal. And Alexa was reminded, with a sudden searing dart of regret, that her pain was Ethan's pain. Her grief was his grief.

Her throat filled. It took a minute before she was able to answer. "The offender seeks weakness to exploit. I suspect he scrutinizes the news releases, so there's no way he's unfamiliar with your name. So, he's put two and two together, understands that we have a past." Reisman hadn't, she recalled. He'd never shown a shred of recognition at Ethan's name. At her urging, she and Ethan had gone to his father first, all those years ago. And although Ethan had wanted to do the right thing and go with her to tell her mother, Alexa had done it alone because she'd thought she'd known how bad it would be.

She'd grossly underestimated the ugliness of the scene. Her mother's cold condemnation. The invective Reisman had hurled at her. The eruption of violence when he'd lunged for her, hands at her throat.

The memory never lost the ability to wound.

Ethan's father had overridden his son's objections and gone to the house alone for her things. She'd thought her world had changed that day. But fate had far more in store for them a few months later.

"As for the image..." It took a moment to steady her voice. "Many cemeteries have a search function to facilitate remote access of gravesites."

"He isn't going to be in a position to 'exploit' anything." He faced her then, his expression implacable. But she recognized the temper he was suppressing. Like a bomb, waiting to detonate.

"He'll try. His focus is me, and I assume that won't change. He shook me up a little." She managed a small smile. "I'm all right now. We're close. I can feel it. And he doesn't know how much we've learned about him. The advantage is ours."

It took long minutes for him to respond. "I know I can't let this get to me. And it won't be allowed to affect the investigation." Fury seeped into his next words. "But I hate him using her like this. It defiles her memory."

She nodded. "I know." Her voice was soft. "It's as if he's stealing a piece of Olivia away, just by thinking of her." The next words were torn from her, accompanied by a familiar pang of loss. "I never even got to hold her."

He was in front of her in two quick steps. Had her wrapped in an embrace in the flash of an instant. "Neither did I. I wasn't even there. Not in time. I've never forgiven myself for that."

She shook her head against his chest. "You couldn't help that. Neither of us could." They'd been two scared kids trying to do their best to navigate their new responsibilities. Muddling through their quickie marriage, moving to married housing on the university campus where Ethan would play hockey. But for all their fears and ignorance of the enormity ahead of them, there had been aching sweetness, too. Out of self-preservation, Alexa rarely allowed herself to recall it. The lust that had still burned between them, hot and reckless. The first time they'd watched their baby on the ultrasound. The awed look on Ethan's face when he'd first heard the heartbeat. The way he'd kissed her, slow and achingly tender when he'd first felt the baby move.

"I always thought I did something wrong," she whispered. It was a shameful secret she'd never fully put aside. "Like I wasn't careful enough. Not knowledgeable enough."

"You read every book in the library on pregnancy. You

set the alarm so you'd remember to take your prenatal vitamins." His arms tightened around her. "But I know what you mean. I felt the same way. Like I should have been able to prevent what happened. But it wasn't us, Lexie. There was nothing we could have done differently. Sometimes life just sucks."

"I was no help afterward. All of the arrangements fell to you." He'd been an eighteen-year-old grappling with the sudden stillbirth of his daughter and a critically ill wife. She hadn't been aware of much of anything for days. There had been no chance to attend the funeral or the burial. No chance for a goodbye she wasn't ready to say.

"It was mostly a blur." She felt him rub his face in her hair. "Dad was there. He walked me through everything. But when I was at the funeral home I felt like I needed to be at the hospital with you. When I was with you, I was afraid..." Ethan paused for a moment. When he continued, his voice was thick. "I thought for a while that I was going to lose you, too."

Her breath hitched once. Because although she'd gradually gotten better, he *had* lost her months later. And every time regrets had reared over that decision, she'd beaten them back with the knowledge that she'd done the right thing.

But that certainty was becoming infused with doubt. He'd accused her once of playing God with his life. And hadn't she, in a way? Because they couldn't agree on the best way to move forward, she'd made a decision and forced him to live with it. And there was no way to know, even given the distance of time, whether the sacrifice had been necessary.

# CHAPTER NINETEEN

ETHAN LIFTED HIS HEAD. Cupped her face in both his hands. And the emotion on his face had her throat clogging. "I spent more time than I care to remember cursing you for leaving. But there was never a moment that I regretted meeting you."

Alexa's heart did a slow, lazy roll in her chest. "You'll never know how hard it was to force myself to walk away," she whispered. Decisions, made for all the right reasons, could still haunt for a lifetime.

His face lowered slowly to hers. She closed the distance between them and brushed her lips lightly over his. Once. Twice. And then settled her mouth more firmly and sank into the kiss.

The gesture began achingly tender. Filled with shared pain and memories. But when Alexa drew away, when her eyes slowly opened, what she saw in Ethan's pale blue gaze had her pulse stuttering.

Desire.

A smoky tendril of heat suffused her. The emotions she'd sought to wall off minutes earlier tumbled forth at the first taste of him. There was too much between them, and their proximity for the last few days had chipped away at the intervening years. The pain was still fresh. The chemistry still existed. And the desire was just as hot and heady as it'd been all that time ago.

Restraint had been too hard-learned to surrender it easily. But with Ethan's arms around her Alexa felt it slipping away even as their lips met again.

Ethan stroked a lazy path up her spine, and she shuddered in response. Now was the time to heed caution and step aside, before there were any more regrets between them. And she would, in a moment. Or perhaps two...

His head dipped, and his teeth closed over the cord in her neck, testing not quite painfully. Reason clouded. Neither of them had escaped unscathed from the hurt of their past. But this aspect of it...She dragged her lips along his jaw, felt the scrape of whiskers against her mouth and the sensation had her senses humming. She'd long thought there was something wrong with her...something permanently broken, because no other man had made her feel like this. Combustible and alive.

There was a flare in the pit of her belly, hot and immediate. He knew how to kiss a woman, hot and devastating. With a single-minded intensity that wiped her mind clean and had the rest of the world dimming. Inner fires flaring. She opened her mouth beneath his and dove into the flames.

His tongue glided along hers. His flavor was dark temptation, lethal to her senses. Her fingers danced up the front of his shirt, undoing buttons along the way until she could slide her hands inside the fabric to skate her fingers over his hard-muscled chest, her fingers flexing in pleasure.

He cupped the back of her head in one palm, but there

was nothing gentle about the gesture. His mouth devoured hers, their tongues tangling, breath mingling, teeth clashing. Swinging her around, he walked her backward until she felt the wall at her back and still he didn't lift his mouth from hers. Her muscles melted, hot wax to molten flame. His hunger summoned an answering recklessness.

He urged her legs apart with his knee then stepped between them. His arousal pressed against her belly and she squirmed against him, wanting to feel him where she was empty and aching. As if aware of her frustration, his hands went to her butt and he lifted her. With her legs wrapped around his hips, Alexa rocked against him, feeling his reaction even if she couldn't manage to drag her eyes open to watch it.

His lips lifted from hers for a moment, and immediately her system mourned the loss. She felt his hand in her hair, and her eyes fluttered open to see him drawing the pins from it one by one, dropping them to the floor. When he had the strands free, he threaded his fingers through them, his gaze slitted.

With sudden urgency, Alexa pushed the shirt over his shoulders, and he finally shifted enough to shrug out of the garment one arm at a time. Her head lolled against the wall as her fingers discovered the planes of his chest, the hollows along his ribs, the angles where bone met sinew.

He began unfastening her shirt, and her breath caught. Held. There was something exquisitely sensuous about focusing on touch alone. The languid slip of each button from its hole. The inch of exposed flesh bathed by Ethan's clever, wicked tongue. Her skin prickled in anticipation of his lips long seconds before it was tasted.

He took his time. Each button was released with deliberate care. Every inch of bared skin treated to the same sensual exploration. Alexa lost herself in the teasing journey she mapped along his biceps. Across his shoulders, her fingers flexing on the cut muscles of his delts, iron beneath her touch.

The rollicking in her pulse felt new. Heady. Every brush of his lips was a promise of pleasures to come. But it also fueled a quiet desperation in her system. She wanted to feel him, all of him. Flesh against flesh. Their bodies sealed so closely that not even a breath of air could fit between them. And she needed him quaking too. Wanted to unleash the primitive nature he'd learned to restrain. She wanted, quite frankly, to strip him of every defense, until there was no guard, no pretense between them.

To that end, she went on a quest to unharness his control. He released her fourth button then, and her breath caught as his tongue delved into her cleavage. Danced along the top of her bra where flesh met lace. It took all the strength she could muster to concentrate on finding the places that made him shudder. The soft velvety skin beneath his arms. A fingernail scraping over one male nipple.

And the feel of his touch faltering, the hiss of his indrawn breath, was its own reward.

She brushed her fingers along his spine, feeling the flesh punctuated by vertebrae. Her fingers faltered when they discovered a knotted ridge of skin below one shoulder blade. It was a reminder of all that had transpired since she'd last seen him. Their romance had lasted less than two years. Their separation, two decades. How, then, could the passion ignite this quickly? This immediately?

His muscles quivered beneath her touch like an impatient stallion, and his hands hurried a bit as he pulled her blouse up to undo the bottom buttons. With one practiced movement, he released the front clasp of her bra, and, with the air of a man contemplating a feast, spread the fabric aside.

Her nipples were tight knots awaiting his touch. And when it didn't immediately come, Alexa dragged her eyelids open, a demand on her lips.

It went unuttered. Ethan was staring at her with a searing intensity. It lingered on her face. Her breasts. The look was a little possessive. Slightly cruel. A man surveying a woman he meant to take at his leisure. She knew intuitively he'd pleasure and take pleasure in return and that certainty sent comets of heat through her veins.

Eyes locked with his, she arched her back, a carnal invitation. Alexa watched the color slash across his cheekbones. The glint in his eyes and his shadowed jaw gave him a sinister cast that was more exciting than frightening.

His jaw clenched, and she sensed that he was battling the urge to rush to fulfillment, an urge she wouldn't protest. Alexa saw the moment he won the struggle, noted the slight curve of his lips as he reached out a finger to brush it lightly over her nipple.

Alexa slipped a hand behind his neck. Obeying her unspoken command, he sucked strongly from her. The slight scrape of teeth against her skin had hunger leaping forth like an uncaged tiger. Her fingers twisted in his hair, urging him to take more.

Her childhood had built a wariness in her, a guard beyond her years. She'd spent decades turning her defenses into a fortress. But Ethan had always been able to dismantle it with an ease that was alarming. He could make her feel things no one else could. Still frightening. Terrifying even. But also rewarding. Because her physical response to him was just as keen.

He lifted his mouth, and the cooler air tightened her nipple almost painfully. She met his lips with her own, an edged blade of desperation slicing through her. She felt alive in his arms. Achingly alive. And the heat careening through her veins chased away the chill that solitude could bring. There was danger here. Alexa wasn't too far gone to be aware of it. Their shared history was fraught with heartbreak and complications. But it faded in the face of the sensation that heightened unbearably everywhere they touched. Every pulse point was razor-edged.

When he swung her into his arms, she opened her eyes dazedly, her wits completely dulled by the passion-induced fog. Ethan moved to the door, flicked off the light and then turned to cross to the bed. He laid her on the mattress and followed her down quickly as if to stem a protest. He wasn't going to get one.

Alexa trailed the nail of her index finger over his shoulder and down his defined bicep over to his pec to trace a teasing circle around one flat nipple. His eyes narrowed in response and a small smile curled her lips. She leaned forward to nip his collarbone as he swiftly stripped off her clothes. Pressing her down on the bed, his arms framed her body, his mouth demanding on hers. The room was draped in shadows except for the jeweled glow from the city lights through the window. They spilled a soft rainbow of color over the bed, a contrast to the shroud of shadows enveloping them.

She savored the tactile onslaught. The stroking of Ethan's heated palms over her skin, hot and demanding on her curves. He trailed a finger up her leg, circling teasingly around the heat centered between her thighs and leaned in for a kiss. Deep. Wet. Rawly carnal. He sent his tongue in search of hers at the same time he parted her slick folds and entered her with one exploring finger.

Her hips arched, twisting beneath him at the dual assault. Her blood was churning in her veins, frothing and crashing like whitewater. There was primitive demand in his kiss. In his touch. It was a demand she reciprocated.

Alexa's hands streaked over his body, tempting, teasing; reveling in the feel of sleek skin covering unyielding muscle. He moved his leg over one of hers as if to hold her in place and she was reminded that he was still half-dressed.

The realization had her eyelids fluttering open. There was something intimately vulnerable lying naked beneath a man who was still partially clothed. Her fingers trailed along the flesh above his waistline; she felt his stomach quiver beneath her touch and smiled, slow and knowing. It was heady to realize he was as susceptible to the barrage of sensation as she was.

He pressed against her clit with his thumb, rubbing rhythmically even as he continued exploring her with his finger. Her vision grayed, sensation arrowing to the pit of her belly. It took effort to gather her scattered senses and work his zipper down, with more than a hint of desperation.

His touch grew urgent. He lowered his head, took a beaded nipple between his teeth and worried it gently. But there was nothing gentle about her response. Her back arched off the mattress in an involuntary reaction.

She felt him smile against her breast and the gesture of male satisfaction steeled her resolve. Pushing his fly open, she freed him from his boxer briefs and took him in her hand, squeezing firmly. His body jerked against her. She had time for one heated glide down the length of him and up again before he lifted his head from her breast and caught her hand with his free one, even as his knowing dancing fingers continued exploring her.

"You...don't...play fair," she gasped. Her muscles tightened as she struggled against giving into the vortex of desire that threatened to draw her toward the inevitable finish.

"Baby..." His kiss was possessive. Primitive. "I'm not playing."

She couldn't summon a response. Sensation slammed against sensation. There was an urgency in his touch. An unvarnished command. And while she could fight the sensual onslaught, the conclusion wouldn't be denied.

He was saying something else, his voice a ragged whisper. but the sound slipped away, as evasive as wisps of fog. Nerve endings formed in a tight waiting ball of urgency. Her control grew tenuous.

And then it snapped, eliciting a cry from her lips as she shattered, falling headlong into a pleasure too long denied.

Her breath panting and uneven, she was aware of his movements on the bed beside her, swift and jerky. She heard a slight sound, realizing he was donning protection, and the realization had reason returning.

But then he was beside her again, the feel of his smooth naked flesh a sensation she couldn't resist. And the longing, recently satisfied, began to climb again.

She leaned over him, intent on exploring his body with her lips one inch at a time. But now he was the eager one. His muscles shuddering with tension, he urged her astride him, his eyes glittering with passion.

Alexa rose above him, and hesitated for a moment, her senses filled with him. There was a sheen of perspiration on his forehead. The skin was drawn tightly across his cheekbones. And the signs of his desire reignited her own. She guided him inside her and the tether on his restraint snapped.

He clutched her hips in hard desperate fingers as he urged her to a faster pace. She braced her hands on his shoulders and met every upward lunge, her movements as urgent as his.

Her blood began to pulse again, scorching rivers under her skin. Need coiled in her belly.

The rhythm quickened. Breath shortened. The climax shook her first, startling in its intensity. Her release triggered his own, and he gave one last violent thrust upward before coming, his fingers hard on her hips. And a sound that might have been her name on his lips.

THE LIGHTS outside the window were keeping Ethan awake. He should get out of bed. Shut the blinds.

But once he was up, he'd have no reason not to keep moving. To grab his clothes. Go back to his room. The idea was curiously unappealing. So, in the end, he did none of those things.

He stroked Alexa's hip, one arm looped around her to keep her close. The position felt foreign. He hadn't slept—actually slept—with a woman since his last marriage. Keeping things casual meant no obligation to spend the night, no awkward morning-afters. He'd gotten used to his own space.

Which didn't explain why he was reluctant to move away from Alexa now.

There would be time enough in the morning to examine the sneaky little doubts that were circling. The ones that said he'd screwed up big time in a big way tonight. But on the heels of that thought came another; he and Alexa were adults, far removed from the two reckless kids they'd been a lifetime ago. They'd both remarried. Had fulfilling careers. And they were both experienced enough to know that great sex didn't have to come with strings.

But that thought was oddly disturbing, so he pushed it away. Instead, he thought of every snippet she'd revealed about her past since joining the team. And it was far more, he was coming to realize, than he'd known even while they'd been married.

There'd been hints of course. The "homeschooling" that required her to educate herself alone in the library. The fact that she'd never let him drop her off in front of her house. That she'd purposefully preempted his intention to accompany her to tell her mother about the pregnancy.

She startled a little in her sleep, and he stroked her delicate spine until her muscles went lax again.

After meeting Reisman for the first time recently, Ethan realized that Alexa's last meeting with her mother had been far worse than she'd ever let on. Somehow, everything was clearer with the distance of time. How a life of solitude and abuse had caused the wariness in her eyes, the guard so at odds with her gut-wrenching beauty. It explained why she'd been slow to smile. Slower to trust. At the time, instead of wondering what had caused her defenses, he'd been focused on slipping beneath them. Each smile he'd teased from her had felt like a reward. Each kiss an unexpected gift.

She'd told him she was leaving him so he could have the life that would have been his before the pregnancy. What he'd never been able to make her understand then was that everything had irrevocably changed once she'd walked into his life. And again, when she'd walked out of it.

It didn't matter. Not anymore. If all they had were a few

stolen moments before they parted again, Ethan wasn't going to deny himself that.

This time would be different. When this case was over, they'd walk away without regrets. He tucked Alexa closer to his side and shut his eyes. And struggled to silence the apprehension that lingered.

ALEXA STILL WOKE UP SLOWLY. There was tossing and turning involved. At one point, she buried her head in the pillow. The early morning sun streaming into the room had awakened Ethan and would eventually—despite her best efforts—wake her, too.

She flopped onto her back, one arm folded over her eyes. Moments later, she lowered it, a frown marring her beautiful brow. And finally, after several minutes, her eyelids fluttered open.

He smiled, charmed. "Good morning." Ethan watched the emotions flash across her face. Shock. Confusion. Realization. Embarrassment. Followed by a languid smile that had his blood heating again.

"Ah...hello." She struggled to sit up in bed, making a desperate grab for the sheet when it slipped below her breasts and pulled it higher. "What time is it?"

"Early." He rolled to one elbow while surreptitiously tugging at the sheet she held. "Should have closed the blinds last night."

She lifted a hand to push her hair back over her shoulder, her gaze going to the window. "That would have helped." She gave another pull at the sheet. He tugged it down another couple of inches, enough to bare one nipple.

Alexa gave a wild grab for the bedcover and found it caught securely by him.

"Then again," he mused, reaching out a finger to tease her breast, "there's something to be said for daylight." He rolled over her, propping his weight on his elbows and kissed her, long and lingeringly.

"Ethan..." she started.

There was a primitive thrill at the sound of his name on her lips, her skin naked against his. And he was beginning to be grateful the dawn light had woken them early. Alexa's arms slowly twined around his neck, one hand going to his jaw while she opened her mouth beneath his.

In the next moment, he stilled, listening. Then mentally cursed when he recognized the small sound that had interrupted them. "My cell."

He moved away unwillingly and rolled off the bed, going in search of his pants. Drew the phone out of the pocket, he answered. "Yeah."

There was a momentary pause and then, "Ethan?" His eyes slid shut for a moment. Jonah Bannon. The jolt back to reality was jarring.

"What's up?"

"I stopped by your room and knocked, but there was no answer."

Because he hadn't been *in* his room. Ethan cut his gaze to Alexa. She was sitting against the pillows, the sheet neatly in place around her now that he wasn't there to devil her. "I'm out for a run." The expression Alexa made at his excuse had him grinning. "DMV send copies of the Tillman licenses yet?"

"Yeah. And you're going to want to see this."

Adrenaline zinged up his spine. "I'll be at your room in a few." He disconnected.

"One of the driver's license photos matched?"

"We'll soon see." Ethan sat on the edge of the bed, reaching for his clothes. He'd have to take a few minutes to shower and change, and he counseled himself to patience. They'd thought they'd been close before, only to have their suspects cleared. His gaze went to Alexa who had apparently forgotten her need for modesty and was swiftly striding, gloriously nude, to the bathroom. He took a moment to enjoy the view as he finished dressing, all the while damning Ian's timing.

The case came first. It was telling that he even had to remind himself of that. But that didn't mean he couldn't feel a lingering sense of regret when he opened the door to her room and closed it softly behind him.

"Far more similarities to Patrick's forensic sketch than Fornier's." Alexa surveyed the copy of the license photo critically, excitement radiating through her veins. "Take away the gray hair and mustache—and the attempt in the fake ID to make his skin look more weathered—and that's this guy."

"No mistake about it," Ethan agreed. They were all huddled around the desk in Bannon's bedroom. "And look at the address listed." He sent Alexa a meaningful look. "Brandon, Manitoba. It's a couple of hours away from the Assiniboine River."

The satisfaction filling her had less to do with her correct assumption and much more with the knowledge they were closing in on the offender. He couldn't know they had descriptions of his vehicles. Or that they knew his name. Where he lived. Those facts were weapons they'd use to track him down. And after the image he'd ambushed her with yesterday, Alexa allowed herself a moment to enjoy their advantage. "What's next?"

"We went to the online local property records and punched in his name," Ethan answered. "He's a property owner. Thanks to Google Earth, we have a picture of his home, although we can be fairly sure he isn't there now."

"Did you find anything online about his marital status?" It wouldn't be unusual for a serial offender like Tillman to have a wife and family who were completely unaware of his activities. But Alexa didn't think that was the case here. He might be divorced or had a failed relationship in his past, but she was betting he was a loner.

"I've got a call in to the Brandon RCMP detachment and the local police department. They can get us all available details about the man and then," there was a glint in Ethan's eyes as he looked at all of them, "once we have a warrant, we're mounting a raid on Amos Tillman's base of operations."

"Bet Friedrich is pissed to be missing this." There wasn't an ounce of sympathy in Jonah's words.

"He's on a plane. He'll be here soon." Ethan gave the equipment in the Halifax RCMP interview room one final adjustment before stepping away, sliding another impatient look at the clock.

"That's good." Ian was bent over his laptop. "He deserves to be here when we take this bastard down."

They were a long way from that point, Alexa thought. She had to keep reminding herself of that fact to keep her excitement in check. But they were far closer than the team had ever gotten before. The opportunity to stop the notorious killer before he struck again seemed within reach.

"Information I've gotten so far is that Tillman is single." Ethan prowled the room as if unable to stay still. "Neighbors don't know much about him. His property is twenty acres, and the nearest neighbor is five miles away."

"The remoteness of the house would have been a draw for him," Alexa added. Tillman had been isolated throughout his childhood in one fashion or another. First with corporal punishment by his father and then by becoming a nameless, faceless child in the merry-go-round of the child welfare system. Overlooked and underestimated. That was part of the profile she'd written from the beginning. But he'd gained the power he'd lacked as a child with his technical prowess. The finder of secrets. The exacter of punishment.

"Finally," Ethan muttered as the screen came to life. The Manitoba ERT command center and team members were parked down the road from Tillman's home, out of sight. "The members are equipped with weapon lights and helmets with cameras and night vision monoculars attached," he told Alexa. "They probably have an infrared lens over their lights so they can be seen only by someone with a night vision capable device."

"Or an infrared-capable camera feed," Ian added, without taking his eyes off the screen. It was divided into five sections, one for each of the cameras' images. The tactical unit moved carefully up the rutted, tree-draped drive for a quarter mile until a clearing appeared. A small white farmhouse was situated on it with an adjacent garage, flanked by another small structure on the other side of it. The old-fashioned wooden swinging doors on the garage would have to be manually opened.

The members of the team halted while they were still under cover of trees. "Change of entry strategy." A quiet voice narrated the scene. "There's a bar placed over the outside of the garage doors. We'll try that way first."

Alexa frowned. As far as security went, locking the structure from the outside made no sense. Unconsciously, she leaned forward on her chair, holding her breath as the team crept up to the garage doors. Lifted away the bar. But when they tried one of the doors, it held fast. Comprehension dawned. The doors were also secured on the inside.

One member used the breaching device on the right door, and after a couple of attempts, it swung open. Two men entered first, weapons ready, followed by the remaining three.

There was nothing of interest in the interior. One man tried the doors on the metal cupboards lining one wall. They were locked. Another member opened what looked like freezer tucked into a corner of the space. An officer splintered off to the right, approaching a single door that would lead to the shed. "Touchpad entry here." His voice sounded on the live feed.

One of the team members picked up the breaching device and used it on the shed door. The entrance held up better than Merkel's had. It took three tries to knock it down.

No one in the conference room seemed to be breathing. Their attention was glued to the scene unfolding in front of them onscreen. Half the team entered through the battered entrance. Flashlights attached to the men's helmets pierced the shadowy interior. The only light inside it came from the center of the space. The men spread across the area, and Alexa's breath caught. "Oh my God."

The screened-in pen took up most of the room in the

area. A strobe of brilliant blue and violet fluttered inside it, a perpetual flash of motion. The scene grew clearer as one of the men approached the enclosure. It was filled with dragonflies.

"He breeds them himself," she murmured. At some point, he had to have come by a pair illegally, but he hadn't left his supply to chance. "How does he care for them while he's gone?" The eggs were probably laid in the child's wading pool in the center of the pen. But the adult insects wouldn't live long without a constant source of food.

"Stand up! Arms over your head! Up! Up! Now!"

Her attention snapped to the screen. The other men raced to join the one who'd barked the order. "It can't be Tillman," Ian muttered. "No way that bastard got out of the province undetected."

"It's a kid," Nyle said wonderingly.

A flashlight pinned a boy against the wall of the building, his slight figure trembling as he squinted against the beam. His hair was ragged as if someone had chopped it off with a knife. His clothes were too small.

"Are you aliens?"

The men lowered their weapons as one. "Son, what are you doing in here?"

"Anis Tera makes me live here. He'll kill us if he finds out you broke his door." His shoulders shook as he started to cry. "I think he's killed people before."

"THE BOY IS TRAUMATIZED, as you can imagine." Ethan had an officer from Brandon's RCMP detachment on speakerphone. "He isn't answering questions at this point. He seems convinced that the man he calls Anis Tera is coming back and will kill him."

A spike of anger ignited in Ethan's chest. Tillman's abuse as a child hadn't kept him from perpetuating the cycle. There didn't seem to be any line the offender wouldn't cross when it came to gratifying his own needs.

"The ERT team found a cell phone in the shed," he told the officer tersely. "One of those old Firefly phones they used to make for kids so the parents could program it to receive and call out only one number. There's no redial function or call history. One of the buttons needed to make an emergency call was disabled. We suspect Tillman used it to keep tabs on the boy, and we need that phone number."

"A warrant..."

"Is in the works. But it will take hours to get the records of incoming calls, and maybe the boy can help. He might have used the cell at some point to call Tillman. We want to ask him a few questions."

"I don't know...the boys' parents are here. I think they're ready to take him home until an official interview can take place."

"We have Dr. Alexa Hayden on our task force, and I think she's the one person who could coax the boy to answer a few questions without further traumatizing him. Run that by the parents." Ethan held while the officer conveyed his request.

"You realize the parents are going to believe I'm a child psychologist." It was clear that Alexa wasn't comfortable with the deception.

"That's what I'm counting on." He was undeterred by her frown. "With your background, you'll know exactly how to speak to him. And he's the quickest avenue to the information we need."

She looked unconvinced, but she subsided. Ethan couldn't stem his feeling of urgency. If the parents agreed, the boy was unlikely to be harmed by answering a few questions. And if he had the information Ethan sought, it would save them hours of waiting for the cell company to come through with records.

When they were this close to capturing Tillman, they needed to take every advantage they could.

"The parents agreed to a *short* interview." The officer had come back on the speakerphone. "I'll set up a video chat if you give me your information."

As Ethan supplied the call details, Alexa pulled the pins from her hair and speared her fingers through the strands to loosen them around her shoulders. His throat dried when he recalled taking the same action himself last night. Logically, he knew she was preparing to face the boy. With her hair loose, she'd look younger. More approachable.

But there was no denying the instant bolt of lust that twisted through him at the sight. It was a byproduct of last night. He knew that. The control he'd maintained since she'd walked into the airport wasn't nearly as easy to regain after it'd been unchained.

He noted Nyle's eyes on Alexa and his slack-jawed reaction. "Roll your tongue back into your mouth," he muttered in an aside to the man. And he refused to label his irritation as possessiveness.

The officer shot him a look. Grinned. "I'm married, not dead."

Ethan's laptop rang. He crossed to where he'd left it on the table and waited for Alexa to join him. She sat down in front of it as he accepted the call. Bannon hadn't returned from getting the warrant signed, but Nyle and McManus drew closer so they could hear the conversation while staying out of the picture.

The boy was older than he'd first appeared. Nine, maybe. And Ethan could see how pale and thin he was. Malnourished, likely. One fist clenched by his side. One more charge to bring against Tillman.

An RCMP officer in the background made the introductions. "Logan Sherwood and his parents, Marcia and Trey Sherwood."

The boy was sitting in between his parents, who both had their arms around him as if they could shield him from future harm. His face was half turned into his dad's shoulder. Ethan's anticipation chilled a bit. The kid didn't look any too cooperative.

"Hi, Logan." Alexa's voice was easy. "My name is Alexa. I'm so glad to be able to talk to you. I've never met a real-life hero before."

The boy shifted his face so both eyes were visible, but made no response.

"You know what a hero is, Logan?" she continued, propping her chin on one fist. "It's someone who's really scared, but they're still brave. I think you've been very brave for a long time, haven't you?"

Logan's expression was uncertain. "I was scared."

Alexa's eyes widened. "Of course you were. Any of us would have been. But you stayed strong and smart and waited for someone to come help. That's what heroes do."

He inched away from his father. "I had to learn things," he said in a near whisper. "I had to learn what he wanted me to know or else he'd hurt me."

Because he was watching so closely, Ethan caught the slight wince in Alexa's eyes, but her voice was steady. "He's a bad man, Logan. He's never going to hurt you again."

Sounding unconvinced, he asked, "Is he ever coming back here?"

She leaned toward the screen, lowering her voice conspiratorially. "Can I tell you a secret?" She waited for his slow nod before continuing. "The RCMP team here is very close to catching him. He won't be getting back there ever again."

The boy said nothing but straightened in his chair. Ethan suppressed a surge of pride. Alexa could establish a rapport with anyone.

"Can you tell me about some of the things you had to learn?"

"Mostly stuff about the insects he kept. The dragonflies, especially. I had to know how to feed them and keep the right temperature during the winter." His voice grew a bit more animated. "I had to learn the real name for them. Anisoptera."

"That's a big word, isn't it? I'll bet you took care of things when the man was gone. Did he ever call and check on you when he was away?"

Logan nodded, but the question drained the bit of animation from his face. "He'd call and see if everything was all right with the dragonflies."

"I'll bet you took good care of them. Did you ever have problems while he was away? Any reason to call him?"

"I never wanted to talk to him. But a few days ago, I ran out of food. I had to call and ask him what I could eat."

Ethan clenched his jaw to keep from cursing. Logan's mother looked like she was on the verge of tears as she tenderly pushed the hair back from the boy's face.

"See," Alexa said encouragingly. "That's another way you were smart. You had to remember that telephone number, didn't you?"

He nodded. "And he gave me the code to open the door into the garage so I could get food from the freezer. I remembered that, too."

"Can you tell me what the phone number was?"

The boy rattled it off, and Ethan scribbled it in a notebook he'd taken from his suit jacket, a feeling of triumph filling him. The ERT team had reported an extensive computer layout in the man's home. Hopefully, Tillman's love of technology extended to cell phones. With the most recent ones, a cell phone ping resulted in an exact location.

"Thank you for talking with me, Logan." Alexa smiled at the boy. "I'll bet you can't wait to get back to your house with your mom and dad."

"And my dog, Dexter," he added. "Mom and Dad say he's really missed me."

"He's going to be pretty excited to see you."

He was quiet for a moment, and his expression screwed up again, as if he were about to cry. "Alexa? Are you afraid of scary movies?"

# CHAPTER TWENTY

"KEVIN DELACORTE." Ethan's jaw was clenched. "The Tailor's first victim." He handed his cell to Ian. The man gave a slow nod of recognition. He'd been one of the original officers on the first task force formed to hunt for the UNSUB.

After Logan's bombshell about the DVD he'd found, Ethan had contacted the forensic ident team he'd dispatched to Tillman's and spoken to the lead investigator. She'd found the DVD exactly where the boy described, played it and took a few videos to send to Ethan.

After the first minute, Alexa turned away. "So much for his claim of a mission sanctioned by God," she muttered. Not all serial killers took souvenirs, but that's what the videos were. A way for Tillman to reenact the moments when he exercised the ultimate control over his victims.

"There'll be a stash of these somewhere in the house." Jonah crowded Ian's shoulder as he strained to look at the video.

"The forensic ident unit will find them." The lead on the team had been texting Ethan every few minutes to update him about what they were uncovering in Tillman's house. "They've gone through the cabinets in the garage. Looks like a lot of the things he needed for his kill supplies. A pile of folded clear plastic bags. Several rolls of duct tape. Syringes. Needles. Thread. Handcuffs. Several small saps." At Alexa's frown, he explained, "Short clubs." He used his hands to indicate the length. "Easy to conceal up a sleeve or in a deep pocket."

"Likely his weapon of choice for incapacitating his victims when he came up behind them," she said grimly.

"Is the Scopolamine supply in there?"

"Not there." Ethan took a moment to watch the next video. "Investigators found several high dosage vials in the bathroom inside the house, though."

Nyle came in, waving a sheet of paper. "Production order in hand, boys and girl. I faxed a copy to the provider as soon as I got this signed. They'll call Ethan with a response."

"Exigent circumstances should speed things up," Jonah noted.

"That and the fact that Captain Campbell at federal RCMP headquarters called the provider as soon as I alerted him that we had the number." Ethan's cell rang, interrupting him.

Ian handed it to him, and he stepped away to answer it. A minute later, his gaze met Alexa's. "I'm not sure. I'll have to get back to you."

The expression on his face had Alexa's stomach plummeting. "What's wrong?"

"That was the Truro RCMP detachment. Patrick Udall's parents just reported him missing. Police want to know if we think it could have anything to do with the UNSUB."

There was a twist of nausea in her stomach. "Did anyone witness an abduction?" When Ethan shook his head, she said, "The boy seems to run the town pretty freely. It's possible he's off on some adventure. But...we know now that Tillman isn't above using children for his own objectives, don't we? I think we have to face the fact that the boy could be in real danger."

"I think it's too soon to make assumptions," Ian said. Jonah nodded in agreement.

Nyle looked thoughtful. "Is there any way Tillman could have learned about the raid on his house?"

"The forensic ident unit hasn't found any recording or security devices in his home that may have alerted him," Ethan responded. But he seemed to give the suggestion consideration. "ERT described the property as secluded. Local police said Tillman was a loner, but it's not out of the realm of possibility that someone saw the ERT command vehicle parked nearby and concluded it was there for Tillman's property. Alexa?"

"That would mean Tillman trusted someone in Brandon with his phone number." It just didn't ring true for this offender. "I think we have to consider all feasibilities, but it's doubtful."

Nyle hitched a hip on the corner of a table and folded his arms across his chest. "Just mentioned it because it seems like if he knew we were closing in on him, he might snatch the kid to have some leverage."

"*If* Tillman is behind Patrick's disappearance," Alexa said slowly, "Leverage would describe his motivation perfectly." But she wasn't so sure the man would be seeking a way out of the province. He'd spent a lot of energy researching her past and letting her know what he'd learned.

Alexa knew better than to mention it in front of Ethan. But she was unable to shake the certainty that Amos Tillman wasn't done with her yet.

Forty minutes later Ethan lowered his phone and lurched from his chair. "We've got a cell phone location."

His words immediately activated everyone in the room.

"Where?" Jonah grabbed the suit coat he'd abandoned and shrugged into as he moved toward the door.

"Between Bedford Street and Saxony Boulevard. Just outside the city limits of Dartmouth." Ethan waited for Alexa to gather her things and join him before leaving the room. "I've been having the provider ping the offender's phone every ten minutes. First three times there was no response, which means the phone was dead or turned off. But a few moments ago, we got a hit." They walked down the hallway toward the entrance. "Probably using a fairly new phone because we're able to zero in on his location."

"Is this really it?" Alexa murmured at his side.

He looked down at her, a hard smile on his face. He knew what she was asking. After all this time of getting close, this time they had Tillman dead to rights. He tried to temper his optimism as he pushed out of the door of the building. Things had a way of going south just when he thought he had the UNSUB in his sights.

"Let's hope so."

"Well, this place has seen better days," Alexa murmured.

Ethan had to agree. The motel's vacancy sign was missing two of its neon letters, and one of the panes in the window of the door to the office was missing and patched with cardboard. The property had four sections. The front horizontal strip held the office, with three rooms on each side of it. Two vertical sections sat to the right and left behind this one, with another between them that ran parallel to the front.

From the image the phone company had sent, Ethan could tell exactly where the UNSUB's room was located. There were parking places in front of it. None held a vehicle that matched the description of Tillman's van or rental. He took a slow swing through the rest of the parking lot while Nyle parked near the room at the far edge of Tillman's section. The three officers got out, walked around the back of the units and disappeared.

Scanning the rest of the lot, Alexa said disappointedly, "He's not here."

There wasn't a van or Camry in sight. A ball of disappointment lodged in his chest, but Ethan said, "His phone was here a half hour ago. He might have hidden the vehicles somewhere and taken a cab. Or left the car in a lot nearby and walked."

"There were no lots nearby," she reminded him, frustration tinging her words.

True enough. The motel was at least a mile from the last establishment they'd passed, a tavern that hadn't had more than three cars in the parking lot.

His cell signaled an incoming text. He swung the vehicle back toward the office and stopped to read the message from Nyle. Sent a response.

"The men will take up position near Tillman's room, remaining out of sight," he explained to Alexa. "We'll see if we can get any details from the manager."

They got out and walked up the two sagging steps toward the office.

Ethan pushed the weathered door open and walked

inside. The floor sloped beneath his feet. He'd hate to see what lay beneath the ratty green carpet.

The man behind the desk looked as rundown at the structure. Deep grooves were etched into his face and the long hair clubbed back in a ponytail was white. He started to smile, showing yellowed teeth until he got a better look at Ethan. Made him as law enforcement. "Don't want no trouble."

"Not looking to give you any," Ethan said evenly as he showed his credentials. "Just need to know if you've seen this man." He showed him a copy of Tillman's driver license photo. The clerk barely looked at it before shrugging.

"Don't believe I have."

"Look again." A note of command entered his voice. "Because we just pinpointed the man's phone to this motel. I have a pretty good idea where the room is situated."

"You need a warrant to get a look at it," the clerk said flatly. He picked up a pen and returned to the crossword puzzle he'd been working.

"And I can get one. But that's not necessary. I already know he's here." At least he'd been when they'd left RCMP headquarters. The cell phone provider had pinged the phone twice more on the way over, to no avail. It was shut off again. "But if I wanted to save time, I could just get a couple of patrol cars over here. Have them start running the plates of the cars in the lot."

The man's expression flickered.

Ethan looked at Alexa. "If we start pounding on all the doors, we're probably going to observe some illicit activity going on. I'd be obliged to act on that information."

"Maybe you should get three or four patrol cars," Alexa suggested. She smiled brightly at the clerk. "Although that could put a scare into your guests. They might not like the police presence. I suppose some of them might be anxious to leave and find a place with more privacy."

"Why you have to be like that?" the older man complained. He snatched the photo from Ethan and brought it closer. Then set it on the counter. "Yeah, he was here. Checked out fifteen minutes ago. Room sixty-one. You just missed him."

"THERE'S A DRIVE OUT BACK," Nyle said as the clerk opened the door to the room. The older man had decided that having Ethan and the officers camped out in the parking lot while waiting for a warrant to come through was a far bigger disadvantage than just letting them take a look at the now-vacant room. "In disrepair, but he could have parked there, keeping the vehicle out of sight."

It was a moot point now. Ethan resisted the urge to send his fist into the crumbling plaster wall. They were destined to creep closer and closer to the man, while each time he wiggled out of reach at the last possible moment.

The five of them filled the small space. There was one sagging unmade double bed. A nightstand with a leg broken on it. An old TV bolted to the wall above a small scarred chest of drawers.

"How long was he here?" Jonah asked disgustedly.

"Told that one." The clerk jerked a thumb at Ethan. "Records say he's been here nine days."

"You don't watch TV? There were sketches of this guy on the news."

"I like to watch sports." The older man jutted out his chin mulishly.

"Ethan."

Alexa's quiet voice had his attention jerking to her. She pointed. There, under the bed, was a bright blue object. He took a couple of steps closer and crouched down. Gingerly lifted the stained coverlet aside where it was dragging on the floor. Recognition punched into him. He reached out for the object. Held it up. It was a Toronto Blue Jays cap.

Just like the one Patrick Udall had worn when they'd spoken to him in Truro.

$\sim$

"The thinking now is that the kid might have been snatched early yesterday evening." Nyle wiped a hand over his face as he walked through the door into the conference room. Jonah and Ian looked weary as they trailed behind him. "Hey, Steve. When did you get in?"

Steve Friedrich waved a hand in response. "About three. Could have walked faster. Nothing but holdups. You talking about the missing boy in Truro?"

Ian took up the thread. "Yeah. Just left there after interviewing the family. Patrick called home yesterday evening and talked to one of his brothers. Said he was spending the night with a friend and then hung up. That's a violation of household rules, apparently. He didn't speak to his parents. My guess is Tillman had him then and forced him to make the call. Slowed down the police response significantly."

"He could have taken the kid out of the motel room in broad daylight today," Nyle said, slumping into a chair. "It had a rear-facing window. If the car was back there, put the kid in the trunk, and no one sees a thing."

Ethan speared a hand through his hair. "Why?" He directed the question to Alexa. "What does he gain with this? What's he planning?"

"Without consulting my crystal ball, I'd guess we're going to learn very soon. He needs the boy for whatever comes next." And it was all too easy for her to imagine the terror Patrick was going through right now, especially after talking to Logan Sherwood earlier today.

"If it's a trade he wants, there's no way."

Alexa met Ethan's gaze, recognized the adamant look there. "He's escalating," she said quietly. She'd spent the hours while the officers were in Truro going through all the information she'd compiled about Tillman's patterns. And this one was fairly clear. "Just like the trigger that provoked the four recent murders in a short period, he's taking bigger risks. Re-exerting the control he lost when he was injured at Simard's direction three years ago. He's redoubling his efforts after being disappointed at the vigil." His disappointment had stemmed from discovering she wasn't there. There was no question that Alexa figured into Tillman's plans, but she wasn't going to voice that thought aloud.

Alexa wondered now if she'd underestimated just how seriously the vigil scene had affected him. Tillman couldn't believe that Ethan would allow her to be traded for Patrick.

So, he had something else in mind. And whatever it was, it'd be far more dangerous for the boy than a simple trade.

ALEXA OPENED HER EYES, disoriented. It took a moment for comprehension to filter in, snippets at a time. Darkness. She blinked a few times. Recalled she was in bed. In her room. Alone.

There was a flash of disappointment, quickly elbowed

aside. Patrick. She sat straight up in bed as she remembered the boy. Tillman had Patrick.

A sound emanated from the tablet she'd laid on the bedside table, and she came totally awake. Alexa snatched it up, her hand shaking a little as she logged in. Checked her email.

Seeing the message in the inbox, she jumped out of bed and raced across the hall to Ethan's room.

The speed with which he opened the door told her he hadn't been asleep yet, although his shirt was hanging unbuttoned and loose from the waistband of his pants. She pushed by him without a word, noting the clock on his bedside table. It was only midnight. She'd slept for less than an hour.

"There's a message?"

Nodding, she sat on the edge of the bed and opened it. Ethan sank down beside her. Neither of them spoke until she'd clicked on the image in the body of the message.

"Oh, God." Alexa clapped a hand to her mouth. It was critical to remain objective, to keep her mind clear, but seeing the picture of Patrick sent objectivity up in flames. The boy's eyes were wide and frightened. There was duct tape over his mouth and wrapped around his body, securing him to a straight-back chair.

"Why has no one recognized the car he's driving?" She set the tablet aside and bounced from the bed, striding to one end of his room and back. "What good is the damn BOLO alert if no one can find the damn him?"

"I'm guessing he changed vehicles." Ethan's voice was expressionless. He had the tablet in his hands and was studying the photo. "Maybe he switched plates. He could have gotten tipped off that we've ID'd him, but I don't think so. He's probably just that fucking cautious. He was driving that rental when he went to Truro last time. Perhaps he was afraid it'd be recognized."

His calm defused her sudden burst of temper. She crossed to the bed and sat beside him again, reaching for his hand. His fingers linked with hers and Alexa leaned her head against his shoulder, dread pooling nastily in her belly. Because there was more coming. Whatever Tillman had been planning the last couple of days was about to come to a head.

Minutes later, when the tablet sounded an alert, she was proven right. As she began reading the email message, her stomach dropped in freefall.

*ALEXA. I didn't have a chance to tell you how much I appreciated your words at the press conference. I think you are coming to know me. Not as well as you will, of course. And I have come to know you. Infanticide is an ugly sin. The worst there is, perhaps.* She gasped, her hand clutching more tightly to Ethan's as pain speared through her. *But there is no sin too great to be forgiven if the sinner is sincerely penitent.*

*I'm offering you a chance for God's mercy. Confession. Penance. Redemption. You can save this boy and receive forgiveness for the child you murdered. But if you don't follow directions exactly, you'll doom him to a grave like the one in which your daughter resides. And doom yourself to the fires of hell.*

*You have six hours before the boy dies. Get in the car and take highway 102 to Truro. Come alone. I'll be in touch soon.*

"When we find Tillman...and we will find him..." Ethan's voice was deadly. "It's going to take every ounce of self-restraint I have not to hurt him."

His response had the darts of pain inside her morph into fiery sparks of fury. "You and me both."

~

It was with a feeling of déjà vu that Ethan nosed the car onto the highway that would lead to his hometown. It wasn't quite one a.m. Traffic was light. And while he was all too aware of the timeline, there had been arrangements to make. He sure as hell wasn't going to allow Alexa to follow the bastard's instructions alone. He suspected Tillman knew that, too.

He sent Alexa a sidelong glance. She was staring straight ahead, silent. Stony-faced. Not the mask she'd worn yesterday when the image of Olivia's grave had nearly unraveled her. No, now she was cool. Self-possessed. While he'd roused the other men, and come up with a quick plan, she'd showered, changed into black jeans, a matching long-sleeved blouse, and tennis shoes. Her hair was pulled back into a braid. She looked a bit like a warrior princess, ready for battle.

"You didn't bring the tablet." Instinctively, he lifted his foot from the accelerator.

"I switched the alert for incoming email to my phone." Her voice was matter-of-fact. "No need to worry about him somehow gaining access to my cell at this point. This way I'll always have connectivity for when the next message arrives."

Because there would be another one. That was certain.

He looked in the rearview mirror. Knew the headlights close behind him would belong to the car carrying the other officers. An ERT team wouldn't be too far behind, along with a crisis negotiator. They hadn't known what awaited them, so when he'd met Captain Sedgewick at RCMP headquarters, they'd prepared for a little of everything.

He hoped he had whatever they needed to get the boy away alive.

"Six hours he said." She turned to look at him. "It doesn't take six hours to get to Truro."

"He isn't there. He'll jerk us around some. Keep us off balance so we can't predict our destination."

"Whatever it is," she said with a thread of quiet determination in her voice, "I'm ready."

Tension settled across his shoulders. He'd give just about anything to figure out a way to leave her out of what was coming next. But he knew that wasn't possible. Tillman's obsession with Alexa wouldn't allow it.

They were still ten minutes outside Truro when the second message arrived. Alexa read it aloud to Ethan.

*I hope you haven't dawdled. It would be a shame if you were too late to save the boy. Onward to Antigonish.*

Ethan pressed the speed dial number for Nyle and relayed the information to him.

"Antigonish? Are we just staying on the Trans-Canada Highway then? That would take us all the way to Cape Breton Island."

"Unless we drop down from there..." Ethan tried to recall the provincial geography of his youth, "...to Sherbrooke. There's a road there that would lead back to Halifax."

"You think he's taking us in circles?"

"Wouldn't put it past him."

"How far behind us is the ERT team?"

"They haven't contacted me yet. So, at least an hour."

Nyle swore, and Ethan silently agreed with the sentiment. But organizing a call-out for an Emergency

Response Team wasn't something that happened quickly. And Ethan couldn't wait until they were mobilized, or he would risk missing the timeline Tillman had set. He suspected the offender realized that, too. They'd wondered what the man's intentions were since the press conference.

In another few hours, they were going to find out.

~

"I've alerted the Cape Breton Island RCMP Ingonish detachment that we're here." Ethan slipped his cell in his pocket and turned to look at Alexa. The first smudges of light were piercing the sky's gray veil. "I told the officer I spoke to that we'd be outside the Cape Dauphin area. When we reach our destination, he'll send someone local who knows the area. He says there's a popular landmark nearby. Glooscap Caves. But past that, there's also the Devil's Fingers Caves. And he warned us away from that spot. It's not open to the public."

"Caves?" Her voice sounded thready. Alexa cleared her throat and tried again. "Surely there's more to the locale than that. Or maybe Tillman will have us keep going to the other side of the point."

He rolled his shoulders. "We're already close to the timeline," he reminded her. And he was ready to face the man who'd played God for too many years. When the alert for another message sounded, a thread of adrenaline entered his veins. He wanted this to be over. And Ethan wanted to be the one who would end it, once and for all.

She read the message aloud.

*By now, you should soon be on the final leg of your journey. You'll have to leave the car behind at Vector Mountain.*

*You'll follow the path, which I've marked for you. I've provided everything you'll need from here.*

*Patrick says hurry.* Alexa's voice shook a little bit on the final words before she visibly steeled her spine.

"Vector Mountain?" Ethan's fingers tightened on the steering wheel as he swore silently. That's where the caves were that the RCMP officer had warned him about. How had Tillman become familiar with the area?

As if plucking the thought from his mind, Alexa mused, "Maybe he lived near here when he was a kid. After his father died, he would have stayed in the child welfare services system until he aged out. There's no telling what part of the province he might have lived in during that time. Or those he visited. We can be sure of one thing, though. He's returning to something familiar to him. He wants that edge."

After another twenty minutes, the road suddenly ended. Ahead was only grass and rock. Ethan braked abruptly. Then sat for a moment, his jaw clenched. "Whatever he has planned, I won't risk you."

"Before you promise that, we need to see what he's got in store for us." She met his gaze head-on. "We can't risk Patrick, either. We'll figure something out. But we'd better make it quick." She pointed to the clock.

He stared at the hands on it, transfixed. Their time had just about run out. A sneaky chill of dread shot down his spine. Without another word, he got out of the car and approached the vehicle coming to a stop behind them. He drew out a cell to call the RCMP officer back. They were going to need that local he'd promised, so they weren't at Tillman's mercy. Now that they could guess what the man had in store for them, it was time to plan a few surprises of their own.

~

"And I'm telling you, it can't be done." Jackson Weaver, a man who lived nearby, shook his head emphatically. "Most adult males can't even move inside these caves. Every single branch is a crawler, and when the space does open up in a few areas, there are keyholes to watch out for on the floor. It's hazardous in there. There's a deep lagoon inside, with treacherous undercurrents. I could get you to it from this side of the cliff. But there are a hundred different passageways that lead to and away from it, all around this bluff."

Which was why, Alexa thought, Tillman had brought them here.

She stared at the jagged side of the cliff that the men were arguing over. They were close enough to make out the dark entrances dotting the stony bluff. None of them were more than a foot and a half wide. The thought of being inside one of those tunnels with glacier-carved rock all around her, made her flesh crawl.

"We know he meant for me to be the one to go in after Patrick." Alexa surprised herself with the steadiness of her voice. The climbing shoes he'd left were close to her size. The helmet with the miner's light attached were too small for any of the men. The knee and elbow pads, the gloves... everything had been chosen for the one person in this party that they'd fit.

And the hand-held radio left with the clothes would be her link to the killer.

"No one's going inside there without proof of life first," Ian declared. With his hands on his hips, he surveyed the bluff before them.

"Damn straight," Ethan agreed. "We have to know the kid's here before anyone goes in after him."

"There are openings on the seaside of this bluff, too," Jackson said. "Three people have died in the last thirty years trying to scale that cliff from there. Lost their balance and fell to their deaths on the rocks below."

"Maybe the folklore could wait until later," Alexa suggested. Her heart was already thumping. Her palms were growing damp. She knew how this was going to end, even if Ethan refused to admit it. Patrick was here. Tillman wouldn't have left him behind. The boy had been taken for one purpose only—to set up this moment.

"Alexa." The radio crackled. A chill broke out over her skin at the sound of the disembodied voice. "I see you disobeyed me. I expected you would. No matter. You'll soon learn discipline. Let's get started, shall we? If you look up to your right, you'll observe our young friend peeking out of one of the entrances. Do you see him?"

Nyle peered at the towering bluff through a pair of binoculars that had been among the equipment they'd hauled from the trunks of the vehicles. He motioned to the others. Pointed.

Alexa looked upward. She saw a flash of white. It still wasn't light enough to make out the shape that far away. She took the binoculars from Nyle and looked through them. And felt a curdle of fear when she recognized the mop of blond hair. The pinched face stamped with fear.

"I think I could make it through the caves," Steve Friedrich said. Everyone stared at him. "I'm long but I'm wiry."

"You're too tall," Weaver responded. "The tunnels would be too cramped for you to maneuver the hairpin turns."

"We've wasted enough time." The result was certain, and Alexa was suddenly in a hurry. Sighting Patrick had ignited a sense of urgency that wouldn't be denied. "I'm going to be the one to go in. We all realize that. Figure out a plan and do it fast."

"No." Ethan's voice was emphatic. "I'll call the local RCMP detachment again. They can round up an officer who's the right size."

"Another stand-in?" She cocked a brow. "That went over so well the last time." And then she jumped when a high-pitched scream of pain split the air. It took a moment for her to recognize that it, too, came from the radio.

"I'm afraid I'm becoming a bit irritated with the delay."

It was all the impetus she needed. Alexa sat down and donned the clothes Tillman had left, her hands shaking.

"Ethan." Jonah drew his attention. "She's right. We're out of options here."

His jaw clenched so tightly Alexa feared it would shatter. For long moments, he stood there, and she knew he was grasping for an alternative. She was also aware that there weren't any. Finally, he squatted down and started sorting through the equipment they'd brought along. "Okay. Here's what we're going to do."

Ten minutes later, Alexa was nodding. "Yes. I've got it." The plan had been polished, re-arranged and then perfected again. She was anxious to get started; to avoid hearing a second scream coming from the radio. Ethan grabbed her arm and walked her several yards away, positioning himself in front of her, his back to the others.

"Remember, you take no chances. Don't deviate from the plan at all. The cellphone we're sending with you is Bluetooth capable, but it won't work when you're deep in the caves. Don't hesitate to use one of your weapons. And if it looks like you can't save the boy, get the hell out of there. I'm serious, Alexa." His expression underscored his words. "We both know who Tillman is after. Patrick is bait. If you can get to him without going near Tillman, fine. If not, we'll find another way."

But she knew there was no other option. She suspected he did, too. "This will work," she said with far more certainty than she was feeling.

"It'd better. We'll have a police presence all over the mountain. He isn't getting away this time." Ethan took her face in his hands and kissed her hard, with more than a hint of desperation. "I don't want to lose you again." He turned and strode away. Despite the gravity of the situation, his statement had her knees going weak. She took a moment to savor his words. The emotion behind them. And then she started to climb, heading toward the cave Patrick had disappeared into.

"Were you wishing her good luck?" The words drifted up to her. Steve Friedrich. "I want to wish her good luck, too."

Alexa smiled at the bit of levity. Whatever awaited her in the caves, it'd help to remember those who awaited her outside them. She wasn't alone. And soon, Patrick wouldn't be either.

She stayed in decent shape. Raiker's training courses were brutal, otherwise. But she wasn't a rock climber, and the bluff was steep, with loose rocks in some areas that made the ascent even more difficult. The utility belt around her waist weighed her down. The radio Tillman had left was clipped to the front of it. An extra flashlight and a bundle of ChemLites to the back. She was panting by the time she got to the narrow opening through which the boy had disappeared. It was marked by a torn piece of white cloth held between two rocks. From Patrick's T-shirt? Alexa paused to switch on her helmet lamp. She checked the length of rope wrapped around her waist. Readjusted the belt. Dropping to her hands and knees at the mouth of the cave, she threw one last look over her shoulder at the men below.

And then Alexa turned to face the yawning dark entrance. She hauled in a deep breath and plunged inside.

Almost instantly, she experienced a clawing sense of panic. She stilled, allowing herself time to become accustomed to the rough-hewn rock pressing in all around her. The beam of light from her hard hat lit the way but showed only inky blackness ahead. She took one of the green Chem-Lites from her belt. With a few deft moves, she bent, snapped and shook it to activate the illumination and set it next to the cave wall. The sticks would serve as her trail of breadcrumbs so she could find her way out again. Ethan said they lasted up to twelve hours.

Alexa hoped she wouldn't be in here for anywhere near that long. Gritting her teeth, she began to crawl.

Twice, she had to get on her belly and worm her way along. She saw skittering movements on the walls as she passed. Did Nova Scotia have cave crickets? She should know the answer to that, but the facts hovered distantly, just out of reach. Better not to think at all. To focus on her mission, on the plan Ethan had drilled into her.

Focus on saving Patrick.

She didn't know how long she moved, alternating between hands and knees and belly before the area in front of her abruptly widened. She sat up and hauled in a greedy gulp of air, rolling her shoulders and lifting her elbows outward, the freedom of movement gratifying until something swooped toward her face. Another whizzed by her ear. Bats. Alexa shuddered and ducked down again, hands shielding her head. Now would have been a great time to have Ethan around to put his vow about dealing with the animals to the test.

She took out another ChemLite to leave. Startled wildly when she heard a voice.

"Welcome, Alexa."

Her earlier fear forgotten, her hand dropped to her side where the Taser was strapped, her eyes straining to see in the darkness. It was another moment before she realized that Tillman's voice was coming from the radio clipped to the belt around her waist. She fumbled to free it, lifting it to her lips and pressing the button to transmit. "You know my name." Her voice sounded husky. "But what should I call you?" He couldn't know that they'd already identified him, and there was nothing to gain by making Tillman more desperate.

"How about...Anis Tera." The staticky voice echoed eerily in the small chamber.

"From Anisoptera? Very clever. And fitting." Bent over, she ran forward until the ceiling and walls closed in on her again, and she had to crouch.

"I knew you'd understand." His words were hard to make out. The radio probably wasn't going to work for long. The further she got into the caves, the less likely it would transmit. "Just as I understand you. We all seek absolution, Alexa. I'm delighted you recognize your need for it."

She bit off the retort she wanted to make. Just having Tillman allude to Olivia might push her over the edge. "How do you know of this place?"

The chuckle that came through the radio had ice bumping through her veins. "Oh, I'm familiar with most of the province. I lived in twelve or fourteen places in Nova Scotia when I was a kid. My time on Cape Breton Island was my favorite. Watch for the glow sticks as you move through the branches of the cave. They signal where you are to turn."

"Where else did you live on the island?" But there was no answer to her question. Ahead she saw a dull glow on her left. Her mouth twisted grimly. Tillman had come up with a similar idea to the Chemlites to illuminate the path forward. She replaced the radio. When Alexa reached the marker, she tried to crawl to the left. The passageway was tight. She had to change position a few times before she was able to squeeze through. A sudden realization hit her then. Tillman was a small man from all accounts, but he could never have gotten himself turned around as she had. Where was he?

Time ceased to exist as she inched her way through the cave. The chill of the surrounding rock seeped into her bones. How was she going to find Patrick if the markers didn't lead to him?

And would she be ready if they instead steered her straight to Amos Tillman?

# CHAPTER TWENTY-ONE

ALEXA DIDN'T KNOW how long it was before the branch she was crawling through widened again. Enough that she could sit up and mentally calm the frantic racing of her pulse. The darkness was oppressive. She took out another ChemLite, bending and snapping it until it shone and set it down near the cave wall. She'd read articles about the effect of sensory deprivation, and she could understand it now, only too well. The lamp on her helmet appeared to dent the blackness instead of splitting it. The shadows on either side pressed against the glow as if seeking to extinguish it. Alexa wondered if she only imagined that the light seemed a fraction dimmer.

The radio on her belt crackled again. She unclipped it to listen, but there was only static. Then a shrill cry sounded. She froze, remembering Patrick's shriek of pain earlier. But this noise was higher. A wavery, high-pitched wail.

A baby.

She shuddered violently. The sound went on and on, the pitch climbing until it raked up her spine. Drilled into her ears. With a brutal knifelike pain, Alexa was reminded she'd never heard Olivia's cry. She'd never been given that gift.

Just as suddenly as it began, the sound was cut off. And the resulting stillness rang with the now silenced cries. "That's what you did when you terminated your pregnancy, Alexa."

"That's not true." She didn't even use the radio; she was shouting the words into the darkness. "Is that was Reisman told you? How would he know? I never spoke to my parents again after I left."

"Don't compound your sin by lying about it now."

She turned around wildly. Because there was no static in the voice this time. Tillman was close enough to be heard.

One shaking hand went to the Taser on her hip. *Keep him talking. Draw him out.* "It was a placental abruption." Where was he? She turned in a full circle, slowly looking for signs of movement in the darkness. "I started bleeding. I had to stay in the hospital. But then..." Oh, God, she didn't want to relive this now. Not with a madman. "Then the bleeding started one night again and..." Her mouth dried out. "The baby was stillborn. I nearly died, too." And a part of her had wanted to, she remembered painfully. When she'd finally gotten well enough to realize what had happened.

"Repent! Turn away from all your offenses; then sin will not be your downfall."

He wasn't here. At least not in this small clearing. Alexa spotted the next slight glow and made her way toward it on hands and knees. "'For nothing is hidden that will not be made manifest, nor is anything secret that will not be known and come to light.'"

"Luke 8:17." Was that approval in his voice? Revulsion

shook her. "One of my favorites. We're well-suited, you and me."

Her stomach heaved at the words. She darted down the next passageway, then froze at the sudden thought of him sliding into the space after her. She threw an agitated look behind her, but couldn't see anything over her shoulder. Where the devil was Patrick?

Alexa heard nothing from Tillman again as she wiggled along as fast as she was able, leaving ChemLites every thirty feet or so and turning into each of the marked passages. He'd gone to a lot of trouble to set this up, and there was no question that he was planning a trap. But she had a few surprises for him, too. He wasn't going to win. Not this time.

The cave grew exceedingly narrow. She belly-crawled again for what seemed like a mile. A bat flew close enough to touch her face and Alexa jerked back, rapping her head smartly against a jut of rock on the ceiling. Even with the helmet, the force of the blow brought tears to her eyes. The rough walls beside her caught and tore at her clothing, and she could feel blood trickling down her limbs. But still, she couldn't slow down.

She struggled to her feet when the opening led to a bigger space. Left a ChemLite and stumbled toward the next marked passage. But this one was wider. There was light coming from the end, although she couldn't see from where. Because there was a bend in the passage, she finally realized. She made the turn and walked in a crouch toward the light. Until she stepped and her foot felt nothingness.

Frantically, she threw herself backward, her arms wheeling. Her body slammed against the wall of the cave with a force that had all her nerve endings screaming. Alexa's heart was in her throat. Panting, she edged along the wall until she was certain her legs would hold her. Weaver had mentioned this, she recalled dimly. That there were areas with keyholes in the floor.

"Alexa." She stilled. The voice was close. Much too close. "That way is dangerous. Come back."

There was a light bouncing in the darkness, approaching her from behind. No, not a light, a *lamp*. Like the one on her helmet.

"I can't. I'm hurt." She inched along the wall toward the keyhole again. Maybe there was a way around it. Maybe...

"Hurt! Do you know what pain is? To have a hammer used on your knee until it shatters and requires three separate operations to repair it? Do you realize what it feels like to have your testicle crushed? For your fingernails to be pulled out one at a time while someone watches and laughs?" His voice raised on each question until it was nearly a screech. "That's pain. The kind you don't think is possible to endure. And I wouldn't have if something hadn't happened that drew both men away so I could make my escape."

He was talking about Simard and Fornier, she realized. And it wasn't gratifying at all to recognize that she'd been correct about the incident that had triggered his escalation.

She kept her head down to better light the floor of the cave. And this time she saw the yawning cavity she'd almost fallen through. A moment later she noticed the boy standing several yards beyond it, in front of an opening with dim light pouring through it.

"Patrick!"

"Ah, you found him." Tillman seemed calmer now. "There are only two ways out from there. Forward, into the lagoon. Or back."

Back wasn't an option. There was a monster in the passage behind Alexa, blocking her way.

"There's only one life jacket. Do you see it?"

She looked around frantically. Finally spotted it lying in front of the yawning expanse on the floor, against the wall.

"If you can get the lifejacket to the boy, he just might survive. He's not a strong swimmer, I'm afraid. And the lagoon below is quite deep, with surprisingly strong currents. If I get to him first...well, let's just say I won't bother with any safety devices."

Patrick's face was drawn, and he was motionless. Utterly terrified.

"You can help him, Alexa, even though you refused to save your own child."

She wanted to cover her ears. That hateful voice, filled with wet, syrupy evil was spouting the most grotesque of lies.

"Therein lies redemption." Tillman's lamp drew closer. "Save the boy, and then choose salvation by coming to me."

Time crawled to a stop. She looked from Patrick to the shadows behind her. A dim glow signaled Tillman's approach. Alexa carried a handgun in an ankle holster. But a bullet could ricochet off the rock surrounding them. Instead, she drew the Taser at her side. Kept her arm down as she sidled her way back toward him.

Her breathing strangled in her chest as his lamp drew nearer. Then even closer. She trembled with the effort it took to remain still, until she could make out his form in the light of her headlamp.

And when she could, she raised her hand and fired.

He gave a keening cry, fell to the ground. She didn't wait any longer. Shoving the spent Taser in the holster, she bent and rolled up her pant leg. She took out the knife Ethan had strapped to her ankle. Then she unwrapped some of the rope from around her waist and sawed at it, the blade slipping and nicking her as her actions grew frenzied. When she had a section in hand, Alexa replaced the knife and reversed course to make her way back to the lifejacket. She picked it up.

"It's okay, Patrick." She tried for an encouraging tone even as her eyes strained to catch a glimpse of Tillman. Was he still incapacitated?

She looked at the gaping hole in the floor. There was a tiny shelf of rock on each side of it. No more than two inches wide. Looping the lifejacket over her arm, she pressed her back against the cave wall and inched along that narrow ledge like she was walking a tightrope.

Alexa glanced down once. She saw nothing but a pit of blackness. She trained her gaze forward again, concentrating on sidestepping a bit at a time. Her journey disturbed several bats hanging from the ceiling of the cave, and they swarmed above her. Next to her. She pressed even closer to the rock at her back, shielding her face, trembling. But her fear of them paled in comparison to her terror of the monster in the back of her.

And when she made it to the other side of the keyhole, she had to bend at the waist and haul in several fortifying breaths. Slowly, she straightened. Urgency began surging through her veins again.

She made her way to the boy. "Hey, buddy." She fit his arms through the life vest and zipped it up. "We're going to get out of here." The garment was too big for him. She cinched the belt as tightly as she could. And only then did she allow herself to look down.

Far below them, the lagoon was an inviting pool of turquoise. The walls surrounding the passage toward it were a smooth funnel on both sides. The calm waters hid dangerous currents. Maybe jutting stones. But the unknown in front of them was preferable to what lay behind.

An enraged roar split the air. Panic sprinted down Alexa's spine. Their time was up. Ahead of them was a dicey chance for survival.

The other direction held certain death.

She took the length of rope she'd cut and tied it securely around her and Patrick until she'd harnessed them tightly together. Then she looked down and gave the boy an encouraging smile. "Ready? We'll jump together. One. Two." Another roar, closer this time. "Three."

Alexa put her arm around Patrick and leaped.

"WHOA, CAREFUL THERE."

Alexa struggled to sit up straight on the blanket. Was thwarted by the ERT member who was applying first aid. "You need to lie down. You were out for a while."

She started to shake her head, then stopped when the action brought to life a chorus of jackhammers. The next time she didn't fight when the officer eased her back down to a lying position. "Where's Patrick?"

"He's okay." She almost wept when she heard the husky voice beside her. Felt Ethan take her hand. "Better shape than you. You got him out of the lagoon, but you fell and split your head on a rock making your way back down the cliff."

"Middle name *is* Grace," she muttered.

His laugh sounded choked, and the grip on her hand tightened. "Well, we won't give you too hard a time seeing how you managed to get both yourself and Patrick to safety."

"I tased Tillman." The memory had her eyes opening again. "Ethan, he knows those caves. Every inch of them. He remembers them from when he was a kid. He'll find a way out. A way no one else will know."

"We've got law enforcement all over this bluff. He's not going to get away."

"Seaside." Did the officer slip her something? Alexa was feeling decidedly woozy.

"He'll go the way you...least expect. And Ethan." She clutched at his hand. "I refused redemption. He'll be compelled to kill me."

"I'm not going to let anything happen to you."

There was a note in his voice she hadn't heard before. *It was...nice,* she thought dimly.

"I know..." she could feel consciousness slipping away, "...how to trap him."

"Just rest now." His hand on her forehead was soothing.

"...just need...to listen...to me..."

"I'm listening, Lexie." She was out before she could feel his lips pressed to her forehead. "This time I'm listening."

# CHAPTER TWENTY-TWO

*For the wages of sin is death...* —Romans 6:23

AMOS TILLMAN STEPPED onto the Halifax Memorial Hospital elevator, his face buried in a newspaper he wasn't reading. The blond wig he wore curved around his chin in a soft bob. His bright pink smock, matching pants, and bright white tennis shoes were similar to the outfits he'd observed nurses wearing as they left duty at the hospital. Everything he needed was in the black purse hanging from his shoulder.

This wouldn't take long.

The passageway he'd used to escape the hapless RCMP officers was as difficult to detect as he'd remembered. It was the longest tunnel in the Devil's Fingers caves. Nearly three-quarters of a kilometer. He'd waited until dusk because he needed some light to climb down to the beach below. To walk the two kilometers to where he'd left the rental with its stolen plate.

The now-constant pain in his knee had slowed his progress, but it took his mind off the raging in his blood.

He'd been wrong about Alexa Hayden. So horribly, laughably wrong.

The elevator doors pinged and opened softly. Someone else got on. The doors slid shut with a quiet *whoosh*. Amos's ascent continued.

Far from being a reward for his many sacrifices, Hayden was the worst of Satan's temptations. She'd nearly fooled him with her shared interests and quiet understanding. She hadn't been placed in his path to be his helpmate; she'd been sent to destroy him.

The doors whirred open on the fourth floor, and he walked out of the elevator to the quiet hospital floor. Two-thirty a.m. The halls were quiet and shadowy. The staff was minimal. He ducked into a door marked laundry. Came out moments later pushing a small foldable cart for soiled linens.

It had been ridiculously easy to discover Hayden's hospital room number. They gave that information out to any interested caller. This would be over in minutes. Then he'd drive to the storage garage where he kept the van. Take off the plates and set it on fire. Maybe burn the whole structure down, to disguise his intent. Then he'd head back home in the rental car. The Lord's weary soldier returning triumphantly from yet another victorious mission.

Room 406. Anticipation filled him. He pushed open the door. The wedge of light revealed the sleeping woman in the hospital bed. There wasn't a stand-in this time. Oh, no. He slipped inside, leaving the cart in the hall, and shutting the door behind him.

Letting the purse slide down his pink-clad arm, he

opened it and drew out the plastic bag. It'd all be over in minutes.

He was going to enjoy every second.

First, he moved the call light out of reach. Then Amos stood over her, the sound of her soft breathing fueling his anticipation. He opened the bag. Raised it toward her head.

And then he felt the kiss of cool steel beneath his right earlobe. "Drop it. Raise your arms. Slow and easy."

Disbelief filled him. This couldn't be happening. Not with the Lord's blanket of protection he'd enjoyed for so many years. He let the bag flutter to the floor, one hand going for the purse where he'd left the syringe. An overdose would work just as well as...

He was slammed painfully to the floor, his arms twisted behind his back. "Amos Tillman." That hated voice was in his ear. Cold and authoritarian. "You're under arrest for the homicides of fifteen victims. And it'll be the greatest pleasure of my life to see you spend the rest of your life in a cage."

## CHAPTER TWENTY-THREE

ALEXA LOOKED up when the hospital door opened later that afternoon. She'd been ready to leave for hours. Her injuries hadn't necessitated even one night in the hospital, much less two. But she'd needed the pretext.

She'd known Tillman would come.

Ethan walked into the room, stopping short when he saw her. A slow smile crossed his face. "It's like you're in a hurry to get out of here or something."

"It's bad enough to be in one of these places when you're actually sick." Far different, she thought with an inward shudder, to lie in one, hour after hour, expecting a madman to try and kill her at any moment. "It's finally over."

Ethan nodded, coming closer to take the seat beside her. "He's behind bars. He'll be transported to a federal holding facility until trial."

The enormity of the past few hours swamped her. "He took the bait so easily. Maybe I was wrong, and he did suffer a psychotic break. He was driven by his compulsion. This final plan of his was far more reckless than even I had expected."

"Yeah, well, I'm not sure I'm up for another two days like this, myself." Ethan picked up one of her hands. Played with the fingers. "We didn't get a ping on his phone since yesterday. He was gone again by the time we reached him then."

"Where was he?" Ethan had been stingy with the details while they'd been waiting for Tillman to make a move.

"A coffee shop down the street where he could watch the people coming and going into the front doors. You were never in any danger." He seemed anxious to reassure her again, even now that it was all over. "We had plainclothes officers near every entrance, elevator, and stairwell. The task force members were spread all over this floor."

"But only one was camped out for a day and a half in my hospital room bathroom," she teased." He'd refused to leave her alone. And in truth, she hadn't tried very hard to convince him to do so. Every officer on the task force was supremely competent. But she'd felt secure with him when she was a girl. And two decades later there was still no one she trusted more to keep her safe.

The knowledge that he was close by had been a quiet comfort throughout the nerve-wracking hours of waiting.

"He was spotted as soon as he entered the hospital." Ethan repositioned himself in the hard chair. "His progress was relayed every dozen feet. I was ready for him."

"And so was I." When he skated his thumb over the back of her hand, Alexa turned her palm in his to capture his fingers. Squeezed them. "I'm glad it's over."

The look in his eyes had the blood in her veins slowing.

Turning molten. "So am I. Losing you once was hard enough. Watching you put yourself in danger, twice...you gave me some bad moments there, Lexie."

"There were one or two." The memory of crawling through those caves was going to haunt her for a long time to come. And she just might develop a walloping case of claustrophobia as a result. But she had no regrets, given the outcome. "Patrick doing okay?"

"Nothing keeps that kid down for long."

She smiled wistfully. They failed to get to Lawler in time. But Patrick and Logan had been returned to their families. Tillman would die behind bars. That would have to be enough.

"So." Ethan dropped her hand and stood up then, jamming his fists in his trouser pockets. "I guess you're planning to fly back to...where do you live?" He crossed to the window. Then to the end of the bed.

"Falls Church. Near DC." Alexa regarded him carefully. She could almost see the nervous energy coursing through him. Wondered at the source of it.

He nodded jerkily. "Got another case lined up?"

The tension that started to build in her began to dissipate. "Nope. I was thinking of taking a few days off. Sticking around for a little while. I'd like to visit Olivia's grave while I'm in the country." It'd been her last stop before she'd left Canada for good all those years ago. All she'd had for comfort in the time since was a picture of their baby's marker.

"I think that's a good idea. To take a few days' break, I mean, after all that's gone down."

She eyed him knowingly. "Is that what you're going to do?"

His answer surprised her. "I don't know." His light-blue gaze was intense, fixed on her with laser focus. "I didn't have the words to keep you from leaving last time. And I'm having a helluva time finding them now. You and I...we both got on with our lives. And there didn't seem to be anything missing in mine until you walked back into it. And now...shit, Alexa. There's no smooth way of saying it. I'm not letting you go again without a fight."

Her heart did a slow dizzying turn in her chest. "I'm not going to put up much of a struggle." His expression stilled. "Our circumstances couldn't be more different now. Leaving you was the hardest thing I ever did. I don't think I have the strength to do it twice."

He was by her side in two quick steps, taking her hand and tugging her into his embrace. And when his arms closed around her, it felt like coming home. Her voice unsteady, she said, "I've loved you since I was a girl, but it's the woman standing here telling you that no matter what happened between us, you were the best thing that ever happened to me." His kiss stole the rest of her words. After a moment, she leaned against him and savored the feel of his lips on hers. Little bursts of heat sang through her veins.

When he lifted his head, his voice was husky. "I want the whole nine yards. House, babies, goofy-looking dog. If that's not what you want, too, better tell me now."

"Because you'd change your mind?"

"Hell, no." His grin was more than a little wicked. "Because I'll get busy changing yours."

"Lucky for you then, that I want the same thing." Alexa brushed his lips with hers before rearing back to survey him critically. "That whole baby thing, though. You *are* a year older than me. And you aren't getting any younger."

He nodded, although the glint in his eye didn't resemble agreement. "You're right. So, in the interest of time, I say..." his mouth lowered to hers again... "we'd better get started."

Don't miss Kylie's next exciting release, *Pretty Girls Dancing,* coming from Thomas and Mercer 1/1/18.

Made in the USA
Lexington, KY
11 October 2017